Seastate
Origins

Nicholas Pichach

Table of Contents

Copyright	1
NEW LIBERTY	2
CHAPTER ONE – A SPARK	3
CHAPTER TWO – A FIRE	13
CHAPTER THREE – DECISIONS	29
CHAPTER FOUR – UNEASE	41
CHAPTER FIVE – A PLAN	48
CHAPTER SIX – COLLUSION	57
CHAPTER SEVEN – INDEPENDENCE	62
CHAPTER EIGHT – FIRST BLOOD	77
CHAPTER NINE – BATTLE OF NAURU	90
CHAPTER TEN – REFLECTIONS	107
CHAPTER ELEVEN – REINFORCEMENTS	111
CHAPTER TWELVE – CONFLICT	119
CHAPTER THIRTEEN – REVELATIONS	126
CHAPTER FOURTEEN – DISCOVERIES	129
CHAPTER FIFTEEN – ESCALATION	136
CHAPTER SIXTEEN – ASSESSMENTS	141
CHAPTER SEVENTEEN – RECONNAISSANCE	145
CHAPTER EIGHTEEN – CHESS MOVES	155
CHAPTER NINETEEN – CONSEQUENCES	164
CHAPTER TWENTY – A TEST OF CHARACTER	181
CHAPTER TWENTY-ONE – OPERATION REUNIFICATION	188
CHAPTER TWENTY-TWO – THE DRAGON COMES	193
CHAPTER TWENTY-THREE – FIRST STRIKES	199
CHAPTER TWENTY-FOUR – A HAIL MARY	210
CHAPTER TWENTY-FIVE - THE BATTLE OF THE SOUTH CHINA SEA	222
CHAPTER TWENTY-SIX – RESOLUTIONS	229
CHAPTER TWENTY-SEVEN – PHANTOMS	241
CHAPTER TWENTY-EIGHT – NEW HOPES	250

Copyright

Published by Defiance Press & Publishing, LLC

Bulk orders of this book may be obtained by contacting Defiance Press & Publishing, LLC. www.defiancepress.com.

Defiance Press & Publishing, LLC

281-581-9300

info@defiancepress.com

NEW LIBERTY

CHAPTER ONE – A SPARK

"If you're not making waves, you're not under weigh."
—Chester W. Nimitz

FEBRUARY 16, 2068
US MARINE HELICOPTER DEFIANT ONE
25 KILOMETERS SOUTH OF MALIANA EAST TIMOR

When it came to describing the situation west of the Rio De Lois River, one word immediately came to mind. "It's genocide," Rear Admiral Richard Davidson hollered over the roaring rotors of the AH-72 Defiant compound helicopter gunship. The fast-moving AH-72 maneuvered just above one of the few permanently flowing rivers in the lush green forests and rugged peaks of East Timor. Over the horizon to the west, Davidson could see pillars of smoke multiplying and advancing on the river. A glance at the heads-up display projected map confirmed to Davidson that the town of Balibo was being overrun.

As if to reinforce the tragedy in Balibo, on the display beside the map still played a video of a US drone flight over the city of Pante Makasar almost a hundred and fifty kilometers to the west. The city skyline was aflame with running gun battles in the streets. The militias invading from West Timor—regular Indonesian troops or not—had overrun the Oecusse exclave and were set to take the rest of the country in a matter of days. Once a Portuguese colony, East Timor had been quickly invaded and occupied by the Indonesian military in 1975 upon declaring its independence. After decades of human rights abuses, Indonesia relinquished control in 2002. Now after half a century, army units out of Indonesia, officially claimed to be irregular and unauthorized militias, were back as if they had never left.

The helicopter pilot to Davidson's right, Army Captain Rodriguez, nodded his head in agreement with a somber "Roger." The AH-72 Defiant built by Sikorsky and Boeing was nimble and, compared to conventional helicopters, fast with not only counter-rotating main rotors but a rear-mounted pusher propeller that allowed it to cruise at more than four hundred and sixty kilometers an hour. Rodriguez lifted the helicopter in altitude as a bridge came into view, jampacked with refugees in vehicles and on foot, pushing their way south toward the small town of Maliana. The town offered hope with its still picturesque setting, attractive town center, and location across the Rio De Lois river where an American company, CanHarvest Renewables, operated a renewable energy facility. Rodriquez reduced the throttle of the pusher propeller as he swung the helicopter to the south where the renewable petrochemical plant stood out from the rainforest landscape of mountains and wet rice fields. "Approaching the CanHarvest facility."

The chief executive officer of the company, Grace Jaden, had informed both the Indonesian and American embassies that she would offer refuge to any who came to the facility. The word had apparently gotten out to the general public as crowds of poor and homeless fleeing the invading militias crowded to get behind the concrete wall surrounding the facility of office trailers, warehouses, storage tanks, and distillation towers.

Davidson could feel the onset of a headache as he considered if Jaden was a hero to be commended or a reckless pain in the ass. *Probably both*, he quickly concluded.

The heads-up display flickered with a projection of the uniformed and helmeted Colonel Chris Florzone in the Combat Information Center of the amphibious carrier *Bonhomme Richard* one hundred and forty kilometers to the southeast on station in the Timor Sea. As the marine commander of the 26th marine expeditionary group, Florzone was anxious to get his men off the ship and on the ground. "Does it look as bad as it sounds?" the Colonel lamented.

Rear Admiral Davidson rubbed his forehead to make it clear he was in desperate need of Tylenol. "Worse, though not sure how we can help," he solemnly admitted.

"You're the political brain on this mission. I'm just the muscle."

"I've got a bad feeling about this," Rear Admiral Davidson said with a frown. He gave a quick salute to conclude the discussion, interrupted by the blinking of an incoming high-priority satellite relayed communication. "Washington finally getting back to me. I'll let you know how it goes." With that, communications with the *Bonhomme Richard* were terminated.

"Identify for retina scan," the feminine-sounding computer announced. Davidson held his eyes open wide while the computer scanned his retina and relayed biometric information confirming his identity back to the satellite. "Identify confirmed. Communication from the White House, Washington, D.C. This communication is classified."

To the admiral's surprise, the new heads-up-display window didn't reveal the secretary of defense but the rather young at thirty-five and well-dressed secretary of state. With his black suit and perfectly combed hair, only the obvious scowl on his face betrayed that the man wasn't a fashion model. "Let's make this quick," the secretary of state began, full of frustration. He raised his hand in the air. "I've got riots over foot stamp program limitations in New York. Simultaneous bombings by extremists in Houston, Chicago, and Los Angeles. Not to mention the bloody stock market being frozen again. In keeping the public calm, I've got no time for high-risk military adventures, Admiral." It was well known that Secretary of State Harris had a disdain for the military reinforced by his all-but-spitting of the word *Admiral*. "So, quickly and without any conflict, secure that facility and await my orders."

Davidson decided to stick to a simple question. "To what end, sir?"

The eyes of the secretary of state squinted with anger. "That corporate shrew is recklessly putting American interests at risk. She is violating the Neutrality Act of 1794 and engaging in unauthorized freebooting and filibustering. She is to be arrested."

What he was to make of the secretary of state's rant left the admiral speechless. He looked down at the refugees and found it hard to contemplate anyone offering sanctuary being considered—having engaged in unauthorized warfare. "Is that really the place of my forces?" He took a deep breath. "Is that even legal?" With his fingers, Davidson enlarged a dossier of Grace Jaden on the screen. Quick facts jumped out at him. "Her husband and eldest son were in the Navy, killed in action in Armenia. The surviving son still serves in the navy."

After a scoff from the secretary of state, safe and sound an ocean away, he virtually pointed directly at the admiral. "You secure that compound and await the president's orders. No engaging any non-American forces."

Before Admiral Davidson could react, the screen went blank.

OPERATIONS CENTER
CANHARVEST MALIANA EAST TIMOR PROJECT

The familiar hum of equipment converting biomass into renewable crude was surpassed by the cries and screams of civilians packing into the petrochemical complex. The operations center was usually quiet for the four operators at the panels that controlled the highly automated plant. The abnormally loud shouts and activity beyond the control trailer were unnerving.

The plant was still operating through the chaos that the disheveled and balding fifty-two-year-old chief operating officer of the company had personally come to observe, overseeing the volunteer operators. "Keep on your screens," COO Luke Zenuck ordered the operators. He partially succeeded in trying to sound calm, but the visible sweat on his oil-stained blue coveralls betrayed that he was anything but. After another look at a camera monitor, which showed the parking lot and warehouse areas crammed with civilians pushing toward the process equipment, he decided there was only one course of action to take. Zenuck turned over his shoulder and declared, "I've got to shut her down."

The tall and slender woman standing to the back of the control room frowned at the request. Grace Jaden, president and founder of CanHarvest Renewables, contemplated the situation. Since meeting decades ago in an engineering class in Wyoming, Zenuck and Jaden's work relationship and friendship had blossomed to the point she always considered his advice. All eyes in the operations center turned to her. She betrayed no hint of emotion, though. Even her dirty blue work coveralls couldn't hide her feminine attributes. "You shut down the plant, we will be on batteries and lose power in a matter of hours." Their air conditioning, communications and the remote-controlled machine-gun placements her security team had rushed into place around the complex were dependent on power from the operating facility.

"But with no one hurt crowding around heat exchangers," Zenuck said. "I've got all the production tanks full of fuel now. And after cooldown, we can let more civilians into the plant."

"Will we lose the gun emplacements and missile defenses?"

Standing next to Jaden, the Chief Security Officer of the company, Andrew Lawrence, shrugged. A tall black muscular former US Army lieutenant, he looked the part of security lead with the demeanor of someone no one in their right mind would ever want to confront. "We can use some on batteries, others on manual."

"Would we have a chance?"

"If they attack the facility with an all-out offensive?" Lawrence asked rhetorically. "No, not really."

A contrast to Lawrence was the slender uniformed Soldier to his side who was anxious to see more civilians in the compound. The East Timor military representative by the name of Jose Guterres gave a tilt of his head. "I have a battalion of troops deployed on the bridge into Maliana. My men will help yours," he said in a pleading tone. His family was among those fleeing the paramilitary groups.

Jaden glanced over the panels showing the facility properly running using the process that had made CanHarvest Renewables a billion-dollar company. One side of the complex produced biomass, which was shredded and slurred, then pyrolyzed in the absence of oxygen to produce crude oil. The other side consisted of hydrotreaters deoxygenating the pyro-oil, which was indistinguishable from petroleum. Not only was the process making a renewable crude oil but fertilizer and power as well. The fact that shutting down the process would cost them their ability to generate power made the decision difficult. "Do it." If the invading forces weren't dissuaded by the sight of the multinational-owned facility guarded by armed personnel and decided to take the complex, there was little her small security detail could do anyway.

The operators called up operating procedures on their tablets and began the process of safely shutting down the facility. The lights flickered as the gensets shut down and the emergency power supply systems activated.

A corner of the main display screen to the front of the operations center flickered and was soon replaced by the image of Jord Laboucan. A larger built man, Laboucan had served as the chief financial officer of the company since its founding decades ago. Jaden had a hard time convincing the man to stay behind and manage the corporate headquarters in Phoenix, Arizona. "Media interview time," Laboucan announced with a forced smile.

There had been a time Grace Jaden had loved presenting to the public—be it board meetings, technology conferences, or media interviews—and it was a surprise even for her to have a racing heart, dreading an interview. She had done countless interviews on the afternoon business news circuit but never from a potential war zone with the media so hostile.

Laboucan saw the look of discomfort. "You've got to fight back. These people need you to tell the world what's going on," the chief financial officer urged with what sounded like the combined wisdom of all the aboriginal ancestors on his father's side. Laboucan was in nothing less than a fighting mood, tired of Jaden staying away from politics while their corporation was being targeted. "Think of it not as an interview but a debate."

But did politics even matter? Both parties seemed to have virtually the same platform, plus or minus a few percent on tax rates. All ran deficits. All used quantitative easing to pick winners and losers in the private sector. Nationalization of company after company was now a normal occurrence. Those who protested foreign interference, the printing of money, and debt found their election results would take days to come in only to at best have lost by slim margins. Jaden closed her eyes and took a deep breath before solemnly making her way into a nearby conference room. They had to at least try to do something. She owed it to her husband and eldest son—both lost to the ideals of freedom.

Grace Jaden stepped out of the main operations center and into the facility board room. The smart screen artificial intelligence automatically detected her presence, activated the wall display, and brought up the visual of Laboucan.

Zenuck took a moment from directing the plant shut down to shout in Jaden's direction as she left the room. "Knock 'em dead!" The engineer took comfort in knowing that safely shutting down the plant was probably far more enjoyable than dealing with the media.

As the conference room door slid shut, there came an uncomfortable silence. The display screen flickered from an image of Laboucan to the network news transmission. Jaden's relationship with the media hadn't always been so strained when she first started CanHarvest Renewables two decades ago at the age of thirty-five. Back then, the interviews were about the business, climate change, and the science of renewable energy. Now at fifty-five with money and power, she found that it was always about politics.

The news reports were all filled with images of the simultaneous bombings in Houston, Chicago, and Los Angeles. Was it a terror cell? The motives and organizations were no longer reported, so as not to inflame extremists. The stock markets remained closed as a result of the bombing. Was America too busy with its own problems to worry about the situation in East Timor?

"You should be on in five," came the voice of a producer. "This will be a live broadcast."

"Looking forward to it." Jaden tried to fake a smile.

The corporate executive got her first look at the handsome young anchorman (with his perfectly groomed brown hair, Italian-made suit, and high-tech anchor desk) who would be conducting the interview.

"And now live over satellite we have Grace Jaden, chief executive officer of CanHarvest Renewables. She is joining us from one of their facilities near Maliana in East Timor, which sits on the path of advancing militias. Thank you for joining us."

"Thank you for having me."

"Grace Jaden, you are opening up your facility to refugees during this attack?"

"Yes," she said and took a deep breath. "We strongly urge the international community, especially that of the United States government, to come to the aid of the legitimate government of East Timor."

The anchorman leaned forward in his desk, reading off a prepared statement. "As we reported last week, you issued formal complaints to the United States government and the United Nations, noting a buildup of activity on the border between Indonesia and East Timor. You also sent letters to the Indonesian government that you will not respect the authority of any forces that cross the border."

"That's correct." Grace Jaden nodded her head. "This facility is operated under the government of East Timor and will answer only to that government."

"If these paramilitaries enter your facility—"

Knowing she had to appear resolute, Jaden immediately cut off the question. "I will instruct our security to prevent that."

"Grace Jaden, politicians in Washington are saying this is a distraction and a stunt meant to distract from negative media attention to your vocal lobbying in opposition to the Accountable Capitalism Act legislation."

Jaden rolled her eyes at how quickly the interview had turned to domestic politics. "Apart from the question as to why the administration has ignored border skirmishes and opened the door to this invasion, the situation in East Timor has nothing to do with the reckless Accountable Capitalism Act that should be defeated," Jaden strongly contested.

Given the impact on the stock market, the debate on the bill before Congress was the focus of the interviewer. "You continue to oppose the Accountable Capitalism Act?"

She tried to slow down her breathing to remain calm and focused despite the surge of anger this line of questioning prompted. "Although we are not on the stock exchange, the act would punish us with high royalties on wells—wells that we use to sequester carbon and generate renewable fuels. The legislation would also require us to accept government-appointed board members."

"To enable you to utilize biomass, which is a public resource," the reporter pressed.

She raised an eyebrow at his matter-of-fact response. "We produce biomass from our private land and wells that we invested in, drilled, and completed using our technology to accomplish both a market and public good. Land and wells we have paid royalties on for decades."

"Making you substantial profits in the process?"

"Yes, profits which we use to fund our operations and allow us to invest in other new technologies."

The anchorman gave her a dismissive look as he gazed over his teleprompter. "Isn't that what the Accountable Capitalism Act calls for?

Charters to be approved by the government? Provision for board diversity? Use of corporate funds to help pay off the national debt?"

"We should have the freedom to use our funds as we see fit. We feel that generic government-provided charters and board members would reduce us to yet another average corporation without technical skill or high-risk tolerance, leaving us mediocre and irrelevant." Grace Jaden turned to the camera, sure that Laboucan would be upset if she didn't take advantage of the airtime to talk up the corporation. "We have been a major supplier of carbon fiber, which at half the weight of steel yet four times the strength, has allowed for electric cars to supplant traditional automobiles. At the same time, our renewable fuel division provides carbon-balanced power and transportation fuels. In meeting market demand, we are doing public good."

"Would not the government ensure that these profits are used for the general good?"

"The government would serve itself first and foremost without the need to take risks for economic gain or enhanced quality of life. Power consolidation always results in economic stagnation and decline." Jaden shook her head, given what she felt was the obviousness of her statements. "The state cannot manage the market as well as a competitive marketplace. If you think you can do a better job, go and do it, but leave our success alone. Statism and out of control bureaucracy has already left the United States with a record-high unemployment rate—twenty five percent—and unmanageable debt—"

The anchorman obviously didn't like where she was taking the conversation, so he immediately cut her off. "What of your diversity?"

"I believe in equality and a merit-based system, period. That is one of our successes."

"But what of historical wrongs. Don't you have—"

"You mean historical wrongs by the state? Isn't that the state's responsibility to deal with? The corporate tax rate has already been raised twenty-three percent in the last two decades. Isn't that enough to—"

The anchorman again cut her off, this time almost smiling at what he was reading off the teleprompter. "We have received information that the US Internal Revenue service is going to review the finances of CanHarvest Renewables over the past decades."

Not wanting to give the anchorman any satisfaction by showing emotion or a hint of discomfort, Grace Jaden leaned back in her chair. "Outside"—she waved her arms—"are twenty thousand people escaping potential death at the hands of an invading army. These are some of the poorest people in the world. We urge the international community to come to our aid."

Knowing that he was not going to get the knockout punch he wanted, the anchorman decided to cut the interview short. "Thank you, Miss Jaden."

Grace Jaden raised her hands in frustration. The transmission cut off, and all she could do was storm out of the conference room.

The chief operating officer had ensured his panel operators were good to proceed with the shutdown without him so he would be free to help calm Jaden down. "You did good," said Zenuck. "That's about as good as it was going to go."

The shockwaves of an echoing explosion thundered down the valley of the Rio De Lois River. Danger was coming.

CHAPTER TWO – A FIRE

"They who can give up essential liberty to obtain a little temporary safety deserve neither liberty nor safety."
—Benjamin Franklin

FEBRUARY 11, 2068

OPERATIONS CENTER

CANHARVEST MALIANA EAST TIMOR PROJECT

The first thought of every engineer and operator in the control room was that a pressure vessel had erupted within the plant. All eyes turned, scanning the various panels, searching for the cause of the explosion. Coffee mugs and panels still shook from the echo of the blast.

"It wasn't us!" Zenuck breathed a sigh of relief, given the fact that all the monitors were green and the live video feeds showed everything was intact with not a flame in sight.

Having been in combat before, Andrew Lawrence suspected the explosion had come from beyond the facility and was already manipulating external cameras on his security panel. "Artillery in the distance," he suggested, and with the flick of a hand over a console, he put the live video feed of the heavily forested valley on the main monitor. He pointed at a column of smoke far off in the distance. "They're still far off but coming."

"Did they cross the bridge?" Jaden reasoned that crossing the lone bridge over the Rio De Lois River would be the point of no return for the invading forces. Should they defeat the East Timor battalion guarding the bridge, the invaders would have free reign to advance unopposed, not only to Maliana but deep into East Timor.

A live camera feed had been set up to keep an eye on the extensive bridge across the Rio De Lois River. There was small comfort in seeing only refugees crowding south on the bridge with the East Timorese forces still hidden among the sandalwood trees and valley cliffs. The video feed left those watching feeling guilty about the relative calm of the control center versus the chaos and panic they witnessed in those slowly trying to make their way east over the bridge.

Hating to be the bearer of bad news, Lawrence nonetheless saw that they were dealing with a new situation. "Ma'am, we've got helicopters coming in from the South."

Jaden gazed up at the large display in an attempt to identify the helicopters. Was the facility about to be attacked from the air? Her heart skipped a beat upon identifying six large V-22 Osprey and five V-30 Valor vertical takeoff and landing craft coming in. They were no doubt American helicopters escorted by at least two AH-72 Defiant compound gunships. She had once longed to serve in the American military, but her eyesight had been too poor. Both her late husband and two sons had ended up naval aviators, only for her husband and the eldest son to be killed in Armenia. "US Marines!" she cheered.

"Thank God for the Calvary!" Zenuck slapped the back of one of the panel operators. He had found it doubtful anyone would come to their aid, but there was no denying the sight of the United States helicopters in route. Zenuck ignored the flashing thought that the presence of the US helicopters was too good to be true—something he would later regret.

US MARINE HELICOPTER DEFIANT ONE
MALIANA EAST TIMOR

"Take us down," Admiral Davidson ordered the helicopter pilot while looking down on thousands of panicked civilians pressing into the CanHarvest facility. The distillation columns and storage tanks of the processing plant were surrounded with crowds of refugees. As the helicopter lowered to the ground, Davidson checked on the positions of various marine units on a projected map while speaking into his headset. "Landing area is clear. I'll take the facility. Alpha Company to deploy with me at the facility. Bravo and Charlie companies at positions above the Rio De Lois River Bridge, which looks defendable. Keep Delta in reserve in the air."

Orders received, six V-22 Osprey aircraft altered their flight paths and broke formation. The Bell Boeing V-22 Osprey was a large American multi-mission tiltrotor military aircraft with vertical takeoff and landing capabilities, so the craft were able to transition from aircraft to helicopter mode by rotating their propellers into a vertical position prior to landing. The unloading process was duplicated by the newer V-30 Valor VTOL craft. Rotors still turning as they touched the ground, each air crew, conscious of being sitting ducks on the ground, rushed to unload a company of marines. Each company consisted of four Stryker vehicles, several TOW missile units and around a hundred infantry. Following the deployment of their precious cargo, the Ospreys lifted back into the relative safety of the air, rotated their rotors back into a horizontal position to accelerate forward, and disappeared to the south.

"I've got four more companies ready to go," Florizone reported from the amphibious assault carrier *USS Bonhomme Richard* in the Timor Sea. "Also have some artillery ready to go." General Florizone bit his lip in apprehension. His units had a collection of mobile Paladin *M109A7* next-generation artillery and M142 HIMARS multiple rocket launcher systems ready to go. "I've also got a couple F-35s on the flight deck. You let me know when you want them."

"Hopefully we won't need them," Admiral Davidson replied into his headset as he took a deep breath and forced himself to think through the situation. "Let's hope the militias, Indonesian forces, whoever the hell is coming up the highway sees us, comes to a stop, and lets things cool down."

Wishing he was on the ground as opposed to stuck watching the situation play out on a computer screen, General Florizone frowned. The two officers had served together on numerous occasions stationed together on the America-class amphibious assault ship *USS Bougainville* on patrol between the Mediterranean Sea and Persian Gulf through a rotation of almost routine crises. While this was, in theory, a different mission in a very different place, Florizone couldn't shake the feeling that this was to be yet another combat deployment. "Better safe than sorry."

With the AH-72 touching the ground Davidson unbuckled his restraints. "I've got a bad feeling about this," he said truthfully to the pilot. "Be ready to take off." Two camouflaged Marines leaped out of the cabin and took positions outside the helicopter with weapons raised. Seeing a thumbs up from one of the Marines, Davidson swung open his door, though the rotors were still turning. His eyes scanned the crowd around the helicopter where he made out Grace Jaden approaching with what appeared to be a security detail of two armed bodyguards at either side.

"Boy, am I glad to see you!" Grace Jaden shouted over the spinning rotors. She paused, gazing at the young marine kneeling with his M2 heavy machine gun raised. Memories of her late son and husband flooded her mind. She saw her eldest son so excited to attend the United States Naval Academy like her husband. The eighteen-year-old in uniform. Her eyes swelled up.

Not having expected such a warm reception, Admiral Davidson awkwardly held his clenched fist to hide a spurt of rather rough coughs. "You"—he pointed right at the corporate executive—"with me!" He gestured for her to follow him into the cabin of the helicopter.

Pushing aside thoughts of her late husband and son, Grace Jaden climbed into the main cabin of the compound helicopter. Behind them, a Marine slammed the cabin door shut.

Able to communicate without screaming, Davidson tapped the shoulder of the Marine manning the main communications terminal. "Get me Washington," he ordered.

Grace Jaden extended her hand, "Grace Jaden with CanHarvest Renewables. You have no idea how much you being here means to us!" She paused upon seeing the admiral turn to her with a sad look on his face.

"Listen." Admiral Davidson's tone was soft and hesitant. "Unfortunately, we aren't here to help these people." Davidson coughed again, this time not out of necessity but to try to hide his sincere regret. He took Jaden's hand and firmly shook it. "I'm Rear Admiral David Davidson of the 26th marine expeditionary group. I'm actually here to bring you home." His tone was one meant to reinforce his mission was not in support of her effort.

Jaden nodded slowly while contemplating the statement. "What do you mean bring me home?"

Not quite wanting to answer the question while at the same time not quite sure of the answer itself, Davidson took the opportunity to turn away from Jaden and focus on the signalman. "Where is Washington?" When in doubt, Davidson always tried to leave politics to the politicians.

The Marine smashed her console in frustration. "I can't seem to reach them."

"What the hell?" The Rear Admiral leaned over to look at the communication screen, which was filled with static across multiple frequencies.

Army Captain Rodriguez turned back from his cockpit display while tapping on a glass indicator. "Definite frequency jamming," the pilot forcefully declared.

Questions raced through Admiral Davidson's mind. Did militias even have the technology to jam their sophisticated satellite communication network? Why would they be jamming their comms? Only one reason came to mind. "Get out of the helicopter!" he shouted at Jaden. "They're coming!" He gestured for the Marines to get back into the helicopter.

Grace Jaden and the admiral met eye to eye. From the serious look of the admiral, Jaden knew exactly what he meant was coming. She at once jumped from the still opening cabin door of the helicopter and raced toward the control trailer.

"Up, up!" Admiral Davidson shouted to Rodriguez while gesturing with his hands lest the sound of the rotor muffle the command.

The marines slammed the helicopter cabin door shut just in time for the first report of activity to resonate through the interior. "Ground contacts coming north up the M8 highway," came a report from one of the Marine companies on the bridge.

BOOM! The first explosion echoed through the valley so loud that Rear Admiral Davidson had first thought that their gunship had been struck. BOOM! BOOM! BOOM! Thunderous explosions continued relentlessly.

As the helicopter raced up into the air, Rear Admiral Davidson watched shells burst brightly both in the direction of the town of Maliana and on the opposite side of the river valley. He struggled to climb from the cabin into the copilot seat while watching in horror as the Maliana police station and city hall erupted into an explosion of flames and debris. A dense smoke cloud engulfed three once-visible churches. Being able to see more as the helicopter rose higher into the sky, Davidson looked to the west along the highway where the entire other side of the valley, packed with crowds of civilians, disappeared into eruptions of smoke and fire. Through the smoke were scenes of chaos as civilians left their vehicles and wagons behind to brave a dash across the bridge. Davidson reached for a radio, "Delta Company, can you help keep that bridge open?" he asked. Before an answer could come back the other side of the bridge, where he had two companies of Marines, was hit by what had to be a spotting shell. "Alpha and Delta, fall back!" the admiral shouted as more artillery rounds came crashing in, blasting the road and the open ground above it. Earth, asphalt, and torn bodies fountained high into the air.

OPERATIONS CENTER
CANHARVEST MALIANA EAST TIMOR PROJECT

Not in her worst nightmares did Grace Jaden expect the complex to come under military attack. Yet, she had been somewhat prepared. "Activate our defense systems!" she screamed into the operations center as the trailer door slammed shut. "Hurry, while we still have time!"

"I'm on it!" Lawrence ran to his terminal where with a few touch commands he activated the weapon systems Jaden had secured from Israelis and American defense contractors—installed with the permission of the overstretched East Timor military.

Lieutenant Guterres with the East Timor military was shouting into the radio, ordering his forces to fall back across the bridge. The forested hillside would be a preferred place to make a stand where they would be less venerable to artillery shells and missiles.

That was where the C-RAM, the Iron Dome, and the Iron Beam trailers were to come into play. Now activated, the Centurion close-in weapons system, also known as C-RAM, was the first to light up the sky. The Vulcan cannon mounted on a swiveling base turned and began to fire at the incoming mortar and artillery shells. Unlike the now obsolete Phalanx naval version, the system fired highly explosive self-destructing 20mm incendiary tracer rounds, which exploded on impact with the target. The small explosions were usually enough to change the course of the shells and prevent them from reaching their intended targets. The occasional shell, which made it past the barrage of C-RAM fire was then hit by the Iron Beam, a 50kW high-energy fiber laser beam. The artillery shells being too many and fast for any human to react to, the fire control system automatically directed the defensive weapons fire.

"I hope to God this works," said Zeniuk, looking over at Grace Jaden.

Knowing it was all in the hands of the fire control computers, Jaden nodded before falling into her chair, leaning back while rubbing her forehead. While not a Soldier, even she could see from the fire control reports that the weapon systems were engaging shells aimed directly at the facility.

US MARINE HELICOPTER DEFIANT ONE
OVER MALIANA EAST TIMOR

American Marines rushed out from behind the cover of the forest to help civilians dash across the bridge. The shells were deliberately aimed to leave the bridge intact. "Move it, move it!" one marine yelled as he grabbed a child from an injured mother, who had blood gushing down her leg. The other Marine had his machine gun up, covering the other side of the bridge, waving the civilians back even while activating his headset. "Getting civilians off the bridge now!"

"Bravo Company under fire!" came the shout of the company commander. He had ordered his Stryker vehicles and over a hundred marines to take cover amidst the wrecked buildings of Maliana. "The city is taking a pounding!"

From the gunship, Admiral Davidson watched as Alpha and Delta companies took defensive positions on the east side of the bridge. To his surprise, the initial shelling had died down, the CanHarvest Petrochemical complex was still untouched, and even the city of Maliana no longer seemed to be under fire. Looking out to make sense of what was happening, Davidson saw the CanHarvest defensive systems taking down the shells. "Well, I'll be damned," he muttered under his breath. He took the opportunity to formulate a strategy. "Companies report position and deploy smoke!"

The Alpha, Bravo, and Charlie Company commanders all reported back that their forces had taken defensive position overlooking the route into Maliana. Bravo Company was deploying around the CanHarvest petrochemical facility. Tossed smoke canisters would hide their exact location and numbers and hopefully offer some cover for the civilians.

"All units, this is Delta Five. We've got company!" came a report over the radio. "Got at least thirty advancing battle tanks heading to cross the bridge!"

Davidson used his heads-up display, controlling various camera systems, to take a look himself from the gunship at the other side of the bridge. On the road coming down into the valley and toward the bridge were at least thirty advancing Chinese-built VT-4 main battle tanks intermixed with Russian-made BTR-80 personnel carriers. The invading formation raced along the highway in the direction of the bridge. Nothing, not even the presence of civilians, was slowing the tanks down. The admiral pushed aside the emotional reaction of seeing crushed bodies to focus on what to do next. The main battle tanks turned their turrets in the direction of the opposite side of the river valley and opened fire—shell after shell.

Captain Rodriquez had dared to approach the river valley only for various klaxons and alerts to fill the gunship indicating that hostile fire control systems had locked onto them. "Hang on!" he cautioned before activating his headset. "Incoming!" Army Captain Rodriguez, having caught the flash of the missile launch and a tactical alert warning sent their AH-72 into a dive straight down toward the tree line for cover.

The pilot of the escorting AH-72 Defiant gunship knew his role in keeping the admiral safe and kept his gunship higher even as it was hit dead-on by the surface-to-air missile and exploded into flames and debris. At such close range, the stealth capabilities of the AH-72 Defiant offered no lifeline for the American crew.

"Air Knight Two down, repeat Air Knight Two down!" Rodriquez shouted.

"*Bonhomme Richard* here," came Colonel Florzone over the radio frequency. "Did anyone see a chute?"

"Negative, negative," Rodriguez reported back solemnly.

Rear Admiral Davidson squeezed the handrails of the copilot seat hard to help regain his composure after the dive of the gunship. *Damn this.* Even more blood pumping then being shot at was the loss of his men. His rules of engagement allowed for defending any US forces under attack. He pushed aside any thoughts as to the comments of the secretary in avoiding a fight. The fight had come to his marines. "This is Rear

Admiral Davidson; all units are weapons-free. We're under attack; prepare for a counter offensive!"

"Engaging now!" came the radio chatter of platoon leaders signaling their understanding. TOW missiles shot out in retaliation across the river valley. Delta Company held the high ground in the hills overlooking the valley, which allowed them to fire over the bridge at the advancing main battle tanks. The TOW missiles hit their designated targets, reducing the invading force to about fifteen armored vehicles within seconds. The remaining tanks scattered off the highway or began to pull back. While the armored advance was blunted, the enemy artillery opened up again with shells on the marine positions. The enemy armored units were no doubt marking the location of the TOW missile launches to train their artillery. Shells exploded once again up and down the east bank of the river. There was too much artillery now for the Centurion C-RAM system to stop all the shells though the deployed smoke canisters kept both civilians and Marines under a haze. "Anyone know where that artillery is?"

"I'll get a drone on it!" Colonel Florzone radioed from the ambitious assault carrier.

"No time," Rear Admiral Davidson whispered as the shells kept coming. He looked to his pilot, Captain Rodriguez. "No time, Soldier."

The pilot nodded in understanding. He confirmed that all the stealth features of the AH-72 Defiant gunship were active and throttled up the pusher propeller, sending the helicopter racing across the enemy-occupied side of the river at more than 460 kilometers an hour. Captain Rodriguez raced the gunship over the dense forests over more enemy VT-4 tanks and BTR-80 armored personnel carriers advancing up the highway. He scanned the radar telemetry, looking for signs of firing artillery.

"There!" Rear Admiral Davidson pointed down at a division of at least thirty NORINCO PLZ-45 self-propelled howitzers set up in a clearing lobbing shell after shell up at his forces to the southeast. "Laser lock if you please."

With a tap, Captain Rodriguez activated a laser identification turret and trained it on the artillery before using the designation to lock the AGM-114 *Hellfire missiles of his own gunship on target.* He gave a quick nod in the direction of the admiral.

"I have an immediate fire mission. Counter-battery mission, target coordinates have been designated! Fire for effect!" Rear Admiral Davidson called out over the radio.

As part of the *Bonhomme Richard's* three warship escorts sailing along the carrier in the Timor Sea was the advanced Zumwalt-class destroyer *John Paul Jones*. Designed to have a low radar cross section, her wave-piercing tumblehome hull made the *John Paul Jones* look more like an ironclad of old than a modern warship. Any hint that she was an obsolete warship, however, was betrayed by the activation of her railgun turret. Both 35MW gas turbines fired up to full capacity powering up the railgun. The projectile had no explosive propellants. Just the electromagnetic force was enough to accelerate the shells over three kilometers a second. The railgun began to pump out shell after shell. "Victor One, shots over," came the report of General Florizone. Despite being over 140 kilometers to the south, it would take only a minute for the first shells to fall from the sky.

WHAMMM! WHAMMM!! WHAMMM!!! Even from the airborne gunship, Rear Admiral Davidson could feel the vibrations of the shells and rockets bursting into the hostile artillery formation. Several PLZ-45 howitzers tried to escape the barrage by driving away from the company. Only one escaped, and the others were brought to a halt as their treads and central firing jacks took damage. The majority of the hostile artillery battery could only sit motionless as shells landed all over their position, toppling trees, shaking the ground, cutting down exposed soldiers, and wreaking havoc on their vehicles.

Seeing the PLZ-45 self-propelled howitzers accelerating away, Captain Rodriguez turned to the rear admiral. "Request permission to engage," he said, gently working his trigger finger.

"Let them have it," said Davidson, nodding.

A Hellfire missile shot out from beneath the AH-72 gunship, streaking off to slam right into the surviving howitzer, which disappeared into a cloud of fire, dust, and mud.

Rear Admiral Davidson turned his attention back to the city of Maliana. According to his tactical display consolidating the reports of all of his forces, it appeared that the hostile armored division was pulling back, blooded by the missiles of Bravo and Delta Company and no longer afforded the cover of artillery. Only Alpha Company appeared to be under sustained attack. "Alpha Company, this is Air Knight One. What's your status?" While waiting for a response, he enlarged the map on the heads-up display and added a waypoint to command Captain Rodriguez to fly the gunship back in the direction of the Rio De Lois River.

"We're falling back!" came the shout of the Alpha Company commander over the radio. A video relay showered his forces pulling back from the bridge where another formation of enemy tanks and armored personnel carriers pushed had emerged. "Hostiles are going to press across the bridge!"

"Bastards." Rear Admiral Davidson shook his head. "We can't let hostiles over that bridge. We'll be overrun."

Back on the *Bonhomme Richard*, Colonel Florzone considered the options, knowing that they couldn't fire their railguns at the advancing enemy with enough accuracy to ensure the safety of the US marines and civilians. "Should we blow the bridge?" the Colonel suggested.

Davidson considered taking down the bridge but was hesitant, given the number of civilians still trying to get across the river. Even now, the bridge was still full of civilians that would be crushed should the tanks make their push across. "We got any Ospreys?"

"They're all yours, Air Knight One."

The forests of East Timor racing below him, Rear Admiral Davidson began to input commands into his console, radioing orders to various aircraft. "All units prepare for targets!"

Having fled to the south, six V-22 Ospreys made hard 180-degree turns while firing up their Rolls-Royce AE 1107C engines to full throttle to accelerate back in the direction of Maliana. The Osprey was primarily built to move Soldiers in and out of battle quickly, but the US Marine Corps had, over the past decades, decided to mount both a laser designator and a .5 caliber GAU-19 three-barrel Gatling guns below the nose along with fuselage-based hardpoints, each with two guided APKWS rockets.

It would be the among the most half-assed air strikes in the history of the US military, Rear Admiral Davidson reflected, but at least he would be doing something to help Alpha Company. Impatient, he looked over at the forest. The highway came into view—filled with burning military and civilian vehicles. Enemy VT-4 main battle tanks navigated around the wreckage, almost at the bridge. "Let 'em have it!" Rear Admiral Davidson ordered.

His targets spotted, Captain Rodriguez fired Hellfire missile after Hellfire missile, taking aim at the VT-4 main battle tanks racing toward the bridge. They would explode seconds prior to reaching the bridge. So close to the objective, the invaders let off smoke to hide their presence while still advancing, one tank ramming the wreckage of the lead tank down into the valley to clear the path. Four V-22 Ospreys flew over the Maliana from the south and opened fire with their GAU-19 Gatling guns, concentrating their fire power directly into the cloud of smoke at the opposite side of the bridge.

Now with the advantage, Soldiers of Alpha Company emerged from their defensive positions looking down on the valley, firing off infrared aimed AT42 Light Anti-tank Weapon missiles. The one-shot 66mm unguided anti-tank weapons propelled by solid rocket fuel slammed into the advancing armored personnel carriers and the tracks of the main battle tanks. Ammunition in one of the VT-4 battle tanks exploded violently blowing off the turret completely off the chassis and into the air.

A BMR80 with an anti-air package responded by firing off surface-to-air missiles as the formation of Ospreys boomed over the bridge. Each Osprey broke formation to take evasive action while deploying flares and chaff.

Rodriguez locked a Hellfire missile on the BMR-80 and took some satisfaction as he pulled the trigger. The armored personnel carrier disappeared into a puff of fire and smoke as the Ospreys turned back to fire APKWS rockets into the now undefended tank formation.

A machine gunner on one of the VT-4 battle tanks made out Davidson's Defiant gunship hovering just on the edge of the valley, correctly guessed it was coordinating the air strikes, and opened fire.

The sounds of bullets ricocheting off the helicopter filled the cockpit followed by the beeping of alarms indicating rotor damage. Captain Rodriguez quickly pushed down his flight stick to drop altitude while raising the nose of the gunship to pull back to the east.

Knowing that the pilot had done the best he could, Rear Admiral Davidson grabbed hold of his restraints and took a deep breath as the gunship dropped.

"Alpha Company to all units," came the exalted report of the Alpha Company commander, "hostiles are bugging out. Repeat, hostiles are bugging out."

The heads-up display was damaged and cracked but still active enough for Davidson to make out the video of enemy units retreating from the bridge, the Rio De Lois still uncrossed by the invaders. "All units, good work but stay vigilant."

As their altitude began to stabilize just above the tree line, Rear Admiral Davidson allowed himself to look over at the pilot with concern, as the flight of the helicopter gunship was now abnormally bumpy and rather noisy.

"We've got to head back. Rotor damage is getting worse," said Captain Rodriguez, confirming the obvious.

Rear Admiral Davidson spent the next five minutes silently worrying that with the pusher propeller at full speed the rotors of the composite helicopter would rip off, sending their gunship crashing into the forest below. He would pat the back of the pilot when the gunship came to a landing on the *Bonhomme Richard*.

"Vampire, vampire, vampire" came a shout over the radio. "We've got incoming missiles—coming in from the West. Range: three hundred kilometers."

Rear Admiral Davidson lowered his headset; not quite sure he had heard the report correctly. "Say again?" He gazed over the monitor, which identified the transmission as coming from the CG-X cruiser *Ticonderoga* as part of the *Bonhomme Richard* battle group.

From deep within the hull of the CG-X cruiser *Ticonderoga*, the anti-air warfare officer watched the display in horror, as ten, now twelve, missile tracks had appeared about three hundred kilometers to the West heading toward their battlegroup of ships in the Timor Sea. "*Ticonderoga* here. We've got multiple tracks inbound from the West, 250 kilometers and closing. Evaluated as submarine-launched!" The AAW officer felt the ship build up speed and turn violently to port. The entire ship rumbled as the cruiser began furiously launching RIM-174 standard extended-range active missiles to shoot down the incoming threat.

"Weapons free!!" the rear admiral ordered, even as he adjusted the flickering heads-up display to project the Timor Sea situation map. The CG-X cruiser *Ticonderoga*, the advanced Zumwalt destroyer *John Paul Jones*, and the upgraded Arleigh Burke-class destroyer *Bainbridge* were now standing between the America-class amphibious assault carrier and a barrage of incoming anti-ship missiles. Radar continued to show more missile launches shooting out from beneath the ocean. "Get me ASW drones over there, now!"

Three CH-46 Sea Knight anti-submarine helicopters were racing in the direction of the submarine missile launches, but already closer were three ASU drones on active patrol. The outer screen of the amphibious battle group was a collection of Sea Ghost, MQ-8B Fire Scout and MQ-25 Avenger drones refueled by Carrier-Based Aerial Refueling System (CBAR) craft. The closest ASU Sea Ghost began dropping sonar buoys into the Timor Sea, which on contact with the water commenced pinging with active sonar.

"Contact!" came the report from the *Ticonderoga* anti-submarine warfare officer commanding the drone. "I've got a Type-093 submarine at missile launching depth."

The report made no sense to Rear Admiral Davidson. The Type 093 Shang-class submarine was a Chinese nuclear-powered submarine—a state-of-the-art one at that. The Chinese commander must not have expected drones to be in proximity to his missile launch, for only upon hearing the pings did they stop firing vertically launched YJ-17 anti-ship missiles and begin to dive to safety. Lest there was any doubt as to the rules of engagement, the rear admiral hollered over the general comms frequency, "Torpedoes away!"

The three drones accelerating in the direction of the sonar contact each dropped a respective Mark 54 torpedo into the ocean, and within seconds, the Shang-class submarine was facing three incoming torpedoes from three different directions. The submarine launched noise counter measures, evading two of the torpedoes, but was simply too shallow and too slow-moving to escape the third. The sonar display lit up with the ensuing signals of the submarine hull exploding as pieces blasted out of the ocean.

Would the Chinese commander take his intended targets to the bottom of the ocean as well? Knowing there was nothing he could do, Rear Admiral Davidson waited. The forests of Timor gave way to the ocean as streaks of light shot to the east across the evening sky. The RIM-174 missiles had shot down about a dozen of the incoming tracks, but radar still showed more than twenty coming in. Some were no doubt decoys. The smaller destroyers were firing their shorter-ranged Sea Sparrow air defense missiles and, now in range, the rail guns and laser systems. The YJ-18 supersonic missiles came in at over Mach 3. The close-in weapon systems were fast, automatically targeting and firing missile after missile, which detonated harmlessly over the ocean. The lasers could hit their targets at the speed of light.

Now close enough to see the four ships of the American fleet, Davidson clenched his fist. "Come on, babies," he urged the ships under his breath, "Dodge those bastards." Even the large amphibious assault carrier *Bonhomme Richard*, over forty thousand tons in weight, was crashing through the water with both shafts at full speed.

There were only a handful of missiles left when the incoming barrage seemed to touch the American ships. The mass drivers of the destroyers took down two while the old-style Phalanx close-in weapon system on the *Bonhomme Richard* downed the third. One missile detonated only seconds from impact, sending a plume of fireballs crashing over the carrier. Some rained over a collection of drones and helicopters. A radar unit exploded on being hit by a rather large piece of debris. Flight crew fell to the flight deck, some on fire, some having shrapnel tear into their bodies.

"All clear, all clear!" came a report from the lead anti-air warfare officer on seeing no more missile tracks on his screens.

More frantic was the report of the flight deck officer. "Fire, fire on the flight deck!"

Under the sun setting over the Timor Sea was a cloud of smoke which had enveloped the *Bomhomme Richard*. Rear Admiral Davidson turned to Rodriguez in the pilot seat as the helicopter gunship approached.

"Can we hold off?" To his relief through the smoke, Davidson made out the carrier, her flight deck on fire but for the most part intact.

With more and more cockpit alarms ringing, Captain Rodriguez shook his head. "Air Knight One to *Bonhomme Richard*. Hate to be a nuisance," he said honestly, "but I've got to come in or bail."

"Uh, give me a minute," came the hesitant response of the *Bonhomme Richard* flight deck controller, who was simultaneously dealing with casualties, fires, and a damaged flight deck. Fire suppression units shot foam and water across the deck, trying to cool the raging infernos.

Captain Rodriguez looked down at the rolling ocean. It looked rough and uninviting.

"Could be worse." Rear Admiral Davidson could see exactly what the pilot was thinking. "This could have occurred over Russia or the Arctic."

The pilot broke out into a laugh. "Whatever you say, sir."

"I've got you cleared on the aft deck," the air controller radioed back, not willing to ditch a multi-million-dollar multi-role compound helicopter for expediency.

Rear Admiral Davidson now only had to worry about crashing down into the flight deck. He patted the back of the pilot when the gunship came to a safe rest on the *Bonhomme Richard*. "Nice flying."

After a salute, Captain Rodriguez proceeded to power down the gunship, relieved that he hadn't lost a multi-million-dollar aircraft on his watch. "It was an honor, sir."

"No, the honor is mine." Davidson firmly shook the pilot's hand. Unbuckling his seat restrains, Rear Admiral Davidson could see from the cockpit that Colonel Florzone was racing from the bridge in the direction of the gunship along with several armed marines. The colonel wore a visible frown, and Davidson was already dreading what the Florzone had to say. The Colonel saluted as Davidson climbed out of the helicopter. Davidson saluted back. "What's wrong?"

"I hate to do this," said Colonel Florzone, shaking his head, obviously disturbed by his orders. He held up a printed piece of paper. "Orders from Washington are for you to be removed of your command and sent back stateside at once."

CHAPTER THREE – DECISIONS

"Is life so dear, or peace so sweet, as to be purchased at the price of chains and slavery? Forbid it, Almighty God! I know not what course others may take; but as for me, give me liberty or give me death!"
—Patrick Henry

FEBRUARY 16, 2068
CANHARVEST MALIANA EAST TIMOR PROJECT
OPERATIONS CENTER

The silence outside the control center was unnerving. The weapon fire had stopped. The civilians, for the most part, tried to hide and keep silent as much as they could. One panel operator looked up at the roof expecting a missile or shell to come shooting down into the control center. Grace Jaden, in standing up from her chair, couldn't help but interrupt the silence. She muffled a cough, being a long-time asthma sufferer.

"Looks like that fight deterred the invasion," said Lawrence, pointing at the cameras still looking out over the Rio De Lois river valley. There was no sign of any hostile activity over the damaged but still standing bridge—just civilians braving the night to flee eastward. It was tough to spot, but US Marines still held positions watching over the bridge.

"They did it," Zeniuk announced. "The good old USA did some good here."

The mention of the American government reminded Jaden that she wasn't out of the woods herself. Her hands were still slightly trembling. Jaden chose her words with great care. "They're going to come back and arrest me, I believe."

Zeniuk tensed up at the serious tone in her voice. "Says who?"

"The Marine commander," said Jaden, then stopped, at a loss for words.

The control center was silent again as all within contemplated the circumstances.

"I need a coffee." Zenuck reached over, poured himself a mug, and took a sip.

Jaden followed suit and found comfort in a mouthful of hot refreshing light-roast coffee.

"So what's our next move?" Zenuck asked.

The chief executive officer shrugged, simply happy at the moment to still be alive before gulping down her sip of coffee. "Is there a next move?"

Punching up his security console, Lawrence tapped on his monitor. "Batteries are too low for our defenses." As if on cue, the lights dimmed and some of the monitors deactivated.

Jaden chuckled. In no way did she want or expect her security detail to take on US Marines. "It's okay, Lawrence. They did good." Whatever millions the company had spent on those systems had been worth it.

"We could just give in," said Zenuck, brainstorming as he sat back in his chair and put his hands behind his head in a stretch. "They get a board seat. So what? We've been doing good for decades. Twenty-five years of tax returns. Do we really think we made no mistakes?"

Jaden shook her head at Zenuck. "No way," her blood boiled as she pointed at the engineer and friend. "This is our company. We built it. It's ours." She had no willingness to lose her freedom to research and build what she wanted, when she wanted. "I'll go to jail, fight the good fight with the lawyers."

There were chuckles across the room, as the way Jaden said the word *lawyer* reminded them all of a collective lack of faith in the legal system. "You mean the civil liberties association that stands for anything but the civil liberties of private-sector civilians?" Lawrence rubbed his forehead in frustration. "A waste of time. It's like fighting in the court of public opinion when the news organizations are all with the state."

All the employees in the room stared at Jaden. Zenick simply couldn't accept that her lot would be jail time. She had probably personally just saved tens of thousands of civilians, not to mention pretty much solved global climate change. He sighed and stood upright. "We've got to get you out of here. We've got the *Shangri-La* in the Banda Sea within flying distance." Far off to the north was a corporate executive yacht that the company used for meetings and wooing investors.

Lawrence raised his eyes and nodded. "Your right," he said, motioning with his hand. "Let's get you out of here."

"What of the Timorese?" Jaden's voice shrank to a hollow whisper.

"You've done what you can," Zenuck urged. "They'll be fine with those Marines here. Besides, Labaoucan will kill us if he finds out we let you get arrested."

Grace Jaden looked slowly around the control center, moving her eyes from person to person, seeking their input. One by one, each shook their head in affirmation. Satisfied, she cleared her throat. "Lead the way."

Lawrence and Zenuck jumped into action, rushing her out of the control trailer and in the direction of a small corporate helicopter. Seeing the executives emerge, security officers began to clear a path for her to approach the helicopter. With a wave of his arms, Lawrence prompted the corporate pilot to start up the helicopter, then opened up the door and had Jaden jump in. "You too." He pointed at Zeniuk. "You're with her."

"You stay safe, Lawrence." Jaden gave the security chief a brief hug. "Evacuate the facility safety and then get stateside as soon as you can."

Lawrence pointed at Zenuck. "Take good care of her," he shouted.

Zenuck shrugged while struggling to lift himself into the back of the small helicopter before finally turning back to wave. "Stay safe, buddy. See you on the flip side."

Lawrence slammed the helicopter door shut and gave a quick thumbs up after which the corporate pilot throttled the rotors and sent the helicopter up into the air.

Jaden leaned back into her seat and allowed herself to recognize how tired she felt as the helicopter shot to the north. It took over twenty minutes before trees and grassland gave way to the coast and the blue waters of the Banda Sea.

Seeing Jaden suppress a yawn, Zenuck tossed her a headset so they could communicate. "You know, this might work out," the engineer said. "Move the company to Singapore."

Even with the sun almost completely set, the calm and inviting waters of the Banda Sea seemed to stretch out forever. "Singapore has an extradition treaty," Jaden replied, not quite feeling up to considering a list of other countries. China was never an option, given full state control. Russia was simply too corrupt. Europe was worse than the United States. The ocean seemed to be calling out to her, though. "What if we fled to our own country?"

In laughing, Zeniuk could feel his body throbbing from a lack of sleep. Stars were becoming visible over the night sky. He leaned against the window of the helicopter and allowed his eyes to shut. "Sure, why not?"

Grace Jaden knew she would no longer be able to sleep, as her mind was now actively engaged thinking through a concept. She had learned to accept and embrace ever since university that once she had an outside-the-box idea—one that had the neurons firing—that any attempt to sleep would just result in a lot of tossing and turning. Instead, the executive reached over, picked up a tablet, and began both researching and taking notes on her concept.

FEBRUARY 17, 2068
CORPORATE YACHT SHANGRI-LA
THE BANDA SEA

Zenuck opened his eyes to see the sun well up over the horizon and the world gently rocking. With a yawn and a stretch to get the oxygen flowing, Zenuck opened his eyes wide enough to confirm the corporate helicopter had safely landed on the corporate yacht, the *Shangri-La*. With a lazy turn of his head, he found the helicopter empty. He pulled hard on the helicopter door hatch only to regret it when he lost his balance as the door slid open faster than anticipated. Zenuck tumbled out of the helicopter with too much inertia and too little motor control to save himself from hitting the deck. He wriggled to pull himself up regardless of the rolling of the yacht with the help of a nearby deck railing. Hoping no one saw anything, he chuckled through the pain. Having learned a lesson, the engineer decided to simply hold on to the railing and allow himself to fully awaken.

The helicopter pad was located just aft and one level down from the bridge deck. Looking aft and down two decks, Zenuck could see the vessel pool below and, beyond that, the wake of the vessel moving through the open water. From the position of the sun, Zenuck guessed they were heading east toward the Pacific. The seventy-four-meter *Shangri-La* was the largest of three corporate mega yachts owned by the company, usually used for various company events and to entertain the media and potential investors. The vessel was an AMELS 242 model, being seventy-four meters, or 242 feet long, with six decks. Grace Jaden had named most of the company vessels after lost cities. *Shangri-La*, of course, was a fictional city—or, rather, a mystical, harmonious valley described in a 1933 novel by James Hilton. Knowing his friend, Zenuck assumed Jaden liked the fact that when President Franklin in World War 2 had been asked where the Doolittle Raid had been launched from and unable to give the real names of the aircraft carriers he had replied "*Shangri-La*." The US Navy too had once enjoyed that joke enough to have named a real aircraft carrier the *Shangri-La* in 1944.

Having regained his composure, Zenuck dashed down a level using the nearest stairway where beyond a couple of observation couches and an outdoor conference table was a glass-enclosed boardroom. Glass doors automatically slid open to let him join Grace Jaden, who stood alone, talking with a projection of Chief Financial Officer Jord Labaoucan on one screen and the Chief Legal Officer Roger Bertrand on another. Zenuck rushed in to take a seat as the conference continued.

"I guess I have no one to blame but myself for the work of that IRS investigation," Labaoucan transmitted from their corporate office in downtown Phoenix. The fifty-year-old of aboriginal background tried to console himself with the view of the Phoenix skyline from the top floor of their twenty-story building.

"Did you know about the IRS investigation?" Jaden asked, even as she waved Zenuck to take a seat at the conference.

"No, it's definitely a pressure tactic."

Jaden shook her head. "It's not your fault. They've changed the rules."

Labaoucan frowned while picking up a tablet off his deck and holding it up to highlight an article. "It gets worse. Media picked up on my domestic dispute from when I was a teenager." He tapped on the rather damning article. "Maybe time to retire."

The chief executive officer tapped her fingers on the boardroom table, continuing to shake her head. "That was a long time ago. You were a kid that married way too early. You sobered up, got a degree. Hell"—she threw up her arms—"You were critical to building this company. You've got a happy wife and five kids now." She took a deep breath. "You're critical to running this company. I will not accept your resignation."

"This ain't Laramie, Wyoming," said Bertrand from his office in New York while raising a finely sculpted eyebrow. The thirty-eight-year-old lawyer was the best-dressed and youngest of the executive team. He always felt that the technical CanHarvest executives were rather unsophisticated in their ways and that, at last, reality had caught up to them. It always bothered him that Grace, unlike most major executive officers, preferred small-town America, where most of their operating facilities were, to the hustle and bustle of the major cities. The lawyer had kept silent, meeting after meeting, with a look of disdain on his face but felt the time had finally come to forcefully join in the discussion. "With all due respect, we need the court of public opinion on our side. They see you as greedy and now backing someone." He shrugged his shoulders before continuing. "*Labaoucan*, a man who had a heated fight with his former girlfriend." He let that sink in and then continued. "Enough is enough. We should submit to the Corporate Accountability Act. Allow the government board representation, agree to an act compliant charter and all these problems should go away."

"Christ," Jaden mumbled to herself before taking a deep breath, struggling to calm down. She stood up and leaned over the board room table. "You're supposed to be defending our constitutional rights. We have a right to own and operate a private company. Why should we want to prop up a government becoming more corrupt by the year?"

Bertrand's lips thinned. "The public needs the government now more than ever. Bombings in the streets, the interest payments on the debt more than most programs. What about the social good?" Bertrand laced his fingers together and sat back in his chair.

Jaden couldn't believe what she was hearing. Her fist crashed down on the boardroom table "You're fired, effective immediately!"

Chuckling, the lawyer crossed his arms. "That's your right for now. But I'm pretty sure your days are as numbered with the company as mine." With the touch of a button the screen went blank.

"He's right, you know," Labaoucan grimly admitted. "Tax evasion charges against the company. Charges of filibustering against you. This scandal on me. I can't see us lasting much longer. Only a matter of time before they start seizing assets."

Grace Jaden took a seat at the conference room desk and put her hands together to make it clear that she was about to engage in serious discussion. "I swear to you, we're not finished yet."

Having listened to the conversion, Zenuck felt resigned to the fact that his time at CanHarvest was almost at an end. "We've got no cards left to play. We fought a good fight."

"Place call to lawyer Kelly Agarwal," Jaden ordered the software running the conference room equipment.

An unused portion of the screen lit up to reveal another company lawyer, this one out in the Phoenix headquarters. A contrast to the pale, slim, and polished Bertrand, Kelly Agarwal was of similar age but of an Indian background, short and slightly overweight. And she was definitely surprised to have gotten a call from the chief executive officer, having instinctively answered the call while still sipping her coffee. "Uh," the lawyer quickly tried to adjust her unsettled hair upon recognizing the chief executive officer on her wall-mounted computer. "Ma'am?"

"You're the lawyer that did the brief on Project Byzantium?" Jaden asked. Subconsciously enticed by the coffee in Agarwal's hand, Jaden stood up to pour herself a cup.

Agarwal's eyebrows went up, as did her excitement level. "Yes, ma'am!" she almost gleefully continued. "The legality of nutrient recycling in international waters! Gotta love a legal grey area!"

The enthusiasm of the lawyer was surprising to both Jaden and Zenuck to the point they both exchanged a glance of disbelief. Jaden punched up the lawyer's resume on her tablet. "Senior analyst, reporting to Bertrand. You have a Masters of Law from London?"

"Yes, ma'am!"

"What's your take on the Corporate Accountability Act?" the executive pressed.

Kelly Agarwal answered, grinning from ear to ear, ecstatic that someone cared enough to ask for her opinion. "It's fundamentally a determinant to our civil liberties, our free market, and our democracy as a whole. Quite frankly, I'm unclear why we're not challenging it constitutionally all the way to the Supreme Court."

Jaden spoke for everyone else on the conference call when she replied, "Well that's a breath of fresh air."

"Why wasn't she running the legal department?" Zenuck added.

Jaden nodded while leaving the question unanswered, knowing it was too late to correct that mistake. Coffee in hand and ready to talk business, Jaden took her seat. "Argarwal, what if I said I wanted to split CanHarvest into two. Most of the company to be spun off as the existing corporate company, minus my shareholdings, to be left to the existing shareholders in the United States." She raised her hand before Zenuck could speak. "But my shares are to be used to purchase the spin-off Byzantium project."

Labaoucan sternly objected. "The Byzantium project is an R&D sideshow that isn't worth a tenth of what your shares are valued at."

Jaden knew Labaoucan had a point, but it was moot. "Then, it's a great deal for company shareholders."

"Better to rule in hell than serve in heaven?" Labaoucan rubbed his chin, warming up to an idea he didn't even fully understand yet. "Still"— he threw his hands up in the air—"that's a lot of money to be giving away."

"I'm feeling charitable," said Jaden, looking directly at the image of Argarwal and waiting.

Argarwal, having given her legal opinion, wasn't accustomed to being actively asked for advice. Realizing all eyes were still on her, she sat up straight and flicked the ball of tape she'd been fidgeting with, sinking it in a nearby wastebasket.

"Just answer the question, Kelly," Jaden urged upon realizing that the delay wasn't simply the lag of the microwave transmissions bouncing to and from a communications satellite in geosynchronous orbit.

Recalling she had an answer to an asked question, Argarwal replied. "We can do the paperwork,"

The response was exactly what Jaden wanted to hear—so much so that the executive broke into a hint of a smile. "Now if we decided to operate the Byzantium project in the Pacific, in international waters, would US law apply?"

Argarwal had been pondering just how, exactly, the current line of questioning fit with her report on the Byzantium project. It had been over a year ago that she had been tasked to formulate a legal opinion on a biomass production pilot to be run in the deep ocean. The technology seemed environmentally safe, using recycled fertilizer to grow seaweed in the ocean where it didn't normally grow, but management had asked just who would be the regulator to approve it. Finding the whole affair irrelevant, Bertrand had passed it on to the analyst. "Per my report, the ship and the project as a whole would be under the jurisdiction of the flag state unless . . ." Her voice trailed off as she realized where the executive was going with the conversation.

"Unless we declared the project was under another flag."

"Yes." Argarwal's answer was short and sweet.

Grade Jaden turned to Zenuck and Labaoucan. Despite knowing the high-level concepts surrounding the proposed Byzantium Demonstration Project, they were still lost as to how it could be of paramount importance to the here and now. "Engineering proposed we could produce a low-cost biomass in the open ocean to safely consume carbon dioxide and boost crude production." She left out the fact that the concept had been developed at her personal request.

With a few taps on his console, Zenuck loaded up the project overview. A map of the Pacific appeared, which zoomed into to show three-dimensional models of ships operating at sea. He had given presentations on the Byzantium demonstration project hundreds of times, and he started to give a briefing semi-automatically. "As you know, terrestrial biomass production is maxed out feeding our renewable crude facilities. To boost production, the idea was that we would use drones and recycling nutrients to seed portions of the open ocean, produce seaweed, and then use dredging vessels to feed a production platform"—he waved his arm like a magic wand in the air—"and voila, new crude production. Just what you asked for."

"Yes," Jaden smiled in appreciation, "But we had serious questions about who the stakeholders for the project were. Who do you ask for regulatory approval in international waters? Since our system disperses nutrients that only the seaweed can utilize or it will drop harmlessly to the bottom of the ocean, who could approve or reject it? I asked the legal team to clarify, and as Argarwal pointed out, the answer was our flag country. But she noted that we could *pick* our flag country. Well . . ." Jaden took a deep breath. "What if we declared our *own* flag country?"

The conference room went so silent, one could hear a pin drop. Jaden cringed at the potential for negative reactions while the other three participants sat stunned—like deer in headlights.

"Uh." Zenuck face muscles tensed up, and he grimaced. He tilted his head one way and then another as if mentally looking at the suggestion from different angles. It was clear he didn't think he heard what Jaden had said correctly. "Our own flag? Like our own country?"

Labaoucan joined in the questioning. "We declare independence?" Grace Jaden nodded.

"Now, wait just a damn minute," Labaoucan protested. "You can't be serious."

"Argarwal." Grace Jaden's tone was one of resolve. "Could we operate the Byzantium demonstration project under our own flag?"

Argarwal played with her hair for a moment while contemplating what to sat. She sighed while deciding between the safe answer and the right answer. At the end of the day, Argarwal wasn't one to choose the safe path. "You would have a legal case to be exempt from US law."

"Ladies and gentlemen"—Grace Jaden turned to look all of the conference participants in the eye—"I propose to hand over the majority of CanHarvest to go build a new company as part of a new country." She finished with a look at Zeniuk. "Zeniuk, you agreed to that last night."

There were chuckles at that, and even Zenuck smiled in response. He half-suspected that her question last night wasn't simply a dream but a trial to gauge his response. "I was half asleep!" It wasn't the first time that they had joked of a crazy plan of action late in the night, not taken seriously at the time, to be later implemented come morning. Still, he added, "And I didn't think you were serious!"

"I can't believe I'm asking this . . ." Labaoucan cracked his knuckles and leaned forward. "But what would this new country be like?"

"Free state. Democracy, limited government," Jaden began, "A condominium constitution with—"

"A condominium constitution?" Labaoucan was waiting for the mere mention of some new concept he would have to learn. He quickly typed the words *condominium* and *government* into his Internet search engine and wasn't surprised when articles came up. "How long did you research this?" He kept skimming over articles. "You were up all night, weren't you? When is the last time you slept?"

Kelly Agarwal felt her heart beating faster as if she was about to be part of something larger than herself. "Ma'am, if it's any consolation, I'd love to move to your country."

There was silence in the room.

Zenuck groaned as he reviewed the assets of the Byzantium project. There were six ships in total, three large tankers, two modified cruise ships, and two modified floating production platforms. "I guess I'd better figure out how to make this practically work. We'd have to be completely self-sufficient."

Chief Executive Grace Jaden gave the order. "You'd better."

"Damn it," came the reluctant agreement from Jord Labaoucan. "My wife hates boats. She gets real sea sick, real fast."

Despite trying to push them from his mind as unrealistic, thoughts of relaxing on a sundeck looking out at a sunset while drinking and listening to soft country tunes just wouldn't give way. Zenuck raised a hand. "I've got a question." The more serious concerns of food and shelter could wait.

"What is it they say? There are no stupid questions?" Laboucan shrugged.

"This one might be," said Zenuck, grinning. "Can we name this new state the Republic of Margaritaville?"

With a groan, Laboucan pointed at the virtual image of the engineer. "That, my friend"—he broke out into a smile—"is, in fact, an excellent question."

Grace Jaden ignored the question and walked away. But a worry did cross her mind: if the concept proved an absolute failure, would she be the woman to blame?

CHAPTER FOUR – UNEASE

"Liberty means responsibility. That is why most men dread it."
—George Bernard Shaw
FEBRUARY 20, 2068
THE PENTAGON

For the first time in his life, Rear Admiral Richard Davidson dreaded stepping into the Pentagon. For decades, he had loved traveling across the Potomac River from Washington, D.C., and took pride in stepping into a building with so much meaning and history. Even after 140 years, the Pentagon was still the world's largest office building, with about 600,000 square meters of office space, where more than twenty-four thousand military and civilian employees worked. Passing through security, he made his way to a boardroom, saluting as he passed security.

The boardroom was large enough for twenty around a table, but for this occasion, only two men sat at opposite sides of the table. It was one of the newer boardrooms built after the 2001 terrorist attacks in which an airliner had been hijacked and rammed into the complex. The secretary of defense, whose last name was Taggart—an old friend from Annapolis— saluted as Davidson entered the room. Secretary of State Harris was with him. Rear Admiral Davidson, the well-built and in-shape-for-sixty secretary of defense motioned for the admiral to take a seat.

Davidson saluted with a stiffened back before pulling out a chair, not quite sure what to expect. At their request, he had been flown from the Pacific and back stateside, where to his wife's happiness, he had been given a week off. It was hard to enjoy the company of his kids and spouse, however, when his future with the military was in question. As he sat down, he took a deep breath.

There was a momentary silence around the table. The secretary of state glared at Davidson, barely containing his rage.

"Listen, Davidson," said the secretary of defense, breaking the silence and pushing his glasses up his nose, "You did good work out there in East Timor."

The secretary of state jumped up from his seat and pointed right at the rear admiral. "You did no such thing!" the younger man screamed. "You disobeyed my direct request not to engage. You did not arrest Grace Jaden."

Rear Admiral Davidson's hope that his transfer from command a week ago had nothing to do with his actions concerning Jaden were dashed. All he could do was sit back slightly and accept responsibility. "Our forces were under attack," he calmly replied. "We were even attacked by a Chinese submarine," he added. "It makes no sense."

"What makes no sense is why you didn't withdraw!" The suited secretary of state paced around the conference table in the direction of the admiral.

"The casualties would have been—"

"None of your concern!" The secretary of state pointed over at a monitor projecting the latest media news broadcast. "The only reason why I'm not urging you be thrown in prison is the positive press making you out to be some hero. Do you understand?"

The secretary of defense stood up with a nervous clearing of his throat. "Listen, I have reviewed the rules of engagement, and Davidson was in the right." He spoke aloud to both the admiral and the secretary of state. Before the secretary of state could turn angrily on him, the secretary of defense quickly continued. "But the administration didn't want a fight. They are now under pressure from the local players and the Chinese " He turned back to the large map projection system with a large-scale display of the Pacific Ocean. "The focus right now is Taiwan, where we've got the Chinese navy making moves, threatening Taiwan and claiming the South China Sea."

"They shouldn't have sent our forces into East Timor then," Rear Admiral Davidson calmly replied. He knew keeping his military career alive past the meeting depended on his ability to remain tranquil no matter how absurd or angering the secretary of state's tirade proved.

The secretary of state nodded his head. "For once, you and I agree." The man shook his head. "I urged the president to use intelligent agencies to retrieve her under the radar as opposed to using the military." The younger man grabbed hold of the desk and looked down, almost upset that he couldn't assign further blame. "I want you out of the military," Harris said without looking up.

Rear Admiral Davidson felt as if he had been suddenly thrown into an abyss, his head spinning at the thought of a life without the Navy. He tried to find solace in the stability of his chair but to no avail. He fell into his chair, silent and defeated.

The secretary of defense made his way toward the veteran sailor. "I have prepared a package for you." He reluctantly threw the papers onto the desk, "An honorable discharge with full benefits."

"You should take it," the secretary of state seethed. "It's more than I wanted them to offer."

While both were in the same administration, the secretary of defense had no love for Harris, annoyed at his lack of respect and understanding that the military was supposed to be run free and clear of the petty politics of Washington. "I know your wife was pressuring you to resign anyway." The secretary of defense tried to sound consoling.

It was true that Davidson's wife had been demanding he resign from the military to spend more time with family in the United States. His kids were getting older, and he had found himself on more than one occasion regretting missing their childhoods while deployed in the Mediterranean Sea. "I'm here to serve, I will not resign."

The secretary of defense gently touched the rear admiral's shoulder. "Take some time. Read through the package."

Rear Admiral Davidson took the papers from the desk, stood tall to give a salute, and made his way out of the boardroom.

Left alone in silence, Secretary of Defense Taggart and Secretary of State Harris mentally worked out how to diplomatically object to each other. Harris continued to look down at the table, unwilling to face Taggart. "I'm going to ensure this Davidson's next job is as a janitor. Send a message to all you reckless cowboys out there."

Taggart sadly shook his head. "You just lost us one of our veteran sailors while we face China in Taiwan and the South China Sea."

Only then did Harris look up from the wooden boardroom table. "There will be no fight with China."

Am I serving the good guys? Taggart was full of doubt. Tired and frustrated, the secretary of defense lumbered out of the boardroom.

OUTSIDE THE PENTAGON

It was cloudy and raining over the Potomac. Davidson, not in a cheerful mood, didn't bother grabbing his umbrella from the car, instead taking in the feeling and sounds of cold wet raindrops colliding with his black trench coat. He cursed under his breath on realizing he was looking at a red Hyundai that was not his. He turned to the nearest sign to find his bearings were so off had thoughtlessly wandered into the wrong parking lot. Off in the distance, he found his red renewable gasoline-powered Ford carbon fiber pick-up truck surrounded by a collection of Tesla cars hooked up to the charging banks. It was times like these that he was glad he had gone for the versatile fire-up-at-any-time convenience of internal combustion engines. To his surprise, standing next to his car under an umbrella was the secretary of defense. Davidson saluted.

After returning the salute, the secretary of defense spoke almost sheepishly. "We need to talk."

His interest piqued, Davidson walked up to the passenger side and pulled on the door handle. He gestured for Taggart to take a seat before walking around to the driver's side and lifting himself in. Slamming the door shut, he turned to his friend—almost with disdain. "What can I help you with?"

Taggart reached into his coat and held up a flash disk. "I know I'm not in a position to ask for a favor, but I need one. That submarine was definitely Chinese-operated."

"You mean the Chinese don't just give away state-of-the-art nuclear submarines to second-tier allies?" Davidson chuckled.

"Something is up in the Pacific." the secretary of defense shifted uncomfortably. "I'm going to quietly demote you"—he made quotation marks in the air to make it clear it shouldn't be seen as a demotion—"to the Office of Naval Intelligence."

The Office of Naval Intelligence was the oldest member of the US intelligence community, tasked with maritime intelligence since 1882. Headquartered in Suitland Maryland, the organization had managed to enjoy considerable independence under the pretext of ensuring real-time reporting on foreign navies, international shipping, and irregular warfare at sea. The thought of such definitely had Davidson's attention. "I'm a sailor," he replied honestly.

"Your wife wants you home," Taggart replied, "And you're of more use to me there. I need to know just what the hell is going on. Honestly," he said with a shrug, "the powers that be aren't as concerned as they should be, and I don't know why."

All of the above statements rang true to Davidson. His wife had been urging him to leave the service. The timing of the East Timor incursions made no sense. And White House disinterest in growing Chinese naval power and movements around Taiwan was equally perplexing. Davidson reached over and pulled the handle to the passenger side door.

The secretary of defense frowned, having expected the rear admiral to jump at the opportunity. If not Davidson, from whom could he get answers? Who could he trust?

"I'll report to Suitland as soon as the transfer is official." Davidson gave a quick salute as Taggart exited the truck. "And I'll get you those answers."

MARCH 1, 2068
HUAIREN HALL,
BEIJING, PEOPLE'S REPUBLIC OF CHINA

The Huairen Hall was built in 1885, over two hundred years earlier, by a Chinese Prince. An outside observer would think it was a Chinese temple or monastery. The Chinese monarchy under the emperor was long gone, replaced by the Politburo of the Communist Party of China, which now met in the hall. In theory elected by the central committee, the politburo was, in practice, very much self-perpetuating by means of predetermined candidates chosen through deliberations by current and retired members. The source of ultimate power was the premier. It was no surprise to find the premier of the People's Republic of China meeting fellow party members in the former imperial garden as opposed to the palaces of the Forbidden City. The current Premier, Xi Shenkum, as the self-proclaimed leader of a new cultural revolution to recapture fortunes lost to the fleeing capitalist class, made it a point to meet in the older halls as opposed to more elaborate and ceremonial buildings. He nodded as members of his defense council emerged from a vast gateway topped by the odd combination of a stone-carved imperial dragon and the hammer and sickle logo of the Party. "What news, comrades?"

"The Americans are accepting that our submarine was acting on Indonesian orders," the foreign minister began with a faintly troubled look on his face.

At the thought of a hundred dead Chinese sailors, the premier slammed his fist against a nearby pillar. "It's the Americans who should be providing excuses to us!" the younger premier shouted. His youthfulness contrasted greatly with the old secretary-general. He pointed at the Foreign Minister as if he were the American president himself. "We had an agreement!"

"Which the Americans still intend to honor," the foreign minister was quick to retort. "Portions of their political balance of power remain intact, and they tell us it will take time."

"I have no time for failing imperialist nonsense! Time is a luxury the Americans do not deserve!" Premier Shenkum chuckled at that. "The foolish spoiled imperialists. We know the state of their treasury; they cannot help but spend capital they do not have." He rubbed his hands together. "It will be their undoing."

The general secretary of China, a relatively ancient man by the name of Jinpin, inserted himself into the conversation to urge caution. "Still, we must keep the ruse going,"

While the secretary-general was an elder statesman, Shenkum had little respect for him, and actively had to hide his disdain for the predictable old man. Jinpin had abandoned his Chinese communist ideology in favor of the stability and riches of the capitalist class. The general secretary had only recently come to work with Shenkum after making it clear he was hunting for capital hoarded by corrupt officials including him should he be uncooperative. Shenkum ensured his tone was unrepentant and uncompromising. "The sooner we replace the ailing United States of America as the lone superpower of the world, the better."

"Comrade Premier," the defense minister said confidently. "With their open borders, we have prepositioned our assets. Why not take that which the Americans provide for us?"

"We have waited this long," General Secretary Jinpin added before breaking into a hoarse cough that betrayed his fear of what was to come. When he was a younger man, Jinpin would have tried to change the course of events to save lives, but feeling his age and on seeing the weakness of the Americans, he knew any attempt to change course would be seen as cowardice. Perhaps he could stall and buy time for rationality and peace? "What is but five more years?"

"Comrades, the revolution must prevail!" Premier Shenkum looked around the room in contempt at his fellow politicians. "There will never be a better time." He spoke the truth. Chinese public multinational corporations were an oxymoron but accepted by cash-strapped and economically stalled Western nations. The West was consumed by internal politics and divisions. "We would already be the hegemon of the world were it not for corrupt officials infiltrating the Party, stealing public money, and fleeing to the West." He purposely spoke with an accusatory tone.

The other council members looked at each other. No one dared object to the Premier for fear that the others would turn on them. Dissenters might be in the majority, in which case the premier could be removed, but then again, they may not have the numbers, in which case their lives would be lost. Even those council members who internally saw madness in the plans of the premier determined that by keeping silent they could rise in status within the politburo.

Shenkum saw the hint of dismay in the faces of the silent council members and smiled. "While we may wait on the final plans," he said as if making a concession, "it is time to bring Taiwan and other inner islands back to the rightful land of our ancestors."

There was no objection. The fellow members of the council had been in politics long enough to know when a course of action was now inevitable.

CHAPTER FIVE – A PLAN

"If you want to build a ship, don't drum up the men to gather wood, divide the work and give orders. Instead, teach them to yearn for the vast and endless sea."

—Antoine de Saint Exupery

MARCH 22 2068

MV BYZANTIUM

THE PACIFIC OCEAN, 200KM SOUTH OF MIDWAY

The *MV Byzantium* was one of three specially modified Floating Production and Storage Units, large floating vessels once used by the offshore oil and gas industry, purchased and operated by the company. Even under clear sunny skies, the three ships—in wide formation with over a kilometer of Pacific ocean between them—looked to most like massive oil tankers. Only close up could one see the extensive helicopter landing pad, the distillation towers of the processing plant, and the odd-looking moon pool where a service rig once sat.

While Grace Jaden had helped engineer the ship, she hadn't yet personally seen a completed vessel. She couldn't help but smile at the satisfaction she was stepping out of the corporate helicopter and onto a design made real.

Two rather tall crewmembers stood at attention to receive her. One was the ship's commander by the name of George Tyson. The man was a rather muscular no-nonsense former drilling ship manager who during the energy transition from petroleum to renewables found himself out of a job. He gave a salute, which Jaden awkwardly returned with a raised eyebrow before she offered her hand. "No salutes required here, Mr. Tyson."

"Sorry, ma'am." Tyson took Jaden's hand and shook firmly. "Was in the British Navy before working the rigs."

The other person standing tall was a slender bioengineer by the name of Doctor Yan Huang. Between her naturally quiet nature and being ill at ease with the rolling of the ship, Dr. Huang was rather soft-spoken as she bowed. "A pleasure to serve, you ma'am."

"It's Grace." Jaden first bowed back before shaking the doctor's hand. "The pleasure is all mine."

Nicholas Zenuck had overseen the commissioning of the vessel over six months earlier, so he knew both Dr. Huang and Captain Tyson well. "Dr. Huang, Captain Tyson." He both bowed and shook their respective hands. "A pleasure to see you out here on the high seas!"

The pleasantries aside, Jaden let her anxieties and concerns surface. "Well, team, the success of our efforts out here depends on being self-sufficient." The chief executive officer knew that they might as well have been on the Moon, so alone was her team now.

"Self-sufficiency you want, self-sufficiency you shall have." Zenuck turned to his project fellows before adding a not-so-confident rhetorical question. "Right?"

Captain Tyson led them off the helicopter deck and onto the bridge of the ship. Display screens and three crew members to the front were focused on the position of the vessel and her two sister ships in the Pacific. "As you can see, we are now two hundred kilometers south of Midway Island in international waters," the Captain began. "Our position is based on both satellite and radar telemetry."

"This location has been selected per the project requirements," said Dr. Huang, pointing to a variety of display screens situated to the center of the bridge away from the windows looking out over the ocean. "Temperature is rather high year-round, and currents are minimal far from any local islands. The perfect place for us to grow the Sargassum kelp. Ocean depth is greater than that of Mount Everest at this location, and there are neither fluvial nor alluvial aquatic systems present." That there was no river or shallow life—be it fish, coral, or crustaceans—ensured that whatever they were doing on the high seas wouldn't put any existing biological systems in danger.

"Are you achieving biomass growth productivity?" Jaden took in the information coming off the displays.

"In a word, yes." Dr. Huang adjusted one of the full-height smart displays and loaded a top-down display of the ocean around the three ships. Clusters of orange appeared on the map, surrounded by large circles. "This is our biomass growth zone at a radius of approximately fifty kilometers surrounding the vessel. These masses are *Sargassum* blooms." Aware that seeing was believing, the former professor led the team away from her displays and out of the bridge complex, down the metallic stairs, and to the moon pool in the center of the vessel.

Within the pool was *Sargassum*, layers upon layers of floating brown seaweed. *Sargassum*, unlike most seaweeds, reproduced vegetatively and floated with berrylike gas-filled bladders on special branches. Several small drones lifted entangled patches—some over seven meters long— and then flew off over the horizon. On noticing Jaden smile at the sight of the drone system in action, Zenuck gave her a thumbs up.

Dr. Huang continued. "Per your patent, the drones are deploying *Sargassum* in addition to floating nutrient dispersion drones into the open sea at set intervals around the production ships. Provided enough fertilizer in the form of ammonium ions, phosphate, and phosphorus, the *Sargassum* grows quickly into large mats similar to those found in the Sargasso Sea over a period of about three months." Walking away from the center of the deck, Dr. Huang took a firm hold of the deck railing before leaning over and pointing out at several small semi-automated vessels. Feeling that her area of expertise was covered, Huang turned to Zenuck.

"Those are the M-1 aquatic seaweed harvesters," said Zenuck, pointing at the bright orange paddle-wheel-propelled vessels filled with Sargassum they had skimmed off the ocean with the use of a front-mounted conveyer. "Using satellite- and drone-provided telemetry, we find the dense mature mats, which are half collected and brought back to the ship. Also, the nutrient dispersal drones are returned when emptied."

Concern about the design of the project was quickly rekindled in Jaden's mind. "With the currents and storms, are we having success in locating the mats?"

Wanting to ensure all his team had a chance to contribute, Zenuck eyed Captain Tyson, who realized it was his turn to speak.

"So far so good." The captain knocked on the deck railing to ward off any bad luck. "Between the satellite telemetry and the buoys, we're able to find the dense mats. Outside the selected growth zone, the *Sargassum* has no nutrients and dies off. It's an art, but it keeps the crew busy and out of trouble. Generally, over six months, we do a complete circle. During hurricanes, we collect what we can and get the hell out of dodge. We've got a team of four meteorologists and pretty much task a private weather satellite full time."

An M-1 harvester had docked with the offloading conveyer and commenced offloading its cargo of green kelp. Upon offloading what was on the deck, it began to pull up a net filled with Sargassum it had been offloading. "The net storage systems are working?" Jaden asked.

"So far, so good," Tyson replied. "Allows each harvester to carry back almost ten times its weight."

That had been a technical challenge during the design of the unit—how to store enough Sargassum. The decision was ultimately made to use off-ship nets that the harvesters would fill up and drag around.

"Provided enough sun and nutrients, we're seeing production at approximately thirty metric tons per acre," Zenuck said rather proudly. "At one hundred square kilometers, each production platform can produce approximately two thousand metric tons of biomass."

Seeing a process come to life always brought a sparkle to Grace Jaden's eyes. She crossed her arms and leaned out over the deck to watch the harvesters link up to a conveyer off the production ship and commence offloading the *Sargassum*. The conveyer offloaded the biomass for processing into the front of the ship, which was filled with a collection of process tanks, heat exchangers, and distillation columns in the same configuration as the multitude of CanHarvest's on-land facilities that had made the company a success. "*Sargassum* mixed with recycled fluids and catalysts, crushed, and brought to a high temperature—350 degrees centigrade—at the pressure of thirty megapascals at high pressure. A hydrogen environment prevents coking poisoning up the catalyst." This process was her life, and she walked through the refinery as if it was her home. "The oil and char are separated. Some of the char is gasified indirectly"—she pointed at an odd-looking piece of pipe—"making hydrogen to treat the oil. The activated char absorbs the ammonium and heavy metals, giving us our nutrients to recycle." She pointed at a large distillation tower. "And a crude tower distills renewable gasoline, jet, diesel, and bunker fuel. And what is our production today?"

Zenuck held up his phone on which real-time production data was displayed. "We're at twenty-five thousand barrels of crude per day, thirty percent capacity, with lots of room to grow. Waste biogas off the digesters alone is producing enough power to operate both the process and the ship."

It took about a billion dollars of investment, but the demonstration project was working as planned. "So, we can power ourselves and make some fair coin"—Jaden pulled on a sample tap to see a clear gasoline product flow into a sampling drum—"but can we *feed* ourselves?" With a touch of a button, a pump activated to transfer the gasoline from the sample drum and back into the storage tank.

Captain Tyson raised his hand with an extended thumb in the air. "Follow me. That is a question best asked of our chief hydroponics officer. It's hard to get her out of her playground." He held open the hatch to the nearest stairwell, waving the team in before closing it tightly shut behind them. Captain Tyson dashed down the rather cramped stairs to lead them into the hull of the ship. The stairway was similar to that of any crude tanker, filled with firefighting equipment and sprinkler mounts, each boot hitting a metallic stair with a resulting echo. Down two decks, Captain Tyson began to manually open a hatch.

While most decks of the ship were filled with oil tanks, processing equipment, generator sets, storage, crew quarters, and the usual maritime lot, this deck had been completely altered. "Ladies and gentlemen"—Captain Tyson opened up the hatch—"one of the most advanced hydroponics and water treatment operations in the world." The sound of rushing water, the hum of pumps and electrical panels, and the ship's engine muffled the sound of Captain Tyson closing the hatch again behind them.

Grace Jaden's eyes had to adjust to focus in the odd combination of artificial sunlight and purple UV light emitters. Looking out, she found the deck was surprisingly open and tall with only the occasional maritime regulation mandated blast wall separating the hull into sections. Rows upon rows of white fiberglass pipe ran down the length of the ship—rows of strawberries, lettuce, and carrots. Beyond these rows was a length of apple and orange trees which amounted to an artificial orchard. Grace Jaden took in the wonderous smell of vegetation.

To the center of the deck was a large open pond where a rather tall blond woman, complete with jeans and a cowboy hat, stood adding drops to a water sample she had just taken. The water evidently turned the color the woman had wanted, as she emptied the sample back into the pond. Only then did the woman turn around and catch sight of the visitors. She seemed to march right up to Grace Jaden. "Have I got a bone to pick with you!"

Not used to even the hint of intimidation, Jaden took a rare step backward that surprised even herself. "Ann Duckering." She offered out her hand while looking around the room. "You've done an incredible job here."

"Which I wouldn't have had to do had you put the Corporate headquarters in Texas instead of that godforsaken Arizona," the frustrated Texas native replied.

"That's debatable," Jaden replied with a shrug, choosing not to comment that the Corporate Responsibility Act was a federal law, which not even the good state of Texas could counter.

Looking the executive up and down, Duckering turned away and activated a nearby display screen. "Well, I've done what you hired me to. Waste water and ash from the process is being used to grow lettuce, strawberries, carrots"—she pointed over at the trees—"apples, and oranges." Leaving the computer screen behind, the agricultural specialist walked over to the pond. Only in peering over did one see the pond was filled with vegetation itself. "Duckweed and sea lettuce are first grown in these ponds, which are treated—being so high in nitrogen. Then, the water gets pumped to the hydroponics system. This kelp we feed to aquaculture fish tanks back there." The Texan pointed aft. "Lots of salmon, trout, tilapia. Got so much fish production now, we're going to have to get into the export game. Thanks to the *ulva* sea lettuce and *Nannochloropsis oculata*, the fish are fortified with lots of Omega three acids," she tapped her head, "Pretty sure lack of Omega-threes has had an impact on those jokers in Washington." She led the team across a bridge over the thirty-meter pond to a hatch to the next hull compartment.

The next compartment was dimly lit with trays stacked upon trays in multiple rows. Zenuck was completely puzzled by what he was seeing.

It took even Grace Jaden, who participated in every aspect of the program design, a few seconds to guess what they were looking at. She peered over a tray to see if she had guessed correctly. Within the tray were mushrooms—rows upon rows—growing in damp ash.

"Mushrooms?" Zenuck asked aloud.

"Damn right." Duckering reached into the tray, picked out a mushroom, and took a bite out of it. "Morels, oyster, and shiitake. Good for you, me, and our fish in the back. Between mushrooms and duckweed, we don't even need to catch anchovies for the aquafarms." She walked over to an oddly placed lab table.

"What's going on here?" Jaden asked.

"We've got one critical problem," Duckering pulled over a microscope and gestured for Huang to take a look into it. "No cows, no meat," said the Texan, scowling. "Trying to grow some artificial meat here using the mushrooms, but so far . . . nothing like the real thing."

Dr. Huang gazed into the microscope to see microbes constructing protein cells. "We're getting close; I can't tell the difference."

Ann Duckering shook her head disagreeably. "She ain't from Texas. Doesn't taste anything like real meat."

"All three ships are set up and producing?" Jaden interjected.

"Yes, ma'am," Duckering replied as proud as she could be, being outside of a farm in Texas.

"Come up with a proposal for a deck to house some cows."

Duckering rubbed her chin, already thinking through her thoughts on the subject. "Will have to be big and custom-designed."

"You keep us alive and fed, and you'll get whatever you want," Jaden promised, even as she felt a vibration from her smartphone. She pulled out the phone and activated it.

"Bridge to Jaden. Incoming communication out of Tokyo," came the voice of a bridge officer.

Jaden exchanged looks with Zenuck and Captain Tyson. "I'm on my way." She quickly shook Duckering's hand. "You've done great work here," she called out before dashing to the nearest stairwell and up to the deck of the ship. Rubbing her eyes and feeling her ears itch, Jaden mentally noted that she would still need to take allergy pills. She took in a breath of saltwater-saturated air to help clear her airways as she dashed across the ship and onto the bridge.

The first officer of the ship waved Jaden over to one of the large flatscreen displays. "Satellite transmission coming in from the Ministry of Energy in Tokyo." Knowing the communication might be confidential the XO walked away to oversee the helm.

The screen blinked, soon revealing the current minister of energy in the Japanese government—namely, Akimoto. Jaden had worked with the minister and met him on countless occasions. "How may I help you, Minister Akimoto?" Grace Jaden asked. "How are our ships?"

The forty-year-old Japanese minister was tense to the point his forehead was wrinkled in concern, making him look ten years older than he actually was. "While I appreciate the work, you have awarded our shipyards, I'm afraid my call is unrelated." The Japanese minister looked troubled enough that Jaden felt unnerved. "The Chinese government has placed a fuel blockade on Taiwan."

Jaden sighed at the troublesome news, though she wasn't quite sure why the minister would seek to consult her on the matter. Perhaps the US government had kept news of her resignation quiet to help calm the markets. "Certainty, the United States government will ensure the flow of fuel to Taiwan, so Japan need not risk any action." Since World War 2, in which Japan had invaded China for her resources, relations between the two countries had always been strained. Back then, China had been the democratic state and Japan had been the authoritarian expansionist regime. Ironically the two countries had switched ideologies. Japan was right to fear directly confronting China.

Minister Akimoto shook his head. "I just got off a discussion with the US ambassador. The United States is reviewing all aid to Taiwan."

Grace Jaden sat down on the closest chair. Feeling events in the outside world were spiraling out of control, the blood drained from her face. She now shared the minister's concern. "Are you sure?" The United States had supported the Chinese Nationalist movement in Taiwan since the Chinese civil war right after World War 2. The Nationalists, weakened by fighting the Japanese and facing defeat by the Soviet-backed communist armies of Mao, had fled to Taiwan. Taiwan was commonly thought of as the Czechoslovakia of the Pacific, and allowing democratic Taiwan to fall to Communist China would seemingly open the door to further Chinese expansionism.

"I'm sure." Minister Akimoto's tone was troubled and serious.

Jaden took a deep breath and mentally tried to put the puzzle pieces of information together. She felt cold, wondering if the American government had gone mad. She rubbed her forehead with both hands. "You *are* aware that I've resigned as CEO of CanHarvest Renewables?"

Minister Akimoto snuck a glance at a file on his desk—no doubt the latest intelligence briefing on what she was up to. "Most unfortunate, as you have been a great business partner for Japan. But our intelligence agencies are reporting that you are up to an enterprise in the Pacific? Indeed, Japanese Gasoline Corporation is reporting you want a crude marketing deal."

The background of the ship's bridge spoke for itself, and there was no point in trying to deny the reports. "And you want me to extend an export deal to Taipei?"

"You'll find we will provide quite a deal on the tankers and ships you require. Not to mention we will help expedite the upgrades in the shipyards."

The middle of the Pacific Ocean felt cloudy, uncertain, and dangerous despite the view from the bridge of a calm rolling sea and blue skies. Grace Jaden gulped down the lump in her throat. She weighted the risk of upsetting China to the gains of friends in Japan and Taiwan. Given the United States government was already out to get her, Jaden knew her team needed all the friends they could get, though. "We'll take care of it."

CHAPTER SIX – COLLUSION

"Timid men prefer the calm of despotism to the tempestuous sea of liberty."
—Thomas Jefferson

APRIL 4, 2068
OFFICE OF NAVAL INTELLIGENCE
SUITLAND MARYLAND, USA

It was a rather cloudy, windy day over Maryland. Rear Admiral Davidson felt his train of thought was like the collection of northern orchids and sundews he could see out his office window, tossing in the wind all over the place. Not even the rather pleasant view of one of the last natural bogs in the Washington, D.C., area helped calm his rising anger. He slowly made his way back to his deck, sat down, and picked up a nearby pair of reading glasses to make sure he had read the wire report correctly. A junior analyst by the name of Rogers knocked at the door, giving Davidson the excuse he needed to not reread the wire report. "Come," he said while waving the analyst in.

The analyst, only three years out of the academy with the rank of lieutenant, nervously saluted.

Davidson saluted back. His presence at ONI, being a rear admiral that had served on numerous campaigns, had attracted Davidson a bit of a following. Davidson, for his part, didn't particularly enjoy the attention and wished the officers would focus on their own jobs.

"Did you see the wire report, sir?" Lieutenant Rogers asked.

"I was hoping it was a joke," Rear Admiral Davidson angrily responded before realizing that Lieutenant Rogers had taken a step back with a frown. "It's not you, Lieutenant. It's the news."

With this reassurance, the lieutenant stepped into the office. "Didn't think you would like it, sir. The president has said that all aid to Taiwan is to be reassessed. They say it's due to corruption."

"Corruption my ass," Davidson irritably retorted. "The president is giving up on a century of deterrence to suck up to the Chinese." Davidson pointed at a computer-projected map of the western side of the Pacific Ocean. He pointed first at the Philippines. "This couldn't have come at a worse time. We've got increased separatist activity in the Philippines "

"Moro separatists," the analyst acknowledged. Conflict was rampant in the Muslim majority Mindanao region where insurgents fought to separate from the Philippines to form an Islamic State.

"Right, but with an odd mixture of Marxism and enhanced weaponry." Davidson pointed to the collection of islands in Oceania west of the Philippines. "In Micronesia, we've got increased militia and pirate activity, bombings, and the like. Chuuk nationalists suddenly using violence to destabilize the region." The once-peaceful Pacific was now a political powder keg just waiting to go off.

"But why, sir?" The lieutenant asked.

It was a good question. The rear admiral's gaze softened, and he nodded. Davidson motioned for the lieutenant to take the seat across his desk. "Makes no sense," Davidson thought aloud while removing his reading glasses. "Why, just a few months ago I sank a Chinese submarine that attacked us."

"That had been leased to the Indonesia government and essentially hijacked by a rouge commander."

Rear Admiral Davidson swiveled his chair to face the lieutenant directly. "Don't tell me you buy into that BS. No way the Chinese Navy would lease out a nuclear missile sub." His head spinning, Davidson thought back to the *Bonhomme Richard* and the sailors injured from missile shrapnel. Enough was enough. "And even then, there's no way the Indonesian military would allow it to be hijacked by a pro-militia commander."

Not quite sure how to respond to the angry outburst, Lieutenant Rogers at first stayed silent before it was abundantly clear the Rear Admiral was waiting for a response. Saying "Yes sir" took all the courage the Lieutenant had in disagreeing with the official line. To quickly change the subject, Rogers handed Davidson a flash drive. "As you asked for, sir. Chatter is showing a lot of activity with the Chinese Navy around Taiwan and in Indonesia. Two Chinese carrier battlegroups put out to sea—"

The news caught Davidson by surprise. "We haven't deployed our carrier groups to shadow?"

"No, sir."

Davidson's eyes narrowed. "Thank you for this. Leave me, please." He took hold of the flash drive while getting up to shut the door behind Lieutenant Rogers. Before even sitting down, he touched a pre-programmed contact on his smartphone while raising the receiver tight against his ear.

"SECDEF," came the response of the Secretary of Defense's personal secretary.

Davidson spoke clearly and urgently into the phone. "Rear Admiral Davidson for Secretary of Defense Taggart, high priority."

"I'm sorry, sir," came an apologetic, almost sad response. "The secretary of defense is unavailable."

Surprised, Davidson raised his voice. "Unavailable? What do you mean unavailable?" He reached into his pocket and pulled out his smartphone.

"I'm sorry, sir," the personal secretary repeated. "That's all I can say at this time."

Knowing that was code for if she said anything else, she would be fired, Davidson reflexively nodded. "Thank you," he said and slammed the phone back onto the receiver. What the hell was the world coming to?

THE WHITE HOUSE

The president was growing annoyed that the oval office, decorated with furniture, exotic drapery, and various progressive and expensive pieces of artwork, didn't placate the two White House correspondents. "Listen," said the president, looking the reporters in the eye, "we're talking peace in our time." He slammed a hand down on his desk. "Gentlemen, the extreme right wants to lead us into a war with China. We cannot allow that to happen."

The two reporters looked at each other before both nodding in agreement with the President. "That's true," the taller of the two reporters said. "Though I don't see the big deal on us reporting on these high-level talks with Beijing."

"It's a distraction from our rolling out of the Corporate Accountability Act," the President stressed. "Our debt is hurting social programs. Market instability is helping the rise of the alt-right. The rich and powerful are trying to use this as an excuse not to pay their fair share. Are you really going to help them?"

"We'll keep it off the top headlines," the reporter offered. "Like the Chicago bombings, the FBI traced to those extremist cells."

"You report on that"—the president pointed straight at the reporter —"and you're playing right into the hands of the racists in America." Satisfied with the nods of the reporters indicating they were going to play ball, the president stood up and offered his hand. "Gentlemen, excellent reporting as always." He made sure his handshake was firm. "One day, you'll be working for the Oval Office yourself." The President threw in the usual line, which generally assured compliance.

"Thank you, Mr. President."

The president led the two reporters out of the Oval Office, where he caught sight of Secretary of State Harris waiting outside. He motioned him in, carefully shut the door behind them, and made his way to his desk to ensure all recorders were off. "We aren't supposed to meet here," the president finally said. Even though his party controlled the presidency and both houses of Congress, one could never discount law enforcement.

"Sorry, Mr. President. Thought you might like this." Harris chose his words with great care before tossing a folder onto the President's desk. "Taggart's resignation letter." He took a seat in front of the president. "Bastard was a mole—wanted to portray us all as another Chamberlain." Chamberlain was the prime minister best known for his policy of appeasing Hitler by handing over Czechoslovakia to Germany in an effort to avoid world war.

The president sat down in his chair and picked up the piece of paper, a wave of relief settling over him on seeing the signature. "How did you get him to sign without raising a fuss?"

"Had the party office make it clear we were aware of where a quarter of his donations came from in his planned future Senate run." Harris snickered. "He knew how we'd let it play out with law enforcement."

"Good thing we've got the career professionals on our side." The president let the piece of paper float down onto his desk.

CHAPTER SEVEN – INDEPENDENCE

"I wish to have no connection with any ship that does not sail fast; for I intend to go in harm's way."
—John Paul Jones

APRIL 4, 2068

THE PACIFIC OCEAN, 200KM SOUTH OF MIDWAY

The helicopter trip from the *Byzantium* to Grace Jaden's new home was a short five-minute dash for the small corporate helicopter. Grace Jaden, Luke Zenuck, and Captain Tyson found themselves hovering right above their destination a further twenty minutes, waiting for a large transport helicopter to depart.

"That a cruise ship or an aircraft carrier?" Zenuck joked into his headset. Even the helicopter pilot was grinning ear to ear while looking down on the massive former cruise ship majestically and making her way through the Pacific.

The former cruise ship, renamed the *New Constantinople*, had been built over fifty years earlier as an entertainment liner capable of holding more than two thousand passengers in style. The top deck was filled with swimming pools, hot tubs, and movie screens surrounding the tall radar-enclosed bridge. The vessel was over two hundred meters long, thirty meters wide, and rose eleven decks out above the ocean. Grace Jaden had spent over three hundred million dollars buying the vessel and retrofitting her hundred thousand tons to operate as a mobile city at sea. Already the two 23MW propulsion motors and three 20MW power generators were running on the low Sulphur bunker fuel produced by the *Byzantium* and her sister ships.

"Tried to buy a mothballed reserve aircraft carrier," Jaden admitted. The America-class amphibious assault ships with their moon pool and helicopter pads would have worked perfectly despite being not quite as luxurious for the crew. "The government blocked the purchase." As it was obvious that they would still be waiting for the helicopter deck to clear for some time, Jaden reached for her tablet and continued scrolling through personnel files. "These are all the candidates that accepted the transfer requests?"

"You bet," Zenuck replied into the headset. "Laboucan tried to get everyone you wanted, plus some of his and my recommendations."

Sliding her finger across the screen, Jaden was met with a surprise profile. A picture of her son, Peter Jaden, seemed to stare right back at her. "Who recommended Peter? Isn't he with some thinktank in Brussels?"

Zenuck felt guilty just thinking of clouding his answer. "*I* did. He's the best aviator we know. He wanted to sign up."

Feeling a flood of conflicting emotions and not quite in the mood to confront them, Jaden quickly slid the tablet to the next personnel file. She tapped the screen, pleased to see a young executive from an outside information technology startup company had accepted the offer. "I don't want to know what it took to get Nolan Ryerson from Cynet to sign up."

"Always knew he was a closet libertarian," Zenuck replied before cursing himself out for using the word *closet* while speaking to a known gay man. One never knew who would find such talk offensive. Typical of most engineers, Zenuck tried to avoid political incorrectness as much as possible. "Though his company is getting a steal of a deal on offshore real estate and power."

The sun was starting to set over the Pacific, and the running lights on the *New Constantinople* were activated. Being a former cruise ship, the running lights included a variety of fancy, attractive, and entertaining displays. One of the engine stacks already had a projection of the name *New Constantinople* and the words New *Liberty* below it. Jaden had begun to wonder if they would be sent back to the *Byzantium* when the compound helicopter lifted off into the sky and accelerated in the direction of Hawaii. The radio squawked that they were cleared for landing, and it took only a minute for the pilot to safely land the small helicopter on the deck of the cruise ship.

"Welcome aboard the *New Constantinople*," said an officer, helping them onto the deck before saluting and pointing in the direction of the nearest cabin.

The three saluted back before dashing out of the wind and into the ship. "We've got to come up with some kind of protocol." Jaden was growing tired of the repeating post-salute dilemma.

"We aren't the Navy," said Zenuck with a shrug.

Captain Tyson directed his comrades down a beautifully carpeted flight of stairs. "But aren't we our own navy now?" Five decks down into the ship, Tyson turned and led them into what was once a large casual restaurant decorated as if a rainforest, complete with waterfalls and a star-filled sky. There were smiles from the hundreds of employees dining in the hall, some meeting with co-workers they hadn't seen in weeks. The far side of the room, once a fully licensed casino, had been brought back into to operation for entertainment and reception purposes. Waiters and waitresses made their way through the crowd while dispersing glasses of champagne.

Scanning the room, Jaden was happy to see Chief Security Officer Andrew Lawrence standing tall near the bar with a glass of champagne. She quickly gave him a hug, having not seen Lawrence since the events in East Timor. "I'm glad you made it out. What news of East Timor?"

Andrew Lawrence had to admit he was glad to have made it out of East Timor. "Well, the US Marines stayed put and kept the militias away. The facility is all shut down."

"Yes." Jaden considered the situation. "I suppose that's no longer our facility now. Hopefully, the militias won't want to tangle with the Marines."

Lawrence took a sip of the champagne, happy to be absolved of the situation. "That's the problem," he said, frowning, "Rumor is that the US troops are pulling out and the new board is going to keep the facility permanently shut down."

"God damn it," Grace Jaden said under her breath. The facility in East Timor was an economic trigger for the small island nation, and she felt guilty about the employees left behind. "We'll help them as soon as we can." She paused, trying to come up with the odds of her being able to honor that sentiment. "I'll feel a lot better when our ships on order arrive." A Japanese company was quickly making requested retrofits to a collection of small but stealthy multi-mission warships she had been able to purchase. She had bought three Tuo-Chiang-class corvettes from Taiwan. A larger Israeli Saar 6 corvette, had been purchased right out of the German shipyard. The Saar 6 itself was a modification of the K130 Braunschweig-class corvettes. All of the vessels were older—from the 2020s—small but fast stealth hulls that with her modifications would give their new nation some badly needed military capabilities. A Swedish-built Gotland-class submarine was part of the purchase order, though Jaden considered simply selling the vessel, still unsure if New Liberty really needed a submarine.

Andrew Lawrence was a realistic man, and he knew that ensuring security for a ragtag fleet of civilian ships would be difficult at best. This was a far cry from his original job protecting on-land facilities. "About that. I'm a former Marine, not a naval commander. Your personal security is one thing, but this . . ." He held his arms up in the air. "Pains me to say it, but we're going to need an admiral or something to back me up. I'm more East Timor than East Timor Sea if you know what I mean."

Knowing she was getting good advice, Jaden nodded. "Let's talk with Jordie. See what we can do."

Having faintly heard his name, Jord Labaoucan turned from leading his wife and three teenaged children, two boys and a girl, around the buffet table to catch sight of Jaden. With a grin, he sprinted in her direction and awkwardly fumbled a salute before offering his hand. "Good to see you, Grace!"

Grace Jaden chuckled as she firmly shook Jord's hand and then gave a crisp salute back. "Jord, nice to have you in the flesh!" Jaden reached around to shake the hands of Jord's wife with whom she had shared many a social setting with. "I'm glad you let him come!"

His wife was all smiles. "Glad to be out of the rumor mill that is America," said his wife, raising her arms in the air. "And I guess if I have to head out to sea, living on a cruise ship is the way to go." Potential seasickness was on the minds of quite a few of the new crewmembers and families coming aboard.

Labaoucan tried his best to subdue his anger he felt about the media's smear campaign involving his own troublesome teenage years.

"Well, this is amazing, Grace. Makes leaving the rest of CanHarvest behind worth it."

"What news of CanHarvest?" Grace inquired, having been too busy with their operation on the high sea to follow the latest business reports.

The chief financial officer shrugged in resignation. "Company went public, and everything you expected to go wrong did. Bertrand was replaced by a government appointment, which was kind of funny." Labaoucan couldn't help but inwardly smile at the thought. "Rest of the board's a bunch of relatives of congressmen, donors—the usual statist board doomed to stagnation and decline. I heard my replacement is from the bloody IRS." The thought of a tax lawyer taking on his position had Labaoucan clenching his fists. "On the plus side, the Department of Justice no longer has you on any official or unofficial most-wanted lists." He looked over to make sure that his children were off to grab soda drinks. "And the media isn't demanding I go to jail for holding down my ex-girlfriend when she was trying to stab me with a broken beer bottle forty years ago."

"But are we in the clear here?" Jaden asked.

"Damn right." The CFO raised his smartphone up with a projection of various signed legal documents. "CleanOcean Energy Corporation out of Singapore." He reached over to grab three champagne glasses and handed one to Jaden and Zenuck, who had tagged along.

All three clinked their glasses together and took a sip, though mention of the company being out of Singapore had Jaden scanning the room for the new company's lawyer. Labaoucan guessed at whom the CEO was looking for and ran into the crowd to grab ahold of Kelly Agarwal. The lawyer was all smiles, almost giddy at the occasion.

"Ma'am!" The lawyer was so excited, she splashed a bit of her drink, leaving others in the room to wonder just how much alcohol she had consumed. "This is so exciting!"

Knowing the conversation was going to be all business, Jord's wife gave a friendly wave before turning her attention back to the children. "Good luck, you three."

"Good luck to us all," said Jaden, smiling back. Finding Agarwal's enthusiasm rather refreshing, Jaden turned to the lawyer. "All right, what's the latest?"

"We sent out emails to all the new corporate, uh . . ." Agarwal struggled for the right word to use. "Employees? Citizens?"

"Both," Labaoucan said resolutely. "We've split those who agreed to come over between those working for the corporation in energy production and those that are going to work for the . . ." He paused, slightly embarrassed that *he* was now at a loss of words.

"Condominium government," said Jaden, finishing the sentence. She had spent countless hours poring over the structure of the new sea state.

Labaoucan nodded at the clarification. "Condominium government," he repeated to make it clear he was on the same page. He pointed over at Nolan Ryerson, who was walking down the rather exotic carpeted stairwell and engaged in a conversation with the equally wealthy Dr. Kraizer. "On that note, you should get us some more corporations."

"We've got everyone voting electronically," Argarwal reported. "Also, call me a modern-day Thomas Jefferson as I have our Unilateral Declaration of Independence ready to go on the results." She held up her smartwatch hand. "The majority have already voted, and the deadline is in twenty minutes."

"You've got twenty minutes before the presentation," said Labaoucan, holding Jaden's shoulder to direct her toward the two wealthiest men in the room.

Nolan Ryerson and Dr. Kraizer were an odd-looking conversation pair. Nolan, in his late thirties, wore a smart black turtleneck, jeans, and sneakers, the preferred style of high-technology executives who had emulated Steve Jobs from Apple for more than half a century. Nolan ran Cynet Systems very similarly to the former Apple executive, who had done away with wasting brainpower on choosing an outfit each morning by wearing the same outfit every day.

The style made sense to Jaden, though her capital-intensive investors generally demanded she wear a more technical office suit. Like her father, she always wore black leather Clark Wallabie shoes, which she considered suitable for the office yet comfortable.

Dr. Kraizer, on the other hand, was in his sixties yet dressed in an expensive and perfectly tailored Italian-made suit. He had made a fortune when he sold the health care cooperative his family had run for generations to a public board under considerable political pressure.

Behind him was his latest twenty-something wife in a no less stunning black dress. The man was a real doctor—world renowned, in fact—but he very much looked the part of a soap opera doctor, albeit one who had been on the show for decades.

Grade Jaden was all smiles, exchanging handshakes with the men, both of whom she respected for having the unique ability to combine business with technical complexity. "Dr. Kraizer, Nolan, a pleasure to have you aboard!"

"The pleasure is all mine," said Nolan Ryerson, passing out glasses of champagne.

"I'm not sure why you wanted me aboard. I'm retired," said Dr. Kraizer with a shrug. "Had to sell the family business."

Jaden took hold of a glass of champagne offered by Ryerson and raised her glass in cheers. "Please, Doctor." Jaden tried to be as flattering as possible. "I'm aware of your volunteer activities working overseas. That being said, we need a health cooperative on board."

Dr. Kraizer seemed to perk up with a raised eyebrow as the three clinked their glasses together. "Why not just hire a medical team?"

"You of all people should know that if we want good sustainable health care, we need a health group invested in the project," Jaden tried to nudge the conversation to a natural conclusion.

"You want me to invest in a health cooperative, one of the corporations of your condominium government?" Dr. Kraizer read between the lines.

"Absolutely," Grace Jaden said matter-of-factly. "You've been emailed the ten rooms and sickbay specifications, not to mention that of the other ships. I think you miss leading a health care company," Jaden said. "Besides, you're retired. What have you got to lose?"

"*Would* be nice to leave the kids a family business as opposed to a large inheritance." Doctor Kraizer looked over his shoulder in the direction of his sixth wife. "I know my wife would love to sit on the pool deck all day." He started nodding to himself as his expression transitioned from one of deep thought to that of resolve. "All right, I'm in—on the condition that you are competitively bidding out services and get me some competition."

"Absolutely." Jaden chuckled, knowing that she had ensured the health of those aboard. "We've separated out the regulator from the implementation boards."

"I was reading that constitution," said Nolan Ryerson, jumping into the conversation. "Limited government, right?"

"The condominium is limited to ensuring utilities are provided for the crew ships like this one, foreign affairs, law enforcement, and the cooperative regulators overseeing boards in health and education," Jaden replied. "Though we need our own currency."

It was Nolan Ryerson's turn to be intrigued. "And that's why I got an email to attend this party, I presume?"

"I'm not going to pretend to be the expert in blockchain and cryptocurrencies, that's where you come in." Jaden took another sip of champagne to obscure any hint of desperation. "I need Cynet Systems to develop us a cryptocurrency."

"There are lots of cryptocurrencies you can use," Ryerson almost scoffed.

"Not backed by renewable crude sales."

Nolan Ryerson was blinking rapidly now, an indication that she had his attention. He slammed down his glass of champagne onto a table. "Right." He grabbed the tablet attached to his belt and began sketching. "Your own national currency backed by your crude sales to Japan and Taiwan, no doubt?" Not even seeing the nod from Jaden, Ryerson was working out the logistics of a cryptocurrency backed by physical product on his tablet. "All right, I'm in on that too," he said before finally looking up, "but I not only get this contract to develop and operate the cryptocurrency but I get to move Cynet here as a condominium member. I'll invest in the whole operation. I get some space for a data center as well."

"Deal. I also need you to talk your friend into setting up a rocket launch platform with the fleet. Getting into the satellite launch business will ensure us telecommunications access." Reusable rockets were often landing on ocean barges, so it made sense to get at least one company—preferably the largest—setting up an operation in New Liberty. Grace Jaden offered her hand, which Nolan quickly accepted before almost leaping away—no doubt to start the work. "We will also need a stock exchange system—"

"That's easy. I'll do that free of charge." Ryerson began dashing up the stairs to his room. "Hell, I'll move Cynet systems off the New York Stock Exchange and list it right here along with CleanOcean Energy." Nolan Ryerson was gone in a flash, leaving just the calm and pleasant Dr. Kraizer still sipping from his champagne glass.

"I presume that went well?" said the doctor, raising his glass.

Grace Jaden clinked her glass with that of the doctor's. "Now we can pay you without fear of the US government coming after us for tax revenue."

"As long as we never head back stateside," the doctor lamented before adding, "Not that I want to go back to that stagnant depressing economy anyway."

If this state were to survive and thrive at sea, it would need a strong economy. Grace Jaden had to play every angle she could. Renewable energy exports. Satellite launches. Cryptocurrencies. Data centers. Seafood. Eventually, they would have to reinvest profits into more complex and high-capital industries like maritime construction. Was tourism a possibility?

While still in thought, Jaden scanned the crowd to detect a familiar face at the craps table. Grace Jaden felt her heart skip a beat, both dreading and looking forward to seeing the man after what had to be at least a year. "If you'll excuse me, Doctor," she said apologetically while taking a long gulp to finish off her champagne.

Seeing her face grow pale, Dr. Kraizer guessed correctly she had personal business to attend to. "The pleasure was all mine," he said and smiled while turning to get back to entertaining his rather attractive wife.

For a moment, Jaden thought she caught her late husband in his usual leather flight jacket rolling the dice at one of the craps tables. It took her mind a few seconds to remind her that his had to be her surviving son, Peter Jaden. She hadn't seen him in almost half a decade. He was still tall and in shape, though years of hard work and the pain of losing both a father and brother had taken a toll on the man in the form of greying and lost hair despite being only thirty-eight. It took all her strength to decide to approach the man let alone think of what to say.

Thankfully, Peter took notice of his approaching mother and lifted the dice. "Care to roll for me, Mother?"

"Why, of course, Mr. Jaden," Grace replied, neither frowning nor smiling. The crowd around the table cheered, however, when she tossed the dice against the back of the table and ended up rolling a winning hard six.

Despite a genuine effort to grin, Peter could at best pull of a sad smile. "You're still in the zone, I see."

Grace sorrowfully looked down. "I haven't been in the zone since Armenia." She could still remember her husband informing her of the eldest son being shot down enforcing a no-fly zone over Armenia only for him and her son to be killed in a rescue mission gone horribly wrong.

After a deep breath, Peter handed the dice to another player and began collecting his chips from the table. "You still had me and Constance."

Grace Jaden led her son away from the table toward an unoccupied corner of the room. "How is your sister?" She often regretted not having spoken more to either of her surviving children.

"Chief executive for a not-for-profit," Peter was able to chuckle. "Trying to save the world just like her mother."

"It's good to see you." Jaden's voice was soft but heartfelt. It felt like Michael and Peter were standing next to her. "I'm sorry we haven't kept in touch." She pushed up against the door to an empty stairwell, and lead her son in where could talk relatively unheard.

"I know why you didn't want me at Annapolis." Peter shrugged as the stairwell door slammed shut. His voice echoed through the stairwell as he began his prepared statement. "And why you buried yourself in your work after Dad and Michael were lost." He took a deep breath to focus on the here and now. "I've resigned from the Navy. I'm here to help."

Knowing they were relatively alone, Grace Jaden wrapped her arms around her son and held him tight as her eyes watered up. Memories of raising her children and working even while her husband served in the military, stressful and chaotic at the time, she now desperately longed for. "I'm glad you're here. And I'm sorry. Truly sorry."

"You have nothing to be sorry for," her son responded unconvincingly. Even now, he felt a hint of anger at his mother, who had begged him not to follow in his father's footsteps. He'd been so angry when he died and then she'd seemingly disappeared into her work. "But I want to help. I got the emails from your team. All that loss for freedom doesn't really mean much if no one is standing up for freedom, right?"

To prevent herself from breaking down, Jaden switched to more practical concerns. "I bought all the drones you recommended for this mission." She smiled through tears of sadness.

Peter chuckled through his own tears. "I didn't think you paid me any attention."

"Of course, I do." Jaden felt her throat tighten up, making it hard to form words. "I'm very proud to be your mother." She brushed her hands down his shoulders as she used to do to clean them of dandruff decades ago. "Thank you for coming. We need someone to manage all these aircraft and keep everyone safe." The smartphone in Grace Jaden's pocket began to buzz. "I've got to go," said Jaden, wiping tears away from her eyes and pulling at her suit jacket to ensure she was presentable. "Presentation time."

Peter Jaden squeezed her hand tight. "You'll do great."

Grace Jaden couldn't help but feel guilty as she pressed open the door back into the conference hall. She held onto the doorframe for strength. "I'm sorry. I took your brother and your father's deaths hard. And this . . ." She gazed across the grey concrete of the ship around her "This is their legacy." With that, she made her way into the conference hall.

The door closed with a slam, leaving Peter Jaden alone. "I'm sorry too," his voice echoed.

Grace Jaden darted to the main stage of the conference center while reaching for her smartphone where quite expectantly was a text asking her to urgently make her way to the front. Jord Labaoucan and Kelly Agarwal were at the podium with the title page of the presentation slide deck on the screen. Jaden gave the two a thumbs up that she was good to go, quickly took her place on stage behind a podium and stood proud, confident, and tall as the cameras activated.

"Ladies and gentlemen," Jord Labaoucan hollered into the microphone while clinking a nearby glass to gain the attention of the room. "Ladies and gentlemen, it is time for what I hope will be a historic presentation." He gestured over to Jaden to take the podium. "Always a pleasure, I present to you Grace Jaden, CEO of CleanOcean Energy."

"Thank you. That was Jord Labaoucan, our fantastic CFO." Grace Jaden adjusted the microphone to ensure her voice was clear. Almost all in the crowded main hall settled down to look over at the large presentation screen. She gave the crowd a quick gaze before focusing on the camera broadcasting her projection across the fleet. There was a moment of silence. "A historic occasion is before us—a historic occasion I don't think any of us expected to be a part of. But I'm glad you're here to share in it. This transmission is being broadcasted to all those on board the *New Constantinople*"—those in the hall cheered again—"our three production ships, the *Byzantium*, *Antioch*, and the *Ephesus*—and a couple of smaller general-purpose vessels. Everyone aboard has come voluntarily despite the potential for great personal sacrifice." She paused for a moment. "Many of you were with me at CanHarvest Renewables, where we were a proud American headquartered corporation. And we did good"—she looked across the room, recognizing various faces—"helping to combat climate change and ensure a secure inexpensive source of energy for consumers around the world." She allowed her anger at having lost the company and the Corporate Responsibility Act to come to the surface with a frown. "But our tax contribution wasn't enough for the state. America, which was founded on the principles of the free market and individual liberty, has lost its way." With a slide of her finger across the podium-mounted tablet she drew up a graph showing the rise in public spending both in the United States and other Western democracies. "Public spending in the United States and other western democracies has gotten out of control—far in excess of the now stagnant population growth rates. And did we see an increase in government services?" The crowd shared her anger with the shaking of heads and a smattering of scornful shouts. Jaden grabbed hold of the podium. "And when we complained, the state came after the corporations, demanding their fair share." Grace Jaden allowed a moment of silence before raising her finger. "Their fair share was our research and development capital. Their fair share was our jobs and salaries. And for what? An unsustainable entrenched bureaucracy that couldn't deliver? Unemployment lines? Economic suicide for our families?" Jaden looked down in silence, knowing that she had reached the point of no return in her speech. There was no point changing her mind now. She looked up again. "Both my son and husband died for the United States of America." She took a deep breath. "A nation that was supposed to be about sacrifice and entrepreneurism. Instead, they pile on debt on generation after generation. Interest payments now exceed funding for universities and schools. Enough is enough; our time in the United States is over." She glanced at Laboucan for a show of support, feeling drained of energy by the last statement. With another slide of the finger, she moved to a slide featuring various electronic election results. "By a vote of over eighty percent, a clear majority has voted for the proposed Constitution of the Free Liberty Pacific Condominium and independence from the United States. I hereby declare these vessels to be under the flag of this new state built on principles of liberty, democracy, and the free market." She advanced to another slide with the proposed organization chart. "Per your votes, Kelly Argarwal has been elected prime minister of the condominium board which will function as our government." She turned back to Kelly and continued. "I invite Kelly to take us through the approved government."

With applause echoing through the room Kelly Argarwal took the podium as an unusually exhausted Grace Jaden fell into a nearby seat. "Thank you, Grace," said Kelly, waving back at her, "Let no one forget that this, like CanHarvest, was your idea. The condominium as ratified under the approved Constitution is a government unlike any other in the world. This ship we are on is being provided, over a set negotiated time period by CleanOcean Energy as a member of the condominium." Kelly used her tablet to point out the structure of the government as she spoke. "The condominium government is responsible for ensuring the well-being of our citizenry by running this vessel and perhaps future vessels, as our home. The condominium board is our elected parliament tasked with selected ministry heads and passing laws. Taxes are collected in the form of rent. To ensure focus, the ministries are limited in scope to treasury, health, education, utilities, defense, justice, and law enforcement. The borrowing of money by these ministers is prohibited. That being said, actual implementation is by competitive boards, cooperatives, and corporations." Kelly looked back at Grace, having been tipped off by Jord that then was a good time to invite Grace to speak. "I think you have an announcement?"

Grace Jaden gathered her strength to stand up from the chair and take hold of a microphone Jord passed over to her. "Yes, I am pleased to announce that Dr. Kraizer has agreed to *invest in our community by founding our* first health cooperative."

There was a round of applause, as many had wondered about health care upon coming aboard. Dr. Krazer's former company had been the health care provider of choice for CanHarvest. The doctor, being singled out by the crowd, happily waved.

"Any additional ministries and changes to the law will require an electronic referendum to be held and constitutional reform." Argarwal smiled at the cheering of the crowd and gave Jaden a wink.

"Which will be quite difficult to enact." Grace Jaden smiled at the positive energy in the room.

"The condominium board has selected Jord Labaoucan as minister of the treasury, Dr. Gord Holden as minister of health, Garry Pehoch as minister of education, myself as the portfolio of justice, Andrew Lawrence as minister of defense, and Grace Janen as minister of foreign affairs and acting *strategos*." Kelly allowed the applause to die down before calling up Jord Labaoucan to the stage. "Jord?"

The chief financial officer of the company came up to the stage, grinning from ear to ear. "It's an honor to be a part of this," Labaoucan said truthfully. "On the treasury side, we have begun working on our state cryptocurrency, which will be backed by our renewable crude sales. I've also been negotiating via email"—he held up his phone—"with Nolan Ryerson to not only manage our stock exchange but have Cynet systems join the condominium."

The slender young technology executive jumped up onto the stage, hands extended with both thumbs up. Laboucan bent over to allow Ryerson to speak over the microphone. "I just got to say that it's amazing to be part of this!" Nolan Ryerson laughed. "Together we're going to change the world for the better!"

"Again," Jord Labaoucan joked, "Not the first time we all did that. Only, this time the government isn't going to screw it up in the end!" Waiting for the laugher to fade, Laboucan turned to face Grace Jaden eye to eye. "Thank you for dreaming this up, Grace, and for letting us be a part of it. I think you should have the last word."

Nodding in agreement, Kelly Argarwal spoke clearly into the podium microphone. "Absolutely."

"We have crude deals in place with Japan, India, and Australia," Jaden said comfortingly though seriously. "Any democratic free market open to us will enjoy open access to our markets. Our goal is to stay out of the world spotlight and do as much good as we can. But we're alone out here." She let the statement sink in. "It's us working together. Even if you're not religious or of another affiliation, I think we could use all the help we can get. I hope even the atheists among you won't mind in joining me in a prayer?"

Some bowed; others simply stood silently. Kelly Argarwal, a Hindu, bowed her head in silence. Jord Labaoucan was Catholic, and he made the sign of the cross before bowing.

Grace Jaden was Byzantine Catholic, and she made the sign of the cross before quoting the Divine Liturgy of Saint John Chrysostom from over fifteen thousand years ago. In the crowd, she made out her son doing so as well before she shut her eyes. "For our new country, for this city at sea, and for every city and land let us pray." She took a deep breath. "Lord have mercy. For our deliverance from all affliction, wrath, danger, and necessity. For the peace from above and for the salvation of our souls, let us pray to the Lord. Do not forsake us who have set our hope in You. Grant peace to Your world, to Your churches, to the clergy, to our civic leaders, to the armed forces, and to all Your people. Help us, save us have mercy on us, and protect us, O God, by Your grace."

"Lord have mercy."

CHAPTER EIGHT – FIRST BLOOD

"It seems to be a law of nature, inflexible and inexorable, that those who will not risk cannot win."
—John Paul Jones

JUNE 20, 2068
REPUBLIC OF NAURU
THE SOUTHWEST PACIFIC

Being just twenty-one square kilometers, the oval-shaped island of Nauru, forty-two kilometers south of the equator in the Southwest Pacific, was tied for being the world's smallest republic. The tying republic was only fourteen hundred kilometers to the southeast, the similarly small island of Tuvalu. Nauru was relatively undeveloped, surrounded by a coral reef that prevented the establishment of a large seaport, and only small boats could come in or go out. Once heavily mined for its phosphate, the strip mine had been exhausted and shut down over a century ago.

On the southern tip of the island was the Westin Hotel situated next to the small single-story building that served as parliament. The acting president of the republic of thirty thousand, Lionel Scotty, took a break from entertaining guests in the ballroom to catch the latest news out of the Federated States of Micronesia. "Has the world gone mad?" he asked himself. There was a humid breeze flowing through the main floor of the hotel, but it brough the president little comfort.

The flat-screen television was filled with images of the tiny capital city of Palikir on Pohnpei Island burning under an evening sky. "The bombings are attributed to Chuuk separates despite denials and the referendum results from last year." Their island neighbors to the northwest, the Federated States of Micronesia, was an independent republic consisting of over six hundred tiny islands and a population of just over 250,000. Despite the small land area, the sizable coastlines made Micronesia the fourteenth largest economic zone in the world. One of the states, Chuuk, had a moderate independence movement which had been over the past fifty years a peaceful nonviolent movement. "The target appears to have been the legislative assembly."

"Should we be worried?" his chief of staff asked, concerned by the unsure look of the President.

"I don't know," said President Scotty, reached for a beer offered by the bartender. He took a long sip before continuing. "Bombings in Palikir might have taken out the Congress in Micronesia." He reached into his wallet to tip the bartender a few bills. "I suppose we should condemn the bombings and offer our support."

A dozen security guards rushed into the open hall of the hotel from the lobby, all with their 9mm pistols raised and at the ready. "Sir, can you come with us?" The lead guard waved upon catching sight of the president.

Startled guests took notice with various fearful and confused reactions, some rushing away while others took cover. President Scotty stood up and slowly raised his hands to motion for calm, worried the tourists, whose presence he so valued, would end up traumatized. "I'm sure it's just a precaution." He turned to one of the guards. "It *is* just a precaution, right?"

The head guard continued to glance back and forth across the room, looking for anything out of place. He had but one focus—to protect the President of the island. "Come with me, now." He signaled for the other guards to fan out and start evacuating the hall to the surprise of those still enjoying the late-night party.

President Scotty knew the guard wouldn't have ignored his question if there was no clear and present danger. The first instinct of the president was to turn to direct those at his function to safely leave the hotel. He never got the chance to act, as his lead bodyguard took a firm hold of his shoulder and dragged him to the lobby.

Looking back in the direction of the bar, Scotty caught sight of multiple figures, all in black, lunging out of the night into the hall. Three Nauru police officers standing watch over the function were struck in the chest by bullets and fell to the floor. The shots were muffled by silencers. With the sights of falling bodies and black-clothed figures with guns drawn came the screams of hotel guests. The President's pulse was racing now, the flight reflex taking over as he dashed toward the exit, surrounded by his security detail.

Hearing a gasp beside him, the president turned in time to see his chief of staff fall face down onto the carpet, the back of his head gone.

"Hostiles! Take cover!" the head body guard yelled into the radio while firing back a barrage of bullets at the invading hostiles. Accuracy was impossible while the guard continued to rush the president through the lobby. His satisfaction in seeing at least one of the hostiles fall was short lived, as he caught sight of night vision goggles on the intruders. For all he knew, bullets could come out from the darkness from any direction.

The sound of gunfire had filled the hotel, bullets ricocheting off walls. Panicked guests fled in all directions, some falling to the ground, hit by shrapnel and stray bullets.

In front of the hotel, a black sedan screeched to a stop in front of the hotel covered by police officers. The rear door already open, the body guard shoved President Scotty into the vehicle even as he felt a sharp pain in his back just below his left shoulder. With his remaining strength, the guard slammed the door shut and yelled to the driver. "Go, go!"

As the sedan raced away, President Scotty looked out the rear window to see his head of security fall to the street, dead, just before the back window was struck by a bullet and shattered. Pieces of glass were flung throughout the vehicle. Scotty grabbed his shoulder, feeling a sharp pain. The situation seemed surreal to the president, who had never seen such violence his entire life. He struggled to keep breathing as the sedan violently turned to the east and rushed by the airport.

"We detected some patrol boats coming toward the island!" a young police officer in the front passenger seat reported before screaming in the direction of the driver. "Keep going, to the safe house!" Having lost his far more experienced commander, the police officer struggled to think. He reached for a radio. "All available officers, converge on the Westin hotel!"

President Scotty was at a loss for words. He struggled not to vomit, his stomach lurching at the thought of the dead and injured he had seen and fear of what was to come. Were they being followed? Why would anyone come after him? He looked down at his hands to find them covered in blood.

NEW CONSTANTINOPLE
THE SOUTHWEST PACIFIC

The buzzing of her smartphone was enough of a disturbance that Grace Jaden slowly transitioned into consciousness from what had been a peaceful sleep. Her head feeling a slight hangover from the late night Jaden had to force her eyes to slowly open. For a brief instant, her dream continued to play out, and she reached to untangle herself from her husband. Not finding his arm, the dream came to a sudden end. With a considerable effort, Grace Jaden rolled out of bed to grab her house coat. In standing up, she could make out the sun beyond just beginning to creep up above the Pacific Ocean. The smartphone buzzed. She groaned, wrapped herself in the house coat, and tried to force herself to at look somewhat awake before tapping on the device.

The smart phone display blinked with an image of a frazzled Jord Laboucan. A just poured steaming cup of coffee and messy hair both indicated he had just crawled out of bed himself. "Sorry to wake you boss," he struggled to say. "Bridge has an urgent communication for you."

"From who?" Grace Jaden pressed hard on her cheeks and forcefully yawned, hoping that the stimulation would help her fully awaken.

"President of Mabu Island," Laboucan replied before being corrected by a nearby officer. "Nauru, sorry. It's early." He shrugged.

"Hell of a time to negotiate a crude deal." Jaden sat down on the bed while taking hold of the phone. "Patch him through."

The phone blinked as the satellite communication link was transferred. The panicked brown face of President Lionel Scotty appeared. "Please!" the man urgently began, "You must help us!"

It took a moment for Grace to acknowledge the man on the display was indeed Lionel Scotty, so panicked and exhausted did he look. The urgency in his voice was unnerving enough to snap her mind into focus. She sat up. "This is Grace Jaden," she said to ensure the President of

Nauru knew with whom he was talking to. Though they were friends, her first thought was that he was trying to reach someone else. "Are you okay? How can we help?"

"I'm in hiding. A militia is on the island killed most of our parliament!" the president was almost incoherent. "The Americans won't help us!"

A puzzled Jaden took a seat on the bed, trying to process the call. Had the man not looked terrorized, she would have thought it all a joke. "What militia?"

"I think they're the same group that struck Micronesia yesterday!" the president hypothesized. "At least two dozen men, a couple gunboats. Came over from the west. I know you helped East Timor. Can you help us too?"

Oh, shit. Grace Jaden could feel a headache coming on. After East Timor was, was she now seen as some vigilante? "Isn't this a job for the US Navy? Or the United Nations?"

President Scotty paused, worried that his long-time friend was seeing him as having lost his mind. "They've lumped us in with the Federated States of Micronesia . . ." The president tried to speak calmly despite feeling drained and shaky. "No military aid as part of their anticorruption effort."

Grace Jaden rubbed her forehead in frustration and took a deep breath. "That was always nonsense." She knew that Nauru had only a small defense force mostly made up of police officers. Only weeks earlier she had been planning to travel to Nauru to work out a crude deal to supply the island, which was dependent on renewable diesel gensets for most of its power. Why not take that trip a little early and with some protection? With newfound resolve, she pushed herself up off the bed, made her way to her desk, and activated her tablet. Still groggy, it took her embarrassingly long to load up a map projection to figure out just where exactly the *New Constantinople* was sailing in relation to the small island. Fifteen hundred to two thousand kilometers southeast of their location. Not that far, relatively speaking. "All right, give me a moment to consult with my management." Jaden tried to sound reassuring to offer the Nauruan President some hope. "We're on our way." She mentally hoped she was telling the truth.

"I look forward to hearing from you," the president replied with sincere gratitude.

The screen went blank, leaving the room dark again.

Alone in silence again, Grace Jaden took a quick look out at the rolling waters of the Pacific. What perilous situation had she gotten everyone into this time?

BRIDGE
NEW CONSTANTINOPLE

Now dressed in the standard-issue blue coveralls of both the "New Liberty Navy" and the CleanOcean Energy corporation, Grace Jaden made her way onto the bridge of the *New Constantinople*. The morning watch continued to sail the vessel as the sun began to peak over the horizon. A rather disheveled Jord Labaoucan made his way to the briefing room. He wore yesterday's suit, having rushed out of his quarters not wanting to disturb his wife. "Over here."

The senior sailors had reconfigured the briefing room as a sort of situation room complete with a large digital projection screen. Within, Andrew Lawrence and three other men in military camouflage uniforms sat around the conference table. They stood up and saluted.

Both Grace and Peter saluted back before taking a seat. Upon sitting down in the rather comfortable chairs, Grace Jaden decided that she needed a cup of coffee and stood up again. "Who needs coffee?" she asked while making her way back onto the bridge where she had seen a brewing coffee pot.

A sailor who had heard the comment soon returned, dashing in with a pot of coffee and a collection of mugs.

Grade Jaden saluted him. "You're a good man, sailor. Thank you." As she poured the pot of coffee into several cups, Peter Jaden loaded up the main screen.

Luke Zenuck entered the room, followed closely by Kelly Argarwal and Peter Jaden. "Thank goodness," he said, immediately grabbing a cup. "No crises this morning until I have some of this."

"You people all have a serious coffee addiction." Labaoucan took a gulp of his coffee. "Is that the crisis? We need a domestic source of coffee out here?"

Grace Jaden blinked. "That *is* a problem," she admitted before shaking her head. "But not a problem for this morning." She looked over at her son, who casually took a seat at the table. "What's he doing here?"

"Grace, I've hired our new head of air operations. You might know him. The rest of you, may I introduce Peter Jaden," said Luke Zenuck with a bow. Before Grace could respond, he added, "Someone on our team has to be a contrarian who isn't afraid to argue with you."

Grade Jaden squinted, clearly unsure of the hire. "You argue with me all the time."

"Yes," Zenuck yawned, "but I always lose. Plus, the man flies fighter jets. I figure that skillset will come in handy out here."

Peter Jaden took hold of the coffee pot and began topping off the cups around the table. "Happy to join the team," he said, pausing to choose his words carefully. "I know you're all aware I am Grace's son, but I don't expect any nepotism or special favors. I hope my aeronautical engineering degree and combat experience speak for me."

"The fact that you managed to put up with your mother speaks volumes," Labaoucan said, somewhat truthfully, raising his coffee cup. "Welcome aboard." Following the clashing of coffee cups, it was time to get to work. The table itself was a tablet which he was able to activate with a touch. The screen lit up with a projection of the Western Pacific Ocean centered on the position of the New Liberty armada of ships. With the swipe of his hand, he was able to offset the project to highlight the location of Nauru to the southwest.

"So"—Labaoucan stared down at the map—"Nauru needs our help apparently."

With a few taps, Peter Jaden projected various circles surrounding the New Liberty armada, the inner most the range of their various sensor platforms and the outer circle the range of their aircraft. Nauru was just outside the circle. "If we move our ships two days west, one of our Osprey transport craft can make it."

"We've only got three of those, and they're bloody expensive!" Laboucan objected. "Plus, it would be a one-way trip."

"We can refuel on the island," Peter replied.

Andrew Lawrence was taken aback at the thought of having to wait two full days to deploy. "Will the Nauruan forces even last two days?"

Grace Jaden took a sip of her hot coffee and took in the soothing taste in her mouth. She had never been nor would be a morning person. She tapped on the conference room desk. "They're going to have to wait two days since we can't get there sooner. But let's move only the *Byzantium*; we can fly off of there." She swiveled her chair to face Andrew Lawrence. "President Scotty was talking about two dozen men, a couple gunboats. What have we got?"

"I can match that." Andrew Lawrence smiled at the thought of being on dry land again, "Twenty-four combat veterans ready to go."

"Plus, we will have the Osprey and her drone for air support," Peter added.

Feeling the caffeine flowing through her veins, Grace Jaden felt refreshed enough to stand up and point at the island on the map. "President Lionel Scotty of the island of Nauru with whom we have been negotiating a crude deal with has gone into hiding and called us for help. Facing a small militia invasion, no doubt connected to recent bombings in the Federated States of Micronesia." She pointed to the larger collection of islands west of Nauru. "We recommend helping our neighbor and potential ally by flying an Osprey with some of our best men to assist."

It took Kelly Argarwal a few moments to realize all eyes were on her. "Oh," she said with a shrug, "I guess I'm the one that signs off on this?"

"You *are* the prime minister," Grace replied. "It's your call."

Leaning back in her chair, Argarwal clenched her hands together. "What's the downside?"

"That Osprey is extremely expensive and one of only three we have," Laboucan began. "And unfortunately, our own gunboats are still in Japan on order."

"Can you rush that?" Grace Jaden asked knowing she would feel a lot safer with corvettes sailing escort.

"How much time do I have to decide?" Argarwal asked, pondering the Constitution they had only recently approved, "I think I need a vote of parliament to approve as well."

Grace Jaden pointed at the map. "Regardless, we have two days to get the *Byzantium* in position." That the *Byzantium* was operated by

CleanOcean Energy meant that the production platform would be moving into position regardless.

The prime minister of New Liberty sat quietly for several seconds, staring at the map. "You know the Federated States of Micronesia, Island of Nauru. All this activity is happening pretty close to us. Can we defend ourselves?"

"The best defense is a good offense." Andrew Lawrence steepled his massive hands and chuckled. "That being said, I've got C-RAM and naval guns on all five of our ships. The *Byzantium* also has a quad-missile pack vertical launch system with RIM-162 Evolved Sea Sparrow missiles and some Mark 46 torpedoes."

"Enough to protect us from any gunboats?" Jaden asked.

"Enough to protect us from a destroyer," Lawrence replied, though not as confidently as he had wanted to. He shrugged while raising up his hands apologetically. "Even so, I'm no Navy man."

"We've got at least twenty drones combat-ready as well," Peter Jaden offered. "Should be enough to take on any local pirates at least."

"Grace, what's your recommendation?" Argarwal looked Jaden in the eye.

There being no way she was going to leave a friend in need hanging, Grace Jaden replied with determination. "We have a duty to protect our ally and stand for free markets and democracy in the region. As strategos and foreign minister, I recommend we proceed. We move the *Byzantium* further west, leave the rest of New Liberty here, fly in, secure the president, and fly out."

"Sounds easy enough." Kelly Argarwal's grin disappeared as she was faced with disapproving stares.

"First rule of CleanOcean Energy," said Zenuck, pointing at Kelly. "Never say anything is easy."

Office of Naval Intelligence
Suitland, Maryland, USA

The Office of Naval Intelligence conference room was packed with officers waiting for the forthcoming presentation. The Pacific was heating up, and it was "all hands on deck" regarding the briefing. Rumors had also circulated that Rear Admiral Davidson and the secretary of state were set to clash, adding to the attendance ratio.

Davidson, in full uniform, pointed up to the projected map of the Federated States of Micronesia. Until only about a decade ago, the republic had been associated with the United States in a compact of free association, and the defense of the collection of islands still felt near and dear to many in the room. Many an American had died fighting for the islands at the hands of the Japanese occupiers during World War Two after which the United States had directly administered the islands as a trust territory. By 1979, the Federated States of Micronesia was granted independence, and after half a century, unlike the Marshall Islands and the Northern Mariana Islands, were no longer defended by the United States. "The capital city of Palikir, located on Pohnpei Island, had reported bombings, including major government buildings. The local government has gone strangely radio silent." The viewscreen flashed with a live satellite feed. "Here are at least five half-a-century old Shanghai Three class gunboats, machine-gun-armed only."

One concerned admiral asked the most obvious question. "So, who the hell are they?"

"Most intelligence reports believe that they're a spin-off of Vietnamese and Indonesian irregular units, which continue to operate off Timor. With US forces having engaged in East Timor"—Davidson stood tall with some pride in having participated in that operation regardless of the career consequences—"it is thought that these irregular pirates have allied with Chuuk separatists."

Many in the room leaned back into their chairs, having already read similar assessments from both the Central Intelligence Agency and the initial reports out of the Office of Naval Intelligence. Even Secretary of State Harris, near the back of the conference table, seemed to settle down at the assessment.

Most were startled when Rear Admiral Davidson continued with a clear and firm tone. "I have to disagree with that assessment." Ignoring whispers and conversations throughout the room, Davidson raised his voiced and spoke slow and clearly, so as to be heard. "I argue that what we are seeing is part of a broader effort to destabilize the region and that we should get a carrier battlegroup into the South Pacific as soon as possible."

Secretary of State Harris, attending the meeting as the president's representative, stood up from the table, seemingly angered by the statement. Harris jumped at the chance to counter. "Based on what facts?" Harris shouted. It was clear he aimed to make the rear admiral, his military record aside, come off as an odd combination of conspiracy theorist and warmonger.

Manipulating the display back to a top-down projection of the Federated State of Micronesia, Rear Admiral Davidson first pointed at the island of Chuuk. "While the Chuuk State, one of the four states of Micronesia, is the most populous and has a history of independence movements, these movements have always been peaceful. The independence movement has primarily been based on a want for isolation as opposed to violence and hostility toward the other states." He raised one finger. "Fact number one is that the Federated States of Micronesia has been relatively peaceful until now." With his fingers, he moved the map to the east. "Number two. Satellite shots are also showing that this so-called"—he made quotation marks with his fingers in the air in protest of the designation—"pirate or militia fleet has three Chinese-built Type 22 missile boats and a Type 037II Houjian-class missile boat, which have moved to the east. These aren't simple gunboats but expensive corvette-class warships. Where did they get the money?" he asked rhetorically— the question he'd been trying unsuccessfully to answer for more than a week now.

"These are forty-year-old hulls and still of the corvette classification," a naval analyst, wanting to show off his knowledge of the designs and simultaneously suck up to the secretary of state, countered.

"Still high-tech warships with anti-ship missiles, surface-to-air missiles, torpedoes, and fire control radar," Davidson pressed, "And in moving them to the east, someone doesn't want us to know they have them." Not hearing any further interjections, Davidson used his fingers to zoom out the map to cover the entire Western Pacific before raising his hand up with three fingers extended. "Third, the entire Western Pacific Ocean is now a hotbed of activity. We have bombings in the Philippines destabilizing the government"—he pointed to the Philippines Islands and then traced north—"Chinese naval units pre-positioning around Taiwan." And finally, he pointed to East Timor. "And only months after militias launched assaults out of Indonesia against East Timor including a Chinese-built submarine—"

The normally model-like face of Secretary of State Harris was now flushed and red. "You and your rouge submarine!" Harris threw a pile of analyst papers he had been holding down on his desk. "Why do you continue to press for a fight, Rear Admiral? A fight you inadvertently started?"

Hoping that cooler heads in the room would see reason, Rear Admiral Davidson made the decision to keep his mouth shut and let the facts speak for themselves.

Realizing he was being politically outplayed, the secretary of state forced himself to calm down. "What do you suggest we do, Rear Admiral?"

"As I indicated, sir"—Davidson had to force himself to not to spit the last word—"I recommend we dispatch a carrier battle group into the region to promote stability."

"With the loss of Diego Garcia in the Indian Ocean and the shutdown of the Okinawa naval station in Japan we have little coverage in the area beyond Guam. We actually have no carriers in the Pacific west of Pearl." The rather concerned admiral seemed almost embarrassed at the statement. Even the once-mighty airbase of Diego Garcia in the Indian Ocean had been handed by the United Kingdom and the United States to Mauritius under heavy political pressure out of the Middle East.

"The president would have to go to Congress." Secretary of State Harris tried to appear to take the recommendations under advisement. "State Department has highlighted a lot of corruption in the Federated States of Micronesia, which is partly why we pressed to end the association status."

The mere mention of the United States having pressed to give up responsibility for defending the islands was too much for Rear Admiral Davidson. "There is a lot of corruption in Washington, D.C., That doesn't mean we should abandon Washington to our enemies."

There was silence in the room, most unbelieving they had heard Davidson correctly.

"You're out of line, mister." Secretary of State Harris pointed directly at the Rear Admiral before sneaking in an angry glance at his superior. "Just like you were out of line in East Timor."

Knowing he had already crossed a line, Rear Admiral Davidson simply concluded the briefing. He sat through the rest of the briefing in silence, content in knowing that the half an hour of reports detailing open warfare in Syria and Turkey while North Africa was on the verge of invading the south would soon no longer be any concern of his. When the meeting concluded, he raced to his superior, the director of naval intelligence, and handed him a piece of paper.

"What's this?" The director of naval intelligence looked down at the paper.

"My resignation."

CHAPTER NINE – BATTLE OF NAURU

"Twenty years from now, you will be more disappointed by the things you didn't do than those you did. So throw off the bowlines. Sail away from safe harbor. Catch the wind in your sails. Explore. Dream. Discover."

—Mark Twain

JUNE 25, 2068, 9:30 AM

MV BYZANTIUM

THE SOUTHWEST PACIFIC

The privately-owned V-22 Osprey dominated the helicopter pad of the *Byzantium*. The large rotors were rotated horizontally, that the tilt-rotor aircraft sat like an awkwardly oversized helicopter. The elevated bridge deck of the production ship offered sailors an unrestricted view of their surroundings, so Grace Jaden was able to silently watch from above as camouflaged men climbed into the lowered back hatch of the Osprey. It was a windy day, and Jaden felt almost guilty watching the team work on the deck from behind glass. Her nerves were on edge, hands slightly shaking in anticipation of the mission to come. She reached over to grab a cup of coffee from the computer station she had been working from over the past three days, careful to hold it tight given the rolling of the ship.

"All radar and sonar systems are showing clear," Captain Tysor reported from the helm console of the ship as he watched over a junior sailor manning the helm. He snuck a quick look at the latest satellite calculated coordinates of the vessel. "That's it. Should be in flight range now."

Peter Jaden tapped a large vertical display to go over the latest navigational data. The island of Nauru was clearly within the theoretical operational range of the V-22. "Looks good to me."

Grace Jaden made her way back to look out over the massive floating production platform of the *Byzantium*. The wind howled under a partially cloudy sky. She would have thought it was too windy to proceed were it not for the multiple drones still flying in and out of the moon pond, distributing *Sargassum* seaweed and fertilizer. "Weather looks good? Wind seems rather strong."

Peter punched up the latest weather reports. "Nothing I can't handle." He had flown numerous missions through far worse weather.

Both Luke Zenuck and Jord Labaoucan had come along on the *Byzantium* and, coffees in hand, they stepped over to review the plots themselves. Laboucan always knew his place as the non-technical voice of common sense, and he looked to Zenuck. "All looks good. So, Peter and Andrew will lead the military mission?"

"I'll come along," Grace Jaden declared, still looking out into the ocean.

It was a statement both Jord and Luke had expected but dreaded to hear. "Certainly, they can handle it," Luke Zenuck began with a sense of déjà vu. Throughout the history of CanHarvest Renewables, from founding all the way to East Timor, Grace Jaden always tried to get into the field as much as possible.

"Definitely not your place." Jord Labaoucan agreed. He looked over to Peter Jaden, the one man who potentially had a shot at changing Grace's mind.

Her son, knowing that there was nothing anyone could say to change her mind, shrugged before leaving the plot with a coffee pot, forcing Grace to turn and face him while he refilled her cup. "Seriously, they're right. Andrew and I can handle this."

"I know you can," Grace Jaden said before adding a definitive, "I'm still coming."

Luke shrugged. "We tried."

The main communication monitor to the center of the bridge was activated with an image of Kelly Argarwal. "*New Constantinople* to *MV Byzantium*, Kelly Argarwal here for Grace Jaden."

Captain Tyson spun the flat screen projector to face the Jadens. "*Byzantium* here, party is ready to go."

"Good morning, Kelly." Grace Jaden put down her coffee cup. "Would be nice to use the whole day. We'd like to get going ASAP."

"You have parliamentary approval to proceed," Kelly announced. "Electronic vote deadline was last night, and the results were unanimous."

Jord Laboucan couldn't help but ponder if this mission was going to end up a costly mistake they would all come to regret. "Doesn't mean we *should* proceed," Laboucan suggested. "We're all sure this is the right move?"

Grace Jaden leaned back against the glass to face both the projection of Argarwal and everyone assembled on the bridge. "Let's do this. Jord and Nick, while I'm gone, I need you two to firm up the crude deals with Taiwan, Japan, and the Philippines. Let's have a crude deal with India and Russia too—ensure we're getting some diversification."

"We're on it," said Zenuck, giving a quick thumbs up.

Jord Laboucan sighed. "All right."

Grace Jaden addressed the bridge. "The Japanese, the Taiwanese, and the Filipinos are paying a premium for our crude. They all see what's going down in the Pacific as a repeat of East Timor with the use of unofficial militias and paramilitaries. They want us going into Nauru as a counter."

"So, we're their paramilitary going in after someone else's paramilitary?" Zenuck asked almost rhetorically.

"Something like that," Grace Jaden replied, seeing no reason to sugarcoat the situation.

That the team was all committed, and Laboucan saw no reason to be anything but supportive of the mission at this point. "Well," Laboucan chuckled, "they'd better buy our oil. At a premium."

"The Japanese are also rushing our corvettes. Got us a great deal on an air-independent population submarine and our own tanker, complete with defenses," said Grace Jaden, summarizing the last few days of intense negotiations. "Should have a whole fleet of third-party tankers showing up over the coming week."

While happy to hear of the renewable crude sales, Zenuck wasn't happy to hear of other nations using them for missions best suited for their respective militaries. "Isn't this supposed to be where Uncle Sam steps in and does all the fighting for everyone?"

Grace Jaden exhaled, well aware that the situation should never have progressed to the point that the only support for the Republic of Nauru would be the new sea state. "There isn't a carrier battlegroup west of Pearl right now. I don't think that's a coincidence."

Zenuck pondered the statement. "Washington is selling out the Pacific?"

"Looks that way, doesn't it?" Grace Jaden said matter-of-factly. "But to whom?" That the United States was drowning in debt, stagnant, and increasingly less involved in the affairs of the Pacific and the growing power of China was known to everyone on the bridge. The American government calling on the Japanese and South Koreans to press for more socialist-style programs had also alienated their once strong friendship. It was only a decade ago when the United States shut down their naval base in Okinawa and pulled out their carrier battlegroup. "And at what price?"

The bridge was silent apart from the whirling and beeping of various radar and sonar systems. All on the bridge coming to accept that the world was changing regardless of their thoughts on the matter.

"Nick"—Grace Jaden turned to Zenuck—"you ensure that renewable crude gets to market. We need those funds."

Zenuck pondered coming along with the Osprey but with bad eyesight and allergies, he mentally admitted to himself that the best place for him was filling those incoming tankers. He gave a salute. "I'm on it."

Grace Jaden reached over to grab her leather jacket draped over her chair. "Let's roll out."

OSPREY ONE

Within the hour, all drone flights off the *Byzantium* were temporarily suspended as Peter Jaden received clearance to take off, sitting in the pilot seat of the V-22 Osprey. With a pull on the throttle, the V-22 Osprey was lifted up off the deck by the two three-bladed eleven-meter-long propellers. Safely airborne, the nacelles rotated ninety degrees for horizontal flight, converting the V-22 into a fuel-efficient high-speed turboprop aircraft.

"Godspeed Osprey One," came the transmission from Captain Tyson, who was aboard the *MV Byzantium*, now far behind the craft.

"Roger that, *Byzantium*," Peter Jaden replied into his headset while he maneuvered the V-22 to face southwest. "On course for Nauru. I'll check in on the hour." He gave his co-pilot and those sitting in the cabin a thumbs-up.

Strapped into her seat in the back of the cabin with Andrew Lawrence and twelve camouflaged infantry, Grace Jaden adjusted her headset, so she could hear over the loud echoing hum of the turboprop engines. "How long?"

"Should be about two hours, thirty minutes," Peter Jaden replied from the cockpit. He pulled back on the throttle, powering up the Rolls-Royce AE 1107C six thousand horsepower engines and accelerating the aircraft to a velocity of over 565 kilometers an hour.

Grace Jaden raised her tablet to face Andrew Lawrence and his men. "All right, First Infantry Platoon—"

"We are a sea state," General Lawrence interrupted while giving his men a morale-boosting grin. "We're all Marines here."

"All right, First Marine Platoon," Grace corrected herself, "According to the Nauru forces we're in contact with the hostile paramilitaries we are going up against." She had decided to call the hostiles paramilitaries, given the fact they didn't seem to deserve the term *militia*. "They are trained infantry holding the Westin hotel, the main port, and the airport. The president of the island is in hiding in an abandoned immigration detention center. Our mission is to retake the airport and create a distraction for the local police force to retake the Westin Hotel and reoccupy the Parliament Building. General?" She looked over at Lawrence.

Andrew Lawrence rolled his eyes and felt somewhat embarrassed hearing his assigned rank of general for New Liberty. "Thank you, Strategos Jaden." He smiled at his men lest they think he had let the rank get to his head. "Listen up, boys. We are the First Marine Platoon of New Liberty. This is our first mission, so let's stay focused here and make it count. Intelligence we have says that we are facing simple infantry of unknown expertise. Let's assume that they know what they are doing." General Lawrence took some satisfaction in knowing that his small platoon consisted of hand-picked infantrymen from among the world's armies. "I've picked you because you are the best of the best from around the world."

"I thought it was just because we were available," one of the Sergeants known by his nickname of Mia joked.

"Regardless, let's go over how we are going to secure that airport."

OSPREY ONE
APPROACHING NAURU
11:47 AM

Though the waters of the Pacific extended in all directions, a beep and flash from the glass cockpit confirmed to Peter Jaden that they were within a hundred kilometers of Nauru. He lowered his headset. "Wake up back there. Twelve minutes to Nauru."

"You going to do your magic?" Grace Jaden asked from the cabin of the tiltrotor aircraft.

"You bet," the pilot responded while looking over at the co-pilot. "Activate weapons systems, Lieutenant Wognar."

With the flicking of various switches Lieutenant Karla Wognar activated the belly-mounted GAU-19 three-barrel Gatling gun. "GAU-19 on." Her glass cockpit lit up with the targeting camera of the Gatling gun.

"There it is," Peter Jaden announced as he made out the dot over the horizon, which was the island of Nauru. The island was relatively tiny, just twenty-one square kilometers in area. The international airport and capital city took up the entire southern quarter of the island, and the northern part of the island pretty much abandoned phosphate mines and stockpiles. "Go for the gunboat first." He titled the plane slightly to face the western part of the island where a small channel allowed for a shallow port to be built—mostly for fishing and tour boats. He snuck a glance at the fire control and radar screens. "Screens showing clear." The island was coming into view now; coral cliffs surrounded Nauru's central plateau—the only fertile green areas the narrow coastal belt where coconut palm trees flourished.

"Roger that." Lieutenant Wognar scanned the port with the targeting camera, zooming in to seek out her target. Anchored just beyond the coral reef was the flotilla of three Shanghai II Type 062-class gunboats. The small vessels were relatively well-armed for their size, each with twin 37mm gun mounts. "Targets in sight."

"Take them out," Peter Jaden ordered. He had ensured that all the radar systems were on passive mode that the gunboats would be caught totally unprepared for what was coming their way.

With the press of Wognar's trigger finger, the GAU-19 Gatling gun opened up with all three barrels pumping out 0.50 caliber M9-linked ammunition. Even from a range of over two kilometers, the rounds strafed across the gunboats. The shots hit their mark, cutting through all three gunboats. The shells penetrated the diesel fuel tank of the center gunboat, causing a small but visible explosion, the fireball engulfing all three gunboats. "Gunboats out of action."

The oval-shaped island and surrounding coral reef passed beneath the V-22 to be replaced once again by the seemingly never-ending waters of the Pacific. The glass cockpit came alive with alarms, and Peter Jaden instinctively dropped the nose of the aircraft while reviewing the warning indicators on the heads-up display. "Fire control radar locked on us, three kilometers to the West!" he shouted while swinging the V-22 Osprey to the east to circle back toward Nauru.

To the west of the island sailed a Type 056 Jiangdao-class corvette. An older Chinese patrol craft, the hull of the ninety-meter-long vessel housed a Type 360 air/surface radar platform, fire control radar, and a variety of machine guns and surface-to-air missiles. The corvette opened fire with a radar-controlled 30mm cannon.

The V-22 was too far and moving too fast for any of the bullets to hit the plane. *Damn it*, Peter mentally cursed. That corvette must have been waiting for trouble with its radar offline, only activated when reports came in of their gunboats under fire. With the radar active, the corvette knew their location, but Peter knew theirs. With its radar active, his own radar could now identify the location, a range, and a predicted vessel class of his opponent. Eyeing his range to the enemy corvette Peter leveled out the aircraft, content that his craft was safe. His heart skipped a beat, however, when another alarm went off. To his surprise, the corvette had an FL-3000 flying Leopard surface-to-air octo-pack missile launcher that had achieved a radar lock on the V-22. "Hang on!" he called into his headset.

The corvette fired off a surface-to-air missile.

Peter swore as he pushed forward on the flight stick, sending the plane diving down toward the ocean while still dodging incoming 30mm shells. He turned sharply to the left as much as he thought he could without stalling over the Pacific. With the press of a trigger button, he had the V-22 deploy chaff and flares which streamed out from behind the aircraft.

The Flying Leopard missile nearly collided with the V-22 but overshot high before arcing around and harmlessly chasing a chaff pod down into the Pacific. "Osprey One under fire. I've got a corvette with some anti-air capability!" Peter pulled up just before the V-22 Osprey hit the water and leveled out, heading straight west toward the island—so close to the surface of the ocean it felt like he could reach out and touch it. "We've got to land." He looked to his co-pilot, "Light up that airfield!"

Wognar caught sight of an infantry-manned security gate dead ahead and took it out with a barrage of bullets from the turreted Gatling gun. She winced at the sounds of bullets ricocheting off the V-22 Osprey. Alarms of various systems taking damage sounded off.

The V-22 shot over the lone runway that was the Nauru international airport. "Taking fire," Peter Jaden yelled into his headset, and he rotated the tiltrotors into helicopter mode, lifting the aircraft's nose to force the ship to hover backwards over the runway. "Prepare to dismount; I'm opening up the hatch!"

The Osprey almost seemed to fall toward the ground, causing the stomachs of those in the cabin to lurch. "Are we okay up there?" Grace Jaden yelled into her headset, wondering if she should brace for impact even as the infantrymen beside her were unbuckling their belts. The Osprey jolted as the landing gear hit the runway pavement hard and the air brakes activated. Before the aircraft came to a halt, Lawrence smashed his fist against a control panel, causing the rear loading lamp to slowly crack open and began to lower.

In the cockpit Peter Jaden activated various infrared cameras to seek out enemies, directing his co-pilot with a nod to fire on a grouping of enemy soldiers shooting at the aircraft from the airport terminal to the north side of the runway. The incoming gunfire came to a halt after a burst of the GAU-19 tore through the building. "Looks clear. You've got houses to the north you can use for cover." He began switching off various systems before unbuckling himself and grabbing his service pistol. "Cover them, but be ready to move out."

With the ramp open, General Lawrence waved for the first six of his infantrymen to run down the platform with M4 carbine rifles at the ready. He tossed out a smoke grenade to hide their position. The grenade also shot out various hot tracers, which would confuse any infrared scopes.

BAM! A sniper shot struck the ramp. Each of the Marines had a small active radar system on their shoulder, which detected the bullet and alerted them to their situation. "Shot, northeast," the electronic monitors reported. Motivated by the knowledge a sniper was actively taking shots at them, the Marines hustled. The parliament buildings and the Westin Hotel were far down the runway to the south side on a narrow strip between the airport and the ocean. Lawrence waved for his men to run north and take cover in a neighborhood of small two-story buildings and warehouses before they disappeared into a haze of smoke. "We're under sniper fire from that terminal!" Lawrence reported.

Peter Jaden commanded the glass cockpit to display the infrared camera of the GAU-22 and pointed at what he thought was the silhouette of a sniper on the second floor. "There!" he said, pointing even as Lt. Wognar aimed the GAU-19 Gatling gun and let the weapon rip.

After rolling down behind a tree and turning to raise his weapon and survey the area, the company leader, an Irish Sergeant by the name of Murphy, radioed back, "We've got cover! Clear for now!"

General Lawrence raised his own M4 carbine up and knelt as he made his way down the ramp. He flirted with the edge of the smoke cloud, using his scope to eye the damaged terminal building to the northeast and the various government buildings and hotels to the southeast. The runway running down the island southeast along the coast was empty apart from a few small passenger planes. "All right, bring down the packs, hurry!"

With the roar of the engine, one younger corporal by the name of Lam started up the Polaris-built MRZR all-terrain-vehicle and drove it down the ramp, mission packs pulled behind in a small trailer. The vehicle skidded while Lam took a hard left and accelerated in the direction of the first squad, as a corporal seated beside him actively scanned for hostiles with his M4 rifle.

"All right, that's it. The rest of us, let's go!" General Lawrence ordered while waving for Grace Jaden to follow. He held down the transmit button on the wrist panel, which controlled his headset and provided him a real-time map of him and his forces. "Osprey one, we're clear. You'd better come with us just to be safe," he recommended, as the large aircraft at the end of the runway made a pretty large and obvious target.

"Roger that," came the crackle of Peter Jaden's response, and his co-pilot emerged out the back ramp. They ran in the direction of the first squad to the north even as the Osprey turboprops were still spinning to a stop.

Grace Jaden gave a quick salute in the direction of her son. "Nice flying there, ace."

Catching up with the group racing across the runway to the north and the relative cover of the warehouse, Peter looked to both Andrew and Grace so they could see his concern. "Enemy corvette off the south coast with some pretty good fire control radar. We might be facing a greater threat than we thought." All three dashed behind the warehouse. "How would a bunch of pirates end up with a Chinese corvette?"

Behind the cover of buildings to every side and with infantrymen deployed to hold the position, the three took a moment to catch their breath. General Lawrence slammed the hood of the MRZR ATV. "Lam, second squad," he said, turning to the pilots and Grace. "You three. Move up north to position Alpha. I'm going with first squad; we're going to secure the airport terminal."

Corporal Lam offered a seat on the ATV to Grace Jaden, who declined with a wave, feeling it was best to have a Marine with a gun occupy the passenger seat, given the less-restricted view. Lam began to drive the ATV along the road to the northwest along the coast slow enough that he could be shadowed by Grace, the two pilots and four other infantrymen on foot. Lam pressed gently on the throttle to accelerate to a speed that those on foot had to jog to keep up.

All spun around at hearing a whistling booming sound echo over the island just in time to see a Chinese built YJ-83 C-802 anti-ship missile slam right into the V-22 Osprey still sitting on the runway. The aircraft disappeared into a plume of flames and debris.

"Must have been that corvette!" Peter Jaden cried, lamenting the loss of his plane.

Grace Jaden couldn't help but think of the forty-million-dollar price tag of the plane. While it was an older used aircraft, it was still rather an expensive item for a private company. "Laboucan is going to kill me." The fire raging on the runway sent adrenaline surging through her body. She struggled to regain her breath and continued the dash to the west.

"If we live through this!" Peter smiled back.

Corporal Lam took a hard right turn in his All-Terrain-Vehicle off the main ring road and inland.

Grace Jaden instinctively took a deep breath on seeing the road head up a rather noticeable incline, where the central plateau of jagged limestone pinnacles rose beyond the fertile coastal belt. She could identify Command Ridge ahead; at seventy-one meters above sea level, it was the highest point on the island. Thankfully, the land around the Euada Lagoon supported banana and pandanus trees that provided some cover along with the buildings. According to the maps, the utility buildings to which the legitimate authorities had fled were still surrounded by some vegetation prior to the barren uninhabited interior of abandoned phosphate surface mines. "Let's see how our allies are faring." She reached for her smartphone and called up the number for President Scotty.

The smartphone screen blinked with a real-time projection of President Scotty. "I assume all that commotion is your arrival?"

"We're running up the road now." Grace Jaden looked around for identifying landmarks. "Passing fuel tanks to the left."

"We've got this road secure; I'm sending security forces now," the president of the island responded.

"Nauruan security forces are coming our way up ahead," she said clearly into the headset, concerned that the sudden sight of the police officers might result in friendly fire.

Encouraged by the thought of meeting up with local allies, the squad doubled their efforts up the hill. About a quarter of a kilometer ahead, armed men poured into the street, machine guns raised up in the air.

Lam hit the brakes of the ATV and raised his binoculars so he could make out the police uniforms of the waving men. The Corporal gave a thumbs up while activating his radio. "Three friendlies spotted near the fuel depot and detention center." Apparently satisfied that they had been spotted, the Nauruan police officers themselves disappeared off of the street.

"You go ahead and set up," Grace Jaden recommended. "The rest of us can catch up."

"Roger that." Wanting to get off the road and out of the open as soon as possible Corporal Lam pulled hard on the ATV throttle, sending it racing up the hill in a plume of smoke. The remaining squad mates dashed to the side of the road, using vegetation and houses for cover. "Alpha One, what's your situation?"

Having slowly made their way east, General Lawrence and his infantrymen in First Squad had reached the airport terminal. With his electronic binoculars set to show infrared, Lawrence scanned the building using a coconut tree for cover. He could see the upper level was still occupied by at least five enemy hostiles. He was too low and surrounded by vegetation and buildings to be able to look across the runway in the direction of the Parliament Building and Westin Hotel. "Alpha One to Strategos. Alpha Squad at the airport terminal, in position. Hostiles are holding their position inside the terminal—at least five on the second floor."

Having brought the ATV to a stop safely in the parking lot of the detection center and behind the manned gate of the Nauruan security forces, Corporal Lam jumped off of the vehicle and ran back to un-tarp the mission packages in the trailer. He threw his package to the sandy ground, knelt down, and opened it up. Within was his M110 semi-automatic sniper system. He lifted out the rifle, attached the scope, and slammed a cartridge into place before running in the direction of the road. He climbed up into one of the observation posts to get above the vegetation. He ignored the rather spectacular view of the coast and focused on eyeing the airport terminal and the collection of government buildings and hotels below to the south. "Bravo One to Alpha One, setting up scope now," he transmitted.

The rest of Bravo raced into the detention center parking lot. Grace Jaden, who normally prided herself on her physical fitness, cursed at her need for deep breathes and a break given the pain in her side while trading salutes with the various police officers that held positions around the building. The Nauruan police officers looked as happy as the members of Bravo Squad at the sight of friendly faces.

A surprisingly young officer approached with his hand extended "Welcome to the island of Nauru. Wish it was under better circumstances. I'm the acting police chief, Detective Waqa. My Dad was the former chief." He tried to remain unemotional despite the pain of having lost his father.

"My sympathies." Grace Jaden firmly took the detective's hand and squeezed.

Peter Jaden gulped, pushing back any memories of the loss of his own father and brother. Knowing that every second counted, he ran beside Lieutenant Wognar, who already had a grip on the largest of the crates, still sitting on the back of the ATV trailer. Peter grabbed the grip for the other side. "One, two, three!" he counted off, then raised the package and dropped it to the ground. Wognar opened it up to reveal their own toy, an RQ-40 Super-Wasp ducted fan vertical-take-off-and-landing unmanned aerial vehicle. The small microdrone powered up as controlled by Peter Jaden's arm-mounted tablet. The drone lifted up into the air and hovered to the south.

Peter Jaden pointed out the displayed view of the airport terminal building. "There's the terminal." Hovering higher up and further south, he was able to adjust the camera to scan the runway in the direction of the Parliament Building and the Westin Hotel. "Hotel and Parliament Building." With a press of a button, he switched to infrared and activated his headset. "All right, all teams, listen up. SuperWasp to all teams, we've got six hostiles on the upper floor of the terminal and I've got six hostiles in the lobby of the Westin Hotel. Parliament Building looks deserted right now."

"Probably trying to lure the president out into the open," Grace Jaden said as she stood over the still kneeling Peter. "Twelve on twelve. Let's work on those odds."

"Alpha One to Bravo One, you got a target," General Lawrence radioed from outside the airport terminal.

Elevated on the observation post, Corporal Lam made out three hostiles on the upper floor of the terminal through his rifle-mounted scope. The hostiles appeared preoccupied with the still-burning wreckage of the Osprey, gazing upon the runway with binoculars. "Targets in sight."

General Lawrence waved Corporal Murphy and the rest of Alpha Squad to emerge from their cover and advance on the terminal. They all hit the terminal wall and began making their way to a back entrance. Lawrence pulled on a door handle to find it locked. "Need some explosives here."

Corporate Murphy ran forward and attached a small detonator to the door. With a nod, the corporal communicated that the charge was ready to go.

"Take the shot," General Lawrence commanded.

From high above, Corporal Lam pulled the trigger to fire the M110 sniper rifle, the first bullet smashing through a glass plane to strike one of the hostiles directly in the head. On seeing his comrade's head explode, a second raised his weapon just in time to suffer a similar fate with a bullet to the chest. The third hostile was better trained and with more time to react dropped to the floor out of sight.

Having heard the sniper shots, General Lawrence knew it was time to move. "Now!" he yelled. The charge on the door exploded; then, he kicked the door open and tossed in a couple of flash-bangs. After hearing the booms of the flashbangs, he ran into the terminal followed by the rest of his men.

There was the harsh rattle of AK-47 fire as hostiles fired down hazy stairwells. General Lawrence caught sight of one rather foolish hostile that ran down the stairs while firing, and he immediately fired a single shot into the man's stomach. The enemy folded in on himself in agony and collapsed.

With the transmitted view from the RQ-40 Super-Wasp drone, Peter Jaden could make out activity now all along the runway. No doubt hearing reports of being under fire, enemy soldiers all grabbed their weapons and rushed out the lobby of the Westin Hotel in the direction of the terminal. The sounds of the waves and the gunfire helped muffle the fans of the RQ-40 SuperWasp drone above.

"This is for my Osprey," Peter Jaden said to himself before electronically ordering the RQ-40 to open fire.

The RQ-40 picked off the two hostiles outside the Westin Hotel before the others had even realized something was amiss. Only the dead bodies indicated they were under fire. It took almost twenty seconds before one of the hostiles pointed up at the drone. He raised his rifle and opened fire, too quickly to be accurate, before being shot by the drone in the leg. The three remaining hostiles retreated back into the hotel lobby.

With the lower level of the airport terminal secure and silent, General Lawrence led Alpha Squad up the stairs to the second floor. Corporal Murphy tossed up a flash bang, which detonated among various chairs usually occupied by travelers.

Unsurprisingly, there came the burst of gunfire at the choke point that was the top of the stairs. Not wanting to send his men rushing into the gunfire, General Lawrence pumped the M203 single-shot grenade launcher attached to his M4 rifle. The grenade fired up and detonated, the blast smashing out the windows of the terminal. Again, he launched another grenade, this time at a slightly different angle.

Satisfied that anyone upstairs would have had to have taken cover, General Lawrence grimaced and then ran up the stairs, rifle firing. The remaining hostiles were completely caught by surprise at the audacity of the General and were quickly picked off by the trained marksmen of Alpha Squad. General Lawrence stayed back as his infantrymen secured the floor. "We've got the terminal," he reported, giving his men a thumbs up on seeing them signal the terminal was secure.

"Okay get out of there in case that corvette decides to take out the terminal" Grace Jaden radioed back while watching a live feed from the SuperWasp drone showing various vehicles coming to a halt at the south side of the runway and police officers with pistols drawn charging the hotel lobby. "The Nauruan police force is moving in to retake the Parliament Building; we figure three hostiles left at most."

"What are we going to do about that corvette?" asked General Lawrence, considering holding the terminal, as it had a strategic view of the capital, but the still burning Osprey on the runway convinced him otherwise. He waved for his men to prepare to pull out of the terminal.

"Leave that to us!" Grace Jaden radioed back from the parking lot of the former detention center. She raised her headset to ensure that her next statement wasn't radioed across the island. "At least, I hope he can leave it to us." She ran over to Peter and the Marines of Bravo Squad, rushing to disconnect, un-tarp, and set up the trailer they had driven in with the ATV. "How are we doing?"

"We're on it." Peter Jaden had set up the trailer, which was in fact a large 76mm gun turret. He flicked various switches to fire up the diesel generators. "By the way, our intelligence was way off," he said, snapping another piece of the turret into place. "That is a full 56 corvette with SAMS." With the press of a button, the unit was activated, the turret raising itself up and rotating into place. He pointed over at Lieutenant Wognar.

Grace looked up into the blue sky and out into the waters of the Pacific, wishing it was instead night that their positions were hidden.

"Where is my damn radar?" Peter Jaden yelled on seeing a blank screen on the human-machine-interface of the turret. Lieutenant Wognar ran a cable from the small quickly assembled radar set over to Peter Jaden, who promptly plugged it into the trailer. The display came alive with a projection of radar waves emanating from the device.

Heartened at the thought of being able to hit back, Grace Jaden scanned the radar display. "Can you find that corvette?" Grace Jaden inquired.

Peter could only shrug, the radar being unable to pick up the location of the corvette, as the terrain blocked the radar signals from scanning the surrounding ocean. The SuperWasp drone had run low on fuel, and he had to land it down on the runway. "We can get the SuperWasp refueled; that should give us some eyes."

"We've got incoming!" came a shout from General Lawrence over the radios.

All eyes looked to the southwest, where on the very edge of the horizon, a plume of smoke rose into the sky before arcing to head straight toward the island.

Peter raced to set the turret to automatic, allowing the automated Super Rapid 76mm gun to go weapons-free, even as the radar screen indicated that the unit had locked onto the incoming missile. The turret turned slightly and then opened fire with a round of shots in the direction of the missile. One of the fired projectiles hit home, causing the missile to explode even before it reached the coast of the island. "Looks like it was going for the airport terminal."

A visibly shaken Grace Jaden slapped the side of the turret. "Let 'em have it!"

Realizing that the enemy had just given himself away, Peter calculated the location of the missile launch and inputted commands into the turret.

"That's going to be a difficult shot," Corporal Lan pointed out as he approached.

"Just fire on that corvette and scare them off! Quickly!"

The turret rotated again and elevated the gun before opening fire. Shell after shell was lobbed high into the air and over the island at such a velocity that they could travel over three thousand kilometers an hour, giving the unit a range of dozens of kilometers. The shells disappeared over the hills of the island, and whether or not any of them would hit the corvette remained a mystery.

Being on the opposite side of the island and without radar, there was no way to tell if any of the shots had hit home. Corporal Lan tried to climb back to the top of the observation post to see if he could get a better view, but he shook his head, given all he could make out was the hills of abandoned phosphate mines. "I'll get eyes on that side of the island!" Lan shouted as he raced in the direction of the ATV.

"What are they waiting for?" Peter Jaden asked aloud. "They outgun us ten to one. That C-RAM will have no chance of keeping the airport and the Parliament Buildings from being hit if they fire a full barrage."

There was only the sound of waves hitting the coast far off in the distance. "They don't know that," Grace replied. "Probably wondering who we are and why we're here. As far as they know, we've got a Sea Sparrow with their name on it."

CHAPTER TEN – REFLECTIONS

"I wanted freedom, open-air, adventure. I found it on the sea."
—Alain Gerbault

JUNE 25, 2068, 9:32 PM
YAREN, NAURU

As the sun set, Grace Jaden took in the waves smashing against the corral ledge that had formed the Nauruan shore. Stars began to twinkle above.

"We're ready for you," said Peter, approaching from the seaside entrance of the Westin Hotel.

"Beautiful, isn't it?" said Grace Jaden, still looking out on the ocean. The wind picked up, providing a nice tropical breeze. "You think we should try inviting Constance to join us?"

"Politics and energy," Peter chuckled while reflecting on his eccentric sister. "No, she's good doing her charity work."

Grace Jaden turned back toward the Westin Hotel with two of Alpha Squads' infantry on guard watching the coast in case whomever they faced tried to stage a repeat attack on Nauru. Further up the coast, the Nauru defense forces had set up a TOW missile launcher aimed out to sea. An additional radar setup provided greater coverage for the C-RAM further inland. The corvette must have deactivated their fire control radar and moved off during the night, as there was no sign of the enemy vessel. "All right, back to work."

The conference center of the Westin Hotel was surprisingly calm and peaceful, given the violence the building had seen over the past day. Both the hotel and the Nauruan Parliament Building were still scarcely occupied, as everyone feared that the hostile corvette would come back and plummet the area with missiles or heavy machine guns.

Jaden entered the hotel where workers were still cleaning up blood. It took her a moment to find General Lawrence at a conference room table working away on his laptop.

Lawrence caught sight of Jaden peeking into the room. "Time already?" A quick glance at his laptop display revealed they were already a few minutes late.

"Hail New Liberty." Grace Jaden instructed.

The display screen flashed to bring up two windows, Jord Labaoucan and Luke Zenuck on the *Byzantium* and Kelly Argarwal on the *New Constantinople*.

"Heard you had a fun day," Jord Labaoucan laughed.

"You could say that," Grace Jaden said, smiling back.

On hearing the conference starting, Peter Jaden rushed into the room with three rather strong Spanish coffees from the hotel bar. "Sorry about that Osprey."

"Don't remind me." Just the mention of the loss of the fifty-million-dollar aircraft brought a frown to Labaoucan's face. "What's fifty million between family? Easy come, easy go, I suppose."

"How go the tanker load-outs?" Grace Jaden interjected in a quick attempt to change the subject to happier news.

The screen flashed with some financial projections and bank transfer data. "First payments came in today," Zenuck said. "Our first ten million in out of Japan. Expecting another twenty-five million out of India shortly."

"Which we're transferring to our new cryptocurrency," Argarwal announced. "The Liberty Coin is now a working currency."

"All right. Well, President Scotty of Nauru sends his regards. The legitimate government of Nauru is back in complete control of the island for now." Grace Jaden smiled and joined in a round of applause from the conference participants "Compliments to the New Liberty First Marine Platoon. Anything from the latest satellite data?"

With a projection of Nauru on the map, Zenuck reported their findings. "We got some satellite shots with the help of Japanese Intelligence. Took all night to find them, but looks like our SAM-armed

Type-56 corvette has moved northwest and met up with two smaller gunboats."

General Lawrence leaned forward in his chair and grasped his hands together. "*Now* what the hell are they up to?"

"I presume they're blockading the island and preventing any more of our aircraft from coming in," said Peter Jaden, leaning over to load up on the display circles showing the projected range of the FL–3000 flying Leopard surface-to-air missile launcher, which were now directly between the ships of New Liberty and Nauru. "Could fly around it."

Jord Laboucan inadvertently slammed his fist against the table he sat at. "No way. We already lost enough aircraft on this mission."

"Agreed." Grace had to agree with Jord that they couldn't go through multi-million dollar aircraft like a commodity. "If they don't shoot it down coming in, they'll hit it when it lands."

"So how do we get off the island?" General Lawrence twiddled his thumbs, hoping there was a plan.

"Got to break the blockade and take out that corvette."

"Hate to be the bearer of bad news"—Zenuck manipulated the map to shift it west—"but another corvette's sailing our way from the direction of the Federated States of Micronesia."

Irritated at facing another warship, General Lawrence grabbed the back of his head with both hands. "Who the hell are these guys?"

It was a good question but one Grace Jaden couldn't answer definitively. "Unfortunately, the Nauruan police report the two infantrymen they had surrounded shot themselves. Makes me think special service—probably Chinese."

"Jesus Christ," said Peter Jaden, frowning. "We're talking World War Three here?"

Taking a deep breath, Grace Jaden shifted uncomfortably in her chair. "These aren't regular units, though, or we'd be toast. I think this is some kind of sideshow. Regardless, we need to break this blockade." She turned the laptop camera to face her directly. "Where the hell are our corvettes?"

"Sailing out of Japan as fast as they can. Still at least ten days out," Laboucan reported. "You sit tight, and we'll come get you."

"Keep the *Byzantium* back," Grace Jaden urged. "Don't want them to come after you. Make sure you keep at least get one of those warships in reserve to defend New Liberty in case they try to rush you." She turned her head from side to side to catch the attention of those in the conference room. "Ten days. Let's make the best of it."

CHAPTER ELEVEN – REINFORCEMENTS

"Leadership consists of picking good men and helping them do their best."
—Chester W. Nimitz

JUNE 28, 2068, 9:30 AM
MV BYZANTIUM
PACIFIC OCEAN

Now having been aboard the *Byzantium* production ship for over a week, Jord Laboucan was getting restless, missing his family, and sick of spending all day on the bridge staring at moving dots on various digital maps. At first, the report of a communication for Grace Jaden from the United States was a welcome distraction. Then, he saw the call was coming from near Washington, D.C. He cringed before answering the call. "Laboucan here," he began while looking down to rub his forehead. "Look, we're free of you crooked crooks. If this is the IRS, you can tell them to kiss my ass." To his surprise, he didn't feel regret but pleasure at the open venting.

An image of former Rear Admiral Davidson filled the display. "I was calling for Grace Jaden."

Recollecting the familiar-looking sailor Jord's, eyebrows went up. "She's busy at the moment." Thinking hard, Laboucan recalled where he had seen the man. "You were the admiral that saved our skin in East Timor?"

"*Former* Admiral," Davidson said, frowning. "I've resigned. And I want to help."

Jord Labaoucan leaned back in his chair. He tried to gauge the sincerity of the offer. "Help with what?"

"Nauru," Davidson replied. "And the Federated States of Micronesia."

What the hell? Was US intelligence watching them? The surprising words forced Laboucan to take the statements seriously. He folded his arms and leaned onto the desk. The admiral had once saved their lives. "You said you're retired?"

"And looking for a job."

"We *do* need an admiral. You interested in the job?" Labaoucan found himself hoping that Davidson was indeed sincere. Would be nice to have an actual Admiral commanding their ragtag fleet of corvettes.

There was a perceptible lag—be it the microwave signal racing back and forth to a communication satellite in geosynchronous orbit or that of the former Admiral engaging in last-minute second-guessing. "I am, so long as my family can come along."

"You don't want to know the pay?"

"I heard it was fair."

Labaoucan smiled to himself. Had the chances of getting their personnel off of Nauru alive just doubled? He tried not to let his enthusiasm show. "All right, how fast can you get your ass to the Pacific?"

JULY 5, 2068, 9:30 AM
MV NEW CONSTANTINOPLE
PACIFIC OCEAN

Bringing his family had taken a day of convincing, and even then, only with the promise that they were headed to something like a former Disney cruise ship on a mini-vacation. Then came another two long days of flying to get to Hawaii and another two days of helicopter jumping from ship to ship to make it to the *New Constantinople*. That they had traveled over the Fourth of July only added to the various emotions of Rear-Admiral Davidson. Was he turning traitor or standing up for the ideals of the US Constitution? Rear-Admiral Davidson, retired, was worried his wife and three kids were going to strangle him when the *New Constantinople* finally came into view. To his relief, it did look like a cruise ship. His wife and kids gushed at the sight of the swimming pools. "See," he said with relief, "a cruise ship! Just like I said!"

"Honey"—his tired wife gave him a hug as the helicopter landed—"I didn't doubt you in the slightest."

Kelly Argarwal was waiting on the helicopter deck and rushed forward to help Davidson's wife and kids into the ship while shaking the retired admiral's hand. "A real honor, sir. You did great work in East Timor."

"Look at the swimming pool!" Even the eldest daughter seemed excited while pointing at the blue pool below.

Both sons were jumping at his leg. "Can we go swimming now?"

"If it's okay, sir, we'd like to get you on your way," said Kelly Argarwal, feeling rather guilty at separating the Father from his family.

Davidson gave his family a tight hug. "I'll be back in a couple of days. I promise." He kissed his wife's forehead.

His wife shrugged her shoulders. She was a Navy wife and understood when duty called. "Well, just make sure you come back in one piece," she laughed. "And be back soon, honey. Kids will be at the pool, and I'll be suntanning."

With that, Davidson was back in the helicopter and flying off to the *Byzantium*. There, he switched aircraft, leaving the helicopters for one of the two remaining V-22 Osprey in the New Liberty fleet under the watchful eye of a rather worried-looking Jord Laboucan. "I'm authorized to assign you the rank of Admiral in the New Liberty fleet. I've informed Captain Reinard you'll be taking command of the fleet." He handed Davidson a tablet. "Here is data on all your senior officers, your ships, and the situation in Nauru. Get in and get out with our people." With that, Laboucan made his way to the pilot and demanded the man take special care of the Osprey.

Within the hour, the V-22 Osprey was in the air, her tiltrotors turning to propel the aircraft forward to the west. It took another two hours of flying to the northwest. With all the available time, Admiral Davidson read through the tablet full of data on the ships and crew.

After about three hours, the four warships of the New Liberty armada could be seen racing across a calm ocean. The flagship of the fleet was the *Ayn Rand*, a Saar 6 corvette that had been in Japan for a retrofit by the Israeli Navy from whom Grace had purchased the vessel. The corvette was noticeably larger than the other three ships at ninety meters. The Saar 6 ships were originally built in Germany, a modification to the K130 German design. She was armed with a OTO Melara 76mm Super

Rapid naval gun, a C-Dome point defense system, the Iron Beam point defense system, a twenty-one-cell Rolling Air Frame surface-to-air missile launcher, thirty-two vertical launch cells for multi-purpose missiles, and two thirteen-inch torpedo launchers. At the rear of the ship was a large helicopter pad and even a hanger. Her two diesel engines could produce 20MW worth of power and enabled the ship to reach a speed of almost fifty kilometers an hour at full speed ahead. With multifunction radar, electro-optical sensors, and sonar, the vessel was the idea flagship to command the fleet from.

To either side and ahead of the *Ayn Rand* in a loose formation was a Tuo-Chiang-class corvette. The Tuo-Chiang was a Taiwanese-designed multi-mission stealth corvettes originally built for the exclusive use of the Taiwanese Republic of China Navy. The three fast corvettes were all named after authors, including the *C.S. Lewis*, the *Tolkien*, and the *Saint Stephen*. While small for corvettes, the ships were built for hit-and-run tactics, as they were fast, able to go double the speed of the *Ayn Rand*, and with very few extrusions and pre-cooled engine exhausts to reduce the possibility of detection. While having no hanger, each still had a flight deck and could handle a helicopter or a variety of multi-mission drones. They were armed with a variety of weapons including torpedo launchers, close-in weapon system lasers and guns, a large traditional 76mm Melara naval gun, and over sixteen missile launchers. A notable downside was that they were coastal corvettes, which would limit their use in rough seas.

Grace Jaden had also apparently bought a Swedish Gotland-class submarine with air-independent propulsion, but with a cruising speed of twenty kilometers an hour, she would arrive far too late for the festivities around Nauru. Still, Davidson was excited about the summary, indicating that the vessel had air-independent propulsion. They were among the world's first submarines to feature a Sterling engine air-independent propulsion system, and the submarine would be missed. The high-efficiency Sterling engines, using heat from the combustion of hydrogen for electrical power generation made her as quiet as any nuclear-powered submarine in a pinch.

The collection of ships that was the Navy of New Liberty was not capable of a fraction of what a Marine Expeditionary Unit could do, let alone a United States Carrier battle group, but it was a capable Navy nonetheless. Admiral Davidson felt his adrenaline pumping as the tiltrotors rotated and the craft came to hover above the deck of the *Ayn Rand*. It was a tough landing, even for a skillful pilot, to bring down such a large vertical take-off and landing craft on the rather small flight deck, and the decision was made to lower him down by wire.

"You ready?" the co-pilot shouted over the engine while unstrapping himself to climb back into the cabin. With the help of another airman, Davidson was connected by carabiner to a winch as the rear ramp cracked open and let in a rush of cold air.

The co-pilot manned the winch and gave a thumbs up. Davidson promptly returned the gesture. He felt old after hesitating prior to stepping off the ramp, only to feel rejuvenated at the feeling of hanging off the end of the rope. The winch slowly lowered the rope with him swinging with the wind. Davidson took in the view of the Pacific before looking down at the collection of sailors waiting to help him on the flight deck of the *Ayn Rand*. On seeing their light blue uniforms, the admiral suddenly felt out of place in his leather jacket and jeans. He also had to worry about his footing; would he crash down onto the deck? It was a relief when one of the sailors took hold of his leg and guided him down onto the flight deck. Admiral Davidson smiled on having his footing on a warship again.

"Welcome aboard, sir!" the commanding officer by the name of Isaac Hayes saluted.

"A pleasure to be here," said Davidson, saluting back while looking up to see the V-22 Osprey's turboprops turn horizontal before the aircraft sped away. Any worry that the commander would be upset with his arrival was washed away by Captain Hayes' smile. According to the dossier, Hayes had quite a resume, having served in the Israel navy for years. The two sailors shook hands.

"You're a submariner?" Davidson recalled. "You're a long way from your sub."

"She's way behind us now." Captain Hayes pointed his right thumb aft to the north. "Glad you're here. I prefer to fight from where I can't be seen."

Admiral Davidson nodded, though he was not sure he'd agree that fighting under a kilometer or so of hydrostatic head was any safer. "Fair enough, but I want you as my XO on this one."

"Looking forward to working with you, Admiral." Captain Hayes led the admiral across the flight deck and through a hatch into the hull of the corvette. A flight of metallic stairs brought them to the Combat Information Center deep within the superstructure, just fore of the main diesel gensets.

The Combat Information Center of the corvette was small but functional. Sailors were manning their control stations with panels providing the latest data from the ship's radar and sonar systems. Two large screens to the front highlighted the position of the ship in the Pacific and her course south along with all known contacts within sensor range.

"Admiral in the CIC!" the senior enlisted sailor called out with a salute.

Returning the salute, ensuring he was following good command practices, Admiral Davidson reviewed the screens, confirming they were clear apart from the usual civilian traffic. Satisfied, he gazed over at the five sailors in the room. All had volunteered, though he to wonder if they had they done so out of loyalty or money. The thought flashed in his mind that perhaps they, and even he, were mercenaries. It was a dirty word for the admiral—soldiers that fought for money as opposed to duty. He pushed the concerning thought aside to focus on the situation at hand. "Hail . . ." He searched for a word, as he was no longer reporting to the Pentagon "New Liberty Command."

The officer on communication duty chuckled approvingly at the phrase. "New Liberty Task Force One to New Liberty Command."

One of the screens flashed to show Grace Jaden and General Lawrence at a table, no doubt on Nauru.

"New Liberty Command has a nice ring to it," said General Lawrence with a smile.

Jaden smiled upon identifying Davidson. "Glad you can join us, Admiral. In person, I'll have to shake your hand for saving us back in East Timor."

"You're just lucky I didn't *arrest* you!" Admiral Davidson's response drew perplexed looks from the sailors in the CIC.

His face serious, General Lawrence virtually looked Davidson in the eye. "General Lawrence here. You on our side one hundred percent?"

"Yes, sir," Admiral Davidson said matter-of-factly. "Resigned my commission with the United States Navy. And I'm on my way to retrieve you." Admiral Davidson looked over at the course projections. "The *Ayn Rand* and the rest of the task force are still at least four days out of Nauru. Should give me time to figure out just who John Galt is.," he said—a reference to Ayn Rand's penultimate libertarian novel.

"I wanted to name them after the original six frigates of the US Navy but was told I shouldn't steal traditions. That being said, it would have been nice to embarrass the US Navy, given the fact that they name everything after politicians now." When first founded, the original six frigates of the US Navy included the *Constitution, Chesapeake, Constellation, President, United States*, and the *Congress* all sounded good to Grace Jaden. She always found it almost criminal that the US Navy now named their flagship aircraft carriers, for the most part, after politicians as opposed to famous battles and carriers of the past like the *Enterprise, Yorktown*, and *Lexington*. Regardless, Grace Jaden had been convinced, instead, that now was a time for new traditions.

"New Navy, new traditions," General Lawrence summarized, having fought for the name changes. Technically, they were his ships. "Admiral Davidson, your orders are to retrieve us."

"Yes, sir." Admiral Davidson nodded. "We could speed up our arrival a couple of days if we came in just the three fast corvettes but I want the *Ayn Rand's* Vertical Missile Launch system when facing that Type 56 corvette." He looked over at Captain Hayes. "What's its current position?"

Captain Hayes frowned as he tried to punch up the latest satellite shot. The screen was static. "Well, I have some bad news. The commercial satellite operator has informed us that their satellite is offline, damaged by a solar flare. We have no live position of that Type 53 corvette, designated Hostile One, or that Missile Corvette, designated Hostile Four."

Grace Jaden and General Lawrence exchanged a look of concern. "No way that's a coincidence, right?" Jaden asked.

"No, no way," said Admiral Davidson, sharing their concern.

"How could that corvette have taken out a satellite?" Captain Hayes asked.

"It couldn't." Admiral Davidson rubbed his chin. "Probably an EMP weapon knocked it out."

"The Chinese?" Jaden questioned.

Davidson nodded silently.

"What the hell are they up to?" Jaden asked rhetorically.

"I presume that our hostiles are still patrolling west and north of Nauru. That being said, I'm going to dispatch a fast corvette—probably the *Saint Stephen* —to protect that production platform"—he searched the screen for its name—"the *Byzantium*, in case the enemy tries to rush it."

"You sure you can take on those corvettes?" Grace Jaden held her hands together, waiting for the response.

"We'll give it our best shot," Admiral Davidson answered, hoping that their best shot would be enough.

CHAPTER TWELVE – CONFLICT

"If fear is cultivated, it will become stronger; if faith is cultivated, it will achieve mastery."
—John Paul Jones

JULY 9, 2068, 9:30 AM
NLS AYN RAND
PACIFIC OCEAN

Sound general quarters," Admiral Davidson ordered from the Combat Information Center deep within the Ayn Rand. He rubbed his chin while taking in the main situation monitor.

Throughout all three ships of Task Force One, klaxons activated and lights dimmed while sailors rushed to their stations. After four days of cruising, the *Ayn Rand, Tolkien,* and the *C.S. Lewis* were approaching the island of Nauru from the north.

After reviewing the status board, the senior enlisted officer gave his report. "All stations manned and ready."

Admiral Davidson turned to Captain Haynes. He decided to keep the deployment simple. "All right, have the *Tolkien* and *Lewis* go into a wide formation." He wanted the corvettes to be close enough to collaborate in supporting each other's air defenses while remaining wide enough to avoid allowing a single torpedo barrage to take out the whole task force.

"Aye, sir" Hayes replied while stepping aside to quietly radio the other ships.

"Keep all sensors passive for now." Admiral Davidson focused on the latest map projection, wishing he knew exactly where his enemies were located. He presumed that switching the radar of the Ayn Rand to active pulsing would give him that answer but at the same time give away the position of his task force. He wanted the element of surprise. "All right, launch the Sea Scout. I want it heading ten kilometers to the west."

On the flight deck of the Ayn Rand sat what for all intents and purposes looked like a miniature helicopter. The MQ-10C Sea Scout however, was completely unmanned. The Rolls-Royce 250-C47E engine fired up on remote command and the rotor began spinning, lifting the craft into the air. When clear of the deck, the MQ-10C's rotor titled to send the craft accelerating to the west, leaving the corvette behind.

Davidson leaned over the console of the Air Warfare Officer to watch the progress of the drone. It took a few minutes for the SeaScout to travel the ten kilometers.

"In position," the air warfare officer flying the SeaScout by remote confirmed.

Admiral Davidson took a step back and stood tall to look over all the sailors manning their stations in the CIC. "Everyone ready?" he asked. "We've only got one shot to get this right."

There were no objections—only the nods of sailors.

Admiral Davidson mentally went through his plan. He still worried it didn't take into account the possibility of submarines being present but decided it was a risk he would have to take. "All right, activate the SeaScout active radar."

The radar of the SeaScout drone powered up and began shooting down waves of energy at the speed of light, many of them being reflected back not only by the ocean but off two waiting corvettes and three gunboats. The SeaScout, in turn, radioed the information to the *Ayn Rand's* fire control system, which automatically updated the situation plot.

"Contacts Hostile One identified as a Type 56 heavy corvette. Contacts Hostile Two, Three, Four in formation as gunboats. Approximately thirty kilometers south. Contact Hostile Five Missile Corvette approximately sixty kilometers west," the Surface Warfare Officer reported as the map was updated to display the contacts.

"Fire control, target twelve harpoons on Hostile One," Admiral Davidson calmly requested.

With quick touches to his panel, the weapons officer locked the missiles on target. "Ready."

"Fire."

The deck of the Ayn Rand disappeared into a cloud of smoke as the vertical launch system doors snapped open, puffs of air threw twelve missiles into the air after which their engines ignited. The missiles at first went vertical before arcing down and racing toward their target just above the waters of the Pacific.

"Vampire, vampire, two missiles on the Sea Scout," the Air Warfare Officer reported as the display showed the missiles racing toward the autonomous drone.

Davidson nodded. The enemy fleet opening fire on the drone wasn't unexpected, the plan had been to sacrifice the drone in return for the position of the enemy ships.

The Aerial Warfare officer deployed flares while sending the SeaScout drone racing forward to close the gap with the missiles in an attempt to force an overshoot. While flares were able to able to confuse the first missile, the second inbound missile smashed directly into the autonomous helicopter, blowing it into a thousand pieces, which rained down into the ocean.

Admiral Davidson kept his attention on the position of the enemy Type 56 heavy corvette, easily the most dangerous of the hostile ships. Sure enough, missile tracks were emanating from the corvette. Given the fact that the enemy corvette was facing missiles, Davidson bet that any incoming missiles would be a subdued barrage.

"Vampires. I've got I think twenty, twenty-two surface-to-air missiles going after our tracks," the radar officer reported. "Six anti-ship missiles coming in at us."

Captain Hayes pointed up at the display. "All hostile contacts have gone to active radar."

There being no point in staying passive now, Admiral Davidson decided to improve their own sensor data and settle his fear of enemy submarines simultaneously. "Go active, all sonar and radar systems." The Ayn Rand's fire control systems and sensors began pulsating in all directions while the bow-mounted sonar began acoustic-pinging the depths of the ocean. "Confirm all missiles on us?"

"Confirmed," came the nervous response of the radar officer. It's never fun having missiles in the air with you as the target.

"Weapons free!" Satisfied, the sonar screen was clear, Davidson grabbed a handheld microphone and pressed the transmit button. "Tolkien and Lewis, start your attack run. Bridge, hard to port."

At full ahead flank, the Ayn Rand's bow cut through the Pacific as the rudder turned sharply to steer the corvette into a circular course. The remaining vertical launch cells held Barak-8 surface-to-air missiles, twelve of which thundered up into the sky in the direction of the incoming barrage.

The *Tolkien* and the *C.S. Lewis* accelerated south toward the enemy formation. The two Tuo Chiang-class fast corvettes were catamarans that at full ahead lifted the center hull completely out of the water, allowing them to reach a speed of eighty-three kilometers an hour.

The first volley of Harpoon missiles launched by the Ayn Rand began to arc down toward the hostile Type 56 corvette at the same time the defensive surface-to-air missile fire reached their position. Flashes erupted in the morning sky as proximity-fused warheads went off, downing Harpoon after Harpoon. Admiral Davidson kept a tight grip hoping that one would make it through the screen. "Spin up another twelve harpoons, and target Hostile One!" he ordered with his eyes still focused on the situation monitor. All it would take is one Harpoon. Come on, make it!

The Type 56 corvette was able to fire eight missiles at a time, but three of the twelve Harpoons made it through the surface-to-air missile screen and continued closing in on the enemy corvette. The automated close-in weapon system of the corvette activated, spraying out bullets. The remaining three Harpoon missiles exploded only seconds before impact, casting flaming debris at the corvette, wreaking havoc on the radar masts.

The situation display showed the radar of Hostile One was down but that that Type 56 corvette was still afloat. Admiral Davidson shook his fist in disappointment. "Another twelve, fire!" he ordered, knowing he had to keep up the pressure, hoping that the damage to her radar system made the enemy corvette particularly vulnerable to another wave.

The air warfare officer quickly input the launch commands before looking up to eye the screen of defensive surface-to-air missiles. Sailors hunched over their displays, sweating as they watched the enemy missile tracks close in. It was a constant reminder that any mistake could bring death to them all. Fourteen Barak-8 missiles streaked into the path of the six incoming YJ-83 anti-ship missiles. With lots of time to adjust course, the first five struck their targets, one narrowly missing. The remaining Barak-8 missiles were automatically re-tasked by the fire control computer.

The radar showing the surface-to-air missiles had shot down the enemy barrage was of little consolation to Admiral Davidson. Instead, he took comfort in feeling and hearing the launches of the Harpoon missiles.

Seeing Ayn Rand's initial missile barrage had failed to finish off the enemy heavy corvette, the commanders of the *Tolkien* and the *C.S. Lewis* launched two additional Harpoon missiles at the enemy heavy corvette while firing torpedoes at the smaller gunboats.

"Bridge, turn us back to the south," Admiral Davidson ordered on seeing the enemy corvette, now facing sixteen incoming missiles, begin to turn to port. "Power up the OTO Melara and open fire on Hostile One."

"A shot at this distance would be the luckiest stroke of luck ever," the weapons officer said, even as he activated the fore-mounted gun.

"Do it!"

The OTO Melara Super Rapid naval gun began lobbying 76mm shells kilometers to the south. The shells missed their mark but confused the auxiliary air search radar of the FL-3000N SAM launcher. The enemy corvette only managed to get off five surface-to-air missiles by the time the first of the Harpoon missiles came into sight in the morning sky. The close-in weapon system went into action, but without the full fire control radar system online, the rapid-fire cannon missed. Two of the Harpoon missiles penetrated the defenses of the corvette just under the speed of sound and slammed dead center into the hull. The warhead then went off. The force of the explosion rippled through the corvette, blasting it out of the water and nearly completely tearing it in two. Water flooded into the hull as the shattered vessel crashed back into the water.

The remaining enemy gunboats focused their machine-gun fire on the *C.S. Lewis*, the shells tearing into her stealthy hull. Both the *C.S. Lewis* and the *Tolkien* responded with 76mm cannon fire at their respective targets, blowing one of the gunboats out of the water. The remaining gunboat had taken evasive action and deployed chaff to successfully dodge the incoming missiles, only to run right into a Mark 48 torpedo. With a blinding flash, the gunboat disappeared into a cloud of brilliant yellow and white.

The gunboats had already launched their torpedoes, and the sonar officer had to remove her headphones at the roar of spinning propellers beneath the ocean. "Torpedoes inbound. Three torpedoes coming in at us!"

"Have the *Tolkien* and *Lewis* engage that missile destroyer." Admiral Davidson pressed the transmit button on his microphone. "Bridge full head flank to the West. Deploy the Nixie!"

Off the aft deck of the *Ayn Rand* shot a variety of towed torpedo decoys, the latest versions of SLQ-25 Nixie. On activation, the decoys emitted a variety of signals to draw the torpedoes away from their intended targets.

The situation projection updated, showing the enemy torpedoes closing in. "Launch disposable decoy!" The admiral turned to Captain Hayes. "Load me two anti-torpedo shots in the torpedo bay."

An autonomous torpedo-looking device was shot off the deck into the ocean to the north. Like the Nixie, the device attempted to mimic the propellers of the *Ayn Rand*.

Wiping sweat away from her forehead, the sonar officer jumped up from her console. "Enemy torpedoes taking the bait!"

Admiral Davidson clenched his fist—this time in satisfaction—on seeing the enemy torpedoes head north as the *Ayn Rand* made her way west. With his own corvette safe, he turned his attention to the positions of the *Tolkien* and the *C.S Lewis* racing to the west toward the sole remaining hostile contact.

The enemy commander on the remaining older Type 37 missile corvette saw the odds were stacked against him and chose to turn to run west back in the direction of the Federated States of Micronesia. "Get us to the *Tolkien* and *Lewis* as quickly as you can."

The radar screen flashed. "Vampire, vampire!" the radar officer reported. The missile corvette launched a barrage targeted at the *Lewis*. "Twelve anti-ship missiles coming in at the Lewis."

The fast corvettes had only the improved close-in weapon systems for anti-air support. Knowing this, both the *Tolkien* and *Lewis* continued to press their attack on the remaining missile boat, each letting loose with a barrage of three Harpoon missiles each at the missile corvette.

"Cover the *Lewis*," the admiral ordered, making it clear that the air warfare officer should fire all the loaded surface-to-air missiles. The *Ayn Rand* fired off sixteen Barak-8 surface-to-air missiles, which raced to catch up with the fast corvettes. Knowing that all he could do was watch, the admiral tapped his finger nervously on the nearest console.

The automated Phalanx close-in weapon systems of both the *Tolkien* and the *Lewis* opened fire on the incoming barrage even as the Barak-8 surface-to-air missiles closed the gap to the incoming YJ-83 anti-ship missiles. Missiles detonated above the fast corvettes, which both deployed chaff pods and flares. The lone remaining Chinese anti-ship missile took the bait and crashed harmlessly into the ocean.

The Type 37 missile corvette, like the New Liberty fast corvettes, had only a close-in weapon system. With a fully functional surface search radar set, the Gatling gun was able to down all six of the missiles prior to impact. The last Harpoon missile, however, was hit so close to the ship that the fireball engulfed the flight deck. Shrapnel rained down on a fully fueled helicopter on the aft flight deck, and the flaming debris cut into a fuel tank. The fuel spraying out of the tank met with oxygen and heat and exploded, engulfing the entire stern of the corvette. The lucky sailors on the flight deck were killed instantly; others found themselves on fire. Survivors rushed to fight the flames and save their ship.

Seeing the detected speed of the enemy missile corvette while its radar went offline, Admiral Davidson guessed that at least one of the missiles had hit the target. "Call back our ships," he ordered Captain Hayes before signaling the bridge. "Bridge, reduce speed to half. Right standard rudder, come to course nine zero degrees. Next stop: Nauru. Let's go get our people." Some of his joy at knowing the Navy of New Liberty had won its first battle at sea surfaced as he clapped his hands together.

CHAPTER THIRTEEN – REVELATIONS

"Democracy and socialism have nothing in common but one word, equality. But notice the difference: while democracy seeks equality in liberty, socialism seeks equality in restraint and servitude."
—Alexis de Tocqueville

JULY 10, 2068, 11:30 AM
NINGBO FLEET HEADQUARTERS
PEOPLE'S REPUBLIC OF CHINA

Premier Xi Shengkun's chest puffed out in satisfaction as he oversaw the busy shipyard before him. He much preferred the action of the East Sea Fleet shipyard to the inaction and politics of the Forbidden City. From an elevated office space, Shengkun could see at least twelve of the large amphibious transports being loaded with infantrymen, armored personnel carriers, and tanks. All seven of the one hundred and ninety-meter-long Type 072 landing ships would hold almost two thousand troops. The closest vessel, a Type 71 Chinese amphibious transport dock being loaded with amphibious assault vehicles, would hold eight hundred troops alone. The real highlight of the yard, however, was the Type 76 amphibious assault ship, the *Yuntai Shen*, which to the untrained eye looked like an aircraft carrier. It was a new generation of amphibious assault vessels in the Chinese navy being able to hold thirty large helicopters. Helicopters could overfly rocky cliffs and deploy forces without the need for a contested beach landing. Just the thought of what was to come brought a grin to the face of the premier.

A uniformed admiral by the name of Jiang nervously approached. The navy was formally a branch of the People's Liberation Army Navy, and the man commanded both the ships and the ground forces being assembled. He gave a perfect stiff salute. "Comrade Premier."

Premier Shengkun held his hands behind his back while turning to the admiral. "I see the loading goes well. When do you leave for Indonesia?"

"We will be ready to depart shortly." Admiral Jiang was easily the most experienced admiral in the Chinese Navy, having engaged in several clashes with Philippine and Vietnamese ships at sea. He would personally oversee the operation from the *Yuntai Shen*. To the admiral, it was a personal honor. Still, it would be a long journey away from home. He could hear the murmurs of the troops upset at the thought of being away from family and homeland for what all intents and purposes seemed to be yet another training exercise. The troops would come to understand the glory of the mission later. It would potentially be the most ambitious naval campaign in the long history of China. To keep up the ruse first would be two months in Indonesia under the pretext of joint exercises.

"Regardless of the American mistakes, the Indonesians owe us." Premier Shengkun was no fan of the Indonesians, but he needed them. For now, both countries were in a mutually beneficial alliance he had to respect.

A grimace betrayed that the admiral had not approached with good news.

"What is it?" Shengkun asked impatiently.

Admiral Jiang handed the premier a tablet showing the latest intelligence report out of Micronesia. "Intelligence reports they lost a heavy corvette and three gunboats off Nauru. A second missile destroyer is also no longer in communication with the staging tanker."

"Impossible." First unbelieving of the report, Premier Shengkun looked down at the tablet to ensure that the communication transcripts were accurate. "Who?" he wondered aloud. He mentally ran through a list of those who were capable and daring enough to take on the irregular intelligence agents he had operating as pirates out of Indonesia. "The Australians? The Taiwanese rebels? Japan?" He continued reading, searching for the identity of the attackers. It certainly couldn't be Nauru itself with just a police force and no real armed forces to speak of. "Can't be the Americans; their politicians have sold them out for debt forgiveness and what they think is our friendship," he said with scorn. The American system, with its greedy incompetent politicians that would do anything for a public dollar, had always been broken, and he looked forward to crushing it once and for all. Still, he had to worry that some American cowboys could be at play.

Admiral Jiang reached over to swipe at the tablet and bring up a dossier. "The American woman."

Premier Shengkun recoiled in shock. He had seen the name and picture come up before—in East Timor—putting a dent in his plans for a quid pro quo with the Indonesians. "The corporate shrill again?

"I'm afraid so."

Premier Shengkun tapped his foot in frustration while reading over the intelligence report detailing her small ocean-based energy company, projections of their renewable crude production, and her purchase of military equipment from American, Taiwanese, Japanese, and Russian defense companies. "Task an attack submarine. At once."

Admiral Jiang considered protesting the deployment of one of his high-technology nuclear attack submarines to go chasing after a collection of civilian ships but thought better of it. These civilians had taken out a heavy corvette. "It shall be done. Shall we delay Operation Storm?"

"No, we push forward with the plan," Premier Shengkun handed the tablet back to the admiral. "Depart for the South China Sea as soon as possible. I'll instruct Jinpin to announce the naval blockade of the rebel Province of Taiwan at once. Proceed to Indonesia. While the world thinks you are engaged in training exercises, you'll be in perfect position with all eyes on the main carrier groups and the blockade of Taiwan. Before the end of the year, we will be reunifying the country and casting the imperialists out of the Pacific once and for all."

CHAPTER FOURTEEN – DISCOVERIES

"Smooth seas do not make skillful sailors."
—African Proverb
JULY 11, 2068, 8:30 PM
NLS AYN RAND
OFF THE COAST OF NAURU
PACIFIC OCEAN

It took a few hours for the small aircrew on the *Ayn Rand* to roll out the Airbus A S565 Panther medium weight multi-purpose twin-engine helicopter from the hanger, given the cramped space and the need to put the remaining SeaScout drone back into storage. The sun was setting by the time the helicopter was in the air and racing toward the island of Nauru under the watchful eye of Admiral Davidson. From the bridge, he watched the craft make the quick hop to land at the international airport among the lights of the capital buildings on the southern tip of the island. Only ten Soldiers could fit in the helicopter at once, so it would take a few trips to retrieve the whole of the First Marine Platoon. Davidson felt his body shake, from the combined strength of a rather cold gale and the thought that a single helicopter could, in a hand fold of trips, carry pretty much the entire army of his new home.

Captain Hayes walked onto the bridge as part of his normal rounds. "Wind is picking up," he said, worried for the smaller corvettes, which were primarily designed for coastal patrols around Taiwan.

"As soon as the first platoon is on board, we'll send the *Tolkien* and the *C.W Lewis* back to New Liberty." Rear Admiral Davidson looked over the sailors manning the helm and the latest weather reports. Captain Hayes handed him a cup of coffee, which he gratefully accepted before again looking south to see the Panther helicopter returning to the *Ayn Rand*. "Let's go meet the new boss." Knowing it would be rather cool outside, he donned his leather jacket before stepping out of the bridge and making his way toward the flight deck. He leaned up against the deck railing and waited.

The Panther helicopter came in slowly before lowering onto the flight deck of the corvette and powering down. The blades spun to a stop before the side hatch slid open. The Marines were anxious to get out of the helicopter and rushed to pull open the crew cabin door and jump out. Grace Jaden was among the last to step out on the deck of the corvette. She gave the 1900-ton Sa'ar 6-class corvette a look; it was hard to believe that the grey warship she had ordered months ago was now physically present.

Admiral Davidson and Captain Hayes gave a crisp salute to greet the Marines before waving them up the stairwell and into the warmth of the bridge. General Lawrence and Strategos Jaden gratefully saluted back.

"Thanks for coming to get us," Jaden said with a smile. "And not arresting me back in East Timor."

Seeing Grace Jaden shivering in the cold wind, Davidson led the new arrivals up onto the bridge. "The pleasure was all mine. Glad someone is standing up for democracy in the Pacific." Out of the wind, the admiral offered his hand to personally greet each of the Marines.

"So, what's the situation?" Grace Jaden inquired while looking over the plot.

"The C.S. Lewis took some superficial hull damage, but other than that, all ships are fully operational." Rear Admiral Davidson brought up the latest radar data on the digital plot table dominating the center of the bridge. He pointed at a radar track to the west. "We were tracking the surviving missile corvette, which was crippled but able to make its way east toward Micronesia. Out of radar range now."

Wanting answers, Grace Jaden looked west. "Can we follow that missile corvette and see where she goes?"

"We've actually got a GlobalHawk stealth drone in storage but no runway to launch it from. Could track it for over a thousand kilometers without being seen," Admiral Davidson suggested while shifting the plot westward to bring the islands of the Federated States of Micronesia to the center. "Could launch from here."

"Now, that's odd," Peter Jaden said, tapping on the plot. "No power signatures or communication in or out of the major Micronesian islands?"

"None." Admiral Davidson looked down at the table, just as perplexed. "No response to any of our hails to warn them about that missile corvette. Their comms went down a couple days ago."

Facing only more questions, Grace Jaden pressed. "Can we investigate?"

General Lawrence nodded in agreement. "I can get us onto Pohnpei safely and make contact with the government in the capital of Palikir."

"Sounds like a plan to me," Davidson looked over at the helm. "Navigator, give me a plot to come around the north side of Pohnpei island."

JULY 16, 2068, 3:00 AM
NLS AYN RAND
EAST OF MICRONESIA
PACIFIC OCEAN

It took four days at cruising speed for the *Ayn Rand* and her two escorts to come into visual range of the island of Pohnpei, on which was the capital city of the Federated States of Micronesia. Grace Jaden played several games of cribbage with her son and off-duty crew, occasionally checking the telemetry, which continued to show complete radio silence out of Pohnpei. Internet news stories circulated, blaming bombings for cutting off communication. It was three in the morning when the *Ayn Rand* was in close enough range that bridge observers should have been able to make out lights along the northern coast of the island. To their surprise, they could see nothing but pitch blackness.

So surprised was Rear Admiral Davidson that he triple-checked their location. "We should see lights on the northern coast. Hell, we should see Palikir from here." Palikir was the capital city of the Federated States of Micronesia with over ten thousand residents.

Jaden suppressed a yawn with a sip of hot coffee. "Should we send in our helicopter?"

"No," General Lawrence commanded, "Let's wait for morning so we can see what we're dealing with here." He ordered everyone back to their bunks to take a pre-mission nap.

Questions racing through her mind as she lay on the top bunk, it took over two hours for Grace Jaden to finally fall back asleep. Her smartphone alarm went off as scheduled, causing her to sit up and slam her head against the bulkhead. She cursed while rolling off the side, only to find the lower bunk empty. "Peter?" Out the nearest porthole, she could see the sun shining brightly. She raced to dash up three flights of stairs to the bridge.

Rear Admiral Davidson had his digital binoculars trained on the island of Pohnpei, which was right where it should be on a beautiful coast line dotted with lush vegetation and small towns. "Good morning Strategos."

Looking aft, Grace Jaden saw that the S565 Panther helicopter had already departed. "Damn it, I was supposed to be on that flight."

"General Lawrence and Lieutenant Jaden thought it best you get some rest." The admiral handed her a cup of coffee, having been told by many of the crew that it helped calm her down. "They've got it under control."

The intercom crackled with the voice of General Lawrence. "First Platoon to *Ayn Rand*. Come in. Over."

Admiral Davidson waved for a Sailor to bring up the communication in the attached briefing room. The screen activated as soon as they walked in to show General Lawrence and Lieutenant Jaden among a collection of small houses.

"You should have waited for me!" Grace Jaden protested.

General Lawrence rubbed his forehead. "Lieutenant Jaden recommended we let you rest."

The lieutenant, knowing he had been thrown under the bus, tried to quickly change the subject. "You want our report?"

Grace Jaden put her anger aside with a nod.

"Sad state of affairs here." General Lawrence rotated his smartphone to show several burned-out buildings and locals still picking through the rubble. "They had some car bombings before losing power, most of their effort was put into fighting the fires without electricity." His expression was one of respect, given the undertaking.

Grade Jaden asked the obvious. "But why did they lose power?'

The answer being beyond his expertise, General Lawrence looked over to the lieutenant.

"EMP." Peter Jaden held up the burned remains of an overloaded transformer. "Electromagnetic pulse detonations took out all their lights, generators, and electronics. We should probably give Constance a call and get some NGOs in here to help clean up the mess."

Not wanting to think of her daughter in a warzone, regardless of her adult age, Grace Jaden quickly changed the subject. "Did you get into contact with the local authorities?"

General Lawrence waved an off-camera local over. "We have, and as you requested, we have offered them our full support."

Taking a seat, Rear Admiral Davidson began pulling up inventory reports. "We've got a spare diesel genset in the hanger. I'll check the other ships. Also, can send over medics."

Nodding in agreement while still standing Grace Jaden placed both hands on the conference table and leaned forward. "The small corvettes—we can bring them into port and use them as gensets as well." Satisfied they could help the Micronesians, she moved on to the next topic. "I want to know where that last hostile corvette is. Can you authorize the GlobalHawk launch with the Micronesian officials?"

Both Lieutenant Jaden and General Lawrence gave a salute. "We're on it."

As the communication terminated, Grace Jaden looked up at the ceiling with questions racing through her mind. EMP weapons and the satellite take-down were too advanced for any pirate or rouge faction that these paramilitaries had to be backed by Chinese Intelligence. "The situation is changing fast. The Chinese are up to something and something big."

"Somehow this sideshow fits in . . ." Admiral Davidson shifted in his chair, frustrated at not being able to put all the puzzle pieces together.

Pulling out a chair, Grace Jaden took a seat beside Davidson. "Call up Zenick, Jord, and Kelly."

With a few clicks on a keyboard, a split-screen communication channel opened with Zenick on the *Byzantium* and Jordi Laboucan and Kelly Agarwal on the *New Constantinople*.

Grace Jaden kept a straight face so as not to alarm them. "Strategos Jaden here on the *Ayn Rand*."

"Glad to see you are all well." Prime Minister Kelly Argarwal looked down into her smartphone while pushing her lunch aside.

"You're calling on the Taiwan blockade?" Zenick got right to business, as the *Byzantium* was in the middle of fueling a tanker bound for Taiwan. "Just saw it on the wire."

Grace Jaden and Admiral Davidson turned to each other in shock and concern. "What blockade?" Jaden asked.

"The Chinese government has announced it will enforce a blockade around Taiwan starting midnight tonight." With a flick of a finger, Jord Laboucan pulled up the latest news report for the teleconference attendees.

"The United Nations is to send a monitoring mission in response?" Kelly Argarwal read aloud in bewilderment. "This is an act of war!"

"Communist China is justifying the blockade, saying the Republic of China is engaging in espionage in Hong Kong." Laboucan summarized various statements from mainland China claiming, as always, that the Taiwan matter was an internal Chinese dispute. Taiwan was founded and ruled by former Chinese Nationalists, who fled to the island after losing the civil war with the communists after World War Two. In some ways, the civil war still raged on, arguably an internal matter. Feeling a responsibility to stand up for the democratic rights of more than twenty-four million inhabitants, however, Jord continued. "Absolute BS." Hong Kong, a former British colony, had experienced years of civil disobedience as the younger generation still held out hope for reforms that would protect the few liberties and democratic councils they still had The "disobedience" in Hong Kong had little to nothing to do with Taiwan.

Grace Jaden leaned forward in her chair. "It has to be connected to all this instability in the Pacific. No way this is a coincidence."

"We're filling up tankers, including our own, for a large Taiwanese contract." Zenick felt sick to his stomach before even asking, "Should I call it off?"

"No," Jaden said while slamming her fist on the table. "You fill those tankers up as full as you can. The Chinese are in clear violation of freedom of the seas, and we will stand by our Taiwanese allies." She corrected herself: "Our *Republic of China* allies. Kelly, set up a conference with Japan, Korea, the Philippines, and Taiwan. We need a united front here."

Having negotiated various monetary agreements over the past few weeks, Kelly Argarwal already knew exactly who to contact. "I'm on it."

Grace Jaden turned to Admiral Davidson next to her. "The Russian Arctic transport company operates some old Typhoon submarines. I want some out here in the Pacific."

"The Russians aren't going to sell us ballistic missile submarines." Davidson entertained the thought that perhaps Jaden had lost her mind.

"They were retired and converted into fuel tankers in the Arctic. Could come in handy to break a blockade."

Happy to hear her idea actually made sense Davidson reached for a tablet and began punching up contacts. She looked back up at the monitor. "Now, Zenick, we've been dealing with some EMP detonations out here. I think it's time we invested in some EMP weapons." Confident in the capabilities of her engineers and somewhat knowledgeable on the theory behind electromagnetic pulses, Grace Jaden already had plans for some devices the little sea state could put together.

CHAPTER FIFTEEN – ESCALATION

"They that go down to the sea in ships, that do business in great waters; These see the works of the LORD, and his wonders in the deep."
—Bible, Psalms 107:23–24

JULY 20, 2068, 8:30 PM
SOUTH OF TAIWAN
SOUTH CHINA SEA

At 200,000 dry weight tons, three Suezmax oil tankers made their way east under the afternoon sun, fully loaded with over two million barrels of renewable crude each. It was a fifteen-day sail from the *Byzantium* in the middle of the Pacific to Taiwan and, thus far, the voyage had been uneventful. Two of the tankers, the *Kyosei Maru* and the *Front Altair*, were third-party owned though the third, quickly re-christened the *MV Freedom of the Seas*, was owned and operated by CleanOcean Energy. Captain Tyson had been transferred from the *Byzantium* to the tanker to personally oversee the effort. As the tankers closed in on Taiwan, only 180 kilometers from mainland China, the commander began to feel apprehensive. The shaking hands of the sailor manning the helm was an indication to the captain he wasn't the only one feeling a little disconcerted at the thought of crossing the Chinese naval blockade.

The arrival of two Taiwanese Kee Lung-class destroyers, the *Tso Yin* and *Su Ao*, to escort the tankers to the island brought little comfort to Captain Tyson, who from the tanker bridge watched them approach through his digital binoculars. Both ships were older—more than half a century old—being former US Navy Kidd-class destroyers with a variety of mark 3 standard surface-to-air missiles. "They're with us," Tyson said to comfort the sailor at the helm. More comforting was a flight of three Taiwanese F-16 Falcon fighters, which did a fly-by over the tankers. Captain Tyson turned away from the open ocean to a large horizontal digital plot projection. The MV Freedom of the Seas had gotten some upgrades, including a sophisticated fire control radar system, two Phalanx close-in-weapon-systems, and a bow-mounted C-Ram Iron Dome system. To the west, he could see multiple air and naval contacts.

"Communication coming in from the *Ayn Rand*," a sailor announced.

Nodding for the hail to be routed to him, a digital window of Strategos Jaden appeared on the plot. "How goes your convoy?"

Captain Tyson took a seat in front of his display, clasped his hands together, and twiddled his thumbs. "Getting exciting now. No sign of any surface combatants, though that doesn't mean we aren't about to be sunk by some sub-launched torpedoes." A noticeable look from the helmsmen had Tyson regretting the statement. "Though we do have some friends nearby."

"We've signed a treaty with Japan, the Philippines, and Taiwan. New Liberty is an official member of the new South East Asia Treaty Organization." Grace Jaden forced a smile. "Working on the Koreans and Australians too." She purposely left out the fact that there had been a SEATO before in the twentieth century to contain communism which failed so miserably in Vietnam it was abolished.

"The more allies in this convoy, the better." Captain Tyson worriedly watched the radar screen blink with data shared by a Taiwanese Early Warning and Control aircraft on patrol. A formation of six Xian H-6 bombers, the Chinese version of the old Soviet Tupolev Tu-16 twin-engine jet bombers, was headed directly at their position from mainland China. "Call you later. We've got company." With urgency, he stood up and made his way to the helm. Radio chatter from the local ships filled the bridge.

"Accelerate to full speed," came a command in broken English from the lead Taiwanese destroyer. The presence of the bomber formation was obviously concerning the Taiwanese warship commanders as well.

Captain Tyson reached to disconnect a microphone and pressed the transmit button. "Engine room, full ahead flank."

All three oil tankers accelerated through the rather choppy sea. High above the tankers, Taiwanese F-16 fighters throttled their engines up to race away in the direction of the Chinese bomber squadron.

"They're going to need a lot more planes," Captain Tyson said to the helmsman as the radar display updated to show at least five Su-35 air superiority fighters, afterburners firing, coming right at the F-16s.

The two squadrons came at each other head-on, the Russian-built Su-35 fighters achieving supersonic speeds. The Chinese and Taiwanese air forces, having spent decades in a state of cold war, often participated in mock dogfights, some ending with midair collisions and lives lost. It was a dangerous game.

The Taiwanese fighter pilots were outnumbered but did their best in doing barrel rolls to come up behind respective Su-35s, only to find their own heads-up display alarms sounding as they were tailed. The Taiwanese pilots had no chance to react when the Chinese pilots pressed down on the flight stick triggers. The Gryazev-Shipunov GSh-30-1 autocannons opened fire, sending rounds slicing through the wings of the F-16s.

The soul surviving F-16 fired off two AIM-120 AMRAAM missiles. With its own fire-and-forget guidance system, the state-of-the-art beyond-visual-range air-to-air missile slammed into an Su-35, engulfing the craft and Chinese pilot in a flaming inferno. The Taiwanese pilot pushed hard on his flight stick to dodge an incoming R-27 missile fired off by a now-trailing Su-35 fighter. His F-16 dove down toward the ocean so fast that he nearly slammed into the ocean, pulling up just seconds before impact.

Free of any airborne threats, each of the six Tupolev Tu-16 twin-engine jet bombers released four KD-88 anti-ship missiles before turning south.

"Vampire, vampire!" Captain Tyson yelled, seeing the missile tracks on the radar plot. "Hard to port." With the knowledge that he was doubling as an air warfare officer, Tyson raced to input orders for the automated defenses of the tanker to go weapons-free. He quickly estimated at least eight anti-ship missiles were coming their way.

The Taiwanese destroyers were close enough that all the sailors on the tanker could hear the roar of standard missile launchers firing up to defend the tankers and provide some cover for the escaping F-16. The remaining fighter of their air support screen was racing away toward Taiwan, pursued by four advanced Su-35s.

The helmsman clutched the ship's wheel hard, sweat pouring down his face. "Are we going to make it, sir?" Even at full speed, the oil tanker seemed to take forever to turn to the East. The Iron Dome and Iron Beam systems picked up the incoming missiles and began firing small interceptor missiles and laser shots. Five of the missiles exploded, hit by the standard missiles of the destroyer and the defensive fire close enough to see over the horizon. Only a last-second shot by the Phalanx close-in weapon system turret caught the final missile and saved the tanker.

The other two tankers weren't so lucky. One missile slammed into the 270-meter-long tanker, the *Kyosei Maru,* dead center, the force of the explosion enough to rupture the reinforced tanks within. The rapid ingress of oxygen and heat into the vessels transformed the tanker into a massive fuel-air bomb with the resulting explosion so powerful it blasted the one hundred and sixty thousand metric ton vessel into the air while tearing it into two.

The shockwave of hot air was so strong that the *MV Freedom of the Seas* rocked from the blast despite being a quarter of a kilometer away. Captain Tyson raised his hand to shield his eyes as the bridge windows shattered and his legs gave out beneath him. As the ship righted itself, he snuck a lookout to the west to see the separated fore and aft sections of the *Kyosei Maru* crash back down into the ocean.

Ahead of the flaming inferno that was once the *Kyosei Maru,* the *Front Altair* tanker was struck in the bow by an anti-ship missile with a WHUMP. Loud fire alarms and klaxons activated as a fire raged on the deck of the tanker. That the ship remained intact was a clear indication that the fuel tanks had not ruptured. The crew rushed to activate firefighting equipment and put on oxygen packs, given the thick black smoke covering the tanker.

Captain Tyson closed his eyes and took a deep breath, wondering just how painful the end would be. After a quick mental prayer and feeling his shoulders and arms to ensure they were still there, Captain Tyson picked himself off the floor to look down onto the radar plot. He was in no rush, dreading to see the radar tracks of the next round of missiles. After taking a deep breath to calm himself, Captain Tyson allowed his eyes to focus on the plot.

To his pleasant surprise, the only inbound track was multiple allied aircraft racing from Taiwan.

Rubbing his eyes to make sure he was seeing clearly, Captain Tyson patted the shoulder of the panic-stricken helmsman, who had let go of the ship's wheel, leaving the tanker on autopilot. "It's okay. We're in the clear." He purposely ignored the possibility of inbound stealth aircraft and stealth missiles and darted to look out the now shattered bridge windows to see five Japanese F-35 stealth Joint Strike Fighters flying over the Taiwanese destroyers.

The Chinese apparently felt their message had been made crystal clear, given the fact that no other bombers or missiles followed the initial barrage. The Su-35 fighters had retreated back to the mainland.

The *MV Freedom of the Seas* would get to unload her fuel, but it was unclear if she would be the last tanker to be able to do so. And since it was an island dependent on renewable crude for her energy supply, Captain Tyson wondered if a surrender of Taiwan was now all but inevitable. "Get me New Liberty Command. Priority urgent."

CHAPTER SIXTEEN – ASSESSMENTS

"No literature is richer than that of the sea. No story is more enthralling, no tradition is more secure."
—Felix Riesenberg

JULY 21, 2068, 2:30 AM

NLS AYN RAND

OFF THE COAST OF MICRONESIA

The live transmission from the Japanese surveillance aircraft showed that, even after six hours, the oil slick that was once the *Kyosei Maru* was still burning. Damage control teams and tugs had been able to recover the *Front Altair* and tow her into Taiwan, but she would never sail as a crude tanker again. The images seemed surreal to Grace Jaden, watching them from a monitor in the small briefing room of the *Ayn Rand*. The corvette sat anchored off the Micronesian coast of Pohnpei Island.

General Lawrence, Peter Jaden, and Admiral Davidson entered the conference room. Peter dropped, exhausted, into his seat, having had, like all in the room, very little sleep. For the past week, the New Liberty task force had been assisting Micronesia, the coastal corvettes had put into the small ports of the two largest cities on the island to use their diesel-powered engines as power generators. Despite the tropical breeze and beautiful blue ocean, Micronesia was, for all intents and purposes, a recovering warzone. "We've got power back up in Palikir," he said, trying to start the conversation with some good news.

Saying nothing, Grace Jaden swiped at her tablet to bring the live video up on the main monitor. "Chinese airstrike took out two of our three tankers."

"The *MV Freedom of the Seas* made it." Admiral Davidson shifted uncomfortably in his chair. "Offloading the crude now."

Grace Jaden clasped her hands tightly. Her determination to sell crude to Taiwan had only intensified with the loss of over two million barrels of crude in what she deemed an unprovoked attack. "Taiwan has a petroleum reserve, but without new crude supplies, the island would eventually have to give in. We've got to keep the crude flowing."

"Shipping crude by supertanker to Taiwan is simply too dangerous." Davidson tilted his head at the tangible evidence to make his case on the display dominated by black smoke emanating from the wreckage of the *Kyosei Maru.*

Knowing Grace would want them to at least attempt to work out the problem, Peter Jaden looked over his shoulder at a brewed pot of coffee. Brainstorming while pouring out gratefully accepted cups of coffee was a regular occurrence on the *Ayn Rand.* "We could air transport crude, but it would be slow and pretty ineffective. A drop in the bucket of what they need."

After taking a sip of her coffee and punching up the latest energy demand data on Taiwan, Grace Jaden stood up and pointed at the annual crude usage. "Even with their nuclear and hydropower plants, Taiwan needs two million barrels a day to stay functional."

"At least a tanker a day." Admiral Davidson reached into his uniform pocket containing his emergency stash of Tylenol. It took him longer than he would have liked to turn the child-proof lock and pop the pill into his mouth. He shook his head in frustration.

"We aren't out of plays yet." Grace Jaden brought up the communications screen and put in a call to Zenick on the *Byzantium.*

The satellite connection broadcasting the image of the *Kyosei Maru* wreckage was replaced with that of David Zenick on the bridge of the *Byzantium.* "What can I do for you, boss?"

"Those Russian Typhoons . . . did they show up?"

"They sure did," Zenuck traced his finger over his smartphone to broadcast the camera image of the *Byzantium*'s port side where a former Soviet Typhoon-class nuclear-powered ballistic missile submarine sat, surfaced. Once the 170-meter-long submarine used to stay submerged for months at a time, constantly ready to fire up to twenty nuclear warhead-tipped missiles on the United States in the event of World War. After the cold war, the longer than a football field submarine had been decommissioned and retrofitted into a massive oil tanker capable of traveling beneath the Arctic Ocean. "Two Typhoon-class tankers and six smaller submarine tankers, courtesy of the Russian Arctic Supply company."

"That'll do the trick," Admiral Davidson said with a smile. The Russian submarines, still among some of the quietest in the world, would most certainly be able to make it into Taiwan short of an all-out naval offensive by Communist China.

"My good man, get those tankers fueled and on a regular route into Taiwan as soon as possible."

Zenuck gave a virtual salute. "I'm on it."

Grace Jaden saluted back while allowing the conference room to enjoy the moment before walking in front of the display screen, placing both hands on the table, and looking Admiral Davidson in the eye. As she often did when upset, she subconsciously ground her teeth. "All right, they fucking attacked our tanker. I want payback. What's the status on that hostile corvette?"

Admiral Davidson grabbed his tablet and made his way to the front. He called up the latest situation plot showing the three corvettes of his task force all near the shore of Pohnpei Island to the middle of the display. With the press on the touchpad, a track appeared, first heading west to Palau and then turning south toward Indonesia. "Corvette Hostile Epsilon managed to head west and then south. Our GlobalHawk drone has been passively following it. Here, north of Papua." He pointed near the southwest corner of the map. "Hostile Epsilon met up with a small commercial tanker here. Must have been acting as a tender."

Grace Jaden took a few steps back to examine the location of the hostile corvette they had designated Hostile Epsilon. With her hands on the smartboard, she zoomed in on the map. "Right on the edge of Indonesian territorial waters."

"Debatable." Admiral Davidson had to admit as much, given the moving currents and accuracy of the GlobalHawk drone.

With countless scenarios racing through her mind, Grace Jaden stood silent for a long minute, eying the projection. Then, with a sigh, she turned back to Davidson. "Do they know we have been following them?"

143

"My thought is no," the admiral speculated before pointing in the direction of Peter Jaden, looking for confirmation.

Still drinking his coffee, Peter Jaden nodded his head in agreement. "The GlobalHawk drone is pretty stealthy, and we've been flying completely passively, using visual detection only. Since the corvette has no working active air radar and it's doubtful she even has passive sensors." He pointed up at the map display. "Plus, given the fact that it took a scenic route west, I'd say those hostiles believe they escaped detection."

Grace Jaden pulled out the closest chair and took a seat. Her brown eyes brightened. "Can you take that tanker?"

Shocked at the question, Peter Jaden took a deep breath before slowly letting the air out past his lips with a low whistle.

Admiral Davidson pondered the question and mentally worked through the assets at his disposal. "I suppose so."

"I want answers." Grace Jaden pointed behind her back at the map screen. "Answers that are on that tanker if we can take it relatively undetected." Jade watched both her son and the admiral, trying to gauge their reaction.

Anxious to be pro-active, Peter Jaden eyed the more bewildered Admiral. "We have shown no active communication in or out of that tanker or the corvette."

Admiral Davidson tapped on the table as he continued to formulate a plan. "That corvette . . . no way we could take her intact, but that tanker," his voice faded momentarily. "We use the GlobalHawk to take out the corvette and then drop the first platoon onto the tanker via helicopter."

Peter Jaden raised his hand up, thumb extended. He had been waiting anxiously—waiting for the opportunity to request a gunship ever since joining the crew of New Liberty. "With a Defiant gunship, I can take out any close-in weapon systems on that tanker and allow a transport helicopter in to land the Marines."

"All right. Work out the plan. Let's be ready to present to Kelly and Jordi in two hours."

CHAPTER SEVENTEEN –

RECONNAISSANCE

"No pessimist ever discovered the secret of the stars or sailed to an uncharted land"
—Helen Keller

JULY 28, 2068, 8:30 PM
NLS AYN RAND
OFF THE COAST OF MICRONESIA2068

After several planning session debates, Grace Jaden was convinced to use a stealthy RQ-170 Sentinel drone over the cheaper bulky GlobalHawk drone on the *Ayn Rand*. The RQ-170 was a tailless aircraft with a wingspan of twenty meters containing a variety of advanced sensor and electronic warfare systems. To Jaden's surprise, the Japanese Air Force was happy to sell one of their RQ-170 sentinels for the mission at a bargain of a price and, more surprisingly, with a rushed delivery. Within the week, an RQ-170 Sentinel arrived from Japan, and upon landing in Micronesia on a piece of highway functioning as a makeshift runway, the drone was refueled for the mission.

"Let's do it," Grace Jaden ordered from the bridge of the *Ayn Rand*.

Piloted by remote from the Combat Information Center, the RQ-170 Sentinel accelerated over the warm pavement of the Sekeren Iap on the southwest corner of Pohnpei island. Lifting into the air, the stealthy aircraft tilted to maneuver south with the help of a strong crosswind. During the day, from a distance, one would have thought the drone was a stealth bomber, but flying at night and with a low radar signature, the chances of spotting the Sentinel were next to none.

Two hours later, the craft approached the island of New Guinea from the north. The world's second-largest island, New Guinea was split into two sections, Papua New Guinea in the east and Western New Guinea, which was part of Indonesia.

Peter Jaden ensured the craft was well to the west to avoid the air defense radar networks along the border. With a population of over three hundred million people spread over more than seventeen thousand islands, Indonesia continually suffered from various rebel movements, coup d'états, and insurrections. A devastating civil war between Islamic State fighters and Republicans had left the state nearly non-functional, with much of the country ruled by local militias. The instability, in turn, left the economy lagging, creating a feedback loop of chaos and decline. In theory, one militia with the support of dissident government representatives had grown so powerful, it had been able to mount an all-out offensive against East Timor, complete with armor and artillery.

Despite being in passive mode, the various sensors easily detected the mysterious tanker to which the damaged Type 53 missile corvette had moored itself to. Scans showed little to no radar activity, so it was doubtful the Indonesian navy knew the location of the vessels or perhaps was backing the operation by purposely leaving alone.

Grace Jaden watched the drone's progress in the darkened Combat Information Center of the *Ayn Rand* while pondering just what exactly that tanker was doing there. Was the attack on Micronesia an Indonesian operation? The use of sophisticated EMP devices still had her betting she was facing a Chinese Intelligence operation. She waited impatiently for a report.

The *Ayn Rand* was farther north, still in the territorial waters of the Federated States of Micronesia but now moving south toward their prey under the cover of darkness at twenty knots escorted by both the *Tolkien* and the *Lewis*.

"There they are." Peter Jaden pointed at his air warfare screen. He put the live video stream from the Sentinel drone on one of the two large plot projections to the front of the CIC. Night vision equipment showed the mid-sized tanker and the Type 53 missile corvette sitting motionless in the Pacific in various tones of grey. "Right where they should be." He took some comfort in the still visible damage to the enemy missile corvette. The hostile warship was clearly missing a radar mast and the aft flight deck was a charred wreck.

Admiral Davidson's voice was filled with suppressed excitement. "All right, let's wake everyone up. Sound general quarters. Report to your aircraft." Davidson stood tall, now committed to taking the fight to the enemy, whoever they may be.

Klaxons activated, and crews rushed to their battle stations on all three corvettes. Handing his console off to the usual air warfare officer, Peter Jaden grabbed his flight jacket.

Grace reached for his hand. "Good luck out there."

Her son winked while putting on the leather jacket. "I've got this." With that, he was out the hatch, rushing to the flight deck where an AH-72 Defiant gunship sat. Calm seas had allowed them to transport the gunship south toward New Guinea. The hanger crew rushed to load the Defiant with Mark 48 torpedoes.

Neither of the smaller corvettes had a hanger, though their respective helicopter flight decks were able to handle craft for one-flight missions. So large was the V-22 Osprey on the Tolkien's flight deck that the commander and flight crew had tied the relatively massive aircraft to the deck lest a wave send the multi-million-dollar craft plunging into the sea. All on the flight deck were nervous while disconnecting the straps holding the Osprey to the deck as General Lawrence led his Marines into the cabin of the V-22.

"All aircraft ready to go," reported the *Ayn Rand's* air warfare officer.

Admiral Davidson exchanged a quick glance at Grace Jaden, knowing this was a point of no return.

Grace Jaden had made up her mind and didn't flinch. "Proceed, Admiral."

"You heard the lady." Admiral Davidson picked up a microphone and hit the transmit button. "All craft, you are cleared to execute. Go, go, go." The hum of subdued voices in the dark quiet Combat Information Center was interrupted with radio chatter of sailors preparing for the aircraft to lift off the decks of the corvettes.

The AH-72 Defiant helicopter gunship piloted by Peter Jaden was the first to take off. Once hovering in the air, Peter throttled the main rotor to full, lifting the helicopter off the deck of the *Ayn Rand*. With a jiggle of his stick and throttle, the pusher propeller to the rear of the helicopter gunship activated, sending the craft forward at over four hundred kilometers an hour.

With the airspace clear, the turboprops of the V-22 Osprey lifted the tiltrotor aircraft off the deck of the *Tolkien*. When safely up and away from the warships of the task force, the nacelles began to rotate, transforming the craft into a conventional aircraft, heading south at over 150 kilometers an hour.

Running lights off on both the Defiant helicopter and the Osprey tiltrotor, the risk of a mid-air collision was enough of a possibility that Admiral Davidson kept a watchful eye on both flight paths and radar tracks. Given the speed of either aircraft, they would both reach the tanker within an hour.

Peter Jaden, at the controls of the Defiant, was navigating completely on telemetry, the sky pitch black with not even a visible moon to guide him. Only the clear sky full of stars made it possible to tell up from down. Jaden kept his altitude low and close to the ocean. He kept all the active sensors deactivated to help ensure that the hostile vessels would have no idea what was coming.

Admiral Davidson on the *Ayn Rand* had the same thought in mind, knowing that the element of surprise was critical to the operation. It was a long half-hour of watching and waiting. Finally, the time had come to take action to ensure the New Liberty forces remained undetected. "All right, order that Sentinel to commence repeater-jamming. I don't want any communication in or out."

With a few commands, the air warfare officer instructed the drone almost 150 kilometers to the south to begin actively jamming both the tanker and the damaged corvette. The drone actively searched the spectrum for incoming and outgoing signals that it could absorb and retransmit as a manipulated signal. The digital radio frequency memory jamming technique was a unique method to keep the intended targets in the dark without them being able to realize they were being jammed.

While holding the fight stick tight to keep the AH-72 helicopter steady in the Pacific winds, Peter Jaden kept a watchful eye on the range indicator, waiting for it to blink below the maximum range of the Mk 48 torpedo. "I'm at fifty kilometers to Corvette Hostile Epsilon. Can you confirm no active radar emissions?"

"Negative," came the voice of the air warfare officer over the radio channel. "You're clear."

Knowing that his target was a crippled corvette—pretty much a sitting duck—Peter Jaden debated with himself the idea of launching now at the effective range of the torpedo versus closing in on the target and risking detection. The drone images had shown that the radar and surface-to-air systems of the corvette had been destroyed. However, the tanker had a close-in weapon system. Still, while standard close-in weapon systems had a usual ammunition range of five kilometers, new rail gun concepts and lasers could extend far past that on a clear day like today. Knowing that the noisy torpedo would alert the hostiles to the attack, he decided to continue to close in on the two vessels, trusting in the stealth capabilities of his aircraft. He looked over to his copilot Lieutenant Wognar. "You have a firing solution?"

"Torpedo locked on Hostile Epsilon." Wognar flipped a switch to arm the torpedoes. "Ready."

Minutes went by over the still calm waters of the Pacific with the steady roar of the rotor and the occasional blowing of the wind. Peter Jaden watched the heads-up display blink at a range of twenty-five kilometers. "Fire torpedo."

The pump jet of the Mark 48 torpedo activated before the weapon splashed into the ocean. Within seconds the torpedo raced beneath the surface at seventy kilometers an hour.

Peter Jaden held down the transmit button to activate his headset. "Torpedo in the water, targeting hostile Epsilon." Without an active sonar buoy in the water, the Defiant had no way to track the progress of the torpedo.

The loud pump jet racing the torpedo could, however, be heard by the Ayn Rand at extreme range, as they knew exactly what they were listening for. "Torpedo running steady," came a report from the surface warfare officer.

Peter Jaden continued to pilot the helicopter gunship close to the enemy ships. "Call up the turret. Get me targets."

Lieutenant Wognar activated the turreted gun system and tried to make out any close-in weapon systems on the tanker. The 20mm XM301 three-barrel rotary cannon had a range of about a kilometer.

"We've got active radar coming up from Hostile Foxtrot!" came a yell over the radio from an excited Air Warfare Officer on the *Ayn Rand*. "Firing HARMs!"

From high above at ten thousand feet, the RQ-172 circled the two enemy warships hidden from sight in the blackness and light cloud cover above. The nose of the Sentinel stealth drone dropped directly toward the tanker before firing off an AGM-88 High-Speed Anti-Radiation, HARM, missile. The AGM-88 automatically detected the active radar transmitter, broadcasting from the tanker with a fixed antenna and seeker head in the missile's nose. A smokeless solid propellant and booster-sustainer rocket motor propelled the small missile at speeds over Mach 2 to guide it right into the radar transmitter, where it then detonated, tearing the radar to shreds, sending quick bursts of light into the night sky.

The actual close-in weapon systems on the crippled corvette remained intact as the enemy switched the guns to automatic and began firing rounds in the direction of the last reported radar tracks of the Defiant gunship, the shots flashing through the night. Knowing at least one torpedo was inbound, the propeller screws of the missile corvette and the tanker began to turn as klaxons blared. Sailors on the tanker rushed to put out the small infernos that were once radar transmitters.

"Get the tanker CIWS," Peter Jaden ordered while pulling the throttle down to rush within a kilometer of the enemy.

Lieutenant Wognar zoomed her display in on the aft-mounted close-in weapon system firing in their direction from the tanker. Satisfied with the position of the targeting receptacle, she pulled her trigger finger, sending over a hundred rounds into the enemy turret. The close-in-weapon-system turret disappeared with a flash of light, and she continued to seek out gun systems on the deck of the tanker.

Moving too slow for any decoys or anti-torpedo systems to be effective, the Mark 48 torpedo slammed into the easy target that was the crippled Type 53 missile corvette. A plume of yellow-stained water and smoke fountained high into the air as the torpedoes tore a hole in the hull of the corvette. Water flooded in, causing the corvette to turtle.

"Direct hit. Hostile Epsilon is no more," Peter Jaden reported. With Lieutenant Wognar taking care of a cannon deck gun with another barrage of over two hundred 20mm shells, he flew the Defiant helicopter over the tanker while broadcasting video live to the Osprey to the north. The camera focused on the tanker below where he could make out only sailors on the deck firing small arms ammunition at the helicopter, a bullet or two ricocheting harmlessly off the armor. Jaden nodded to himself. "All right, General Lawrence. Looks clear."

V-22 OSPREY BRAVO

The pilot lowered the nose of the V-22 Osprey with the turboprops at full throttle to drop under the clouds and quickly close in with Hostile Foxtrot below. The tanker was easily visible, given the light provided by the still-burning inferno of the sinking missile corvette. With most of the sailors on the tanker trading shots with the Defiant gunship, the Osprey took no fire as the nacelles were rotated to hover just over the bow.

"All right, Marines"—General Lawrence slapped the side of his M16 assault rifle—"open that hatch!" He ran forward anchored by rope to the winch and pulley system along with the rest of the First Marine Platoon. "Let's find out who these assholes are once and for all."

Once the hatch lowered, Corporal Lan ran to the end of the ramp and raised his M110 semi-automatic sniper system.

"MANPAD on portside bow!" came a concerned yell over the radio from Peter Jaden. The helicopter pilot had caught sight of a sailor lifting up a man-portable surface-to-air missile easily capable of shooting down either the Osprey or the gunship.

Through the scope of his rifle, Corporal Lan surveyed the deck of the ship and felt his heart skip a beat on seeing a Chinese sailor raise a QW-1 Vanguard missile launcher right up at him. Instinct kicked in and he quickly pulled the trigger. The missile launcher fell harmlessly to the deck of the tanker as the soldier took a bullet right to the chest. "Tango down!" Corporal Lan gave a thumbs up.

All too aware of the urgency and with a strong desire to get off the aircraft, all five marines took a deep breath and jumped out the hatch of the Osprey, falling quickly to the deck, trailed by the rope. Only the sophistication of the winch system prevented them from slamming into the deck or snapping their necks as the ropes tightened up.

Despite multiple combat jumps, General Lawrence had to breathe a sigh of relief on stomping his boot firmly onto the deck of the tanker. Running forward, he waved his Marines to use the burning wreckage of the forward close-in weapon system for cover. Peering around a wrecked cargo container, he picked out enemy hostiles further back on the bridge deck exchanging fire with the Defiant gunship. He raised his rifle and opened fire. Not wanting to get caught in the crossfire, he radioed the gunship. "Okay Defiant, we're going for the bridge. Let us know what we're facing."

"Thermal scan shows twelve remaining hostiles on the bridge and below decks," Peter Jaden reported as he watched the thermally-imaged gunfight from above. "Scratch that, eleven. Good shot."

On seeing his intended target down, General Lawrence waved for the men to advance down the deck of the tanker. The wind gusted across the deck as above the Osprey, nacelles rotated and the turboprop disappeared into the night. "Lan, you take the bridge. Fuhr, you stay back and cover him. Corporal Murphy and the rest of the Platoon, we're going in!" The sound of bullets whizzing over them and ricocheting off metal was nothing new to Lawrence, and he was able to keep calm and slowly advance on the enemy positions.

Corporal Lan set up his sniper rifle and began picking off the armed soldiers he could make out on the elevated bridge deck.

Satisfied with the sniper coverage, General Lawrence forced himself up and bolted down the deck, followed by nine Marines. The platoon used various cargo containers for cover between dashes. Lawrence often looked over his men to ensure none had been hit in the advance. Hundreds of bullets cracked across the tanker deck at supersonic speed, shattering windows and punching metal.

The entire deck rocked violently as a grenade detonated ahead with a boom. His ears ringing, General Lawrence found he welcomed the tanker deck being flooded with smoke. With an opportunity to reach the elevated bridge structure unseen, he ran down the deck so quickly he had to slam into a bulkhead to come to a stop.

Three hostile troops, on losing sight of their, enemy darted down the stairwell from the elevated bridge only to be struck down by the well-placed shots of waiting Marines. "Three tangos down!" the squad leader hollered.

Slowly creeping up the stairwell, General Lawrence's heart skipped a beat as yet another armed sailor emerged from the bridge. With the pull of the trigger, his M16 sent rounds directly into the chest of the man who fell down the flight of stairs, lifeless. "Go, go, go!" Up the stairs, his troops poured fire into the doors and windows of the bridge. On reaching the hatch to the bridge, General Lawrence tossed in a grenade before slamming the hatch closed. The entire bridge lit up in a flash of fire, smoke, glass, and shrapnel. "Get me a thermal scan!"

A younger Marine ran up with a thermal imaging screen and aimed it at the bridge. Three bodies were sprawled on the ground with no hostiles up and about.

General Lawrence pulled open the hatch and waved Corporate Murphy in. Marines kicked weapons from the bodies of the injured. Lawrence knelt down above one of the enemy combatants that appeared to still be breathing. He felt the pulse of what appeared to be a Chinese sailor. "Get me a medic!" he radioed before the sailor's head exploded. To Lawrence's horror, he turned to see that only a quick shot from Murphy had saved him from a rushing attacker who had targeted not him first but the injured sailor. Whatever intelligence they could gather was lost among the blood splatter he wiped off his uniform.

"We've got a problem!" Corporal Murphy dropped his rifle to point at a couple of charges of C4 set up on the bridge.

"Secure engineering!" General Lawrence ordered while impulsively running forward to pick up the charge and throwing the still-beeping detonation device over the side and into the Pacific. The device detonated against the hull of the tanker with an echoing blast. Lawrence leaned out over the railing worried that he had just torn a hole into the hull of the tanker. Satisfied that the ship was intact, he turned around only to hear the sounds of gunfire and radio reports from below deck.

"Four tangos down. Engine room secure!" Corporal Murphy radioed.

Shivering in the crisp air, General Lawrence made his way back into the heated bridge. His nose wrinkled at the smell of blood. He looked down at the corpses of the enemy. "Has to be Chinese intelligence," he said, pointing at a headless body. "Only they would take out their own to keep us from interrogating him."

The young Marines in the room shrugged in response, just happy to have survived the battle, machine guns still at the ready to face potential threats. The sound of running gun battles had faded, and they could only hear the unsettling hum of the ship's generators

His heart pounding, General Lawrence allowed himself to take in a deep gulp of air to catch his breath. Feeling his age, he grabbed his knees and bent down to stretch. Satisfied that he no longer sounded like he was about to have a heart attack General Lawrence straightened up and adjusted the radio frequency of his headset before transmitting a triumphant. *"Ayn Rand, we've got Foxtrot."*

CHAPTER EIGHTEEN – CHESS MOVES

"At sea, I learned how little a person needs, not how much."
—Robin Lee Graham

JULY 31, 2068, 8:30 PM
OSPREY BRAVO
OVER THE SOUTH PACIFIC

The rear ramp of the V-22 Osprey clanged to life and began to lower, revealing both a star-filled sky and the dark waters of the Pacific below. It was hard to hear anything in the cabin now, apart from the roaring of the turboprop engines. A nervous Grace Jaden tried to calm herself by taking a deep breath of the influx of crisp salty air before Marines lowered a diving helmet over her head. Only Admiral Davidson looked like he was enjoying the experience with Dr. Haung and Cynet Systems Executive Nolan shaking as a result of both fear and an ill-timed gust of air.

Helmet clamps secure, Marines began to open valves of the tank strapped to her back. She could hear the flow of oxygen into the helmet. "We really have to do this?" Jaden asked.

Admiral Davidson couldn't help but chuckle at the uncomfortable looks of the civilians. It had been years since he had done his last drop into the ocean from a helicopter. He snapped his own helmet into place. "Best way to not alert any hostile forces is to keep our ships away" he radioed. "We go in at night and swim our way over." It had been over three days since General Lawrence had secured the tanker, and time was becoming increasingly imperative.

"Do you really need us?" Dr. Haung also inquired while mentally trying to not hyperventilate. "I'm a researcher, not a Navy diver." She clenched her fists in a vain attempt to not feel nauseous as her helmet was secured.

"We need you for your Chinese fluency"—Admiral Davidson pointed at Nolan—"And you for your computer skills."

"Looking forward to it." Nolan, unlike his counterparts, loved risky activities. That being said, he had never jumped into the ocean from a moving plane, and even he seemed to breathe heavily.

With an eyebrow raised, Jaden turned to the corporate executive. "I thought you were this wild risk-taking skydiver."

"Over land," Nolan lamented, "and with a parachute."

Admiral Davidson slapped Nolan's back. "First time for everything." He pointed over at a Marine. "Let's do this. Range to the Intrepid?" Now under their control, Jaden and Admiral Davidson had chosen to rename the captured tanker formally known as Hostile Epsilon the *Intrepid*.

"You're about five miles out," Peter Jaden reported from the cockpit as he adjusted the nacelles and reduced the throttle. "Ready for drop?"

Admiral Davidson gave the team a thumbs up. The gesture was rather unenthusiastically returned. "Ready for drop. We jump off, grab the drone, and should be about four hours to the *Intrepid*."

With a few throttle adjustments, the Osprey transitioned into hover mode. Peter slowly dropped the craft down in altitude to the point it looked as if one could reach out from the ramp and touch the ocean. Water thrust upward by the wind from the propellers sprayed into the cabin. He doubled-checked the airspeed. "You're cleared for jump." Peter Jaden's voice betrayed his own amusement at the discomfort of the civilians, particularly his mother.

A group of four Marines, two on each side, took hold of the rather large submersible unit and pushed it forward off the ramp. It fell into the ocean with a splash and disappeared beneath the waves for a few seconds before buoyancy took over and it remerged. The small semi-submersible hydro pump drone could propel the team underwater at over thirty kilometers an hour.

"Move her a little forward," Admiral Davidson instructed the pilot, not wanting the risk of inexperienced members of his team jumping down onto the drone package and breaking bones. When he was seeing the open ocean, he stepped down the ramp before reaching back to take Grace

Jaden's hand, leading her to the edge of the ramp. The fury of the water splashing up made the experience of walking down the ramp more terrifying than the actual plunge into the surprisingly warm waters of the Pacific. The wet suits had been specifically chosen to operate as floatation devices, and despite the rough waters brought on by the tiltrotor, all were able to stay afloat.

Seeing all four team members in the water, Admiral Davidson waved his arm in the air to indicate that the drop had been successful.

The turboprops created a variety of waves, making it difficult for the team to stay above water as Peter Jaden very slowly lifted the Osprey into the air.

Treading hard to maintain his position, Davidson made it difficult to wave the team members over. "Come to me," he urged, swimming over to drag Dr. Haung in the direction of the drone.

Above, the nacelles of the Osprey turned, and the tiltrotor aircraft disappeared into the night. Without the blasts of air from the turboprops, the ocean was left relatively calm.

Admiral Davidson reached the drone package and with a couple of touches of the control panel, the unit activated. He tapped on a bar in the rear of the drone. "Everyone, grab on." He helped Dr. Haung take a firm hold of the handle before securing her to the drone by a carabiner.

"That's wasn't so bad," Dr. Haung chuckled.

"All right, I'm going to fire this up." Admiral Davidson secured the rest of his team and last himself to the drone, "Just hang on tight." With a few more touch commands, the submersible turbines activated, and they accelerated under the water in the direction of the tanker.

The trip took over two hours, but for Dr. Haung and Grace Jaden, it seemed to take a lot longer. The heaters of their wet suits maintained body temperature, but the rush of turbulent water flowing rapidly around their wet suits and being reliant on the oxygen in their packs as they traveled beneath the waves made the journey uncomfortable. Nolan, on the other hand, closed his eyes, visualized getting a hydro massage, and ended up so relaxed it was a struggle to stay awake.

"Imagine you're Super Girl," said Admiral Davidson, trying to comfort Dr. Haung.

"Been a long time since someone called me a girl!" Dr. Haung laughed through the unpleasantness.

Unsure, the admiral followed up. "Is there a Super Woman?"

"Isn't that Dr. Haung's real identity?" Nolan continued to enjoy what he had come to consider a virtual massage.

After another five awkward minutes of silence, Dr. Haung asked. "So, why the *Intrepid*?"

"What?" Admiral Davidson didn't quite register the question.

"The tanker. Why did you two name it the *Intrepid*?"

Grace Jaden had finally figured out how to keep herself from rolling by twisting her shoulders. "It's named after a small ketch captured by the US Navy from the Corsairs of Tripoli during the First Barbary War." She tried to think of the year, but it didn't come readily to mind. "What year?"

"1803," Admiral Davidson replied with a firm grasp of American naval history. "The original Intrepid was used to sneak aboard and scuttle the frigate *Philadelphia* to keep her out of enemy hands."

Grace Jaden hoped history wouldn't repeat itself quite so accurately. "Hopefully, we won't be burning any of our ships."

The conversation went on for over two hours as the drone raced toward the tanker using global positioning system telemetry. The discussion then took a tangent into Objectivism and the philosophy of Ayn Rand. Ayn Rand had escaped communist Russia at the age of twelve to achieve fame in the US in the 40s and 50s for her novels *The Fountainhead* and *Atlas Shrugged*. Her philosophy was based upon laissez-faire capitalism, which she defined as the system based on recognizing individual rights. In art, she had promoted romantic realism.

"You an objectivist?" Admiral Davidson asked of Jaden.

"Not fully," Grace Jaden admitted. "I'm Byzantine Catholic. I believe the Universe was created."

The conversation then went into the nature of the universe itself Grace Jaden made the case for the universe being a simulation designed to teach and test, given the fact that it had a beginning and an end and that, despite years of searching the sky, there had been no hint of other artificially generated transmissions.

To Admiral Davidson's relief, he didn't have to come up with an opinion on the subject of the origin of the universe, as the drone controls began to light up and indicate that they were approaching the tanker. With the squeeze of a trigger, he took manual control of the craft and brought it up to the surface. The craft slowed down, emerging from beneath the ocean and experiencing more drag.

Fully awake, due to the adrenaline and thought-filled conversation, Grace Jaden took in the star-filled sky. She could see why Admiral Davidson had been so pleased that there was no moonlight; it was so black, the chances of them being seen from above were next to nothing.

Admiral Davidson still worried about thermal sensors that brought them right up against the hull of the motionless tanker as quickly as possible where they were welcomed with cables.

Having been manning the *Intrepid* alone with his Marines, for over three days straight, General Lawrence welcomed the company as he leaned over the siding to fetch Dr. Haung. "I've got you." The forty-something woman was shivering as she was drawn out of the warm water of the Pacific. With the help of Marines, she was brought aboard and wrapped in warm blankets. Next to come up was Grace Jaden. "Cutting it close, only half an hour to sunrise."

"That was perhaps the longest three hours of my life." Grace reached up to take a firm grip of Lawrence's hand.

Marines helped Nolan and Admiral Davidson aboard. Davidson promptly tied the drone to the side of the tanker. "I'm getting too old for this."

"That was awesome!" Nolan smiled on being brought up onto the deck, "That should be a sport!"

"Welcome aboard the *Intrepid*," said General Lawrence, saluting. "Can I be relieved of my command? Me and my men are anxious to get back to some good old ground combat. This sailor shit isn't for me." The past three days had been angst-filled for the Marines that had to wonder if and when missiles would come raining down on their ship. One missile strike would make short work of the undefended tanker. That was if a simple storm didn't come and set the tanker aground.

Admiral Davidson returned the salute. "The Navy will miss you. You did fantastic for your first command. We might make a sailor of you yet."

Still recovering his breath and freezing, despite being under multiple blankets, Dr. Haung reached over to take an offered thermos of hot tea. "Is there ever a dull moment with you crazies?"

"You said you wanted adventure," Grace Jaden chuckled.

"Your wish is our command," General Lawrence led them up the stairwell to the bridge, where dry clothes were waiting. All five of the new crew members were anxious for the comfort of dry clothes, and they were already unzipping wet suits while grabbing their outfits. The noticeably shivering Dr. Haung was allowed by the rest into the washroom to change first.

"Over here," said General Lawrence, pointing at a rather complex piece of machinery. "I assume this is the radio?"

Admiral Davidson nodded, as he recognized controls for both a Very High Frequency and Super-High Frequency transmitter. He turned up the volume. Over the static were recognizable patterns and beeps.

Nolan's eyebrows went up as he listened to the patterns. "Definitely a code channel—all encrypted. Bring me my computer."

Marines rushed to haul in the water-tight case containing his computers.

"Occasionally I can hear a word or two—I assume in Chinese." General Lawrence handed over his smartphone. "I've managed to record a couple of them."

Admiral Davidson handed the phone to Dr. Haung as she emerged from the washroom, having overheard some of the conversation.

"I'm a researcher, not a crypto-programmer." Dr. Haung wasn't able to make any sense of the distorted words and shook her head in frustration.

"I'll do the decoding. You just help me with my Chinese." Nolan pulled out his laptop computer and began hooking up the equipment to the terminal. "I feel like James Bond. This is great." Having coded his entire life, he was already able to pick out useful information. He pointed at the occasional ripple in the audio wave display. "This is our automatically generated reply transmission confirming our location."

Admiral Davidson turned to General Lawrence. "Good thing you didn't deactivate the communications terminal. Definitely would have given away the fact that something was up."

Nolan scrolled down the audio file. "I don't know what any of this is, all encrypted. Give me a couple of days, and I'll have this worked out. Might need the help of our supercomputers at Cynet."

With a long night ahead, Grace Jaden started to search the bridge for a coffee pot. "Anything you need, it's yours."

JULY 31, 2068, 8:30PM
BEIJING CHINA2068

Premier Xi Shengkun found the whole American political system perplexing. The American secretary of state had to communicate with him using Chinese Intelligence to ensure that the message wasn't recorded. What was the point of transparency if American politicians could just go around the system? It was all evidence of America being a corrupt and decrepit nation. Pushing such questions aside, he played back a portion of the message.

"American public opinion is turning against the president," the voice of Harris stated. "The government will take action if this continues another month." The recording had been made at the Chinese embassy in Saudi Arabia, so he knew the message was authentic.

So angered was Premier Xi Shengkun that he inadvertently crushed the glass cup he had been sipping tea from. Staff rushed to sweep the glass off his desk.

Shengkun swiveled his chair in place to face the two military generals standing at attention behind him. "You heard the Imperialist bastard." He rubbed his pounding forehead. "Your projections indicated that Taiwan should be out of fuel supplies by now."

Expecting the question, the chief of the defense staff handed the Premier a tablet. "We weren't accounting for this."

Premier Xi Shengkun stared at the image displayed on the tablet. It appeared to be satellite photographs of a harbor. "What am I looking at?"

"Crude unloading terminals." General Ming tapped on the tablet to highlight the crude storage tanks.

"How can the Taiwanese rebels be unloading crude given our blockade?" The Premier used his fingers to zoom the display in on what had to be an offloading vessel. So unexpected was the image that it took him almost twenty seconds to come to an understanding. "Submarine tankers." He tossed the tablet onto his desk. "Can we intercept these crude shipments?"

The general, having played politics for decades, knew that now was not the time for half-truths. "Doubtful. Not without commencing the invasion of Taiwan." The Typhoon-class submarines were designed to be ballistic missile submarines, not to be found.

"Inability to deal with this potentially scuttles the liberation of Taiwan." The Premier tapped his fingers on the desk. "Who is responsible? The Japanese? Russians?"

"We believe the tankers are being loaded with crude supplied from a private American company in the Pacific."

Premier Shengkun didn't hide his surprise, slamming his fist hard against the desk. "What are you fools rambling on about?"

"Per the intelligence report a couple months ago, the US corporation claimed to declare independence from the United States—"

Premier Shengkun all but screamed out a response. "The woman?" He stood up from his chair in anger while shaking his head in confusion. How could all their best-laid plans be undone by an American woman? "A private American woman?"

"Perhaps the United States government can deal with her?" the general offered.

Trying to calm down, he walked over to snatch a replacement cup of tea from his rather attractive secretary. "The American government is too unreliable." He took a sip of tea. "Their administration goes back and forth like the wind. Can you deal with this American woman yourself?" He looked General Ming eye to eye while mentally wishing he was instead looking at Admiral Jiang. Admiral Jiang was off waiting in the South China Sea with his battle group.

"We have an attack submarine shadowing her fleet," General Ming recollected. Knowing his position was on the line, he didn't hesitate in adding, "We can deal with her."

"Do it," Premier Shengkun ordered. "And prepare contingency plans against the United States and her allies." The time to strike had come.

General Ming suddenly felt cold as he processed the premier's orders. "Sir. To do so risks full-scale world war."

"Then so be it," the premier said firmly. "There will never be a better time."

CHAPTER NINETEEN – CONSEQUENCES

"The sea drives truth into a man like salt."
—Hilaire Belloc

AUGUST 10, 2068, 6:30 AM
PRC ATTACK SUBMARINE CHANGZHENG 25
THE SOUTH PACIFIC

The Chinese Type 093 second-generation nuclear-powered attack submarine, the *Changzheng 25*, sat at a depth of over half a kilometer beneath the surface of the ocean, putting significant hydrostatic pressure on the hull. At that depth, there was little to no light, so the submarine was completely dependent on the skills of the sonar operators for navigation.

When the submarine's commander, Captain Yunsheng, had first received his orders months ago to track a fleet of civilian vessels, he had been outraged. The seven-thousand-ton, 110-meter-long attack submarine had been designed to take on American Carrier battle groups, not babysit and harass civilian ships. Orders from the Politburo, however, were not something to ignore, and so he set sail east to the middle of the South Pacific. He was pleasantly surprised he had to halt their approach on the flotilla of civilian ships giving off a multitude of active sonar pings that would reveal even his ultra-silent submarine. Seeing it as a personal challenge, it took the Captain over a week to work out a pattern in the active sonar coverage and figure out how to get closer to the ships without being spotted.

Sneaking above the thermal gradient, his sonar operators had determined the civilian fleet he was tasked to pursue was made up of at least one cruise ship, several tankers with a variety of escorts, including at least one corvette, a variety of helicopters, and four Orca-class submarine drones, all with active sonar seeking out submerged threats. Even more of a surprise was the detection of Russian Typhoon-class submarines coming and going from the tanker.

"This is no normal civilian convoy," his sonarman had reflected on the composition of the fleet.

Indeed, Captain Yunsheng had come to appreciate he was facing an actual challenge. It would take an additional two weeks for him to finally strategically position the submarine at extreme depth beneath a thermal gradient ahead of the civilian vessels such that the Changzheng 25 could drift right under them undetected.

He was on the bridge overlooking the sonar station when the silence was broken by the Extremely Low-Frequency sensor console beeping and lighting up.

"Incoming communication from Beijing," his communication officer reported. Such communications were always critical, given the huge size of the transmitter required for such a transmission. China had constructed the world's largest ELF facility, roughly the size of New York City. It was the only way to communicate with submarines at such excessive depths. Being under so much water so far from Beijing, it would take hours for the communication equipment to decipher the orders.

Knowing there was nothing that could be done to speed up the process, Captain Yunsheng decided to take in a quick nap as the submarine continued to silently drift.

AUGUST 10, 2081, 8:00 AM
TANKER INTREPID
NORTH OF WEST PAPUA

It had taken tasking his entire information technology company and the use of all eight of their supercomputers over four days to break the algorithm, and that was after reverse-engineering the terminal, but triumphantly, Nolan finally had a program that, in theory, would be able to translate what, for the most part, looked like static being transmitted to the Intrepid. Nolan crossed his fingers and swallowed hard before punching his finger down on the enter key of his laptop. "Let's see what we can find out." He waved for Dr. Haung to approach.

Dr. Haung took no notice of the gesture. Being no fan of computers, she had become bored of waiting on Nolan and chose, instead, to focus on the view of the Pacific beyond the windows of the bridge. It was a warm, sunny, cloudless day. Taking in the sun and the gentle waves rocking the anchored tanker she could almost picture being on the beach somewhere.

Nolan's computer screen filled with various Chinese words and numbers. "Dr. Haung over here!" he shouted.

The older research scientist jerked her head at the interruption. Her focus back on the task at hand, she crossed her arms and bent over to get a good view of the screen. She quickly skimmed the communique but, in disbelief, had to re-read the message three times to ensure she had read it correctly. She pointed to one particular sentence in purple. "Why the different color?"

"That's an extremely low-frequency communication," Nolan replied. "A very expensive and slow method to communicate. Pretty much for submarines only." The mere mention of the word *submarine* in a sentence picked out by Dr. Haung sent chills up his spine. "Why?"

"It's an order to attack ships at the latitude and longitude of New Liberty," Dr. Haung said matter-of-factly, trying to keep her emotions in check.

With urgency, Nolan stood up from the computer terminal and yelled at the nearest Marine. "Get me Admiral Davidson and Grace Jaden here right fucking now! Where the hell are they?"

Admiral Davidson, having heard his name in the commotion on the bridge, rushed out of the boardroom. "What's up?"

"We've got orders being sent to a submarine to attack New Liberty!"

New Liberty being an unlikely priority for China, Admiral Davidson raised an eyebrow. "You can't be serious."

"Does this sound like a fucking joke to you?" Nolan made sure his tone stressed that time was of the essence while pointing to the computer screen.

The serious look on the usually no nonsense Dr. Haung's face had Admiral Davidson reach for his radio. "Flash to New Liberty. Attack by enemy submarine imminent!" The admiral suddenly felt powerless and far from where he should be.

CHANGZHENG 25
SOUTH PACIFIC
THIRTY-FIVE KILOMETERS SOUTHEAST OF NEW LIBERTY

Awakening to a buzzer, the still-in-uniform Captain Yunsheng jumped up from his bunk and stormed out of his quarters to the command center of the submarine *Changzheng 25*. To his dismay, he found himself still having to stare anxiously at the printer. It took twenty minutes longer than the communication officer had estimated for the computer to finish comprehending the message. All he could do was stand and wait. Finally, the cursedly slow machine began to print out the orders. Before the printout was even complete, Captain Yunsheng snatched the piece of paper and read his orders. He blinked a couple of times in surprise. What he had thought was going to be among the most boring and irrelevant of assignments was turning out to be the most exciting of his naval career.

"Our orders, Captain?" his Executive Officer inquired, having also been silently standing next to the Captain. It was very rare for the attack submarine to receive high-priority transmissions from transmitters usually reserved for nuclear ballistic missile submarines.

"Sound general quarters," Captain Yunsheng calmly ordered. "We're going into battle."

The executive officer bowed his head in acknowledgment and scurried off to alert the crew. No klaxons would be activated given silence was critical in keeping the nuclear attack submarine undetected.

The captain made his way to the plot table. His submarine sat just northwest of the civilian convoy where a gap had developed in the sonar coverage of the three drones, the corvette, and the civilian tankers, which all had active sonar systems. "Helmsman." He waved the officer over before drawing an imaginary line over the plot through the gap toward the last estimated position of the large civilian cruise ship. "We are going to come in at quarter speed—nice, slow, and quiet." His strategy was simple: traverse the sonar gap while staying as close to the bottom as he could, rely on the thermal gradients and reflective coatings of his submarines to absorb some of the active sonar pings energy, and then come up to take out the civilian ships at point-blank range.

"Yes, sir," the navigator responded before returning to the helm of the submarine to carry out the orders.

Stepping backward and leaning against the fire control computer, Captain Yunsheng looked down at the weapons officer manning his console. "Load all torpedo tubes."

"Yes comrade sir," came the response of the weapons officer. The Shang-class submarine had six twenty-six-inch torpedo tubes, which would be loaded automatically with Yu-6 torpedoes. The Yu-6 was the latest version of the domestically produced Chinese torpedo originally reverse-engineered from a captured US Mark 48 torpedo in the 1980s.

A very real concern for Captain Yunsheng was the potential for his crew to hesitate at the rather irregular orders he would have to give. In the heat of battle, there would be no time for his crew to mentally debate the ethics of firing on a rather large cruise ship possibly with thousands of civilians aboard. He bent his knees and lowered his torso, so he could look the weapons officer right in the eye, and spoke softly that only he would hear. "Our primary target is the civilian cruise ship and tankers. Understood?"

The weapons officer had been well-trained, aware that his place was to follow orders to the letter. "Understood, sir."

NLS SAINT STEPHEN

The Combat Information Center of the Tuo Chiang-class corvette *NLS Saint Stephen* was silent. Sailors watched their panels, intently babysitting the *Byzantium* and the production tankers. Unlike her sister ships, the *Saint Stephen* had sat back to escort the civilian ships, which were the heart of New Liberty. That suited Captain Semko just fine, given the fact that his wife and four kids were on the *Byzantium*. That his family was on the ships he escorted was a reminder he had an important job to do. He constantly performed rounds, checking between the main screen, the air warfare officer, and the anti-submarine warfare officer. The corvette was rocking in the waves, given a particularly strong wind, so Captain Semko had to hold the ASW station for balance. The Tuo Chiang-class was built primarily for the coastal waters of Taiwan, and on more than one occasion, she'd had to moor up with one of the larger tankers when faced with rough waters. "Have New Liberty change course to the northwest," Captain Semko ordered his executive officer. He had made irregularly moving the armada of ships around the biomass production area a routine practice.

"Aye, sir," the executive officer sighed at the need to once again radio out new courses for each of the ships.

While his actions were probably overkill, Captain Semko took his responsibility as a defender of New Liberty seriously. Continuing his rounds, he made his way to the anti-submarine warfare station.

The *Saint Stephen* had variable-depth sonar actively pinging, but the majority of the sonar information on the displays was being provided by the larger production vessels and the submerged Orca drones.

All three Orca drones were armed with two torpedoes each and had a full sonar suite. The extra-large unmanned undersea vehicles had boxy hulls akin to a small submarine communicating with the larger ships by fiberoptic cables and sound waves. The shrouded propellers kept the Orca's quiet. The drones could dive to a depth of more than two kilometers—deeper than most submarines—making them invaluable. Each had to be refueled every three months, so Captain Semko had them on rotating patrols.

The Orca submarines were at a depth of about four hundred meters, the anti-submarine officer wanting to keep close tabs on the drones. "Looks clear," the sonar officer reported while holding the headset close to his ear. It had been over two weeks since his last non-whale sonar contact—an American Virginia-class submarine that passed beneath the fleet on what was presumed to be a standard patrol of the Pacific.

"Can you project your sonar coverage on the screen?" Captain Semko inquired. It was often said that the price of freedom was eternal vigilance. He turned to the main display to the front of the Combat Information Center and adjusted his glasses to ensure he could make out all the data presented.

The sonar officer punched up the ranges of the active sonar pulses, which almost covered a 360-degree circle in a fifty-kilometer radius around the *Byzantium*. "On the board."

Despite his best efforts in positioning the drones and vessels, a small gap in the sonar coverage still presented itself to the northwest of the formation. Captain Semko walked to the plot to make notes in his log. "We need one more Orca drone."

"Originally, there were supposed to be three more corvettes," the sonar officer offered. "They're out on wild adventures while we babysit tankers in the middle of the Pacific."

Captain Semko tapped on the monitor of the anti-submarine warfare station. "Watch your monitor, Lieutenant. And be careful what you wish for."

The communications officer jumped up from her console. "Urgent communique coming in from the *Ayn Rand*." She ran a tablet over to Captain Semko. "Imminent subsurface attack against New Liberty expected."

Reading the report, Captain Semko felt his heart skip a beat. "Sound general quarters! All ships to battle stations" he ordered while sprinting back to the anti-submarine warfare station. "Show me the thermoclines!"

The sonar officer punched up the last estimated depth-temperature profile. "On the screen."

The graph showed a sharp temperature drop at six hundred meters. A thermal gradient enough to hide a submarine. "Get Orca Alpha down to eight hundred meters depth and move Beta to the Northwest." Captain Semko turned to the navigator manning the plot and pointed. "Change course to the northwest, full speed ahead." Semko cursed at the realization he had left the *Saint Stephen* southeast of the *Byzantium*, out of position to counter an enemy attack.

The propellers of the *Saint Stephen* cavitated while accelerating the craft to over forty-five knots. Klaxons activated and the lights of the Combat Information Center dimmed in preparation for battle.

CHANGZHENG 25

"Sonar reports that one of the submersible drones is dropping rapidly in depth! Also, high-speed screws bearing eighty degrees, Comrade Captain!"

Captain Yunsheng's head snapped up from the plot. He closed his eyes. How could his nuclear submarine have been detected? Regardless of how the enemy was aware of his oncoming attack, there was only one course of action to take. He knew he had to move fast. "Go to full speed ahead, depth to three hundred meters, quickly!"

The propellers of the Chinese Type 093 second-generation nuclear-powered attack submarine spun to life as the diving planes of the submarine titled to send the submarine accelerating up from beneath the thermal gradient.

The captain looked to the sonar officer while watching the depth gauge, waiting impatiently for his submarine to emerge above the thermal gradient. "Anything?"

"Sonar contacts on the board." Unaware of what was to come, the sonar officer's voice was rather jubilant, as he had the exact locations of the five tankers, the large civilian cruise ship, the three submersible drones, and the enemy corvette. "Corvette coming right at us, still southeast of Alpha, though."

Captain Yunsheng felt his heartbeat accelerating with the report of each contact. He turned to the weapons officer. "Get me firing solutions on contact alpha. Prepare a spread of four torpedoes on Alpha and two on that corvette!"

"Should we come up to periscope depth for a visual sighting?" the first officer asked.

The captain shook his head dismissively to make it clear everything at surface was to be considered a valid target. "You have a firing solution on Alpha?"

"We have a firing solution, Comrade Captain. Contact bearing sixty degrees at five knots and accelerating. Estimated range at 920 meters, torpedo run time nineteen minutes."

Damn it, thought Captain Yunsheng. He had hoped to come up a lot closer to his prey. Time was of the essence with the corvette coming closer with each passing second that Yunsheng vacillated. "Fire torpedo spread."

The *Changzheng 25* shuddered as six Yu-6 torpedoes were shot out of their tubes and accelerated toward the ships of New Liberty.

NLS SAINT STEPHEN

The vibration in the deck plates as the central hull elevated out of the water told Captain Semko that the *Saint Stephen* was racing as fast as she could to catch up to the *New Constantinople*. He hoped his nimble corvette would be fast enough to quickly catch up. He subconsciously tapped his finger on the plot, waiting for a report from the Orca drone still dropping in depth. Would the drone find the enemy submarine before it was too late?

"Torpedoes inbound!" came a frantic shout from the sonar officer as his display lit up, the sonar detecting the loud thrashing of fast-spinning propellers.

The blood drained from Captain Semko as he reached for a phone transmitter. He was out of time. "Flash message to all New Liberty ships: torpedoes in the water!" He dropped the phone to his side. "Snap counter torpedoes, get me a solution, and fire every Seaspider we've got! Priority on the torpedoes targeting the *Byzantium*."

"Four torpedoes coming in on the *New Constantinople*," the sonar officer said, frowning. "Two coming in on us." No matter how many times they had trained for the scenario, sailors always found their worldview shattered on hearing an active weapon was coming in on them.

"Seaspider launcher ready!" the weapon officer reported.

Time was of the essence. "Release now!"

On the deck of the corvette, the Seaspider torpedo launcher rotated and then began firing off eight Seaspider anti-torpedo torpedoes. The Seaspider was among the world's first anti-torpedo hard-kill systems designed to be an effective and affordable active defense against incoming torpedoes. Splashing into the water, the propulsion system of each respective Seaspider fired up. Unique for guided underwater weapons was the use of a solid-propellant rocket motor. The rocket motor and small nonstandard dimensions of the units provided maneuverability that was greatly superior to conventional torpedoes despite the traditional rudder and fins arrangement.

The production tanker *Byzantium* also had a Seaspider torpedo launcher rack, so Captain Semko quickly did the mental math to see if she was in range for an intercept. Unfortunately, to the northeast, any attempt would be futile, but the system still might prove useful in the event of a second salvo. If they survived the first torpedo spread. "Priority message to *New Constantinople*. Accelerate to flank, and deploy passive countermeasures." He looked over the plot. "Helm, change course to two-seven-five."

"That will put us right behind the *New Constantinople*!" the executive officer cautioned.

Captain Semko felt no hesitation in making clear what the priority of his crew should be. "My family is on that ship—along with countless others."

Nods of understanding came from all the senior officers, including the XO. "You heard the captain." The executive officer turned to the helm. "Course two seven five, full ahead flank!"

It was only a matter of time before a new barrage of torpedoes would be coming their way unless they dealt with the hostile submarine itself. Captain Semko leaned over the sonar officer. "Sonar, get me a target!"

The sonar operator frantically searched through the live consolidated acoustic data from both the *Saint Stephen* and the three Orca drones. An algorithm highlighted a wave file with a possible contact before blinking that a match had been registered. Data on the predicted identity of their attacker winked onto the screen. "Conn, sonar contact, Chinese Shang-class submarine at 270 degrees, range ten kilometers, depth four hundred meters! She's loading more torpedoes!"

"Firing solution now!" Captain Semko shouted with urgency, the clock ticking.

The weapons officer quickly inputted the information into his terminal. "Got it!"

"Lock all torpedoes on target and fire!"

The port-side torpedo launcher fired three Mark 46 torpedoes, which dropped down into the ocean and began seeking its prey beneath the waves. The sound of the torpedo propellers was so intense that the sonar operator had to remove his headphones.

Captain Semko looked to the main situation display. The six Chinese torpedoes were still closing in on the *Saint Stephen* and *New Constantinople* to the northwest. "Hail *New Constantinople*. Have her turn hard to starboard and come to the east, full flank! Helm to come in right behind her." As officers rushed to carry out his commands, Captain Semko knelt down beside the weapons officer and spoke softly, so only he and the officer could hear. "Get our ASW drone airborne and order those Orca drones to open fire." He took a deep breath before adding solemnly, "While we still have time."

MV NEW CONSTANTINOPLE

Both Zenuck and Argarwal had been in a routine operations meeting in the briefing room when the klaxons sounded throughout the ship. Emergency drills had been conducted on a weekly basis, so families knew to report to the lifeboat stations. Sailors were already inflating and lowering zodiacs on the main deck in case the order came to abandon ship. Zenuck took a second to pull out his smartphone, only to pause in disbelief at the rush of incoming messages. "We're under attack!"

"To the bridge," Kelly Argarwal suggested, wanting to know exactly what was going on.

Both rushed up a stairwell in the direction of the elevated bridge deck of the former cruise ship, trying to balance themselves with the handrails as the vessel accelerated to its maximum speed of thirty knots and took a hard starboard turn. Zenuck turned back to grab hold of the Prime Minister on seeing her lose her balance and nearly tumble over the rail. For the most part, the immense size of the ship had left all aboard accustomed to relatively steady decks, but at this speed, the entire ship violently rocked. Even from over fifty meters above the water line, ocean water sprayed up across the open decks from the churning of the hull into the Pacific.

Any hope that this was a drill faded on seeing the bridge a flurry of activity and the worried looks of the sailors. The commanding officer had his up binoculars looking directly aft. Beyond the glass windows, the corvette *Saint Stephen* skimmed over their wake, racing toward them.

"We're too fast to abandon ship," one sailor reported to the commander.

"We're committed to evasion now!" the commanding officer by the name of Lars advised his senior crew. While he had spent most of his life with a Norwegian cruise line, Lars had spent his twenties and thirties learning to sail in the Navy. Lars double-checked all the passive anti-torpedo equipment provided to him. "Deploy all countermeasures. Release the Nixie!"

Aft of the ship, a variety of passive anti-torpedo countermeasures, including a towed AN-SLQ-25 Nixie, were projected into the water. The decoy automatically began emitting signals to mirror that of the large cruise ship to draw away torpedoes. A variety of smaller disposable devices were also thrown into the ocean, but none had the same ability to emit simulated propeller and engine noises. The *Saint Stephen*, too, deployed its own Nixie as its anti-submarine warfare drone, a helicopter-looking MQ-8B Fire Scout, lifted off the helicopter pad and raced away to the west, no doubt to engage the hostile submarine.

"Confirmed torpedoes in the water!" a communications officer reported.

Kelly Argarwal clutched her stomach, feeling nauseous at the rocking of the vessel and the knowledge that someone had fired off torpedoes with the intent to kill her and everyone aboard. Zenuck and another sailor saw her turn pale and lose her balance. She caught ahold of Zenuck to steady herself. "I'm okay."

"It's going to be okay," Zenuck said, hoping the prime minister wouldn't regret her decision to join the New Liberty effort. He closed his eyes in prayer that a higher power would protect the men, women, and children of the ship. He could feel the powerful engines spinning the propellers and thrusting the ship through the water faster and faster. Would it be enough?

Captain Lars turned a nob on one of the consoles to increase the intercom volume, over which the voice of the anti-submarine officer on the *Saint Stephen* was broadcasted. "Seaspider intercept!" came a jubilant cry, "Two torpedoes down now!"

Beneath the waves, nimble Seaspider anti-torpedo torpedoes detected their close proximity to the incoming Chinese Yu-6 torpedoes and detonated, the explosion enough to sever the propeller of one of the intended targets while ripping off the sensor dome of another. Another Seaspider detonated beneath the waves.

"Four torpedoes down!" the intercom broadcasted. Any hint of triumph was quickly offset. "Two still incoming, coming in fast!"

"Look!" one of the sailors on lookout duty pointed to the southwest where just aft of the two New Liberty ships, a wake was visible from the surface. The two remaining Yu-6 torpedoes were coming in and coming in fast. The race was on, with the two remaining torpedoes chasing the fleeing *Saint Stephen* and *New Constantinople*.

There was a small burst of water aft of both the *Saint Stephen* and the *New Constantinople* as one of the Yu-6 torpedoes exploded, prematurely set off by the Nixie decoys.

Overwhelmed by multiple noise decoys and torpedo explosions the fire control systems of the last Yu-6 torpedo were went into an override mode and locked onto the nearest distinguishable target. The torpedo turned and smashed dead aft into the hull of the *Saint Stephen* before detonating.

The explosive power of the warhead blasted the small corvette forward at such a force it almost caused the ship to roll mid-air, surrounded by a plume of ocean water fifteen meters high. Debris plumed as the corvette disintegrated before crashing back down into the ocean where water rushed to flood compartments now accessible between the shattered decks. Most of the men and women aboard were killed instantly by the fireball of the blast or the concussions of being thrown against bulkheads at high velocity. The unlucky survived long enough to drown as the sea poured into the wrecked hull of the corvette.

The sonic boom of the explosion echoed through the bridge of the *New Constantinople*, only to be followed by stunned and saddened silence. The *New Constantinople* was still intact at full flank speed, leaving the wreckage of the *Saint Stephen* behind.

Seconds passed before Captain Lars turned away from the wreckage to his bridge team. "There is still an enemy submarine out there," the urgency in his voice brought the attention of everyone who could hear them back to the situation at hand. Lars cursed, knowing full well he had no sensors or weapons but was still facing a hostile submarine. "Get me an uplink from all available drones! Hurry!" He raised his binoculars and sought out the helicopter-looking drone of the late *Saint Stephen* with a new commitment to the universe that the sacrifice of the corvette's crew would not be in vain.

CHANGZHENG 25

While most of Captain Yunsheng's attention was focused on the plot where he watched the reported positions of the three torpedoes closing in his nuclear submarine, he did sneak a look at a nearby timing clock. It was too late now to fire off another spread before the incoming torpedoes came into range. "Make our depth six hundred meters, and come around to course 320 degrees." It was time to get back down under the thermal gradient.

The officer manning the sonar turned triumphantly to Captain Yunsheng on hearing the sounds of the corvette breaking up. "Corvette destroyed. Definite break up."

Captain Yunsheng raised an eyebrow. "What of the large civilian liner?"

The sonar officer shook his head, perplexed at the strange reaction of the Captain. The corvette was the obvious military target and the first kill of the *Changzheng 25,* so why would the captain be upset at the news? "Contact Alpha at thirty knots heading on course eighty-five degrees, range twelve hundred meters."

"She's getting away," said Captain Yunsheng with a curse. He would have to deal with completing the mission objective later, given the three incoming torpedoes, which were so close now, the sonar officer had to remove his headphones. "Standby countermeasures! Full ahead flank!"

"Noise decoys ready!" the weapons officer reported, watching as the torpedoes tracked closer and closer.

The rods of the nuclear reactor of the Changzheng 25 had been lowered to generate more heat and more steam to spin the propellers of the submarine.

Seeing that the incoming Mark 46 torpedoes were now almost at point-blank range, Captain Yunsheng gave the order. "Launch counter-measures!"

Three noise decoys were launched from the hull of the nuclear submarine and commenced spinning and broadcasting propeller-like noises. The sound of the noisemakers and incoming torpedoes could be heard through the metallic hull of the attack submarine.

Captain Yunsheng smiled on hearing the sounds fade. All three Mark 46 torpedoes took the bait and accelerated harmlessly over the attack submarine safety beneath a zone of cold water. The changing water temperature acted as a reflector for sound waves. "Reduce to quarter speed!" The enemy corvette would not avenge herself as the captain expected, given the time and distance he had to work with. It was time to get back to the business of completing the mission objectives and sinking the now undefended civilian ships above. "Turn to course nine-zero. Get me a firing solution on Alpha, and bring us back to a depth of three hundred meters."

To the surprise of the captain, there came the echoing of active sonar pings.

"Captain!" the sonar officer shouted. "The submersible drones! They're beneath the thermocline at a range of fewer than three hundred meters!"

Fulfilling the last command received from the *Saint Stephen*, each of the three Orca submersibles had silently dived beneath the thermocline while slowly moving to the last reported position of the Chinese attack submarine. Upon crossing the thermocline at five hundred meters depth, the artificial intelligence systems switched to active sonar. On confirming the presence of a submarine, the fire control computers worked out firing solutions. The first Orca submarine opened fire with two Mark 46 torpedoes. Then came another four from the second.

The captain bowed his head in shame. It had been a mistake to assume that all the drones would be out of action, given the destruction of their mother corvette whose crew would get their retribution after all.

The sonar officer relayed what the Captain already knew. "Torpedoes in the water! Six torpedoes coming at us!"

Captain Yunsheng closed his eyes. To come to the surface would do nothing but attract the other torpedoes circling noisemakers above the thermal gradient. Two torpedo barrages on active sonar would be impossible to evade.

"Captain!" shouted the executive officer, protesting the captain's inaction. Though it may be hopeless, the captain still had to try.

"Launch countermeasures," Captain Yunsheng said robotically to appease the XO. "Dive to crush depth." It would be a futile effort but an effort nonetheless.

The first two Orca-fired Mark 46 torpedoes took the bait of the noisemakers and missed the *Changzheng 25*. The submarine titled down as the submarine dropped deeper and deeper beneath the ocean. Another torpedo chased one of the countermeasures. The fourth, however, steered down, corrected its course slightly, and smashed straight into the *Changzheng 25* just below the conning tower before exploding and tearing a hole in the hull of the submarine. At this depth, any loss of integrity was too much, and the submarine imploded.

MV NEW CONSTANTINOPLE

There were no skilled sonarmen on the cruise ship, so the report had to come from the lone remaining trained anti-submarine weapons officer on the *Byzantium*. "ASW drone showing definite target break up."

Captain Lars raised his binoculars and looked far off to the west where the MQ-8B Fire Scout had taken station and dropped a sonar buoy into the ocean. He raised his fist in triumph.

There was a chorus of cheers from all the sailors on the bridge.

Even Kelly Argarwal, after vomiting in a nearby trash can, smiled at the report and the knowledge they would live another day.

"Can we communicate with the Orca drones? Get them back on patrol?" Zenuck asked.

The operation of the submersible drones was beyond the knowledge of Captain Lars, and he could only shrug in response.

"I'll check with the ASW officer on the *Byzantium*." Zenuck took a seat at the communications terminal and decided to hail the *Ayn Rand* first.

The main monitor showing the plot of the New Liberty taskforce was replaced with an image of Grace Jaden. "What's your status, New Liberty?"

"We were attacked by a Chinese submarine," Zenuck said, frowning. "The submarine has been dealt with, though we lost the *Saint Stephen*."

Behind him, Captain Lars ordered the cruise ship to reduce speed and begin to circle around to search for survivors.

Kelly Argarwal leaned over Zenuck, squeezing his shoulder for balance. "That was close. *Too* close. Where are you?"

"I came aboard the *Ayn Rand* so we could communicate freely." Grace Jaden rubbed her chin in frustration.

Admiral Davidson dropped his head into view. "Your orders are to play dead and flee east. Keep our families safe."

Grace Jaden nodded her head in agreement. "Understood, Prime Minister?"

"Yes, ma'am."

"We need more aircraft," Admiral Davidson injected.

Zenuck spoke up. "The modifications on the last production tanker were completed to Peter's specifications; she's on her way south."

"Good. Things are about to get even hotter out there," Grace Jaden said with an ominous tone. "Play dead. Deactivate all active comm systems."

"How will we be able to help you?"

"We aren't going leave you out there!" Kelly Argarwal protested.

"If you don't hear from us, you won't be leaving anyone behind. Just keep those families safe; all other priorities are secondary. What are your defensive capabilities?"

Zenuck called up the latest information on his display. "We've still got the three Orca drones, which should come to surface soon for orders. We'll reattach the fiber optic cables. Torpedoes and missile defense on the production tankers. We'll have to coordinate our defenses from the *Byzantium* with the *Saint Stephen* gone."

"I'll send the corvettes back as soon as we can."

"Yes, ma'am."

"*Ayn Rand* out."

Turning around to face Captain Lars, Zenuck stood up from the chair. "As soon as rescue operations are completed, we are to move the task force southeast and go passive on all radio and radar transmissions. Use satellite comms only. There could be more submarines out there, so let's be ready."

CHAPTER TWENTY – A TEST OF CHARACTER

"There is a certain enthusiasm in liberty, that makes human nature rise above itself, in acts of bravery and heroism"
—Alexander Hamilton

AUGUST 11, 2068, 11:12 AM
NLS AYN RAND
SOUTH PHILLIPINE SEA

Grace Jaden took in the spray of the ocean brought on by a gust of wind while standing motionless on the deck of the *Ayn Rand*. She shook her head wearily as her mind reflected on the families of the New Liberty ships far in the East, who had almost been lost. She had personally hired Captain Semko as commander of the *Saint Stephen* and knew his wife, son, and three daughters well from church services. Now he was gone, and they were fatherless. Was it her fault?

General Lawrence approached from behind, having seen her look in the faces of commanders who had lost good men and women under their command over a hundred times before. "Staff is ready for the briefing, Grace." He saw the frown on her face and added "Everyone chose to be here, Grace."

"No one chose to end up fighting a war in the Pacific." Grace Jaden bowed her head.

"We chose to be free." General Lawrence kept staring at her until she looked up. "You've given us the chance to be free. Many have fought and died for freedom; at least you kept the cause alive." He looked back at the raised bridge and sensor masts of the frigate. "No one else could have done that. No one."

Not wanting to be seen engaging in self-pity, Grace Jaden turned on her heel and strode into the superstructure of the *Ayn Rand* and down a stairwell into the briefing room just aft of the Combat Information Center. Her eyes narrowed as she looked down on the electronic plot table, dominating the center of the room, which was showing a map of the Western Pacific with a scattering of markings.

Nolan, Dr. Haung, and Captain Hayes stood around the plot table. Nolan and Doctor Haung looked tired but not exhausted after the long helicopter flight back from the *Intrepid*.

Grace Jaden took her place around the plot. "All right, gentleman. Let's get to it." She turned to Nolan and Doctor Haung. "That was good work on learning of that Chinese submarine. You saved New Liberty."

Nolan grinned. "Glad we could help."

Even Doctor Haung seemed proud of the accomplishment. "It was a team effort."

The main projection screen at the front of the conference room activated with an image of Admiral Davidson on the bridge of the *Intrepid*, which was still far to the south, just off the coast of West New Guinea. "Got a laser signal going from the *Intrepid*, but if I cut out, I'll try to reconnect."

The crewmembers adjusted to face the projection. General Lawrence entered the briefing room and took a seat as well.

"All right, let's start with an overall brief," said Grace Jaden, tapping on the plot.

"New Liberty is now over five hundred kilometers to the east and proceeding at quarter speed to the Southeast Pacific." General Lawrence bent over the map table and pointed. "We have our Orca submersibles on patrol, and the *Byzantium* has full air defense capabilities. That being said, Japan has tasked one of their few nuclear submarines capable of operating that far out to assist, and the Philippines has sent an older Pohang-class corvette to ensure we can keep the shipments of crude going to Taiwan."

"Nice to know our allies are committed." Grace Jaden clasped her hands together. "Admiral Davidson, what is your status on the Intrepid?"

"Throughout the night, we've loaded the modified M142 and Yun Geng missile launchers onto the *Intrepid* along with the EMP generator warheads completed by Zenuck and his engineering team." Admiral Davidson, by remote, presented various ranges for each of the weapon systems. One of the circles now enclosed the South China Sea. "The modified MGM-140 missiles give me a range of three hundred kilometers."

"Currently, off Micronesia, we have the *Ayn Rand,* the *Tolkien,* and the *C.S. Lewis.* We've moved northwest in the direction of Taiwan to ensure we don't end up the justification for a repeat Chinese attack on Micronesia." Captain Hayes adjusted the display. "The fifth uncompleted production vessel has been modified to act as a drone carrier—a sea control ship as it were—based on designs by Peter."

Peter Jaden had departed the *Ayn Rand* to personally oversee the outside-the-box kit-bashing of the tanker hull. Jaden had to wonder how her son was coping.

"Crews spent the night installing deck plating and fuel lines. She's still about six hundred kilometers to the east but should join us within the day to give us some additional air coverage. Our Gotland-class submarine is sitting south of Taiwan being refueled by a Japanese tanker." Captain Hayes longed to be united with the submarine he had been hired to command.

"All right. This is what we are thinking," Nolan pointed down at Indonesia. "We believe that the Chinese are communicating with various third-party tankers pre-positioned in the South China Sea, which are acting as refueling vessels in collaboration with Indonesia."

"What's in it for Indonesia to cooperate with China?" General Lawrence asked.

Grace Jaden pointed down at Micronesia and East Timor. "Divide and conquer. China gets Taiwan; Indonesia gets Micronesia. Both split the Philippines potentially."

"Exactly." Admiral Davidson had been suspicious of the level of cooperation between Indonesia and China since East Timor. "Taiwan's defenses are positioned based on an attack from the mainland, not from the south. Sure enough, China has a marine expeditionary group doing joint training with the Indonesian Navy as we speak. I also think we should expect the use of EMP weapons as tested in Micronesia."

Grace Jaden stepped back from the display. "The Chinese were expecting their naval embargo to leave Taiwan short of power and on the verge of collapse. Micronesia was supposed to stay crippled and occupied. We've been a thorn in their side the whole power play, leading to that submarine attack on New Liberty. Wither we like it or not, we're at war." She paused to reflect on the fact that the tiny sea state of New Liberty was facing the entire Communist state that ruled mainland China.

"There is absolutely no way we can win this conflict," General Lawrence protested. "I don't like it"—he sighed—"but this just might be the time for negotiations."

Grade Jaden held up her hand to keep the room silent. "I'm not interested in backing down. We expect an attack against our allies in Taiwan, and we are to do our part to thwart it. Taiwan and Japan have supported us from the start, and I intend to support them. I'm ordering Admiral Davidson to move the *Intrepid* into prime firing range to EMP-pulse the Chinese fleet in the event of an attack. Keeping our taking of the *Intrepid* as secret as possible will be imperative to the success of that operation."

"I have recorded scheduled reports to the Chinese fleet that they should continue to believe that it is on station and operated by Chinese Intelligence," Doctor Huang offered.

"Which are preprogrammed to send per our artificial intelligence algorithm and what we believe are the expectations of Chinese Intelligence," Nolan continued. It was the best they could do with the time they had, and he hoped it would be enough. "But if they do any kind of pro-active checking up on their agents . . ." he allowed his voice to drift into silence.

"After any EMP attack, we are to move to point-blank range with our corvettes and engage the Chinese troop transports—in particular, their helicopter carrier, which would allow them to overfly beach defenses and gain complete access to Taiwan." Grace Jaden turned to Captain Hayes. "And to push the fleet toward the pre-positioned *Nautilus*."

"If it's all right with you, I would like to be on the *Nautilus*," Captain Hayes requested.

"Better get out there quick. Keeping your position undetected will be essential."

"Understood. I'll take precautions." Captain Hayes saluted and rushed out of the boardroom to hand command of the *Ayn Rand* to his executive officer.

NEW LIBERTY FLOATING PRODUCTION SHIP FIVE
THE PHILLIPINE SEA

Peter Jaden stood on the bridge of floating production ship five, an older production platform built more than a hundred years ago. It was to have been the fifth production platform of New Liberty, but the conversion had only just commenced when the East Timor incident occurred, after which most of the construction was put on hold.

That was when Peter Jaden had come up with an idea based on an old concept from the Royal Navy. Back in April 1982, when facing the Argentinian air force during the battle for the Falkland Islands, the Royal Navy would only be able to deploy from the task force twenty Sea Harrier jets jumping off the aircraft carriers, *Invincible* and *Hermes*, against near-continuous airstrikes from the mainland. The Sea Harriers had proven invaluable, shooting down twenty Argentine attack jets. Within a month, the Royal Navy commandeered two fifteen-thousand-ton G2-class roll-on-roll-off container ships two football fields in length, the *Atlantic Conveyor* and the *Atlantic Causeway*. Both were modified with an aviation refueling system and makeshift hanger structures and flight decks. Just as early U.S. and British escort carriers during World War II were converted from civilian ships, the *Conveyor* and *Causeway* were to be converted into impromptu aircraft carriers for helicopters and Harrier jump jets that didn't require a long carrier deck. While the Conveyor would be lost, the Causeway operated as a helicopter carrier for the remainder of the conflict.

Given an air force of a single VTOL fighter craft and an assortment of drones, Peter Jaden presented a modification to Production Ship Five to serve as an aircraft carrier.

"Are you nuts?" was the first feedback more than a month ago from Jord Labaoucan. "Don't aircraft carriers cost billions?"

"Not *this* aircraft carrier." Peter Jaden had planned his response well in advance with an already prepared budget. "This one will cost less than $5 million and save you some aviation fuel over the coming decade while you're at it."

That was enough to get Jord onboard. The conversion was to be done cheap and dirty—a flat deck for VTOL and drones and modification of the piping beneath to provide for refueling capabilities.

Peter fought hard to win approval for the conversion, getting both Admiral Davidson and Kelly Agarwal on board with presentations on how the ship could be used to escort fuel tankers and provide air support for chasing away enemy submarines.

"I'll get this approved at once," Admiral Davidson had promised months ago, and within hours the authorization for expenditure had been approved using funds from the naval budget.

And so, fulfilling a dream he'd had since aviation school, Peter Jaden found himself in command of an aircraft carrier . . . of sorts. *But what a carrier*, he acknowledged, while looking her over from the elevated bridge. Welded steel plates provided a flight deck beneath which fuel hoses had been run to provide for the ability to fuel aircraft. So quick was the conversion that he had the crew installing fire suppression equipment, practice-firefighting, and training to abandon ship even as the vessel made its way southwest to rendezvous with the other warships of New Liberty. The vessel was a floating fire hazard with only a single Phalanx single close-in weapon system welded on the bow for defense, so he made the fire suppression equipment and training a top priority.

"Sir," said his executive officer, a civilian sailor by the name of Susan Andrews, handing Peter a tablet. "Orders from the *Ayn Rand* to stay east of the fleet about fifty kilometers."

Peter Jaden read the notes issued by his mother. "All right, let's get all the drones ready for launch." The air group of his makeshift aircraft carrier consisted of twelve stealthy-looking RQ-180B Sea Ghosts and twelve more conventional MQ-10B Sea Avenger drones. He had only one piloted aircraft—a single-seat, all-weather, stealth multirole vertical takeoff and landing F-35 Lightning II retired by Japan and bought for his exclusive use. The F-35, being a jack of all trades, was generally the master of none—especially the short-take-off and landing variant before him, which had been the subject of much scrutiny and criticism. There was a reason that Japan had chosen to sell the STOVL versions of the craft while sticking to the higher-performance runway-launched versions and newer aircraft designs. "Also, we need a name for our aircraft carrier." He looked out over the drone-filled deck. "How about the *Bonhomme Grace*?"

"Sir?" Andrews raised her eyebrow.

"The last aircraft carrier to save us was named after the frigate of the American Revolution. She, in turn, was named by John Paul Jones himself in honor of Benjamin Franklin who got her from the French." Peter handed back the tablet. "Makes sense for New Liberty that we would have the Poor Grace."

"Does that make you John Paul Jones, sir?" Andrews beamed as she asked.

Any comparison to the Father of the American Navy had Peter Jaden blush. He was not of the same caliber, in his opinion. Not even close. "Certainly not." Peter Jaden looked down the length of the flight deck, hoping the deck was long enough. Usually, a ski jump was necessary to launch an F-35 up into the air off a carrier but at the expense of a great amount of fuel, the vertical landing system could be used to lift the craft into the air. "Make sure that if I don't have enough thrust off that F-35 and fall overboard that the divers are ready to come get me," he said half-jokingly. Realizing she might take it completely as a joke, his grin faded. "Seriously. Have a trained recovery team ready to come get me."

CHAPTER TWENTY-ONE – OPERATION REUNIFICATION

"The price of freedom is eternal vigilance."
—John Philpot Curran

AUGUST 22, 2068, 10:31 AM
BEIJING

Premier Xi Shengkun angrily slammed the official letter received from the president of the United States of America onto his desk.

"It's just the United Nations." A top Chinese diplomat stepped forward. "The United Nations has no power in the South China Sea. We can ensure enough votes that no resolution passes the Security Council. Plus our veto—"

"We had a window in which the American Navy would do nothing, and it slips through our fingers!" Premier Shengkun interrupted while looking up in disgust at the diplomat and his lack of understanding. The tall premier stood up from his desk and blustered over to come face to face with his senior Generals. He paced before the Generals, shaking his head in disappointment while clasping his hands together behind his back. So displeasing was the Premier's scowl that more than a few of the generals took a step back despite their years of military experience, above-average height, and uniforms covered in metals.

The defense minister snapped to attention. "We have developed a contingency plan for this situation." The time for diplomacy was over. "We can proceed even with the Americans no longer promising to stand aside."

There was clear surprise in the faces of the Senior Generals at the declaration of the defense minister. Sweat dripped down their foreheads.

"Surely we should re-evaluate the situation. Our covert operations —" the general to the immediate left of the defense minister protested, only for Premier Shengkun to wave for a security officer to approach.

"You are relieved of your command, General Yun." The security officer standing guard over the room moved quickly, removing the relieved General's pistol at his side before leading him away. "Embarrassing!" Premier Xi Shengkun snorted. "I expect better of our armed forces. The time for reunification has come. Implement Operation Reunification at once!"

SEPTEMBER 2, 2068, 2:15 AM PST (6:15PM TAIPEI TIME) THE PACIFIC

It had taken decades for Chinese Intelligence to work out exactly how to pre-position the electromagnetic pulse generators, but given the relatively porous borders of the United States and with ample time, the operation was eventually a success. In San Diego, near naval base Point Loma and naval base Coronado, the pieces were moved across the border piecemeal out of Mexico to be assembled in strategically selected storage trailers over years. Several more devices were similarly moved into the United States to be shipped under the cover of a multi-national communications equipment company to Washington State, Hawaii, and Japan. Each component was purposely segregated to look nothing like a complete weapon system that they could sit waiting in storage lockers, some north in Seattle near naval base Everett, another west of Honolulu in close proximity to Pearl Harbor, and three more by naval bases in Japan.

The deployment in the Republic of the Philippines was accomplished with the assistance of the separatist Moro National Liberation Front. Chinese intelligence was never keen to work with Islamic extremists, but with Indonesian Special Operations doing much of the fieldwork, three complete pulse generators were smuggled in by submersibles during one of the many political corruption-induced unrests in Manila.

Despite being scattered across the Pacific, each of the electromagnetic pulse generators received the same cellular phone call within a few minutes to trigger the explosively pumped flux compression generators and their firing sequence. All the pulse generators were of a similar design, consisting of aluminum tubes surrounded by copper wire helixes. Each unit was of a size easily carried by a person yet could produce electromagnetic pulses in the millions of amperes and tens of terawatts. Over time, they had been combined that most of the packages had over a hundred such charges. Explosive charges within the aluminum tube detonated, blowing out the tubes along the axis and propagating the coil-covered tube radially outwards, deforming the discoid protuberances and pushing the coils outward. As the explosion progressed in an instant, a magnetic field was compressed within each module by the conductive piston and the simultaneous drawing together of the inner faces, also creating an inductive current. As the induced current attained its maximum, the fuse opening switch fused and the load closed simultaneously, allowing the current to be delivered to the load. The device itself was destroyed within a few seconds of operation, which was more than enough time to generate an intense yet short burst of electromagnetic energy.

Hit by the pulse at the speed of light, power went out in large swaths of the Philippines, Tokyo Japan, Hawaii, California, and Washington State as transmission lines were overloaded with induced high currents and voltages. Transformers arced, causing circuit breakers to close if fast enough, igniting from intense heat and exploding if too late. Radios crackled, and television screens went blank. Computers running within twenty kilometers were almost instantly subjected to high-current arcing and rendered inoperative.

The Chinese military engineers had selected key frequencies to take advantage of the fact that the warships in nearby naval bases were for the most part running on shore provided auxiliary power. So close were the selected locations to naval bases that even warships designed with some nuclear EMP protection were impacted. It was seemingly random which magnetic drives and computers had enough shielding and which were wiped clean by the electromagnetic pulse.

Air force bases fared little better with pilots left wondering just how much of the electronics in their warplanes had been lost and whether the planes would ever be air-worthy again.

For many personnel and civilians, they at first thought they were dealing with a power outage, only to find electronics burnt out, various small fires raging outside, and every light and electronic device inoperative. For those suffering the consequences of the electromagnetic pulse, there was no way to even call for help leaving soldiers, sailors, police officers, firefighters, and civilians feeling vulnerable and defenseless.

SEPTEMBER 2, 2068 6:15 PM
WEST OF TIAWAN

Twelve Chinese Xian H-6 bombers in close formation made their way from the mainland to just south of the island of Taiwan before turning north. The pilots listened for any counter order over the radio. Hearing none, they ordered their respective weapons officers to proceed.

Sitting on each bomber wing were a total of three YJ-12 supersonic missiles. At the scheduled time, each supersonic missile detached and dropped before the integrated ramjet booster propulsion system activated to rocket the supersonic missiles to over four hundred kilometers an hour down toward Taiwan.

The Republic of China air defense systems covering the entire island of Taiwan were always active, and the missiles were quickly detected by multiple AN/MPQ-65 radar sets with alerts issued. Sky-Bow III missile launchers automatically fired off Tien Kung 3 interceptor missiles.

The seventy-two YJ-12 missiles faced more than three times the number of interceptors, some of which hit their mark. The objective of the YJ-12 supersonic missiles, however, was never to strike any targets on sea or on land but instead detonate their EMP warheads as close to the island as possible. Sensing their impending demise, the surviving YJ-12 missiles detonated, beaming concentrated electromagnetic energy racing at Taiwan.

Radar systems pulsed with electromagnetic radiation, overloading their capability to process information. Cities went dark as power transmission lines overloaded and surge protection systems tripped at the high voltage. Various weapon systems operators cursed, finding that there was just too much damage to certain portions of their integrated electronics and that the system as a whole was rendered inoperative. Crews rushed to prioritize, determining which air defense batteries were still operational, calling up backup units and manning older anti-aircraft guns while commanders used backup phone systems to mobilize soldiers in preparation for an amphibious landing.

A real shooting war was being waged for Taiwan once again. In some ways, this was the latest chapter in the civil war that had gone cold yet continued to fester. The People's Republic of China was, after more than a century, acting on its threat to use force to take the island.

CHAPTER TWENTY-TWO – THE DRAGON

COMES

"Those who deny freedom to others, deserve it not for themselves"
—Abraham Lincoln

SEPTEMBER 2, 2068 5:15 AM
PRC AMPHIBIOUS CARRIER FUJIAN
SOUTH CHINA SEA

At long last the power of the Chinese navy was being unleashed. So proud of the moment was Admiral Luo Yan that he chose not to direct the operations from the Combat Information Center safe within the superstructure but from the bridge of the Type 75 amphibious assault ship, so he could witness the deployment in the flesh. The warship before him, all running lights on, was nothing less than a helicopter carrier, the Chinese version of American Landing Helicopter Docks (LHDs) such as the Wasp and America class. The *Fujian* combined the functions of helicopter carrier, command center, and transport dock into one being fully capable of deploying landing craft, hovercraft, and helicopters. Within her hull were thousands of soldiers for the liberation of Taiwan. She measured the length of two and a half football fields and displaced more than 3500 tons.

The Type 75 amphibious assault ship sat to the center of the task force, dwarfing the five smaller 2500-ton Type 071 Yuzhao-class amphibious transport docks around her. The Type 071 amphibious ships, looking more like landing ships than carriers, simply didn't exude the same might as the Type 075. Those smaller dock ships would land troops on the beaches while the Type 75 would launch penetrating raids further inland. Around the landing ships were a variety of escorting warships, including an advanced Type 055 destroyer and four Type 054A frigates.

Beneath the waves, a Type 39A Yuan-class attack submarine escorted the task force.

At the moment, the admiral was content to listen over the intercom to the battles raging across two dozen islands in the South China Sea. His helicopters had pre-deployed Marines and half an hour ago received the order to engage the Filipino and Taiwanese rebels on the contested islands of the South China Sea. Caught by surprise, with no United States Navy support and no hope of reinforcements from their now besieged homelands, the defenders were being quickly overrun. Everything seemed to be going according to plan, and Admiral Luo Yan couldn't help but smile as he looked down on the flight deck. To his disappointment, he made out four Marine-filled helicopters still on the flight deck where they had been ten minutes ago. He turned to the executive officer with a scowl and pointed down at the source of his displeasure. "Those helicopters should have been off this deck five minutes ago!"

The executive officer turned from his display. "Philippine Naval Forces on Second Thomas Shoul still have an operating surface-to-air missile battery. We lost a transport helicopter." On seeing the startled reaction of the admiral, the executive officer quickly handed him a tablet with the latest situation map. "A momentary setback. All other operations are on schedule. We have just secured Nansha Island from the rebels."

Second Thomas Shoul was well known by the admiral. Back in 1999, the Philippines' navy had intentionally run around on the shoal an old World War Two American LST-542 tank landing ship to serve as an outpost asserting the Philippines' sovereignty in the South China Sea. The Philippines' marines had, over the years, added a surface-to-air missile battery and a makeshift flight deck capable of launching up to four helicopter gunships. He pondered an all-out missile strike but decided against it, given missiles were better saved for the battle for Taiwan and the risk of counter-missile fire at his warships in shallow waters. "Send gunships!"

"We were planning to use amphibious marines as to not risk surface-to-air missiles" Executive Officer Wan explained. "We're preparing divers—"

Admiral Luo Yan shook his head to display his impatience. Did the officer not understand that time was of the essence and that they should be moving on to the real prize of Taiwan? He grabbed a transmitter and pressed down on the transmit button. "Get me two gunships on the deck."

"Yes, sir," came the voice of the flight deck officer.

The executive officer bowed his head in subservience to the authority of the admiral. "As soon as the SAM site is destroyed, I will deploy those helicopters." The executive officer set about tasking the gunships with destroying the platform.

The admiral spun around to look back down on the flight deck. The two flight deck elevators were raised, each with a respective Z-10 helicopter gunship. The Soviet look of the gunships was no mistake, as the Z-10 was based on a Russian design from the Cold War.

The executive officer, wanting to quickly alleviate the frustration of the admiral, radioed the flight deck crew to launch the Z-10 attack gunships right off the elevators. The gunship rotors began to spin and lift the helicopters into the air. Both gunships disappeared over the horizon to the East and the first hints of sunrise.

A flight officer turned up a volume knob that all could hear the radio transmissions of the helicopter gunships. Radar displays showed the position of the gunships approaching the platform.

"Arming missiles" boomed the voice of one of the pilots. The gunship pilots would use GJ-10 missiles, the Chinese equivalent to the laser-guided US Hellfire missiles.

"Incoming miss—" came a shout over the radio frequency followed by a burst of static.

"Bravo Two is down!" the remaining Z-10 pilot declared. The first Z-10 had fallen victim to a MANPAD shoulder-launched surface-to-air missile. "Engaging target."

The executive officer considered giving the admiral a stern look for the loss of the gunship but decided against it.

The Chinese gunship pilot opened fire on the the Filipino soldiers still manning the platform with the autocannon chain gun he achieved a target lock and fired off a GJ-10 missile at the center of the former landing ship. "Target destroyed."

The admiral lifted his arm and gestured for the transport helicopters to take off. "Secure that island." Seeing the four transport helicopters begin to lift off the flight deck, the admiral decided it was time to head below deck to the Combat Information Center to better implement the next phase of the operation. So large was the Type 75 ship that it took eight staircases to reach the CIC deep within the hull. The admiral was greeted by a room full of salutes as he entered. "Situation report Vice Admiral He."

His deputy flag officer raised his head in the direction of the main display. "Our forces have secured the Spratley islands. The mainland has commenced missile bombardment of Taiwan. The first and second carrier battle groups remain north of Taiwan, having commenced air superiority flights and strategic bombing of the island in preparation for our landing. Some reports of South Korean and Japanese forces aiding the Taiwanese rebels, but nothing unexpected. The EMP blasts have certainly put a damper on their response." He pointed at the position of their task force far to the south. "As expected, the Taiwanese forces are all focused on the mainland and the north."

"That's our window." Admiral Yan knew that having the two large aircraft carrier task forces to the north was part of the plan as both a distraction and to counter any American, Japanese, or Korean intervention, but he grew uneasy at the mention of their activities nonetheless. His task force wasn't yet part of the primary campaign to reunify China, the South China Sea being but a stepping stone. Would his fleet even see any combat? Would the rebels of Taiwan be so surprised by the amphibious assault coming from the south that the island would fall without a chance for him and his men to earn glory in battle? "Order our task force to proceed north to Taiwan at twenty knots. What of the Philippine Navy?"

"I don't foresee any threat, given the fact that they are somewhat occupied by our Indonesian allies." The Vice-Admiral didn't speak with confidence, having little faith in the Indonesian Navy. Still, the display showed numerous Indonesian warships up and down the coast. The Philippine islands themselves were under missile attack from both sea and air. "Many of the Filipino warships were caught by complete surprise and sunk while still in harbor by our air force."

The admiral rubbed his hands together. The southern coast of Taiwan beckoned on the display. "Range to our objectives?"

"Our lead warships are nearing missile range of Pratas. The air force is bombing their missile sites, but we still risk anti-ship missiles." The Pratas Islands were three atolls just north of the South China Sea occupied by the Nationalist rebels.

"Commence missile bombardment of Pratas as soon as in range. Once their missile batteries are confirmed destroyed, land marines and capture the islands," Admiral Yan ordered. He looked up at the radar display to take in the western coast of Taiwan being pounded by missile strikes launched by H-6 supersonic bombers. The Taiwanese rebels did manage to get at least a hundred aircraft in the air—F-16 Fighting Falcons and AIDC Ching-kuo multirole combat aircraft, which were engaged in a fierce air battle with Chengdu J-20 and Su-30 air superiority fighters. That he had no true aircraft carrier of his own was of no concern, given how close to the mainland his fleet would be. The admiral entered a few commands into his tablet before handing it to the officer manning the sea warfare station. "These are a list of surface-to-air batteries and anti-ship shore defenses on Taiwan we are to target with cruise missiles in preparation for our invasion."

Eyebrows were raised by most of the officers manning the CIC. To maintain secrecy, most of the crew had only been told they would be going into combat within the last twenty-four hours, and even then, they'd been told only of the mission to take the South China Sea. There was always a worry of Nationalist sympathizers in the ranks, even after more than a century.

With a loud cough, Admiral Yan both cleared his throat and ensured he had the attention of every man in the operation center. "Our mission is to proceed north to Taiwan, bombard key targets, use our helicopters to penetrate island defenses, and then proceed with an amphibious invasion via the more accessible southern beaches. The aircraft carrier battle groups to the north are nothing more than a distraction from our effort, the liberation of the rebel province of Taiwan. The Nationalist regime will finally be put out of its misery once and for all." He stamped his foot. "Glory and honor are ours."

A younger communication officer cheered at the order to be joined quickly by a bandwagon of clapping and hollers from officers and enlisted men.

Admiral Yan nodded his approval at the euthanasic reaction while reflecting again on the situation presented on the main display. Between the position of his task force and the southern beaches of Taiwan was open sea. The final defeat of the Nationalists in Taiwan was all but guaranteed. Nothing could stand in his way.

CHAPTER TWENTY-THREE – FIRST STRIKES

"God grant me the courage not to give up what I think is right even though I think it is hopeless."
—Chester W. Nimitz

SEPTEMBER 2, 2068, 6:35 AM
NLS AYN RAND
EAST OF THE SOUTH CHINA SEA

Grace Jaden rushed into the Combat Information Center of the *Ayn Rand*. Over the past few days, the *Ayn Rand*, the *Tolkien*, and the *C.S Lewis* had made their way up the Sulu Sea in the direction of the South China Sea. Both the Saar 6 and the Tuo Chiang-class corvettes were made to be stealthy and with a slow course purposely right along the coast the ships were virtually undetectable.

The new commanding officer, Commander Norman Berg, pointed up at one of the main display screens where he had projected various news reports. "Flash message from SEATO. Taiwan, the Philippines, Japan reporting major power outages, radar systems going offline. At least six civilian jetliner crashes as well."

General Lawrence sat at an empty station trying to make sense of the news reports. "Electromagnetic pulses?" he guessed.

Grace Jaden nodded in agreement. "It's begun."

As commander of the armed forces of New Liberty, it was technically General Lawrence's role to order their forces into combat. He leaned over in the direction of the nearby communications officer. "Get a word out to the *Intrepid* that they are to proceed." He grabbed hold of the console as if the rolling of the ship had suddenly increased in intensity.

"Wish this wasn't all going down at sea so I could have boots on the ground."

"Not entirely unexpected for a sea state." Nolan stood next to Jaden with a forced smile to lighten up the mood. "I understand the Philippines and Taiwan, but the wire is showing power outs in Japan and the United States West Coast as well. Coincidence?"

"Doubt it," Grace Jaden said. "Though I predict it will be extremely difficult to prove it was the Chinese government."

"Well, hopefully, we take some of those bastards with us." General Lawrence leaned back in his chair, knowing that all he could do now was offer the sailors some moral support. "Make them pay."

"Hopefully Admiral Davidson takes it to them."

"Should we order the Bonhomme Grace to get her birds in the air?" General Lawrence asked of the commanding officer.

"Not yet," Commander Berg walked over to his electronic plot. "With full radar capabilities, that Chinese task force would make short work of our aircraft. And we don't want to give away our position."

"*Bonhomme Grace?*" Jaden looked over at Lawrence.

"Your son named the carrier," said the general, smiling.

Grace Jaden couldn't help but roll her eyes while hoping she would one day be able to protest the naming of the ship in person. She tried not to think of the odds of that occurrence, given the fact that their small three-ship taskforce was about to join in an all-out shooting war against a Chinese battle group.

"Have the formation go to general quarters," Commander Berg instructed his executive officer.

The sharp blaring sound of the *Ayn Rand's* klaxon filled the electronics-packed space. On all three warships, headset-wearing sailors hunched over glowing screens and consoles, speaking quietly over radio and intercom circuits while preparing the vessels for battle.

Grace Jaden kept her eyes on the main display and watched as the status of every weapon mount and sensor system in the task force switched to a status of "manned and ready." "You think we've got a good plan?"

"A *crazy* plan," Commander Berg chuckled. "But any plan that gives us even a fraction of a chance for three small ships to change the course of the war, though, is a stroke of genius. I'll try my best to carry it out."

"Passing between the Calaman and Palawan Islands," the navigation officer reported. "Entering the South China Sea."

Commander Berg knew that their ability to survive long enough to engage the enemy depended on hiding among the coast of the islands. "Keep all radar systems passive and keep her as tight with that shore as you can without running her aground."

SEPTEMBER 3, 2068 10:21 PM
INTREPID
SOUTH CHINA SEA

Admiral Davidson had kept as few personnel onboard the captured tanker as possible—an engineering staff of twelve, four sailors to help navigate her, and six officers to man the missile launchers they had snuck aboard and installed under the cover of blue tarps. The *Intrepid* was at twenty knots heading northwest through the South China Sea as fast as he dared move without attracting the attention of the large Chinese task force to the West. Admiral Davidson stood on the bridge, staring out at the Pacific as the sun set to the west. "Keep a parallel course with the Chinese task force." He looked at the helmsman, "No drastic moves. What's our position?"

"Fifty kilometers south, 102 kilometers east of Pratas Island," the sailor manning the helm, Lieutenant Ristov, reported.

Admiral Davidson turned away from the still-dark sky and made his way to a console, communicating over Wi-Fi to a rather unique piece of equipment. Nolan's company, Cynet, had provided a piece of equipment installed near the fore of the ship capable of sophisticated passive radar detection. The rather exotic artificial intelligence system was detecting multiple radar signatures and attempting to identify them with very little data. Surprisingly, the artificial intelligence system managed to detect contacts and provide identifications. Several were third-party tankers similar to the *Intrepid*, which no doubt had kept the Chinese fleet secretly supplied and on-station for over two months.

The strongest signal was identified as the Type 55 Renahi-class guided-missile destroyer *Nachang*. The type 55 destroyer was almost a third larger than that of a US Alleigh Burke-class destroyer, 108 meters long and armed with over a hundred vertical launch systems, long-range surface-to-air missiles, anti-ship cruise missiles, a rail gun, and two anti-submarine warfare helicopters. The *Nachang* appeared to be covering the east side of the Chinese task force with the majority of the ships positioned north to face the Taiwanese navy.

"Chinese task force moving north toward Taiwan now at ten knots. I've got at least one Type 55 destroyer to the east, three Type 52 Luyang III-class destroyers to the north, and four Type 54 frigates. At least eight tankers." Davidson pointed to the display. "These radar returns are pretty close together. I bet that's four seventy X-type landing ships and the Type 75 helicopter carrier. That Type 75 is our primary target."

A flash of light in the night sky to the northwest caught the attention of Lieutenant Ristov. "Visual contact bearing about two-seven-zero degrees."

"Missile launches." Admiral Davidson watched his screen fill up with symbols representing airborne contacts. The passive system was good but not good enough to generate complete tracks, so the exact targets were unknown. Even so, it was obvious the targets were to the North. Taiwan was about to get hammered. "It's dark now, let's get ready to take our shot while we still can."

Days ago it had been a pleasant surprise when Davidson learned that the weapons officer who had volunteered for the mission, Lieutenant Matt Lauinger, was an expert on the missile launchers brought aboard. On hearing the need for a volunteer while serving on the *Ayn Rand*, Lauinger had quickly raised his hand. His late wife had escaped Hong Kong years ago before passing away from a rare form of cancer. Fighting Communist China felt like he was honoring her memory. "No way I can get a shot off. No radar to lock on."

"Objective isn't to hit the ships. These missiles all have EMP warheads. We want air bursts before they arc down." Admiral Davidson pointed at his screen, which was filled with detected missile launches. "Even with the element of surprise, there's no way we'd ever get a shot from this hulk through their air defenses for a hit anyway."

Lauinger nodded in understanding while working out how to program the missiles. "Can do. Just get me in as close as you can."

It was a dangerous game. The closer the admiral brought the *Intrepid* to the Chinese battle group, the more attention she would draw—but the more likely it was that the missiles would do their job before being shot down. "Will get you to within one hundred kilometers."

The thin-bearded weapons officer rubbed his jaw in thought. "I think we might as well take the shot from here."

Admiral Davidson was so surprised he turned from the display to face the weapons officer. "Really?"

"By the time the interceptor missiles come into range, we'll be detonating them."

"Let's give it an hour and get within one hundred kilometers."

The weapons officer had to admire the courage of the naval commander. "You aren't afraid they'll sink us?"

"Why would they? We are part of their happy fleet," Admiral Davidson tried to sound as brave as the sentiment while straightening his stance and making his way back to the sailor manning the helm. "Hopefully they're too busy firing at our allies to notice us." He patted the shoulder of Ristov at the helm. "It's night now. Let's set up the missile launchers. Set her to auto-pilot and have your bridge team and the engineering crews start to prepare to abandon ship."

The sailor double-checked the auto-pilot on the ship and the course that would swing north in half an hour and put the tanker on a parallel course with the Chinese task force. "Aye, sir."

It took over half an hour for the crew to un-tarp the missile launchers with little to no light. Hydraulic rams were activated, raising the two M142, and three Yun Geng missile launchers sprawled out on the deck. The trailers were meant to be towed by trucked vehicles but seemed to work fine having been lifted by crane and placed directly on the deck.

During that time Lauinger made his way from launcher to launcher with his laptop which he used to program the missiles.

Admiral Davidson did one last walkthrough of the tanker he had called home for the past couple of weeks and made his way up to the empty bridge. The occasional flashes of light over the horizon coupled with the decreasing temperature of nightfall sent shivers up his spine. He took in the warmth of the bridge as he closed the hatch behind him, knowing it would be the last heated room he would be in for quite some time. With a few touchpad commands at the helm station, he deactivated the propellers of the tanker. The lights blinked momentarily as the electrical generators ramped down. The noises of turning turbines were replaced with that of wind and waves as the tanker came to a halt. The massive tanker began to gently rock with the waves of the Pacific.

Lauinger marched his way up the stairwell and entered the bridge with a salute. "Now or never, Skipper."

"Key in the firing sequence. Give us thirty minutes," Admiral Davidson ordered. He did a quick check to ensure that no sailors were left behind.

The weapons officer held his hand in the air with his pointer finger aimed down at the keyboard. "Last chance to change your mind."

Closing his eyes and taking in the heat one last time, Admiral Davidson nodded. "Go for it."

With the tap of his finger, Lauinger activated the firing sequence. The radar images were replaced with a thirty-minute countdown.

"Let's get the hell out of here." With urgency, Admiral Davidson and Lauinger dashed out of the bridge and down onto the main deck to meet the assembled crew of twenty-two sailors. The first group was already in their diving suits and lowering themselves into the Pacific. The most courageous of the lot leaped off the side and disappeared with a splash.

Tied off to the *Intrepid* were four of the large semi-submersible hydro jets, each with two large fuel tanks attached. He hoped his calculations were right—that they would have enough fuel to get close back to the Philippines. It would be a long, slow trip. "Everyone off!" he shouted as he began to put on his diving suit.

Lauinger screamed "Geronimo!" before jumping off the side of the ship, falling more than three stories and splashing into the Pacific.

The admiral stood alone on the tanker beneath the star-filled sky. After one last look to ensure he was the final party to leave, he untied the semi-submersibles and dropped the ropes down. The waters were calm. Careful not to end up landing on the vehicles or crew, nor hit the side of the *Intrepid*, he leaped from the side and dropped ten meters into the ocean. He reached around to open his air tanks and flush out the saltwater.

Wanting to get as far away from the *Intrepid* under the cover of night as possible, Admiral Davidson activated the hydro-jets as soon as he saw everyone was tied off. The vehicles accelerated under the waves and automatically turned to the east. Unfortunately, being underwater, there would be no way for him to see if the firing sequence would be effective nor the fate of the *Intrepid*.

Thirty minutes later, the programmed firing sequence issued the command for the modified M142 and Yun Geng missile launchers to fire. Over a dozen modified MGM-140 missiles shot into the air before streaking to the west. Unlike most anti-ship missiles, these were programmed to gain altitude and speed fast and arc in on their target.

PRC DESTROYER NACHANG
SOUTH CHINA SEA

The air weapons officer on the guided-missile destroyer *Nachang* was the first to raise an eyebrow at the missile launches, which he at first thought was perhaps a stealth Indonesian or Navy special operations warship joining in the barrage against Taiwan. For the past hour, the warships of the Chinese task force had been clearing a path for the landing ships, destroying several corvettes and twelve aircraft, hitting at least twenty defense batteries, and simultaneously downing any counter-missile fire coming their way. But then the missile track was projected to be directly coming in on the Chinese warships. "Vampire coming in from bearing nine-zero degrees!"

His commanding officer rushed to confirm the radar detections. "Engage!" the commander demanded while helping to key in commands for the automatic firing of HHQ-9 surface-to-air missiles. The H/PJ-11 close-in weapon system and the HHQ-10 short-range surface-to-air missiles were already set to automatically fire within a range of twenty-five kilometers without any action on the part of the sailors.

Given the speed of the incoming missiles each of the MGM-140 missiles reached their destinations and began to detonate in the air a full minute before they would have been intercepted by the HHQ-9 anti-missile missiles. The traditional warheads of the MGM-140 had been replaced with explosively pumped flux compression detonators. Deep within each warhead, small explosives blew coils outwards, which for a brief instant, prior to their destruction, generated an electro-magnetic pulse that propagated at the speed of light focused forward on the Chinese task force.

The Chinese task force of seven destroyers, four frigates, a large helicopter carrier, and six landing ships was bathed in electromagnetic radiation. Radar screens went dead, either as a result of being overloaded with information or damage as receivers were subjected to high voltage. One older Harbin Z-9 helicopter without adequate electronic shielding lost power and, hovering just over the ocean, fell powerless into the Pacific.

PRC AMPHIBIOUS CARRIER FUJIAN
SOUTH CHINA SEA

Minutes ago, Admiral Luo Yan had silently yet contently watched the main situation display deep within the Chinese amphibious assault ship. He had to actively stop himself from smirking with each missile track emanating from the ships of his task force as they pounded Taiwanese and Filipino air and anti-ship missile batteries to the north and west. Then, without warning, the screen went blank. The blood drained from the admiral's face. "What just happened?"

The surface warfare officer pounded both fists against his terminal in frustration. "We've lost radar telemetry from the majority of the fleet!"

Admiral Yan stormed over to the air warfare officer, shouting into his headset. So engaged was the air warfare officer that despite seeing the admiral approach, he continued to converse with the destroyer *Nachang*. With no reported visual sightings of more incoming missiles, the officer spun his chair around to face the admiral. "Missile attack against the task force from the east. Looks like an EMP detonation." Having given his report, the officer spun back to his terminal and began to rewind the recorded radar data, looking for the source of the missiles.

The admiral stood, perplexed. Had the Philippines' Navy decided to target his task force? What course of action should he take? Realizing he had no idea what was coming next, he focused on the survival of his task force. "Any more incoming missiles?"

"Hard to say, sir." The air warfare officer pointed at an icon on his display. The radar played back the incoming missile track clearly launched from the contact right into the taskforce at near point-blank range. "Looks like it came from our own tanker!"

Friendly fire? Or traitors? The admiral urgently shouted at the communications officer. "Raise that tanker!"

"Tanker not responding to our hails," came the response of the perplexed communications officer.

This wasn't the time to take unnecessary chances. "Order the *Nachang* to take out that tanker. Anti-ship missiles now!" the admiral commanded. With sailors still assessing the damage, he had to worry how long would it take for the order to be transmitted, received, and implemented. Would they have to use signal lights?

A small victory came with new symbols on the screen; enough electronics were still in place for the order to be broadcasted from the *Fujian* to the destroyer *Nachang,* and at least one radar system was able to confirm a resulting missile launch. The admiral kept his eyes glued to the track of the YJ-19 anti-ship cruise missile from the vertical launch system of the stealthy Type 55 destroyer all the way to impact.

NLS AYN RAND
SOUTH CHINA SEA

The passive EL/M02247 MF-STAR radar on the *Ayn Rand* detected the momentary electromagnetic pulses before the screen went practically blank. "They did it," Grace Jaden pumped her fist in the air at the good news. While they couldn't make out the positions of the Chinese warships, it would be increasingly difficult for the fleet to make out the small stealthy corvettes of New Liberty. While still outnumbered at least thirty to one, the odds had shifted, however slightly, in their favor. "Gentlemen, start your engines."

Adrenaline surged through Commander Berg, who was anxious to join the battle. For the past hour, the CIC had echoed with reports of missile strikes and air dogfights over the Philippines and Taiwan. Doing nothing but staying hidden was unnerving, to say the least. "All right, fire up the radar systems for a few minutes, and see if you can get me some targets." He picked up a receiver and pressed down on the transmit button. "Engine room, full ahead flank!"

The three corvettes of New Liberty began to tear through the waters of the South China Sea in pursuit of the Chinese fleet.

The radar now actively transmitting three close-proximity contacts came up on the screen. "Contacts Alpha, Bravo, and Charlie. Alpha signatures are of an LST-542 landing ship. Must be the Teluk Saleh!" The old United States landing ship was among the largest amphibious assault ships in the Indonesian navy, and she was racing toward Palawan Island. "Bravo's a Clurit-class fast-attack craft. Charlie is a Komar-class missile boat!"

Estimating the range at fifty kilometers on the plot, Captain Berg issued orders before even hearing the exact range and bearing. "Harpoon missile, take out that Komar!" He had only sixteen anti-ship missiles that he intended to save for the Chinese task force but one well-aimed shot from the Komar would end his mission before it even began.

The foredeck of the *Ayn Rand* disappeared into a burst of smoke as a Harpoon missile shot up into the night sky. It would take five minutes for the missile to crash down on the Komar.

Commander Berg held his breath, hoping that the missile would hit in time before the Komar could get off a shot. A minute passed with all eyes on the continually updated situation plot. "Naval gun, target the Clurit class."

"Vampire, vampire!" the air warfare officer yelled as the Komar fired off a barrage of P-15 Termit anti-ship missiles. "Engaging!" With a few keystrokes the C-Dome fired off three Tamir interceptors downing two of the older Termit missiles. The automatically aimed Phalanx close-in-weapon-systems of all three frigates detected a missile that had made it through the screen and opened fire pumping a stream of depleted uranium shells into the air. One shell hit the missile, causing it to explode just as it entered visual range.

Without similar air defenses, the Komar missile boat had no such recourse as the Harpoon missile came crashing down and exploded.

The *Ayn Rand*'s Italian built Oto Melara 76mm main gun was loaded with Vulcano guided projectiles. Through the use of targeting computers, the gun turned, aimed, and opened fire. It took only sixteen seconds for three projectiles to smash into the still-approaching Clurit-class fast attack craft. There was no need for explosives. The projectiles were at a high enough speed that they tore through the vessel, puncturing the fuel tank. The fuel vapors soon ignited, and the entire ship erupted into flames.

"Good shooting!" said Captain Berg, leaning over the shoulder of his surface warfare officer. "Now the landing ship."

"Try to limit casualties," Grace Jaden urged, knowing that the Indonesian forces were of limited capability compared to that of the Chinese task force.

Berg nodded. "Target their engines. Fire!"

The *Ayn Rand* opened fire with her naval gun yet again. The large slower-moving Indonesian amphibious landing ship was an easy-to-hit target. The shells smashed through the engine compartments, destroying four gensets and leaving the vessel without power.

"So far, so good," General Lawrence

"Now on to the *real* threat. The hunted become the hunters."

The *Ayn Rand* and her escorts cut through the waves, racing toward the Chinese taskforce.

CHAPTER TWENTY-FOUR – A HAIL MARY

"Damn the torpedoes! Four bells. Captain Drayton, go ahead! Jouett, full speed!"
—David Farragut

SEPTEMBER 3, 2068, 11:36 PM
NLS BONHOMME GRACE
SULU SEA

Its engines roaring, the F-35B Lightning II lifted off the deck of the Bonhomme Grace. It took firing the engines over their rated power to lift the plane vertically up. Peter Jaden waited for the makeshift aircraft carrier to pass under him before making what would be his one and only attempt at getting completely airborne and, even then, took a deep gulp of air. He swung the rear thrust vectoring nozzle into the horizontal mode while tilting the nose of the aircraft down. The aircraft dropped even as it accelerated forward, and it looked to the deck crew watching that it would crash straight into the ocean. Pulling with all his might Peter Jaden was able to keep the aircraft in the sky, skimming over the waves with just enough speed to finally pull up and gain in altitude. He turned the plane around to get a look at the production-ship-turned-makeshift-aircraft carrier.

The *Bonhomme Grace* was at full speed to help with the launching of aircraft but had no active radar and only two running lights on for the deck crews, so she was hard to spot. Given the Frankenstein of a ship was arguably a floating fire hazard with only one close-in weapon system for defense, that suited Commander Jaden fine. "All right, *Bonhomme Grace*, let's get those drones in the air."

"Launching all squadrons!" Andrews oversaw the aircraft launch operation from the bridge of the Bonhomme Grace. Drone after drone raced off the flight deck. Both the Sea Ghosts and the Sentinel drones had bat-wing fuselages and both emissions and bandwidth management for multi-spectral stealth. The RQ-180B Sea Ghosts looked like baby B-22 stealth bombers while the MQ-10B Sea Avengers looked more like miniature F-22 fighters. Once clear of the carrier flight deck, the black drones disappeared into the night sky. With a glance at the flight deck controller, confirming all the drones were away, Taggart picked up a receiver and pressed the transmit button. "All drones in the air. Godspeed, Hail Mary Leader."

The radio crackled. "Appreciated, Poor Grace Command."

Her mission was complete, as all her drones were in the air, and since she had no practical weapons of her own, the further the *Bonhomme Grace* was from the battle, the better. Andrews squeezed the shoulder of the rather young officer at the helm. "Turn East. Get us out of here as fast as she can."

The sailor had no objections to turning away from danger. "Yes ma'am." The rudders of the *Bonhomme Richard* turned hard to port as the propellers ramped up and cavitated to turn the modified tanker around.

Andrews took a look out the bridge windows into the night sky. It was pitch black that none of the drones were visible. Wanting to see how the drones were making out in the air she made her way to the back of the bridge and down a stairwell to where the drones were being piloted remotely.

HAIL MARY LEADER
SOUTH CHINA SEA

Commander Peter Jaden pulled back on the throttle to accelerate his F-35 Lightning II to cruising speed while dropping as close to the ocean as possible. It would be hard for the Chinese radars to detect his aircraft flying low under the horizon but not impossible. He hoped that the element of surprise would be worth the risk of flying so low. All he could see out the cockpit was pitch black, so he had to fly using only his instruments. Not trusting the autopilot, he held his flight stick with one hand, even as he reached over to switch on a transponder to allow the squadron of drones to follow. The RQ-180B Sea Ghosts were to engage aircraft, and the MQ-10B Sea Avengers were to engage the surface ships. Knowing it was futile, Peter looked back anyway to see if he could make out the drones in formation behind them, and sure enough, all he could see was blackness with hints of cloud cover. He turned back to the glass cockpit and prepared his aircraft for combat, being sure to keep his radar on passive mode, lest he alert the Chinese fleet to his presence prematurely. After minutes of just listening to the spinning of his aircraft turbine, worrying that the relative calm would dull his senses, he unsnapped his oxygen mask while activating his headset transmitter. "*Bonhomme Grace*, this is Hail Mary leader. You receiving?"

Within the hull beneath the bridge complex of the *Bonhomme Grace*, Lieutenant Karla Wognar watched over a variety of crew members at their monitors in a darkly lit control center. Each was flying a drone by remote. Although the drones had artificial intelligence capabilities and could be directed by Commander Jaden's F-35, the craft would be flown by remote for as long as possible to enhance their effectiveness. Twelve of the Sea Ghosts formed a v-formation with the F-35, and twelve of the Sea Avengers took up formation about half a kilometer back. "Roger, Strike Leader, this is Alpha and Bravo command. All drones are reporting, and the squadrons are formed up according to plan. Wish you had bought me an F-35. Would have loved to have flown beside you."

Commander Jaden felt a little more comfortable knowing that he had essentially manned fighters covering his back. Had communications not been established, the drones would have been going into combat with artificial intelligence systems that, while better than nothing, weren't particularly impressive in combat. "Aren't you flying beside me now?"

Flying drones always felt more like a video game than piloting to Wognar. No turbulence, no knowing that if you were shot down you were subjected to free fall and certain death. "This just isn't the same, Commander, and you know it. But I've got your six." She was no stranger to combat to the point she was somewhat jealous he was personally heading into a firefight while she only got to participate by remote.

An alarm sounded. Commander Jaden's eyes immediately looked over at the radar screen. Far to the north, the combined passive radar arrays of his fighter and those of the drones were identifying aircraft. "I've got contacts." As he looked in the direction of the contacts, his virtual HUD lit up with ranges showing them almost a hundred kilometers away. They were missile launches, a combination of Taiwanese and Chinese anti-air missiles. "Looks like some action to the north." The IFF transponders came up on the display, identifying contacts as three F-16 Fighting Falcons putting up a valiant fight against at least several Chinese Su-30 fighter craft.

Given the capabilities of her ship was limited to fleeing east, Andrews decided to make herself useful in the drone flight center by relaying the latest intelligence. "Looks like allies in distress."

Commander Jaden had to resist the urge to deviate from his flight path straight to the South China Sea to turn and hit the afterburners to help the beleaguered Taiwanese pilots. "We've got to focus on the mission. Note their position, though." Not wanting to get caught unprepared, he snapped his oxygen mask into place lest he have to pull some high-gravity evasive maneuvers.

Ten more minutes passed as he watched life and death battles play out before his eyes on the radar screen. Every few minutes, the hum of the turbine would be interrupted by the alarm of a radar contact blinking in and out of existence on his display. Some were so fast, they had to be cruise and interceptor missiles being fired to and from Taiwan and the Philippines. He tried to break the silence by radioing. *"Poor Grace, explain to me why I'm up here flying when I could be doing this by remote?"*

"Just not your style, Hail Mary Leader." Lieutenant Wognar's chuckle was loud enough to be carried over the radio frequency. "Can't let the robots have all the fun."

"Right." Commander Jaden nodded to himself, mentally agreeing that no remotely controlled drone would be as good as a pilot in the air. The conversation did remind him to ensure that his own electronic orders were ready to be sent to the squadrons of drones in case they lost contact with the makeshift aircraft carrier. In case contact was lost with the carrier the RQ-180B Sea Ghosts would continue to engage any interceptor aircraft, only engaging the surface vessels were there no airborne contacts left. The MQ-10B Sea Avengers were to always attempt to sink the largest surface ship detected afloat. The orders were so simple, he hoped even an artificial intelligence system could carry them out.

"This is supposed to be the future," Andrews said aloud.

Commander Peter Jaden and Lieutenant Wognar both shook their heads in disagreement. "Call me a Luddite then." Looking over at the electronic map screen, Jaden saw his fighter was now more than five hundred kilometers from the carrier and halfway to the intended targets in the South China Sea. The pilot reminded himself that time flies at more than a thousand kilometers an hour. "All right." He swallowed hard. "Let's light up the night."

Lieutenant Wognar nodded over at one specific electronic warfare specialist remotely piloting two of the Sea Ghosts.

These Sea Ghosts had no weapons of their own but instead were full electronic warfare packages. With the touch of a screen, both EW packages activated, sending out electric signals at various rotating frequencies, making it almost impossible for the Chinese fleet to figure out what they were facing. "ECM and ECCM systems are active."

PRC AMPHIBIOUS CARRIER FUJIAN

Fearful of the unknown the blank situation monitors represented, Admiral Luo Yan rushed to order early warning radar-equipped helicopters be dragged out of hangers and put into the air. After the electromagnetic pulse had knocked out most of the radar systems of his tank force, the admiral had expected the worst in an all-out counter-attack by the Taiwanese air force, navy, or in the worst case, both. Whatever radar was functional and still communicating with the fleet, including mainland launched combat air patrol fighters, he had scanning the north seeking out any such offensive.

The admiral could feel the seconds tick by. How much time did they have before the first missiles struck his ships? It was all but inevitable. Nationalist sympathizers must have infiltrated their tanker. He found himself wishing once again that he was on a real aircraft carrier with Ilyushin Il-76 airborne early warning and control, AWAC, craft. All he had, instead, were some fighters from the mainland and a couple of helicopters with limited AWAC capabilities.

The situation display blinked as the first radar sets scanned the north to find . . . nothing.

To the surprise and relief of himself and his officers, the initial radar returns showed no incoming attack from the North. Admiral Yan closed his eyes in relief as he mentally thanked fate for allowing his fleet to undeservedly dodge a bullet. He opened his eyes, not quite believing the initial radar data. His eyes again came into focus to find nothing apart from the expected air battle raging over and around Taiwan. He allowed himself to commence breathing normally and contemplate the invasion of the rebel island just as the air patrol began to circle to the east. His heart skipped a beat on making out a noticeable gap in the radar returns. He pointed up at the screen. "What's going on there?"

The nearest air warfare officer saw the admiral's concern and immediately tasked the squadron of Su-35 and J-20 fighters to focus their active radar on the blind spot. To the surprise of the officer, the display updated to reveal a muddle of symbols. "Electronic countermeasures to the east!" the officer reported.

The jamming could only have one explanation. His fleet was under attack from the air, not from the north but the east. "Order the combat air patrol to engage!"

HAIL MARY LEADER

At the controls of his F-35 Lightning II, Commander Peter Jaden allowed himself the flicker of a smile at having the advantage. The Chinese air combat patrol, three SU-35 fighters, and two J-20 stealth fighters all had their active radar on, so he knew exactly where they were. He armed two of the AIM-260 Joint Advanced Tactical Missile (JATM) missiles and pulled the trigger. "Fox Three," he radioed to his remote wingmen while switching targets, "Fox Three!" he fired again.

The rocket engines of the American beyond-visual-range air-to-air missiles ignited, lighting up the night sky as they shot out and up in the direction of the Chinese air superiority fighters racing in his direction.

Similar shouts from his remote wingmen joined his announcement over the radio frequency as six of the Sea Ghosts, each targeting a different fighter, fired off one or two missiles in the direction of the incoming Chinese fighters.

The Chinese pilots flying toward what they expected were perhaps three or four Taiwanese aircraft pulled up in surprise. The first J-20, specifically targeted by Jaden due to its advanced stealth capabilities, exploded before the pilot even had the chance to launch chaff pods and flares.

The element of surprise had allowed Jaden to get his fighters in close enough that he could see the fireball of another exploding J-20 along with additional far-off flashes of light in the night sky. The radar blinked to show the second J-20 and most of the SU-35s were no longer detectable.

Two of the SU-35 Flanker-E fighters were able to pull up and survive, using the Russian design's high maneuverability and ability to achieve supersonic speed without the use of afterburners while launching chaff pods to avoid destruction. They leveled off and each fired off R-77 medium-range active radar homing air-to-air missiles.

An alarm flashed to indicate that at least one was locked on his fighter. Peter Jaden forced himself not to instinctively pull up but to continue to skim the sea as the missile closed in on his position. Only after a long breath did he pull up while simultaneously launching countermeasure flares and chaff, causing the two missiles locked on him to detonate against the surface of the ocean. He leveled off in time to see two more R-77 missiles after the Sea Ghosts on his screen. One hit home, causing the drone to explode. The other missed, the Sea Ghost being able to evade with countermeasures.

Sea Ghost drones maneuvered to avenge their fellow drone. "Fox Three!" Lieutenant Wognar's voice radioed as six AIM-260 Joint Advanced Tactical Missiles blew one of the Su-35 fighters out of the air.

Seeing that the lone remaining Su-35 was in a good position to evade the missiles locked on it high up in the air with distance, Jaden had his F-35 shoot up in altitude in pursuit. As soon as he was within a kilometer, he fired off two more AIM-260 missiles which struck home. So close was he to the exploding Su-35 that he had to pull left on the flight stick to avoid crashing head-on into the debris. Breathing heavily, he snuck a look at the radar screen, which showed that all was clear. He quickly used one hand to access to the virtual HUD commands. "Did anyone see what happened to the second J-20?" he shouted into his headset while rewinding the electronic record of the battle.

That's when he saw the tracers of bullets shoot past his cockpit. Only his instinctive need to rock the fighter back and forth prevented the automatic gunfire from tearing up his F-35. Time being of the essence, he pulled back, sending the F-35 into a barrel roll. "Under fire!" he yelled.

The J-20 had survived and was on his tail. With radar not active, the Chinese stealth fighter was impossible for the other drones to lock onto.

"Damn it!" Commander Peter Jaden shouted at himself, in part to distract his mind from the pain of crushing g-forces brought on by the roll. His flight suit pressured up to help regulate blood flow and prevent the pilot from passing out. Still, the bullets shot out from behind him. Jaden reached down and activated the air brake flaps while pulling hard on the flight stick, sending the craft up and into an uncontrolled stall. He had escaped the incoming fire of the J-20 only to now be falling toward the ocean below with only seconds to impact. With only one trick left to play, Jaden put all his effort into reaching over to adjust the engine nozzle, turning it slightly to try to stabilize the craft. The strain was so excessive that, for an instant, Jaden thought he had miscalculated and the whole engine would rip away. Only a look at the horizon indicator, showing he still had some velocity, told him otherwise. As soon as he had enough speed, with two hands on the flight stick, he fought to stabilize the craft. With a grunt, he locked the engine nozzle back into the horizontal mode only seconds from crashing into the ocean. He ignored the ironic thought that the very VTOL capability of the F-35, which he had condemned again and again as a jack-of-all-trades-and-master-of-none—not even close to the F-22 in performance—had just saved his life. Still, the aircraft had taken some damage, given the level yet turbulent flight. He had to just hope the aircraft would hold together, as there was no way he could repair the damage. "Where the hell is he?"

"Switching to thermal infrared imaging," Wognar radioed as she searched the display screens of the control center. The drones searched the sky, but trying to find the stealth aircraft in the night sky was next to impossible.

"He's going to use his guns!" Jaden urged over the radio knowing the Chinese pilot would avoid using active radar to pick off the drones one by one. "As soon as he opens fire you cut engines."

It took a few seconds for Wognar to understand what Jaden thought her remote pilots should do. Her flight crew nodding, Wognar gave a thumbs up to no one in particular. "Wilco!" Taking the strategy a step further, Wognar pushed her chair back and sought out the console of the Sea Ghost at the highest altitude. She pushed the drone pilot aside and quickly acted to reduce the speed and straighten out the course of the aircraft. Another button switched the radar of the drone to active.

"What are you doing?" the drone pilot protested, only to be silenced by her serious glance.

As predicted, the purposely slowed Sea Ghosts was shot up by the Gatling gun of the J-20 stealth fighter that had come up just behind it "Eat this, asshole." Lieutenant Wognar issued the command to activate the air brake flaps. The drone, stabilizing to a virtual halt in mid-air, was pulled back by the turbofans of the J-20 before colliding with the stealth fighter. The shock of the impact caused the J-20 stealth fighter to begin to disintegrate into a shower of debris. The pilot ejected off to safety just as a ruptured fuel tank exploded.

"That is a kill," Commander Jaden confirmed as he watched both the flaming debris of the J-20 and the Sea Ghost fall to the ocean. With the screen clear of airborne threats, the strike formation now had a clear path to the Chinese fleet, but for how long? "Attack drones, light up your targets! Let's give them hell!"

PRC AMPHIBIOUS CARRIER FUJIAN

Admiral Luo Yan adeptly hid his surprise and fear on seeing the telemetry from the air combat patrol disappear off the situation monitor. Mentally, he knew he had to face the reality that his air support had fallen victim to whatever foe he was now facing. The priority now had to be self-preservation, the survival of his carrier, and the thousand Marines aboard. "Turn West, full ahead flank. Order the *Nachang* to cover us!"

The surface warfare officer turned from his display with a horrified look on his face. "But the landing ships are to the east!" At least four slower-moving Type 73 landing ships were positioned to the east of the carrier. The large 850-ton vessels resembled freighters, each loaded with five hundred infantry and four amphibious tanks. Like freighters, they were slow and difficult to maneuver.

"We have a battalion of troops onboard ourselves!" the admiral Luo Yan angrily shouted back. Now logically was the time for rationalism but was he being seen as a coward? He pushed the thought aside before quickly adding, "Have the *Sanya* and *Handan* stay back to cover the landing ships." The two Type 54 frigates to the east would have to cover the four landing ships to starboard. He wanted the advanced anti-air warfare systems of the Type 55 destroyers covering his amphibious carrier. "All weapons-free. Ensure whatever operational radars we have are active."

As the power plant and propellers of the Chinese amphibious carrier powered up the rudders turned almost violently to port. The deck, along with the entire forty-thousand-ton mass of the carrier, leaned sharply to the left as the blaring sounds of the klaxons echoed in the night.

"Inbound missiles!"

HAIL MARY LEADER

The air battle finished, and the path was now clear for the airstrike. The formation of twelve MQ-10B Sea Avengers overtook Peter Jaden's F-35 and the remaining six Sea Ghosts. "At least eight landing ships. These radar returns are pretty close together. Further west is the Type 75 helicopter carrier. That Type 75 is our primary target." Between his air group and the Type 75 were at least three frigates. "She's moved north. We'll have to take out the two frigates and knock out some of these straggling landing ships."

The first pair of Surface To Air Missiles flashed up out of the darkness, blasting off the Chinese Type 54 frigate, *Sanya*. More than twenty miles away, Peter Jaden could make out the spectacular and frightening sight. "We've got incoming. Better start your attack run!" All of the Chinese ships had their radars active, so there was a good chance the Chinese frigates would be able to spot the stealth drones despite their small size.

"On it." Wognar watched the range to the Chinese fleet decrease to less than twenty miles. The General Electric TF35 turbofans went to full power as the Sea Avenger drones began their dive at the Chinese task force.

The barrage of surface-to-air missiles passed over the formation of Sea Avengers and instead took down the Sea Ghost, still jamming various frequencies.

"Targets in range and selected. Commencing attack run!"

Each of the MQ-10B Sea Avengers opened their bomb bay doors, exposing their position. But before Chinese fire control radars could lock on, they released a barrage of AGM-123 Skipper IV laser-guided missiles. Compromised of a Mark 83 bomb with a stealthy case fitted with a Paveway guidance kit and two solid propellant rockets, the munitions rained down on the targets. Three of the Sea Avengers were engaging the frigate, *Sanya*; another three were on the *Handan*; and each of the others was taking on a landing ship.

New pairs of fiery streaks of SAMs leaped up from the frigates, followed by the gunfire of automated Gatling guns. Some of the AGM-123 munitions were downed and went off, yet others hurtled closer.

The landing ships could only fire their heavy machine guns into the air, the tracer fire lighting up the night sky.

An enormous explosion flashed, blindingly bright, ahead. One of the slow-moving Type 73 landing ships left without cover was struck by an AGM-123. From his cockpit, Jaden could see a dull orange glow far off in the distance. He switched to infra-red to make out the gray-white freighter-looking silhouette of the landing ship growing whiter by the second as fires raged out of control. "That's a hit on a Type 73." Steadying on a new course, more to the west, Jaden scanned the southern sky, noting the glowing sparks streaking low over the water. It was impossible to see the details, as the frigates launched SAM after SAM as the munitions closed in.

An AGM-123 struck the Type 54 frigate, *Sanya*, dead center. Any hit on a frigate-sized ship by a modern anti-ship missile essentially put her out of action, killing dozens of sailors in a searing blast and condemning survivors to deal with raging, out-of-control fires and potential sinking.

Three of the Sea Avenger drones exploded as they were hit by more sophisticated surface-to-air missiles from the more advanced guided-missile destroyer *Nachang*. A Sea Ghost was downed by a hail of rail gun shells.

"Damn it." Commander Jaden could see, too, that the primary target was getting away to the west. The Chinese were using early warning helicopters with advanced radar to detect his drones enabling the warships to pick off with missile and gunfire. "Sea Ghosts, with me. Sea Avengers, take out those landing ships."

The F-35 and the Sea Ghosts accelerated toward the Chinese amphibious carrier and the *Nachang* as the Chinese frigate *Handan* disappeared into a giant white fireball.

Another Sea Ghost exploded just to the left of Jaden's F-35. Knowing he was running out of time and drones he pulled the trigger as soon as he had a lock on the first of the AWAC helicopters. The AIM-260 Joint Advanced Tactical Missiles made short work of the helicopters, sending them crashing into the sea.

The victory was short-lived, as a stream of Gatling gun shells tore through the left-wing of the F-35, sending it into an uncontrollable spin.

"Eject, eject." the flight computer's calm and feminine voice advised as the airframe continued to break apart.

"Punching!" Peter Jaden's hands grabbed hold of the yellow-and-black-striped loop beneath his legs, and after a deep breath, he pulled hard. Small explosives blasted the canopy clear of what was left of the F-35 before the ejection seat was rocketed out of the fighter. The blast was quick and disorientating. He could see nothing but black as he was tossed and jolted in the open sky, spinning into freefall. Bracing for a high-speed collision with the surface of the ocean sure to kill him, Jaden cursed that he never got to take a shot at the Chinese flattop. He closed his eyes tight and prepared for the end. Instead came a hard jolt upwards, a jolt so hard he could feel muscles pull. He looked up to see his chute deploy automatically.

CHAPTER TWENTY-FIVE - THE BATTLE OF THE SOUTH CHINA SEA

"I have not yet begun to fight!"
—John Paul Jones

2:07 AM
NLS AYN RAND
SOUTH CHINA SEA

The *Ayn Rand*, *Tolkien*, and *C.S. Lewis* plowed through the South China Sea. In the CIC, Grace Jaden, General Davidson, and Commander Berg stared at the life-or-death battle raging on a monitor. Symbols crawled, appeared, and disappeared. There were far fewer blue dots representing New Liberty drones than there had been. Grace Jaden felt faint on seeing the symbol that had been her son's F-35 aircraft blink out of existence.

"*Hail Mary* bailed," came the transmitted voice of Lieutenant Wognar.

Had she lost her last son in battle? Grace Jaden could feel her resolve slipping away.

General Davidson squeezed her shoulder. "He'll be all right. He's a survivor."

What was the point of all this death? Grace grabbed hold of a console to keep herself from falling as the world continued to spin. It had to mean something. She had to ensure it meant something. Her muscles tensed and neurons fired. "Did we accomplish our objectives?"

Commander Berg pointed at a display while explaining what he was seeing. "We got at least four of their landing ships and two frigates. Peter took out their helicopters, reducing the radar coverage, so the Sea

Avengers were able to get these landing ships, but further in is that advanced missile frigate which made easy work of them."

Grace Jaden continued to process the information. The amphibious carrier was getting away. Would the losses be enough to cause the Chinese fleet to break off their landing?

"Can they kamikaze the drones into the carrier?" Nolan suggested.

Commander Berg frowned. "Their air coverage is still just too good —just lost another Sea Avenger. We've got only a handful of drones now."

General Lawrence rubbed his chin. "It's not enough."

The Chinese task force kept moving north. "It's not enough," Grace Jaden agreed. "Project the course of the amphibious carrier."

The surface warfare officer punched up a plot that ran north.

It was east of where Jaden wanted that carrier. "Damn. We have to take out that carrier or push her west. You said those AWAC helicopters were down?"

Commander Berg hunched over the display. "Yes. Peter and the Sea Ghost drones took care of them."

"Can our ships approach undetected?"

Berg took another moment to examine the display before swiveling around. He considered advising against any more offensive action but decided to do so would be dishonorable. "We can probably get a shot or two in. Very unlikely we'll be able to get close enough to that Chinese carrier."

"Commence surface attack," Grace Jaden added. "Push them west."

Reaching up to grab the nearest headset, Commander Berg began issuing orders. "Bridge, full ahead flank, course two seven zero. Laser the *Tolkien* and *C.S. Lewis* to follow us in loose formation." He tapped on the monitor. "Primary target is that Type 55 destroyer and then the Chinese Type 75 carrier. I want a missile barrage in the air to the south at least five minutes before engagement."

Under the cover of darkness, the corvettes raced toward the Chinese taskforce. They could only hope that the Chinese radar was so damaged by EMPs and the airstrike that they could sneak in close enough to get off some shots.

PRC AMPHIBIOUS CARRIER FUJIAN

How could this have happened? And on his watch! Admiral Luo Yan hung his head in disgrace trying to cope with his losses. Only a disconcerted look from a young surface warfare officer reminded him he still had a job to do. The enemy aircraft—most if not all of them drones—had to have come from somewhere. He would find their base of operations and obliterate it.

"Only three drones remain," the air warfare officer reported, trying to lighten up the mood in the Combat Information Center.

Admiral Luo Yan reviewed the order of battle. He still had the majority of his fleet but had lost more than a quarter of the landing force. Enough to proceed with the invasion of Taiwan, he calculated. Perhaps he could still play a vital role in the Communist victory over the Nationalists. "Order all ships into close formation and resume course to the north." He clenched his fists. "Victory will be ours."

The surface warfare officer stood up from his panel. "Surface contacts to the East!"

NLS AYN RAND

"Vampire, vampire." Using the radio shorthand for anti-ship cruise missiles, the air weapons officer alerted the crew that missiles were coming right at the New Liberty corvettes.

The report of the incoming missiles made it clear that at least one of the corvettes had been spotted. "Open up!" Commander Berg instructed.

The deck of the *Ayn Rand* disappeared into plumes of smoke and fire as Harpoon missiles shot out into the air followed by a barrage of surface-to-air missiles. The Gatling gun of the C-RAM system began pumping shells into the night sky at the incoming Chinese missiles.

Having fallen behind and too far to engage the guided missile corvette, the naval gun of the *C.S Lewis* opened fire on nearby landing ships. The gun sent guided projectile shells at high kinetic energy right into the engine room of a large Type 73 landing ship.

The fuel tank of the Chinese troop carrier exploded with such force that the entire 850-ton hull capsized, plunging hundreds of soldiers beneath the waves in a matter of seconds.

The naval gun on the *C.S. Lewis* sought out a second target when Chinese anti-ship missiles penetrated through her screen of Sky Bow interceptor missiles and the C-Ram close-in weapon system fire to hit her flight deck. The entire aft portion of the corvette exploded into flaming debris, sending the rest of the hull twisting forward.

"Lewis is hit!" the surface warfare officer grimly reported.

Commander Berg felt his blood boil at the thought of the sailors he would never see again. "Bring our barrage in from the south!"

The combined barrage of twenty Harpoon missiles from the late *C.S Lewis* combined with missiles from the *Ayn Rand* and *Tolkien* and accelerated down at the guided-missile destroyer *Nachang*. Some fell from interceptor missiles, others from rail and Gatling gun fire. Another fell harmlessly into the ocean, going after a decoy. In came four more missiles from the south; these had been fired earlier on a long trajectory to be called in later. The sea and sky lit up again as a Harpoon missile struck the bow of the *Nachang*, followed seconds later by a second hitting the guided-missile destroyer dead center in the superstructure. Fragments reached her missile and gun magazines, after which the guided-missile destroyer disappeared into a plume of multiple smaller explosions.

PRC AMPHIBIOUS CARRIER FUJIAN

One minute, Admiral Luo Yan was listening to a steady stream of reports and orders being issued from the darkened Combat Information Center. The next minute, it was replaced with an eerie silence as all eyes looked up at the main display. A real-time infrared image from a deck-mounted camera showed what was left of the guided-missile destroyer *Nachang*, a fiery wreck.

Sailors in the Combat Information Center were glad the room was dark, as it hid the tears in their eyes as they watched the burning wreckage.

Luo Yan's taskforce's most advanced escort warship and hundreds of sailors gone. The admiral wanted to close his eyes as if he could wish away the scene, but a battle still raged on. Casualties were to be expected. The Politburo demanded sacrifices to be made for the Communist Party. The normally calm admiral was unable to contain his rage. He also still had a landing force to get to Taiwan. Enough was enough; the time to storm the beaches and take Taiwan had come. And still on the plot was an enemy corvette. "All landing ships to the northwest!" said the admiral, pressing down on a transmitter. "All frigates to finish off that flotilla!"

NLS AYN RAND

Racing toward the *Ayn Rand* were the Type 52 destroyers, *Xuchang* and *Yiyang*. With less sophisticated fire control systems, they were only able to fire on the *Ayn Rand* with a barrage of anti-ship missiles, but the *Yiyang* had a powerful railgun, which pumped out shell after shell.

The entire Corvette was rocked by the impact of shells crashing into the superstructure of the ship. One hit the flight deck, sending an unfueled helicopter crashing into flight personnel before tumbling into the sea.

Ayn Rand's Oto Melara 76mm Super Rapid naval gun returned fire, the surface warfare officer, finding comfort in the fact that the *Yiyang* was taking as good as she was giving.

The CIC filled with smoke from the engine room, which was now engulfed in flames. Grace Jaden fell to the deck, struggling to breathe through toxic smoke. Blood oozed from various cuts from the broken glass of monitors.

The power went out momentarily leaving the sailors in pitch black before the emergency lights activated. Without the power plant, the naval gun was nothing more than an expensive paperweight. Commander Berg grabbed a handheld radio. "Emergency power. Switch to batteries. Prepare to abandon ship."

General Davidson grabbed hold of both Grace Jaden and Nolan and dragged them to the hatch. "Let's go!" he called back at the sailors of the CIC.

NLS ATTACK SUBMARINE NAUTILUS

It had been a frustrating couple of weeks for the crew of the New Liberty submarine *Nautilus*. First, they had to sit for weeks motionless on station hundreds of meters below the surface towed into position by a Japanese freighter. Then, there had been hours of listening to a battle raging above on the surface, as Captain Hayes had to order his crew to do absolutely nothing.

The Swedish-built Gotland-class submarine was powered by two sets of Kockum-built Sterling engines with tanks of onboard oxygen. The Sterling engine was operated by cyclic compression and expansion of hot gas heated only by the combustion of hydrogen and oxygen-producing water. For a couple of weeks, his conventional submarine would be as quiet as—perhaps quieter, than—any nuclear-powered submarine.

At long last, the sonar officer, Lieutenant Jenkins, could hear the approach of the expected Chinese landing force from the south. Even then, as the ships of new Liberty attacked, Captain Hayes had to order his sailors to do nothing but watch the passive sonar in silence. The Chinese amphibious carrier was too far off for a guaranteed torpedo strike. Jenkins could make out the twin screws of the Chinese amphibious carrier *Fujian* propelling her right toward the *Nautilus*.

Hayes hovered over the computer display watching the sonar-station-produced waterfall chart confirming the findings of the sonar officer. "Prepare for attack," he softly ordered. "Get me a firing solution. All torpedoes on that carrier."

Every sailor on the submarine held his breath as the carrier drew nearer. Some of the landing ships passed overhead. The swishing roar of a frigate rushing south echoed through the submarine.

Captain Hayes kept his eyes on the display, the range decreasing. The submarine was too deep for a good shot. "Diving officer, bring her up to seventy-five meters."

The submarine came alive as valves opened to release compressed air into the ballast tanks, making her slightly buoyant as the water was pushed out of the hull. The *Nautilus* slowly rose.

"What about those frigates?" asked his executive officer, pointing at the screen.

"Racing to the south, no doubt to engage our forces. Hopefully too fast to worry about us." Captain Haynes mentally prayed he was right.

Once the depth stabilized, Captain Hayes did a last-minute check of their position. He turned to the fire control officer, who nodded to indicate without a word that his firing solutions were ready and loaded. He grabbed an overhead support and took a deep breath. "Shoot!"

The torpedoes were blasted out of the tubes by a pulse of water before their own propellers activated to speed them toward their target. The high-pitched screw noises made by eight torpedoes were unmistakable.

PRC AMPHIBIOUS CARRIER FUJIAN

Aboard the *Fujian*, the officer manning the high-frequency sonar frantically screamed into his headset. "Incoming torpedo barrage, due north!" The amphibious carrier was headed right into the path of the oncoming torpedoes.

Admiral Luo Yan dashed to the anti-submarine warfare station, not believing he had heard the report correctly. "Did you say torpedoes?"

That the entire carrier was swinging to port while collision klaxons activated was all the confirmation the admiral needed. Reports were coming in left and right. He heard the ship's captain order decoys to be launched.

Time seemed to slow down for the admiral.

The enemy fleet had pushed them right above an enemy submarine waiting for them the entire time. What had destroyed his fleet? A couple of drones and corvettes? One submarine. He chuckled at the thought that at least his defeat was at the hands of a strategist to admire. He closed his eyes and waited.

Three torpedoes slammed into the *Fujian*. Three plumes of yellow-stained water and smoke fountained high into the air, the detonations enough to break the back of the carrier. Water flooded into the hull.

Having been flung into a bulkhead, Admiral Luo Yan fell to the deck, unconscious with a deep gash in his head, so he didn't hear the screams of the drowning marines nor experience the CIC filling with the saltwater of the South China Sea.

CHAPTER TWENTY-SIX – RESOLUTIONS

"Thank God, I have done my duty."
—Horatio Nelson
SEPTEMBER 3, 2068, 3:36 AM
NLS NAUTILUS
SOUTH CHINA SEA

Contact is breaking up." The sonar officer of the *Nautilus* could hear the hull of the amphibious assault carrier filling with water, numerous explosions, and alarms. Listening closely, the officer thought he could hear the shouts of sailors trying to extinguish one of many fires and the calls for survivors to abandon ship. The massive carrier with helicopters and soldiers still in the hanger began to submerge and split in half.

There was no time to celebrate. Captain Haynes knew his submarine was detectable above the thermocline. All three Chinese frigates above would have their location marked by sonar and be out to avenge the loss of their flagship. They had to escape. "Dive! Dive! Depth to three hundred meters, ahead full!"

The diving officer allowed the ballast tanks to fill with water as the propeller of the *Nautilus* began to power up.

The first incoming torpedo came not from the surface but from a Chinese submarine below a temperature gradient. The sonar lit up with the shrieking of incoming torpedoes, which emerged from the depths.

"Torpedo! Bearing Seven Eight!" the sonarman shouted.

Panicked faces turned aft in the direction they could hear the torpedo.

The Gotland class submarine was running out of time. "All ahead full! Diving planes down!" Captain Haynes had ordered not just the rapid filling of the ballast tanks but the force of the propellers to send the ship racing to the bottom of the sea. The hydrostatic pressure on the hull was increasing with every meter in depth, resulting in the hull creaking ominously. "Load counter-measures." He considered the use of active anti-torpedoes but placed his bet on leaving countermeasures above the thermal gradient as *Nautilus* slipped beneath. A thermocline is a thin but distinct layer of water in which temperature changes more drastically with depth, dividing an upper mixed layer from calm deeper water beneath. As the density of water changes with temperature, thermoclines will reflect sound and potentially conceal a submarine from sonar above. "Come on. Dive, baby, dive!"

The control room crew kept their eyes on the rapidly increasing depth. "Two hundred meters," the diving officer announced.

The thermocline was somewhere between 210 and 220 meters, or at least it had been earlier in the day. Captain Haynes made his play. "Launch counter-measures!" Please, Lord, let us make it. As the submarine passed where he believed the thermocline was, he added, "Right full rudder!". The submarine tilted abruptly as it turned. He leaned back against a bulkhead to await the fate of him and his crew.

From dedicated launching barrels, two on each side of the submarine, shot a variety of Leonardo-built C304/S countermeasures designed to draw off the incoming torpedoes. Each functioned as both a jammer and a mobile target emulator. The jammer had a highly efficient transducer covering the whole receiving bandwidth of the torpedo's sonar with a switching amplifier and high-energy-density thermal battery. The jammer generated a very high amount of energy spread over the reception band that would mask the sound of echoes from the intended target, making it hard to sort out any data. The mobile target emulator was a sophisticated transponder to simulate a real Gotland-class submarine, generating in real-time acoustic echoes. The trick in the programming was making the countermeasure appear to be easier to detect than the submarine but not so easy to detect that it would be discounted by any torpedo fire control computer. The countermeasure would move as well and generate propeller noises.

The torpedoes, propellers, pings of active sonar, and the loud simulated screw noises of the countermeasures dipped in intensity as the submarine passed beneath the thermocline. The torpedoes took the bait, skimming the thermocline but not crossing, each pulling up to pick off the more detectable Gotland-class contacts.

"Torpedo screws fading." The sonarman knew not to sound pleased. It may be superstition, but any premature celebration would be condemned as jinxing the boat.

There was still an enemy submarine hunting the *Nautilus*. Where was she? "Quarter-speed. Rig for silent running!" Hopefully, they could disappear in the confusion of torpedoes and noisemakers. "Sonarman, find me a target!" The *Nautilus* had turned around to face the direction of the incoming torpedoes. She would be hard to spot by the Chinese submarine given the thermocline, but the Chinese submarine would have the same advantage.

Lieutenant Jenkins realized that it was now a battle of sonar skills, both the New Liberty and Chinese submarine trying to find the other first. His eyes focused on the waterfall plot as he ran algorithm after algorithm, seeking a pattern in the sound waves. All of the active sonar pings were above from the warships. Both submarines were playing cat and mouse with passive sonar. But who was the cat and who was the mouse?

The Godard-class had many features to enhance stealth with all shipboard machinery isolated and mounted on rubber dampers, a hydrodynamic hull design, infrared signature, and no less than twenty-seven independent electromagnets to counteract the magnetic signature of the hull. Captain Haynes tapped on a monitor to ensure short-circuiting extremely low-frequency electric field generators were on and the Sterling engines were fully functional. The captain, as with many in the control room, wiped the sweat from his forehead waiting. There was nothing to say, the sonar operator knew his job and how critical it was.

The submarine was near the maximum depth the submarine could operate, the hull having to counter the force of thirty thousand kilopascals of hydrostatic pressure. Internal piping, not having been tightened, began to leak. Sailors had to wonder if the submarine would implode, given the various metallic creaking and groaning.

"Three hundred meters," the diving officer reported while leveling out the dive planes.

"Keep her there." Captain Haynes patted the arm of the equally anxious diving officer.

A slight wave form appeared at thirty degrees on the sonar screen. Was it a wave form? Jenkins tried to get the computer to identify it as at least a potential contact, but there just wasn't enough of an echo for it to register. Could it be a whale? He listened to the headset for the hint of any sound that might warrant a torpedo. He didn't hear anything biological, but did he hear something mechanical? Was he hearing a nearly silent turbine spinning?

Haynes saw the perplexed look and rapid typing of the sonarman. "You've got something?" he asked quietly.

Jenkins pointed at the slight waveform. "Maybe. Could be nothing."

The submarine commander knew the look of a man afraid to make the wrong call. "Better to make a call than no call at all."

Lieutenant Jenkins made the call. Perhaps it was his mind seeing a pattern where none existed but the sonarman decided he indeed was seeing a waveform. "Weak signal—could be a reactor of a creeping boat."

Captain Haynes had a conundrum. He could shoot on the contact and probably take out the Chinese submarine, but the attack submarine would certainly snap shoot a couple of torpedoes in their direction. At this depth, he had nowhere to go but up where the Chinese frigates would make short work of a noisy submarine at full speed. Any fancy maneuvering and the hull might give in.

The weapons officer had already worked out that he would program the torpedoes to head in the direction of the contact, get to the approximate range of where he had thought the last pair of incoming torpedoes had originated, and then go active and hit whatever they found. "Shall I prepare a firing solution?"

Turning to the first officer, Captain Haynes decided to commit the submarine to action, although with unorthodox tactics. "Full stop. Drift."

"Sir?" The executive officer raised an eyebrow. Drifting at this depth would be dangerous and leave them unable to take evasive maneuvers.

Captain Haynes nodded. "Full stop, XO. Load forward tubes with Mark 60 CAPTOR mines into the tubes, and set to this depth."

The propellers of the *Nautilus* came to a halt. The submarine drifted with the calm but present currents of the ocean at such depth.

Crewmembers loaded Mark 61 CAPTOR mines into the tubes. The Mark 60 Encapsulated torpedo was a deep-water anti-submarine mine, which within held a Mark 46 torpedo. Within a minute, the display showed the torpedo tubes were loaded.

Haynes had hoped the time to load the torpedo was enough for the propeller to have completely come to a stop without cavitation but knew that in the ocean, wrong assumptions cost real lives. He double-checked the sound signature and propeller rotations. Both read zero.

Captain Haynes had to make yet another bet. "Set the CAPTOR mines to activate in twenty minutes. As soon as they are released, back away gradually."

The propellers of the *Nautilus* slowly began to spin the other way, propelling the submarine in reverse and leaving the discharged mines ahead. At such a slow speed, five minutes didn't give the submarine that much time but Haynes had worked out that it should be enough. He patiently waited next to the helmsman. "Start to turn her around, five degrees per minute."

With minute turns of the rudder, the *Nautilus* slowly began to come about. At five knots, it would take a painful amount of time for the submarine to completely come about. The submarine had turned from facing due-south to the west, ninety degrees, by the time twenty minutes had passed.

"CAPTOR mines active," the weapons officer replied, hoping that the programming was good enough that they wouldn't fire on the *Nautilus*. So slow and silent was the submarine that if detected, the mines would probably open fire on them.

Haynes stared at the sonar plot, which remained empty. He looked down to see Lieutenant Jenkins shake his head; he could no longer make out any hint of a sound echo. Another twenty minutes passed before the submarine was facing north.

The Chinese submarine commander must have worked out that Haynes would either shoot or run and had bet that his submarine could outrun and outlast his. With just a diesel and a Sterling engine, Haynes had to admit, that the Chinese Commander would be right. Hopefully, he wouldn't be expecting a surprise along the way, however. Captain Haynes reached up and grabbed a transmitter. "Engine room, activate diesel engine. I'll need full ahead flank, twenty knots in a minute."

"Ready, sir," came the response of an engineer.

All eyes in the control center turned to the Captain. On diesel, the Chinese submarine would easily make out their position.

Turning to the first officer, Captain Haynes also committed the submarine to action. "Full ahead flank, twenty knots to the north-east."

"Ballsy, Captain. An honor to serve with you whether this works or not," the XO chuckled before having the engine room switch fire up the diesel genset. The crew felt the *Nautilus* roar to life and leap under their feet. With the propellers accelerating, rapid changes of pressure led to the formation of small vapor-filled cavities, which then collapsed and generated shockwaves. The collapsing voids not only resulted in severe surface fatigue but were noisy—so noisy, the cavitation echoed throughout the submarine.

The Chinese attack submarine, immediately identified on opening fire as a Chinese Type 093 second-generation nuclear-powered attack submarine, fired off four torpedoes in the direction of the *Nautilus*.

The sonar of the CAPTOR mines detected both the Chinese Type 093 and the *Nautilus*, but the latter was so noisy, it was easily identified as a friendly Gotland-class submarine. That left only one target. Each Mark 61 CAPTOR fired out a Mark 46 torpedo from the aluminum shell. Being within half a kilometer of the Chinese submarine, which had sat waiting for its prey, the torpedoes closed the distance quickly—too quickly for last-second countermeasures to be effective. The torpedoes detonated against the hull of the Chinese submarine, causing it to lose any ability to resist the hydrostatic pressure. The hull of the Chinese submarine imploded, crushing most of the sailors. Water flooded the wreck in seconds, leaving no survivors.

"Full speed!" Captain Haynes shouted. The *Nautilus* had a head start, but the Chinese Yu-6 torpedoes could make more than sixty knots at full attack speed.. "Get me a firing solution on those torpedoes!"

Heart racing, the weapons officer tried to keep as calm as he could while working through the firing solution. He had some room to play with, but the torpedoes were closing in fast. It was a race, and the Gotland-class sub at twenty knots had no chance of staying ahead. He had two of the rear-loaded Bofors Type 2000 torpedoes set to head right at the torpedoes and proximity-detonate just ahead of them. "Solution ready."

Now was not the time for mistakes. Haynes looked at the chronometer and saw he had another minute. "Verify!"

The weapons officer double-checked his calculations and made a slight tweak to ensure the torpedoes were constantly matching the depth of the incoming torpedoes. "Verified."

Captain Haynes clenched his fist. "Shoot!"

Racing at full speed, the rear torpedoes shot right into the wake of the *Nautilus* and on stabilizing after all the turbulence, raced directly aft. The Chinese torpedoes didn't flinch and continued to race full speed at the New Liberty submarine.

"Load more torpedoes, quickly." Another look at the chronometer and the Captain saw the order was redundant. There wouldn't be enough time to fire off another barrage.

"This one's going to be close!" Jenkins called out while removing his headphones.

The sonar of the Type 2000 torpedoes showed they were directly ahead of the Chinese torpedoes. After undergoing slight adjustments to ensure they were right in the path and at the same depth, the torpedoes detonated. The shockwave at this depth was enough; four of the incoming torpedoes arced down further into the depths of the ocean where they were crushed by the hydrostatic depth. The two others lost their ability to navigate and raced harmlessly and randomly through the ocean.

Lieutenant Jenkins reviewed the sonar information. "No torpedo screws coming in on us."

"Full stop!" Captain Haynes snapped out the order, not wanting to attract any more attention. "Switch back to the Sterling, quickly!"

The XO shouted orders over the intercom, not used to the engines so loud. The diesel engines shut down, temporarily cutting off power as the control room lights flickered. The submarine went eerily silent.

All eyes turned to Lieutenant Jenkins on the sonar. Would the surface frigates be on them despite their depth? Or were they still preoccupied with the battle above?

NLS AYN RAND

Flinging the hatch open, General Lawrence dragged both Grace Jaden and Nolan onto the deck. Smoke enveloped the *Ayn Rand*.

The general cursed, having no idea which direction to go due to the thick smoke. He saw sailors rush toward the flight deck with firefighting equipment. On seeing the injured crew, one medic ran up and put an oxygen mask on Grace before opening up the valve.

Gasping for air, Grace Jaden took in the fresh oxygen. Only the oxygen kept her lungs breathing, given the soot she had taken in. Fire-suppression foam shot down from the bridge structures, mixing with saltwater. Klaxons and the shouts of sailors trying to keep the ship from being consumed by flames had her ears ringing. She was able to take off the mask, grab a rail, and look out over the deck.

The sea was dark, lit only by the flickering glow of ships on fire

With oxygen masks on and sailors putting out flames with extinguishers, Commander Berg tried his best to keep the Combat Information Center operational. The main display was out, so he could only see the plot on the surface warfare terminal. The *Ayn Rand* was hurt but still fighting on. The C-RAM system was constantly firing now, downing incoming missiles at point-blank range, the occasional flash of light from an intercept casting debris down on the crew, which was trying to keep the flames from spreading to the weapons magazines. It was a losing battle. Berg grabbed a radio. "All hands, prepare to abandon ship." At the same time, he wasn't going to give up without a fight. "Engine room, can you give me naval gun power?"

The plot showed the Type 52 destroyers *Xuchang* and *Yiyang* closing in on the *Ayn Rand*. The *Yiyang* had lost her railgun in the exchange, so the frigates would have to get into cannon range to finish her off. That is, if they didn't finish her off with missiles first.

"Sir, it's the *Tolkien*!"

The *Tolkien* had come up alongside the *Ayn Rand* and was exchanging Harpoon and interceptor missile fire with the frigates. The battered *Ayn Rand*, in turn, was making a radar lock on the stealthy *Tolkien* difficult.

The radio crackled. "*Tolkien* to *Ayn Rand*, get everyone's ass on the deck. We're coming to get you!"

NLS TOLKIEN

Sailors strapped to water jetpacks shot off the flight deck of the *Tolkien* carrying ropes and chains before crashing down onto the smoke-filled deck of the *Ayn Rand*. They rushed to tie the ships together, grateful that the ocean was relatively calm. As soon as the lines were tied together, winches activated to draw the two ships together.

The sky was alight with tracer fire from the two Gatling guns. An anti-ship missile streaked down, only to be downed by the C-RAM shells of the *Tolkien*. Shrapnel smashed against a radar stack on the crippled *Ayn Rand*, which crumpled overboard opposite the *Tolkien*. The *Tolkien's* naval gun powered up and began lobbing shells to ward off the Chinese frigates while interceptor missiles were fired off the bow.

Ropes and chains were tightened with the metallic screeching of the hulls rubbing against each other. Ladders from the flight deck of the *Tolkien* were raised and caught on the higher decking of the *Ayn Rand* to allow crews to cross between the two ships. Untrusting sailors quickly tied up the ladders. Any crossing between ships in the waters of the Pacific was unnerving.

"Get on!" sailors from the *Tolkien* shouted while grabbing their counterparts and dragging them to the fully intact frigate.

The fire suppression systems on the *Tolkien* were activated and aimed at the *Ayn Rand*. The leader of the rescue effort, a lieutenant commander, shook Commander Berg's hand as he came up on the deck. "You think we can tow her back to New Constantinople?"

"Not a chance," Commander Berg admitted, not wanting to put any more people in danger. "We're a sitting duck! I give it five to ten minutes before the fires reach the magazines." He pressed the transmit button. "*Ayn Rand* crew, this is Commander Berg. Abandon ship, halt all firefighting and get onto the *Tolkien* as fast as you can. That is a direct order."

General Lawrence led Grace Jaden and Nolan to the ladders. The rolling of the waves combined with the smoke was nauseating. Hand after hand, they kept climbing down, motivated by the worry a sudden jolt would send them crashing into the ocean below where they would no doubt either be drowned or crushed by the hulls pressed together.

The Captain of the *Tolkien* by the name of Sean Mackenzie watched the rescue effort silently and impatiently in the CIC. Was he to save one crew or doom two?

Berg looked back at the *Ayn Rand* one more time to see no one among the fires raging out of control. "Anyone still on the *Rand*?" he radioed.

There was no response.

Given the fact that waiting any longer could mean the loss of both ships, Commander Berg jumped off the deck of the *Ayn Rand* and crashed hard onto the deck of the *Tolkien*. "*Tolkien*, this is Commander Berg. Let's haul ass. We've got everyone off." He yelled at sailors to start cutting the ropes tying *Ayn Rand* with the *Tolkien*.

The *Tolkien* took off at full speed, ladders and planks falling down into the ocean. The C-Ram cannon was commanded to no longer attempt to protect the *Ayn Rand*. With all incoming missiles targeting the *Ayn Rand*, the autocannon ceased firing for a few seconds.

Two anti-ship missiles slammed into the port side of the *Ayn Rand*, one right onto the bridge and another into the vertical launch system magazines. Sections of the *Ayn Rand* superstructure collapsed before what was left disappeared into a raging inferno.

Medics rushed Grace Jaden, who was still disoriented and struggling to breathe, below deck with her arms hung over her shoulders.

General Lawrence was about to follow when he caught sight of Commander Berg communicating over his radio. He held his hand up against the Commander's chest to get his attention. "What's going on?"

"We're getting the hell out of dodge as fast as we can." The commander felt the corvette tilt in a hard turn to the east at forty-five knots. Water shot over the hull, and they dashed through the nearest hatch lest they be swept overboard.

A panicked shout over the radio caught the attention of all aboard. "Incoming torpedoes. I've got six . . ." There was a pause. "*Eight* torpedoes inbound. Range six kilometers and closing!"

General Lawrence and Commander Berg dashed down the stairwell to the Combat Information Center. They raced in to find the captain of the *Tolkien* calling out a list of orders.

"Anti-torpedo torpedo systems, fire a full spread! Reload and shoot. All VLS magazines to interceptor missiles. Task the naval gun for long-range missile defense." Commander Mackenzie took a deep breath while spinning to catch the attention of each of the sailors, "We're all on defense now. We run to the coast of the Philippines and we hide." On seeing Commander Berg and General Lawrence enter, Captain Mackenzie made his way in their direction so they could speak privately. "Welcome aboard."

"Thanks for coming to get us." General Lawrence shook Mackenzie's hand.

Commander Mackenzie sighed. "Well"—he shrugged—"we haven't gotten you out alive yet." He pointed at the plot. "We kept the frigates busy trading missiles, but they got smart and launched a full spread of torpedoes at us." Mackenzie then turned his attention to the missile magazine status monitor. "We're running low on interceptor missiles. I've got no anti-ship missiles left."

Anti-missile torpedoes dropped into the water from port and starboard launchers. Six hard-kill Seaspider anti-torpedo torpedoes shot back in the direction of the incoming acoustic torpedoes.

At forty-five knots, the *Tolkien* was moving through the water at the same speed as the torpedoes, though enough rouge waves or unexpected drag and the Chinese torpedoes would still catch up.

"You've got to get those frigates off your back. Why not return the favor?" Commander Berg suggested, on seeing the Chinese frigates at full speed themselves. They no doubt were preparing another barrage of missiles or calling in an airstrike from the mainland.

With an appreciative grin, Commander Mackenzie tapped the shoulder of the surface warfare officer. "Load both triple torpedo launchers, target those Chinese frigates, and shoot. And launch every decoy we've got."

Chaff shot dispensers, lobbed more infrared and radiofrequency chaff canisters into the air and the ocean in an attempt to keep the Chinese guessing as to their exact location.

Six torpedoes shot off the port and starboard sides and splashed beneath the ocean where they raced toward the Chinese warships. The chances of the weapons hitting the enemy were low but would certainly force them to slow down if not abandon the chase.

The race was on, the *Tolkien* at high speed rushing to disappear along the coast of the Philippines and the Chinese frigates in pursuit. The Chinese commanders were conflicted by a need to protect the remaining landing ships and the desire to avenge the loss of their flagship. Radio intercepts showed that they were constantly calling for an airstrike from the mainland but that any planes were tied up in the air battle raging to the north or engaged in search and rescue efforts.

While outmanned and outgunned, the Tuo Chiang corvette had speed and stealth. Commander Mackenzie knew that only the pre-cooled engine exhaust, used to lessen their infrared signature, and a reduced radar signature by means of a clean structure had kept them afloat thus far.

In the medical bay, sailors lifted Grace Jaden onto a bed. She tossed and turned, struggling to regain a sense of her surroundings. "It's okay!" a medic called while injecting a sedative, lest she go into shock, and pressing her to lie down.

"Mom!" a familiar voice in the bed next to hers rang in her ears. "Mom!"

Grace Jaden's head flopped to the one side of the bed. She struggled to force her eyes to stay open and focus.

Was it a dream? Through a haze, Grace made out the face of Peter Jaden. "Peter?"

Peter Jaden, loaded on sedatives given his back pain, could barely tap his flight jacket. "Saw my transmitter. They pulled me out of the ocean with a drone." He meekly extended his arm. "We do it?"

"We did it," Grace Jaden replied while taking hold of his hand and squeezing.

"I think Dad and Peter would be proud."

"I think you're right." With a combination of drug-induced and emotional satisfaction, Grace Jaden passed into peaceful subconsciousness.

CHAPTER TWENTY-SEVEN – PHANTOMS

"He that will not sail till all dangers are over must never put to sea."

—Thomas Fuller

SEPTEMBER 4, 2068 10:16 AM

BEIJING, CHINA

T

he premier of the People's Republic of China sat at his desk, mentally going over the timeline of events. Twelve hours since the commencement of Operation Liberation and Nationalist Taiwan had failed to fall as planned.

The operation had started well. As planned, electromagnetic pulse generators had crippled key installations across the Pacific to throw any rapid response by allies into disarray. The impressive radar and air force of Fortress Taiwan had been crippled. Taiwan's financial system and key infrastructure were out of action on an island already short on supplies. The message had been sent loud and clear to the United States that, with Taiwan occupied, any attempt at liberation would be seen as an attack on the mainland itself to the point Beijing would use nuclear weapons.

After bloody battles and the losses of countless ships to Feng IV anti-ship and Sky Bow V surface-to-air missiles, the army had taken the Penghu archipelago of ninety islets that lay thirty miles from the main island. The landing fleets were no longer subject to missile strikes against its flanks.

The main carrier battle group, including two aircraft carriers, went toe-to-toe with South Korean and Japanese support craft while launching airstrikes against Taipei and sinking much of the Taiwanese navy. Airstrikes had taken out top political and military leaders. Thousands of paratroopers managed to establish beachheads, where landing ships stormed the accessible western beaches.

The Philippines was unable to help their Taiwanese allies, having been hit by the Indonesian airstrikes in the surprise southern campaign. The South China Sea had fallen quickly to the combined Chinese and Indonesia fleet.

Victory seemed assured. The southern fleet would come up and flank any potential counter-attack against the beaches and clear a path for forces to move into Taipei. The Chinese fleet should have been able to steam into the ports of the capital virtually unopposed.

But the southern fleet never arrived, freeing up Taiwan's helicopter gunships and jet fighters to push back the Chinese air force while tanks, artillery guns, and missile batteries pummeled targets on the pre-targeted and heavily mined beaches.

In attempting to regain control of the skies, the northern fleet diverted its squadrons south, allowing the Japanese and South Koreans to fly in reinforcements and perform sorties over Taiwan.

With at least five thousand dead, the army had pulled back whatever marines it could back to the Penghu archipelago.

The senior Politburo cabinet entered the room and stood at attention in front of the desk. They each were expressionless, apart from crisp salutes from the military delegates. All dreaded the conversation to come.

Premier Shenkum didn't look up, even as a senior General placed a tablet on the desk with the latest military intelligence reports. "Premier Shenkum, the beach landing has been repulsed," his Senior Military Advisor acknowledged. "Without the planned southern front, the Nationalist rebels were able to concentrate their firepower."

At the time the People's Republic of China was be securing the Nationalist capital of Taipei, there wasn't a PRC soldier on the entire island of Taiwan apart from stranded paratroopers deep behind enemy lines without supplies. How could the situation have changed so quickly? What should have been the greatest military victory of the Chinese military since repulsing the US in North Korea was now perhaps its greatest military defeat.

More startling for the Politburo members was the report of the younger Minister of Internal Affairs. "At this rate, we will need all our forces to maintain order on the mainland. Hong Kong is practically in open rebellion."

"Your police forces have massacred thousands in Hong Kong," the General protested. "We will have to declare martial law and storm the city to regain law and order."

"How could the military have allowed those EMP weapons to strike the mainland?" the internal affairs minister retorted, unable to control his anger. "We've lost power in more than a dozen cities!"

Embarrassed for the politburo members bickering among themselves, Premier Shenkum looked up to eyeball the cabinet members while speaking in an unrepentant and uncompromising tone. "Enough, comrades. Enough." He reached over and gestured at his personal guards at the office door. "Send in the secretary-general and General Cho."

The politburo members looked at each other nervously, having expected more time to prepare for the head of the party to be brought in.

The premier's security detail brought in the elderly Secretary-General Jinpin and General Cho. The older man seemed to have more energy than he'd had in years, storming to the front of the desk and forcing the cabinet ministers to step out of the way. "You have failed, Mr. Premier. Forget Taiwan. We'll be lucky to still be in control of the mainland!" He slammed a diplomatic report on the desk. "The Americans are threatening nuclear war in response to our EMP attacks unless we immediately recall our forces, announce a ceasefire with the SEATO forces, and agree to recognize the sovereignty of Taiwan!" The Secretary-General's face was boiling with anger. "I will not fight a nuclear war to make up for your failings!"

The premier ignored the outburst. He glanced down at the paper and slid the report back in the direction of the secretary-general. "Nor should you have to." He looked up from the desk at what he considered to be a hapless old man. "You will sign this treaty."

The secretary-general took a step back in surprise. The world seemed to spin. He was supposed to be the one doing the demanding; the failure was that of the premier. The older man looked from side to side at the politburo cabinet members in puzzlement. He tried to refocus and get back on track, staring the premier eye to eye and pointing. "This is your failing."

"You are mistaken." Premier Shenkum pushed back his chair to stand tall and look down on the secretary-general. "This was all on *your* watch! This is *your* failing." He lowered his voice and spoke in a flat matter-of-fact tone. "You will sign the treaty and then resign. The committee has already met; the decision is made. You will name me the new secretary-general." He looked to the minister of internal affairs, making it clear that his loyalty would be rewarded. "I will declare martial law and crush these riots."

"You?" The secretary general recoiled in horror as if about to have a heart attack. "You are an epic failure!"

Premier Shengkun chose his words carefully. "I have reviewed the operational timeline. The failure was that of your supporters in Chinese intelligence allowing the South China Sea fleet to be compromised and costing us our best military commander." He eyed General Cho. "You as leader of the Armed Forces, including military intelligence, are to stand trial before a worker's court."

Having reservedly stood at the table, General Cho interjected. "On what charge?"

"Charges of high treason."

General Cho shivered in despair. His forces had been defeated and disgraced. He considered simply accepting his fate but decided to at least try to save his life. "Nothing more could have been asked of our forces. We inflicted serious damage—"

"Enough," the premier interjected. "This failure is on your command. You should be relieved to be sentenced to death." Shenkum nodded in the direction of a guard, who reached for the pistol in his holster.

The secretary-general shook his head in disbelief. A general who had personally led forces into combat, who had commanded men to storm the fortress of the Penghu Archipelago, was being sentenced to a humiliating trial and dishonorable death by the politician whose strategy was ultimately responsible for the failure. It was too much. He raised his hand while nodding almost uncontrollably. "General Cho and his forces fought with honor. You c—"

"Comrade Secretary-general." Premier Shengkun cleared his throat. "We had a window, and General Cho did not take advantage of it." He changed the topic of conversation while leaning across the desk. "You will sign the treaty and resign, naming me the new secretary-general." He turned in the direction of the politburo members, who knew the stage was set for them to nod. "The senior party officials have discussed the matter and have come to an agreement that it would be unsuitable for you to continue in your post after bringing such humiliation on the People's Republic."

With a snort, the secretary-general clenched his fists while analyzing the situation. So, it was a coup? He looked over General Cho, but the man was already in handcuffs, being led away. He tried to show defiance while wanting to slap the slight but noticeable grin off the Premier's face. "Are you mad?" he chuckled. "I may resign, but I certainly will not name you —"

"Your daughter has over five million in a Canadian bank," Premier Shengkun loudly interrupted. while opening his desk drawer and presenting documents. "Your son, a factory manager, has over twelve million. You don't sign that treaty, resign and name me secretary-general, they'll be brought up on corruption charges with General Cho. You know the sentence."

Feeling as if he had aged a century in less than a minute, the secretary-general reached to pull over a wooden chair at the side of the desk and took a seat, scanning the various bank reports gathered by Chinese Intelligence. He had no doubt they were authentic. That being said, most politburo families and senior union officials had stockpiles of money. To say that aloud, though, was to admit they were all criminals. "Very well." Defeated, he slumped back into his chair. "What must I do?"

Premier Shengkun waved for the foreign affairs minister to step forward and present a folder. "You will sign that treaty and sign this confirming me as the new secretary-general."

Saying nothing, the nodding secretary-general took the folder with tremulous hands, struggled to stand up, and stumbled out of the office.

Satisfied, Premier Shengkun sat back down into his office chair while dismissing the Politburo cabinet. "Emergency committee meeting in thirty minutes. Be prepared to sign off on declaring a state of emergency, so we can take drastic actions to restore peace and order on the mainland. He waved at the internal affairs minister. "My first act is to name Liu head of military intelligence in preparation for operations to restore control over strategic coastal ports."

The politburo awkwardly turned away, satisfied that despite the failure of the operation, the supremacy of the Communist Party was still intact. And was that not what really mattered?

With a last-second curl of his finger, he waved Liu to approach, so he could whisper into the man's ear. "You personally report to me now."

Liu nodded, fully understanding.

"Former Comrade Secretary-general Jinpin is to commit suicide in disgrace, following signing the treaty? Understood?"

"Completely, comrade."

Sitting at his desk, Premier Shenkum felt as if the sun was again shining. Was that not the ultimate lesson of Sun Tzu, to ensure that even in defeat one could find victory? Suddenly, the loss of forces in Taiwan was just a temporary setback on the road to restoring the ideology and integrity of the party. China was indeed victorious!

Alone, he sifted through his intelligence papers. One paper, in particular, had his attention. He opened up the brief detailing the actions of the American cowgirl in the South China Sea. Had she really cost them the Southern fleet, including the brilliant Admiral Luo Yan? It seemed too hard to believe. Still, he mentally committed to the universe, she would pay. One way or another, her little experiment at sea would pay.

SEPTEMBER 4, 2068 7:00 PM
ABOVE WASHINGTON DC

The Boeing E-4 Advanced Airborne Command Post was a modified 747 jumbo jet to serve as the National Airborne Operations Center in the event of a potential nuclear exchange. While the official designation was "night watch," the plane was commonly referred to as the "Doomsday Plane." Unlike the *Air Force One*, this plane was specifically designed to survive an EMP attack, had state-of-the-art active countermeasures, and was filled over a hundred personnel and stations to command the entire United States government and military.

The plane had been in the air with the president, secretary of defense, and secretary of state only half an hour after the first EMP attacks against Pearl Harbor, Seattle, and San Diego came in and had been in the air for over two days now. Aerial refueling could keep the plane in the air indefinitely. US military forces were at DEFCON One, the highest state of alert, ready to fire a barrage of nuclear-tipped ballistic missiles from silos and nuclear ballistic missile submarines to decimate the Chinese mainland. The Chinese, too, had nuclear missile silos and submarines. Would both nations annihilate each other?

The president had expected the Chinese to take the island. The two parties would broker a ceasefire in which the United States would accept the reunification of Taiwan in exchange for reparations and a non-aggression pact ensuring Japan and South Korea would remain untouched. It would take months to mobilize the ships to even attempt to liberate Taiwan, and even then, it would cost tens of thousands of American soldiers' lives. Certainly, no American would want to see a nuclear war over Taiwan. The maddening days of sacrificing millions of lives for the concept of freedom were over.

"This just came in over the hotwire!" An intelligence agent rushed a tablet into the conference room where the three senior leaders sat around in private debating the next steps of the United States.

The president was the first to read the report, and he breathed a sigh of relief. "China has agreed to sign the treaty. The CIA also reports that Secretary Jinpin is to resign with . . ." The President paused, not quite sure he read the next sentence right. "Premier Shengkun as the new secretary-general." He looked to Secretary of State Harris with a puzzled expression.

Harris ignored the gesture and smiled. "Excellent news."

"But what of the EMP attacks?" The secretary of defense raised his arms in protest. "Those were acts of war on the United States of America!" He pounded the table. "Should we not respond in kind?"

The secretary of state took the tablet and held it up. "The Chinese are paying consequences. Forced to recognize Taiwanese independence, pay reparations. Surrender islands in the South China Sea. Besides, the civilian casualties are light."

"We've lost critical infrastructure," the secretary of defense urged, "Parts of those cities still don't have power."

"Haven't several Chinese cities been hit with EMP devices?" the president added rhetorically.

The defense minister went on. Having lost personnel and equipment, not to mention American cities having been attacked, he wanted some type of action on the part of the US armed forces. "From Japan and Taiwan!" he countered. He slapped on a report from the intelligence services, "And that rouge American company!"

"Which I authorized," said the president, gazing over at Harris for support.

Unclear just how much the president's "authorization" was part of the decision by the Taiwanese and Japanese governments—the latter in a struggle to survive—the secretary of defense shifted awkwardly in his chair. He shook his head, still not contemplating why the American President was willing to let the Chinese off with what he saw only as a stern talk. He got up and stormed out of the room.

The secretary of state stood up, closed the door to the conference room, and then locked the door.

The president looked up from his desk while raising his hands in despair. "I suppose it's all I can do." He pondered the situation while rummaging through the various military options. "Though maybe we could do this demonstration nuclear detonation in the South China Sea. That would make us appear tough."

I'm almost glad this all went south, Harris reflected. No more pretending. He let his honest emotions show. The president was a pawn— and a pathetic one at that. "I think you take credit for the peace treaty and then resign."

The president was so confused that he blinked uncontrollably. "Excuse me?"

"Look." Harris pulled out the chair, sat down, and leaned forward. "You will resign or we will expose your entire plan to divide the Pacific for Chinese funds."

"Wasn't that *our* plan? The party's plan?" the president tried to recall just how exactly it had come to this. And why was Harris sounding more like a backstabber than a confidant? "You were in on that plan." He drew himself up. "If I go down, you all go down with me."

Idiot. "We'll all go down with *you*. Keep in mind that includes your son with the shady business deals with the Chinese. Chinese money in and out of accounts. Not to mention the sex—"

The president waved his hands in the air, surprised by how dark the conversation had turned so quickly. "Enough." He took a deep breath. "I'll resign. Just make sure I'm taken care of." He brainstormed various options. "Speeches, diplomatic missions, all of that."

Pouring the man a final cup of tea, Secretary of State Harris unlocked the door. "Done." He stepped out of the conference room.

"Where are you going?"

Secretary of State Harris considered telling the truth—that he found the President so boring and thoughtless that he didn't want to spend another minute in the same room as him. Or that he was about to make phone calls to his campaign that would secure him the presidency. But why tell the truth when you could lie? "To the washroom."

The president was left alone with just his thoughts.

Walking down the aircraft, seeing the various staff that would soon be reporting to him, the secretary of state had to admire Shengkun. Their scheme to rebuild the Pacific Rim had been a failure, and yet the overall objective, absolute power, had been achieved. As if to reinforce the point, his satellite phone rang with the identifier showing it was his executive assistant. "The president will resign. You make sure my nomination papers are in."

"The party is concerned about that American woman."

He waved his hands, frustrated that the political operative would be dumb enough to talk about it over the phone. "The accusers? They can be dealt with, as usual." He rolled his eyes.

"No, the entrepreneur in the Pacific. She's being honored by Taiwan as an ally, and the Japanese are doubling their tanker contracts."

Harris stopped and contemplated.

"Sir, is something wrong?" a young communication officer asked on seeing the blood drain from his face.

"Nothing we can't deal with in the future."

CHAPTER TWENTY-EIGHT – NEW HOPES

"Humanity has won its battle. Liberty now has a country"
—Marquis de Lafayette

SEPTEMBER 14, 2068
NEW CONSTANTINOPLE
PACIFIC OCEAN

There was applause as Grace Jaden stepped out of a Mitsubishi H-60 twin-turboshaft engine helicopter and onto the deck of the *New Constantinople* to a cheering crowd assembled around the flight deck. She turned back to salute the Japanese pilots as Admiral Davidson stepped out. She gently pressed closed the hatch to the Japanese version of the Sikorsky S-70 helicopter. The Japanese pilots saluted back, freeing her to turn back to the assembled crowd. Was the cheering the crew of the *New Constantinople*? Citizens of New Liberty? *I guess you could call them both*, Grace thought as she took in the joy of seeing everyone again. That she could take a deep breath of ocean air and not break out into uncontrollable coughing was a personal victory. "Thank you, thank you." She made her way down the luxurious flight of stairs, shaking the hands of those rushing to congratulate her.

General Lawrence, Kelly Agarwal, Jord Laboucan, and Nicholas Zenuck waited patiently at the back of the crowd.

Zenuck crossed his arms, trying hard to suppress a grin. When Grace had made her way close enough, he tried his best to sound stern. "About time you got back."

"I brought friends." Jaden laughed while shrugging to the port side. Off in the distance was the Japanese Hyuga-class flagship, the *Ise*. She was, for all intents and purposes, an aircraft carrier, two hundred meters long, featuring a flat top with an elevated bridge. Different than most supercarriers, she had no catapults and was armed with a vertical launch missile system, a C-RAM, and a rail gun. Under the pacifist constitution of Japan after the Second World War, the nation was forbidden to deploy nuclear weapons, strategic bombers, or aircraft carriers. The *Ise* was thus a "helicopter carrier" under the Japanese Maritime Self-Defense Force. The Japanese Prime Minister had, himself, ordered the carrier to bring a replacement F-35 Joint Strike Fighter and V-22 Ospreys to honor the contributions of New Liberty.

Over the past two weeks, the carrier had sailed east from Japan into the Pacific. The *Ise* had fought hard in the battle over Taiwan, losing numerous helicopters and F-35 Lightning II fighters. While her official mission was to rendezvous with the ships of New Liberty to present Jaden and various awards, the ship was to continue east to pick up replacement ammunition and aircraft. Her sister ship, the *Hyuga*, had been struck by a Chinese anti-ship missile and would be out of action for months, so the Japanese Maritime Self-Defense Force was rushing to get the vessel back to full fighting capacity.

"Not every day you get medals of honor from the prime minister of Japan and the president of the Republic of China." Kelly beamed. "It's like we're a world power!"

General Lawrence couldn't help it. He had to laugh. "Because we *are* a world power!"

"Let's not do that again, okay?" Jord Labaoucan urged. While the cost of the corvettes and aircraft lost in the battle of the South China Sea was very much on his mind, more so were the lives lost and those returned home. *Home.* Jord chuckled to himself, realizing home was no longer some house on the continental United States but the hull beneath his feet.

"Agreed," Grace Jaden laughed while shaking their hands. She put her arm up over Admiral Davidson's shoulders. "Hopefully, you'll only have some light patrol duties from here on in."

The admiral laughed. "I wanted action. I suppose I got action." He recollected the tense hours of rushing for the Philippine coast, only to be saved by the crew of a small fishing trawler. It took him days to get to Manila.

The team made their way down into the reception hall where a celebration had been prepared. In the background, Jimmy Buffet and the music of other classic country artists played. Those in the hall could smell the various appetizers ready to be brought out.

Of those waiting, licking their lips, were Dr. Kraizer along with Dr. Haung and Peter Jaden. Peter Jaden was still on crutches, unable to walk from the back strain of the ejection.

On seeing her son, Grace Jaden ran up and hugged Peter. They hadn't seen each other since the Philippines, Peter having required additional medical attention. The pressure sent pain pulsing through his nerves. "Ouch, gentle!" he half-cried/half-laughed while trying his best to hug back.

Grace Jaden turned to Dr. Kraizer. "Is he okay?"

"He'll make a full recovery," said Doctor Kraizer, squeezing Peter's shoulder.

Peter wasn't as confident as the Doctor that he would end up with no chronic pain, but he smiled regardless, just happy to be alive. "Wait until we tell Constance about this!"

"Let's not." Grace handed Peter a glass of Prosecco. "Or we'll never get her out here to visit." The mention of her daughter brought with it a rush of emotions. Her hand shook. For so long she had wanted to live up to the legacy of her husband and son. She took a deep breath, confident she had done right by them, wherever they were. Were they watching her right now? It was time to move on. To reach out to her daughter. To reflect on the lives lost. Was it worth it? Holding tight to the glass of vibrant-looking sparkling wine, Grace Jaden sought out distraction in the form of the nearest microphone.

Nolan approached while taking off his smartwatch. With a press of a button, he was able to connect it wirelessly to the sound system. "My lady."

"Thank you." Grace Jaden took a deep breath while awkwardly speaking into the phone. She raised her glass. "A toast first to those we lost."

The room went silent. Glasses clinked.

"The former UK Prime Minister, Margaret Thatcher once joked that the problem with statists is that they're just not at home with freedom. They don't like ordinary people choosing because they might not choose statism." Grace Jaden spoke firmly but femininely. "That we should all be equally reliant in sitting back in subservience. Well, my friends"—she raised her glass up—"there are still individuals who want to get up and go. Mothers, fathers, workers, inventors, entrepreneurs, and fighters with pioneering spirits!"

The assembled crew hooted and cheered.

"Hell yeah!" Nolan raised his glass up high.

"We're not numbers in a machine. They thought that with the United States gone that there would be nowhere else for us to go. That we would just accept the stagnation, grateful—in the unlikely event they didn't starve us to death—to enjoy waiting for the sun to run out of fuel. Yet, you can't keep the individual down. We will never stop fighting to survive, to prosper, and to be free. We didn't have generations fight against the destructive forces of totalitarianism and stagnant statism to give up now!" Grace Jaden scanned the men and women assembled and found strength in their determination. "Our vision will live on. A person's right to work as he or she will, to spend what he earns, to own property, to have the state as servant and not as master. And on that freedom, all other rights depend. Thank you."

The ballroom erupted into cheers.

Grace Jaden took a sip from her glass and savored the taste. The sound of the music was raised, indicating that the party had started. Appetizers were brought in. She nearly spit out her drink on catching sight of a robed man off in the distance. She dashed up to him. "Father Mark?"

The man spun around, clearly uncomfortable being on a ship at sea. He breathed a sigh of relief at hearing his name. "Grace Jaden?" he said, finding the loud music disconcerting.

Grace led the priest into a nearby stairwell so they could talk. "The Vatican sent you?"

"Yes, apparently I'm to set up an Eastern Catholic Church?" he said, squinting his eyes, not quite sure what exactly he was doing on the ship. He just went where he was told—his mission to spread the word.

"At my request." She sought out a terminal so she could load up the space she had dedicated to the church. "I can show you the space, but we'll need to have a service for those lost in the conflict."

"Of course." The priest could see the hurt in her eyes. "Of course."

The stairwell door swung open slamming the bulkhead hard. Zenuck ran in. "No time for a dance I guess," he handed her a tablet, "You've got a flight to catch. The *Ise* has a cargo plane ready to go!"

Grace Jaden took the tablet and immediately noted it was an official communication from the South East Asia Treaty Organization, the new alliance of the Republic of China, Japan, South Korea, and the Philippines, which New Liberty had coordinated with during the battle of the South China Sea. "I *do* have to go!" Grace Jaden handed back the tablet before darting back into the hall and up to the flight deck.

Seeing her rush up while enjoying a shrimp appetizer, Jord Labaucan raised his thumb. "Where is she off to?"

Zenuck handed the tablet to the chief financial officer. "You'll have to read it to believe it. Oh, and you'll be happy to know Japan just gifted us four Osprey and two F-35s."

His jaw dropping, Labaoucan put aside the appetizer and took a firm hold of the tablet. "Really?"

On hearing of a second F-35 Lighting II, Peter Jaden was already wondering just where they could operate it from. He caught sight of Lieutenant Wognar on the dance floor with a few fellow aircrew members. He struggled with the crutches to get close enough to talk. "I think we just got you your plane."

"I love planes," said the Lieutenant, smiling, "but right now, all I want to do is dance."

Despite the crutches, dancing suited Peter Jaden just fine.

OCTOBER 1, 2068

MANILA, PHILIPPINES

Manila, the capital of the Philippines, was the most densely populated city in the world. Located on the eastern shores of Manila Bay, the city had been considered among the original set of global cities, being so strategic to traversing the Pacific. Manila had been chosen to serve as the new headquarters for the Southeast Asia Treaty Organization, one of the few government buildings overlooking the beach tasked to the organization.

That wasn't where the convoy of limousines carrying heads of state was headed, however. Not wanting the treaty to be seen as overly militaristic in nature, despite it ending a very hot war, the official ceremony for the signing of the treaty between the People's Republic of China and the nations of the Southeast Asian Treaty Organization was conducted at the Manila Metropolitan Theater. The façade resembled a stage being framed by a proscenium-like central window of stained glass, an almost churchly open forum. In the middle of the plaza was the signing table with photographers taking pictures and journalists taking notes from above.

The ceremony was long, with various speeches calling for cooperation, good sense, and decency. The president of the Republic of China was consolatory, hoping that one day, the mainland could be reunited with Taiwan but in a free democracy. Grace Jaden certainly could clap for that speech. She looked over at Communist China's delegation and could see no emotional reaction.

The Chinese speech by Secretary-general Jinpin was short. The frail-looking man seemed pale and weak. He apologized for the error of rushing and forcing reunification. Reunification would happen but without the use of force.

This time, she spotted Premier Shengkun, who clasped his hands anxiously. Why did he look so chipper?

Next up was the president of the United States. His call for peace was repetitive with little the audience had not heard before. More than once, Grace Jaden had to suppress a yawn.

After dozens of more speeches came the signing ceremony. First, the People's Republic of China and the Republic of China signed the agreement. The People's Republic of China would halt all hostilities and return to pre-war boundaries, formally agreeing not to attempt unification through military force. The Republic of China would do the same, normalizing relations and gaining a symbolic seat at the otherwise ineffective and irrelevant United Nations. The Indonesian President was called up to sign, agreeing to return to pre-war boundaries. Then, the heads of State for the Southeast Asian Treaty Organization were called up one by one to sign the cease-fire agreement, including reparations for the EMP attacks against Japan and the Philippines. After the Japanese prime minister had signed, the next state was called to sign.

"Southeast Asian Treaty Organization member New Liberty," the moderator called out.

Grace Jaden stood up and made her way to the signing table to the surprised conversations of delegates, journalists, and reporters. She looked left and right while smiling. This was real recognition of the small sea state, and she intended to play it for all it was worth.

Not surprisingly, the PRC delegation looked none too happy. In particular, Premier Shengkun seemed to seethe, despite having agreed in advance to the signature. More of a revelation was the disturbed look of the United States delegation. Was it concern over Grace Jaden? Concern over the fact some sea state was being asked to sign where the great world power was not? It was a mystery for another day.

Grace Jaden reached the center of the forum and looked down at the official paper. The treaty would provide New Liberty with a maritime exclusion zone to be respected by the signatories. The Taiwanese President had insisted that New Liberty sign as a SEATO member country. Technically, Kelly Argarwal was supposed to sign, but she had delegated the responsibility to Grace. She took a seat, blinded by camera flashes.

Taking a firm hold of the pen, she signed the treaty. Grace Jaden, Strategos of New Liberty.

THE END

www.ingramcontent.com/pod-product-compliance
Lightning Source LLC
Chambersburg PA
CBHW051104030726
47504CB00006B/1784